Sanctified and Chicken-Fried

SANCTIFIED AND

SOUTHWESTERN WRITERS COLLECTION SERIES
The Wittliff Collections at Texas State University–San Marcos
Steven L. Davis, Editor

CHICKEN-FRIED

The Portable Lansdale

By **JOE R. LANSDALE**

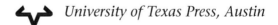 University of Texas Press, Austin

The Southwestern Writers Collection Series originates from the Wittliff Collections, a repository of literature, film, music, and southwestern and Mexican photography established at Texas State University–San Marcos.

Requests for permission to reproduce material from this work should be sent to:
  Permissions
  University of Texas Press
  P.O. Box 7819
  Austin, TX 78713-7819
  www.utexas.edu/utpress/about/bpermission.html

♾ The paper used in this book meets the minimum requirements of ANSI/NISO Z39.48-1992 (R1997) (Permanence of Paper).

Library of Congress Cataloging-in-Publication Data

Lansdale, Joe R., 1951–
  Sanctified and chicken-fried : the portable Lansdale / by Joe R. Lansdale.
  p. cm. — (The Southwestern writers collection series)
  An anthology of short stories, excerpts from the novels The magic wagon and A fine dark line, and previously unpublished tales.
  ISBN 978-0-292-71941-5 (cl.: alk. paper)
  I. Title. II. Title: Portable Lansdale.
  PS3562.A557S26 2009
  813'.54—dc22   2008049636

Contents

Foreword: Joe R. Lansdale

Bill Crider

I've known Joe R. Lansdale for nearly thirty years. That's hard for me to believe, since it seems more like a few weeks, but it's true. I remember our first meeting with such clarity that I can play it back in my head like a movie.

The year was 1979. The place was a hallway in the Memorial Student Center at Texas A&M University, just outside the dealers' room, and the occasion was AggieCon X. It was the last day of the convention, and I suppose my wife, Judy, and I had made one last round of the dealers' tables before leaving for home. As we stepped out the door of the room, I happened to glance at the name tag on a guy standing over by the windows: Joe R. Lansdale.

The name was familiar. While I'd never seen Joe before, I'd read his letters in *The Mystery Fancier*, a "fanzine" devoted to mystery fiction. The editor, Guy M. Townsend, published articles and book reviews written by mystery fans who wrote them for the love of the genre and who received no payment for their work. There was also a section devoted to letters from readers who had something to say about the contents, and that's where I'd seen Joe's name. As anyone who knows him can tell you, Joe always has something to say.

I walked over to Joe and his wife, Karen, and said to him, "I think I know you from another fandom."

Joe looked at me as if to say, "What on earth are you talking about, you old coot?" (I was not yet forty, Joe not yet thirty.)

I introduced myself and explained where I'd seen his name. He warmed up a bit then because he'd seen my name in the same publication. We introduced our wives and started a conversation about writers, writing, books, and movies. We discovered that we had a lot in common, and the conversation we began then has lasted from that day to this, although it's expanded to include many other topics. At first the conversation was conducted in large part by letters, the kind we banged out on old manual typewriters. Later it included e-mail and phone calls, and of course we've talked face to face at many a convention over the years.

I've always felt privileged to take part in this extended conversation and in my friendship with Joe. Try to imagine how exciting it would be to read *Act of Love* and *The Nightrunners* in manuscript, to see bits and pieces of "The Fat Man and the Elephant" before they coalesced into a story, or, best of all, to hear Joe tell the story that became "Mister Weed-Eater" before a word was ever set down on paper. Those were the days.

Or maybe not, because Joe wasn't yet selling steadily, much less making any money on his writing. There were times when his agent would have to send him stamps so he could mail his manuscripts, times when Joe and Karen would bring a loaf of bread and a jar of peanut butter to a convention to save money on food.

The lean times, however, did nothing at all to change Joe's mind about his talent and where it was going to take him. I've never met anyone more fiercely committed to his writing or more certain that sooner or later his name on a book or story was going to make people eager to read it. I've never forgotten how angry he became once when someone called him a "neo-pro."

Sometimes I wonder if Joe ever expected to be renowned not only in this country but in France and Italy, where he's now regarded as a literary figure on a par with Hemingway and is treated more like a rock star than a writer. But then I remind myself that he probably expects to attain that kind of recognition right here, any day now. I, for one, think he deserves it, and I believe that after reading the stories in this book, you're going to think so too.

Ah, the stories. Hilarious, vivid, vulgar, poignant, profane, profound, colorful, and unforgettable. Not to mention unique. There's nothing else like them, because a Lansdale story is *sui generis*. A lot of younger writers have clearly been influenced by their reading of Lansdale's work, and their stories have traces of Lansdale DNA in them, but no one has ever duplicated the singular qualities that make a Lansdale story his own.

This collection begins with a little tale I've already mentioned,

"Mister Weed-Eater." Joe swears that the tale is based on actual events, and long before he wrote it down, I heard him relate some of the incidents it contains to rooms full of people who were laughing so hard that I thought they might strangle themselves. Anyone who doubts that Joe is a natural-born storyteller would have all disbelief removed after hearing him launch into some supposedly true story like this one or the one about the telephone woman (which isn't included here).

"Tight Little Stitches in a Dead Man's Back" isn't funny at all. It's a post-apocalyptic science-fiction horror tale that will give you bad dreams, the kind you awaken from in a cold sweat, hoping that you don't go back to sleep for a while. On a more cheerful note, the narrator of the story refers to martial arts on the very first page. Did I mention that Joe, in addition to being a fine writer, is also superbly skilled in the martial arts? He devised a system known as Shen Chuan and has his own school where he and others teach. He's been inducted into both the International Martial Arts Hall of Fame and the Texas Martial Arts Hall of Fame, and he holds any number of black belts. In other words, you don't want to mess with him. I've seen him in action, and I know.

Speaking of the apocalypse, many of the people living in Galveston, Texas, on September 8, 1900, must have thought it had arrived. In "The Big Blow," Lansdale imagines what might have happened if Jack Jackson had been in a prize fight that night with a man paid not just to beat him but to kill him. The storm and its aftermath are terrifying in themselves, but the human story is what takes center stage here, and what a story it is, laugh-out-loud funny at one point, frightening at the next. This story alone could make a writer's reputation, but it's just one of many in the Lansdale canon.

The Magic Wagon is a western novel, true, but that's like saying that the Grand Canyon is a hole in the ground. This slim book is one of the wildest westerns ever written, and even that understates the case. I remember that when it came out in paperback, James Reasoner, a writer friend, said that he loved to think of someone going into a bookstore for a Louis L'Amour book and spotting *The Magic Wagon* on the shelf next to it, thanks to alphabetical order: "Well, I guess I might as well pick this'n up, too. Looks short, and it's got a covered wagon on the front." Sure enough, it does, but the contents are a long way from Louis L'Amour. It has a wrestling ape, the trick-shooting son of Wild Bill Hickok, and Wild Bill himself, or at least his petrified corpse. Also one of Lansdale's classic nose-picking scenes, maybe his best. You have to wonder what that fellow must have thought when he read it. I'd like to have seen his face.

The Great Depression was the time of Bonnie and Clyde, and of other bank robbers, like the ones in "Dirt Devils," a story with sudden, sharp violence with a sense of doom hanging over everything like the dust cloud that the wind twists into a dust devil in the story's opening scene.

In "The Pit," a man named Harry takes a wrong turn. A really wrong turn. He winds up fighting for his life in the pit, after the warm-up dogfight, with an audience screaming for blood. Throw in a crazed preacher and a rattlesnake named Sapphire, and you have a combination of such grisly humor and bloodletting that you might want to turn away. But you won't be able to, and after you think about what you've read for a while, you might just discover that it's also a scathing commentary on the issue of race in this country.

"Night They Missed the Horror Show" is one that Lansdale himself labels "a story that doesn't flinch." I couldn't have put it better myself, and this might be my favorite of all his stories. I like the black humor and the horrible inevitability of the plot as it uncoils like a rattler, with a bite that's just as vicious as any snake's.

"Bubba Ho-Tep" attained fame far beyond its print origins when it was filmed by Don Coscarelli. It became known as the funniest, most satisfyingly entertaining movie in a generation. Or maybe two. But don't let the fact that it was a great movie experience deter you from reading the story. When Elvis and JFK battle the mummy in the nursing home, it's more stirring than anything on the screen. Funnier, too, and more touching.

It's impossible for me to describe "The Fat Man and the Elephant." I can tell you it's about a failed preacher named Sonny Guy, who thinks he's found his totem animal in a sad and sickly sideshow elephant, but that doesn't come anywhere near to getting at the heart of the matter. Just read it.

Lansdale's fascination with drive-in theaters has shown up often in his fiction, but he's never put it to use more effectively than in *A Fine Dark Line*, a novel set in the not-too-distant American past that captures a lot of the good and the bad about that time and brings it all home in a fine coming-of-age novel. There's only a taste of it here, and it will leave you wanting more.

BILL CRIDER

When Lansdale was asked to write a story for an anthology about horse racing, he naturally couldn't quite follow the guidelines. Readers can be happy he didn't, because what he came up with was "White Mule, Spotted Pig," which marginally involves a mule race but is a lot more about freedom and friendship and responsibility than about racing. It brings the collection to a fitting close.

And there you have it. High art and low comedy; sex and violence; humor and sadness; love and death; all in one package. Not a neat package, never that, because it holds living, breathing people who lead often messy lives, people whose stories will keep you riveted while you read and who will stay with you long after you've closed the book, even if you try to forget them. I've taken up enough of your time here. Go read the stories. You'll be glad you did.

Sanctified and Chicken-Fried

Mister Weed-Eater

Mr. Job Harold was in his living room with his feet on the couch watching *Wheel of Fortune* when his five-year-old son came inside covered with dirt. "Daddy," said the boy, dripping dirt, "there's a man outside wants to see you."

Mr. Harold got up and went outside, and there standing at the back of the house next to his wife's flower bed, which was full of dead roses and a desiccated frog, was, just like his boy had said, a man.

It was over a hundred degrees out there, and the man, a skinny sucker in white T-shirt and jeans with a face red as a baboon's ass, a waterfall of inky hair dripping over his forehead and dark glasses, stood with his head cocked like a spaniel listening for trouble. He had a bright-toothed smile that indicated everything he heard struck him as funny.

In his left hand was a new weed-eater, the cutting line coated in greasy green grass the texture of margarita vomit, the price tag dangling proudly from the handle.

In the other hand the man held a blind man's cane, the tip of which had speared an oak leaf. His white T-shirt, stained pollen yellow under the arms, stuck wetly to his chest and little pot belly tight as plastic wrap on a fish head. He had on dirty white socks with played-out elastic and they had fallen over the tops of his tennis shoes as if in need of rest.

The man was shifting his weight from one leg to the other. Mr. Harold figured he needed to pee and wanted to use the bathroom, and the idea of letting him into the house with a weed-eater and pointing him at the pot didn't appeal to Mr. Harold 'cause there wasn't any question in Mr. Harold's mind the man was blind as a peach pit, and Mr. Harold figured he got in the bathroom, he was gonna pee from one end of the place to the other trying to hit the commode, and then Mr. Harold knew he'd have to clean it up or explain to his wife when she got home from work how on his day off he let a blind man piss all over their bathroom. Just thinking about all that gave Mr. Harold a headache.

"What can I do for you?" Mr. Harold asked.

"Well, sir," said the blind man in a voice dry as Mrs. Harold's sexual equipment, "I heard your boy playin' over here, and I followed the sound. You see, I'm the groundskeeper next door, and I need a little help. I was wonderin' you could come over and show me if I've missed a few spots?"

Mr. Harold tried not to miss a beat. "You talking about the church over there?"

"Yes, sir. Just got hired. Wouldn't want to look bad on my first day."

Mr. Harold considered this. Cameras could be set in place somewhere. People in trees waiting for him to do something they could record for a TV show. He didn't want to go on record as not helping a blind man, but on the other hand, he didn't want to be caught up in no silliness either.

Finally, he decided it was better to look like a fool and a Samaritan than a cantankerous asshole who wouldn't help a poor blind man cut weeds.

"I reckon I can do that," Mr. Harold said. Then to his five-year-old who'd followed him outside and was sitting in the dirt playing with a plastic truck: "Son, you stay right here and don't go off."

"Okay, Daddy," the boy said.

The church across the street had been opened in a building about the size of an aircraft hangar. It had once been used as a liquor warehouse, and later it was called Community Storage, but items had a way of disappearing. It was a little too community for its renters, and it went out of business and Sonny Guy, who owned the place, had to pay some kind of fine and turn up with certain items deemed as missing.

This turn of events had depressed Mr. Guy, so he'd gotten religion and opened a church. God wasn't knocking them dead either, so to compensate, Sonny Guy started a Gospel Opry, and to advertise and indicate its location, beginning on their street and on up to the highway, there was a line of huge orange Day-Glo guitars that pointed from highway to Opry.

The guitars didn't pull a lot of people in though, bright as they were. Come Sunday the place was mostly vacant, and when the doors were open on the building back and front, you could hear wind whistling through there like it was blowing through a pipe. A special ticket you could cut out of the newspaper for five dollars off a fifteen-dollar buffet of country sausages and sliced cantaloupe hadn't rolled them in either. Sonny and God most definitely needed a more exciting game plan. Something with titties.

Taking the blind man by the elbow, Mr. Harold led him across the little street and into the yard of the church. Well, actually, it was more than a yard. About four acres. On the front acre sat Sonny Guy's house, and out to the right of it was a little music studio he'd built, and over to the left was the metal building that served as the church. The metal was aluminum and very bright and you could feel the heat bouncing off of it like it was an oven with bread baking inside.

Behind the house were three more acres, most of it weeds, and at the back of it all was a chicken wire fence where a big black dog of undetermined breed liked to pace.

When Mr. Harold saw what the blind man had done, he let out his breath. The fella had been all over that four acres, and it wasn't just a patch of weeds now, but it wasn't manicured either. The poor bastard had tried to do the job of a lawn mower with a weed-eater, and he'd mostly succeeded in chopping down the few flowers that grew in the midst of brick-lined beds, and he'd chopped weeds and dried grass here and there, so that the whole place looked as if it were a head of hair mistreated by a drunk barber with an attitude.

At Mr. Harold's feet, he discovered a mole the blind man's shoe had dislodged from a narrow tunnel. The mole had been whipped to death by the weed-eater sling. It looked like a wad of dirty hair dipped in red paint. A lasso loop of guts had been knocked out of its mouth and ants were crawling on it. The blind had slain the blind.

"How's it look?"

"Well," Mr. Harold said, "you missed some spots."

"Yeah, well they hired me 'cause they wanted to help the handicapped, but I figure it was just as much 'cause they knew I'd do the job. They had 'em a crippled nigger used to come out and do it, but they said he charged too much and kept making a mess of things."

Mr. Harold had seen the black man mow. He might have been crippled, but he'd had a riding mower and he was fast. He didn't do such a bad job either. He always wore a straw hat pushed up on the back of his head, and when he got off the mower to get on his crutches, he did it with the style of a rodeo star dismounting a show horse. There hadn't been a thing wrong with the black man's work. Mr. Harold figured Sonny Guy wanted to cut a few corners. Switch a crippled nigger for a blind honkey.

"How'd you come to get this job?" Mr. Harold asked. He tried to make the question pleasant, as if he were asking him how his weekend had been.

"References," the blind man said.

"Of course," said Mr. Harold.

"Well, what do I need to touch up? I stayed me a line from the building there, tried to work straight, turn when I got to the fence and come back. I do it mostly straight?"

"You got off a mite. You've missed some pretty good-sized patches."

Mr. Harold, still holding the blind man's elbow, felt the blind man go a little limp with disappointment. "How bad is it?"

"Well . . ."

"Go on and tell me."

"A weed-eater ain't for this much place. You need a mower."

"I'm blind. You can't turn me loose out here with a mower. I'd cut my foot off."

"I'm just saying."

"Well, come on, how bad is it? It look worse than when the nigger did it?"

"I believe so."

"By much?"

"When he did it, you could look out here and tell the place had been mowed. Way it looks now, you might do better just to poison the weeds and hope the grass dies."

The blind man really slumped now, and Mr. Harold wished he'd chosen his words more carefully. It wasn't his intention to insult a blind man on his lawn skills in hundred-degree heat. He began to wish the fella had only wanted to wet on the walls of his bathroom.

"Can't even do a nigger's job," the blind man said.

"It ain't so bad if they're not too picky."

"Shit," said the blind man. "Shit, I didn't have no references.

"I didn't never have a job before, really. Well, I worked out at the chicken processing plant tossing chicken heads in a metal drum, but I kept missing and tossin' them on this lady worked by me. I just couldn't keep my mind on the drum's location. I think I might actually be more artistic than mechanical. I got one side of the brain works harder, you know?"

"You could just slip off and go home. Leave 'em a note."

"Naw, I can't do that. Besides, I ain't got no way home. They pick me up and brought me here. I come to church last week and they offered me the job, and then they come and got me and brought me here and I made a mess of it. They'll be back later and they won't like it. They ain't gonna give me my five dollars, I can see that and I can't see nothing."

"Hell, man," Mr. Harold said, "that black fella mowed this lawn, you can bet he got more than five dollars."

"You tryin' to say I ain't good as a nigger?"

"I'm not trying to say anything 'cept you're not being paid enough. A guy ought to get five dollars an hour just for standing around in this heat."

"People charge too much these days. Niggers especially will stick you when they can. It's that civil rights business. It's gone to their heads."

"It ain't got nothing to do with what color you are."

"By the hour, I reckon I'm making 'bout what I got processing chicken heads," the blind man said. "Course, they had a damn fine company picnic this time each year."

"Listen here. We'll do what we were gonna do. Check the spots you've missed. I'll lead you around to bad places, and you chop 'em."

"That sounds all right, but I don't want to share my five dollars. I was gonna get me something with that. Little check I get from the government just covers my necessities, you know?"

"You don't owe me anything."

Mr. Harold took the blind man by the elbow and led him around to where the grass was missed or whacked high, which was just about everywhere you looked. After about fifteen minutes, the blind man said he was tired. They went over to the house and leaned on a tree in the front yard. The blind man said, "You seen them shows about those crop circles, in England, I think it is?"

"No," said Mr. Harold.

"Well, they found these circles in the wheat. Just appeared out there. They think it's aliens."

"Oh yeah, I seen about those," Mr. Harold said, suddenly recalling what it was the man was talking about. "There ain't no mystery to that. It's some guys with a stick and a cord. We used to do that in tall weed patches when we were kids. There's nothing to it. Someone's just making jackasses out of folks."

The blind man took a defiant posture. "Not everything like that is a bunch of kids with a string."

"I wasn't saying that."

"For all I know, what's wrong with that patch there's got nothing to do with me and my work. It could have been alien involvement."

"Aliens with weed-eaters?"

"It could be what happened when they landed, their saucers messin' it up like that."

"If they landed, why didn't they land on you? You was out there with the weed-eater. How come nobody saw or heard them?"

"They could have messed up the yard while I was coming to get you."

"Kind of a short visit, wasn't it?"

"You don't know everything, Mister I-Got-Eyeballs. Those that talk the loudest know less than anybody."

"And them that believe every damn thing they hear are pretty stupid, Mister Weed-Eater. I know what's wrong with you now. You're lazy. It's hot out there and you don't want to be here, so you're trying to make me feel sorry for you and do the job myself, and it ain't gonna work. I don't feel sorry for you 'cause you're blind. I ain't gonna feel sorry at all. I think you're an asshole."

Mr. Harold went across the road and back to the house and called his son inside. He sat down in front of the TV. *Wheel of Fortune* wasn't on anymore. Hell, it was a rerun anyway. He changed the channel looking for something worth watching but all that was on was midget wrestling, so he watched a few minutes of that.

Those little guys were fast and entertaining and it was cool inside with the air conditioner cranked up, so after a couple minutes Mr. Harold got comfortable watching the midgets sling each other around, tumble up together and tie themselves in knots.

However, time eroded Mr. Harold's contentment. He couldn't stop thinking about the blind man out there in the heat. He called to his son and told him to go outside and see if the blind man was still there.

The boy came back a minute later. He said, "He's out there, Daddy. He said you better come on out and help him. He said he ain't gonna talk about crop circles no more."

Mr. Harold thought a moment. You were supposed to help the blind, the hot and the stupid. Besides, the old boy might need someone to pour gas in that weed-eater. He did it himself he was liable to pour it all over his shoes and later get around someone who smoked and wanted to toss a match. An accident might be in the making.

Mr. Harold switched the channel to cartoons and pointed them out to his son. The boy sat down immediately and started watching. Mr. Harold got the boy a glass of Kool-Aid and a stack of chocolate cookies. He went outside to find the blind man.

The blind man was in Mr. Harold's yard. He had the weed-eater on and was holding it above his head whacking at the leaves on Mr. Harold's red-bud tree; his wife's favorite tree.

"Hey, now stop that," Mr. Harold said. "Ain't no call to be malicious."

The blind man cut the weed-eater and cocked his head and listened. "That you, Mister I-Know-There-Ain't-No-Aliens?"

"Now come on. I want to help you. My son said you said you wasn't gonna get into that again."

"Come on over here," said the blind man.

Mr. Harold went over, cautiously. When he was just outside of weed-eater range, he said, "What you want?"

"Do I look all right to you? Besides being blind?"

"Yeah. I guess so. I don't see nothing wrong with you. You found the leaves on that tree good enough."

"Come and look closer."

"Naw, I ain't gonna do it. You just want to get me in range. Hit me with that weed-eater. I'll stay right here. You come at me, I'll move off. You won't be able to find me."

"You saying I can't find you 'cause I'm blind?"

"Come after me, I'll put stuff in front of you so you trip."

The blind man leaned the weed-eater against his leg. His cane was on a loop over his other hand, and he took hold of it and tapped it against his tennis shoe.

"Yeah, well you could do that," the blind man said, "and I bet you would too. You're like a guy would do things to the handicapped. I'll tell you now, sir, they take roll in heaven, you ain't gonna be on it."

"Listen here. You want some help over there, I'll give it, but I ain't gonna stand here in this heat and take insults. Midget wrestling's on TV and it's cool inside and I might just go back to it."

The blind man's posture straightened with interest. "Midget wrestling? Hell, that's right. It's Saturday. Was it Little Bronco Bill and Low Dozer McGuirk?"

"I think it was. They look alike to me. I don't know one midget from another, though one was a little fatter and had a haircut like he'd got out of the barber chair too soon."

"That's Dozer. He trains on beer and doughnuts. I heard him talk about it on the TV."

"You watch TV?"

"You tryin' to hurt my feelings?"

"No. I mean, it's just, well, you're blind."

"What? I am? I'll be damned! I didn't know that. Glad you was here to tell me."

"I didn't mean no harm."

"Look here, I got ears. I listen to them thumping on that floor and I listen to the announcer. I listen so good I can imagine, kinda, what's goin' on. I 'specially like them little scudders, the midgets. I think maybe on a day I've had enough to eat, I had on some pants weren't too tight, I'd like to get in a ring with one of 'em."

"You always been blind? I mean, was you born that way?"

"Naw. Got bleach in my eyes. My mama told me a nigger done it to me when I was a baby, but it was my daddy. I know that now. Mama had a bad eye herself, then the cancer got her good one. She says she sees out of her bad eye way you'd see if you seen something through a Coke bottle with dirt on the bottom."

Mr. Harold didn't really want to hear about the blind man's family history. He groped for a fresh conversation handle. Before he could get hold of one, the blind man said, "Let's go to your place and watch some of that wrestlin' and cool off, then you can come out with me and show me them places I missed."

Mr. Harold didn't like the direction this conversation was taking. "I don't know," he said. "Won't the preacher be back in a bit and want his yard cut?"

"You want to know the truth?" the blind man said. "I don't care. You're right. Five dollars ain't any wages. Them little things I wanted with that five dollars I couldn't get no how."

Mr. Harold's mind raced. "Yeah, but five dollars is five dollars, and you could put it toward something. You know, save it up till you got some more. They're planning on making you a permanent groundskeeper, aren't they? A little time, a raise could be in order."

"This here's kinda a trial run. They can always get the crippled nigger back."

Mr. Harold checked his watch. There probably wasn't more than twenty minutes left of the wrestling program, so he took a flyer. "Well, all right. We'll finish up the wrestling show, then come back and do the work. You ain't gonna hit me with that weed-eater if I try to guide you into the house, are you?"

"Naw, I ain't mad no more. I get like that sometimes. It's just my way."

Mr. Harold led him into the house and onto the couch and talked the boy out of the cartoons, which wasn't hard; it was some kind of stuff the boy hated. The blind man had him crank the audio on the TV up a notch and sat sideways on the couch with his weed-eater and cane, taking up all the room and leaving Mr. Harold nowhere to sit. Dirt and chopped grass dripped off of the blind man's shoes and onto the couch.

Mr. Harold finally sat on the floor beside his boy and tried to get the boy to give him a cookie, but his son didn't play that way. Mr. Harold had to get his own Kool-Aid and cookies, and he got the blind man some too.

The blind man took the Kool-Aid and cookies and didn't say thanks or kiss my ass. Just stretched out there on the couch listening, shaking from side to side, cheering the wrestlers on. He was obviously on Low Dozer McGuirk's side, and Mr. Harold figured it was primarily because he'd heard Dozer trained on beer and doughnuts. That struck Mr. Harold as a thing the blind man would latch onto and love. That and crop circles and flying saucers.

When the blind man finished up his cookies and Kool-Aid, he put Mr. Harold to work getting more, and when Mr. Harold came back with them, his son and the blind man were chatting about the wrestling match. The blind man was giving the boy some insights into the wrestling game and was trying to get the boy to try a hold on him so he could show how easily he could work out of it.

Mr. Harold nixed that plan, and the blind man ate his next plate of cookies and Kool-Aid, and somehow the wrestling show moved into an after-show talk session on wrestling. When Mr. Harold looked at his watch nearly an hour had passed.

"We ought to get back over there and finish up," Mr. Harold said.

"Naw," said the blind man, "not just yet. This talk show stuff is good. This is where I get most of my tips."

"Well, all right, but when this is over, we're out of here."

But they weren't. The talk show wrapped up, the *Beverly Hillbillies* came on, then *Green Acres,* then *Gilligan's Island.* The blind man and

Mr. Harold's son laughed their way through the first two, and damn near killed themselves with humor when *Gilligan's* was on.

Mr. Harold learned the Professor and Ginger were the blind man's favorites on *Gilligan's,* and he liked the pig, Arnold, on *Green Acres.* No one was a particular favorite on the *Beverly Hillbillies,* however.

"Ain't this stuff good?" the blind man said. "They don't make 'em like this anymore."

"I prefer educational programming myself," Mr. Harold said, though the last educational program he'd watched was a PBS special on lobsters. He'd watched it because he was sick as a dog and lying on the couch and his wife had put the remote across the room and he didn't feel good enough to get up and get hold of it.

In his feverish delirium he remembered the lobster special as pretty good 'cause it had come across a little like a science fiction movie. But that lobster special, as viewed through feverish eyes, had been the closest Mr. Harold had ever gotten to educational TV.

The sickness, the remote lying across the room, had caused him to miss what he'd really wanted to see that day, and even now, on occasion, he thought of what he had missed with a certain pang of regret; a special on how young women were chosen to wear swimsuits in special issues of sports magazines. He kept hoping it was a show that would play in rerun.

"My back's hurtin' from sitting on the floor," Mr. Harold said, but the blind man didn't move his feet so Mr. Harold could have a place on the couch. He offered a pointer, though.

"Sit on the floor, you got to hold your back straight, just like you was in a wooden chair, otherwise you'll really tighten them muscles up close to your butt."

When *Gilligan's* was wrapped up, Mr. Harold impulsively cut the television and got hold of the blind man and started pulling him up. "We got to go to work now. I'm gonna help you, it has to be now. I got plans for the rest of the day."

"Ah, Daddy, he was gonna show me a couple wrestling holds," the boy said.

"Not today," Mr. Harold said, tugging on the blind man, and suddenly the blind man moved and was behind him and had him wrestled to the floor. Mr. Harold tried to move, but couldn't. His arm was twisted behind his back and he was lying face down and the blind man was on top of him pressing a knee into his spine.

"Wow!" said the boy. "Neat!"

"Not bad for a blind fella," said the blind man. "I told you I get my tips from that show."

"All right, all right, let me go," said Mr. Harold.

"Squeal like a pig for me," said the blind man.

"Now wait just a goddamned minute," Mr. Harold said.

The blind man pressed his knee harder into Mr. Harold's spine. "Squeal like a pig for me. Come on."

Mr. Harold made a squeaking noise.

"That ain't no squeal," said the blind man. "Squeal!"

The boy got down by Mr. Harold's face. "Come on, Dad," he said. "Squeal."

"Big pig squeal," said the blind man. "Big pig! Big pig! Big pig!"

Mr. Harold squealed. The blind man didn't let go.

"Say calf rope," said the blind man.

"All right, all right. Calf rope! Calf rope! Now let me up."

The blind man eased his knee off Mr. Harold's spine and let go of the arm lock. He stood up and said to the boy, "It's mostly in the hips."

"Wow!" said the boy, "You made Dad squeal like a pig."

Mr. Harold, red faced, got up. He said, "Come on, right now."

"I need my weed-eater," said the blind man.

The boy got both the weed-eater and the cane for the blind man. The blind man said to the boy as they went outside, "Remember, it's in the hips."

Mr. Harold and the blind man went over to the church property and started in on some spots with the weed-eater. In spite of the fact Mr. Harold found himself doing most of the weed-eating, the blind man just clinging to his elbow and being pulled around like he was a side car, it wasn't five minutes before the blind man wanted some shade and a drink of water.

Mr. Harold was trying to talk him out of it when Sonny Guy and his family drove up in a club cab Dodge pickup.

The pickup was black and shiny and looked as if it had just come off the showroom floor. Mr. Harold knew Sonny Guy's money for such things had come from Mrs. Guy's insurance before she was Mrs. Guy. Her first husband had gotten kicked to death by a maniac escaped from the nuthouse; kicked until they couldn't tell if he was a man or a jelly doughnut that had gotten run over by a truck.

When that insurance money came due, Sonny Guy, a man who had antennas for such things, showed up and began to woo her. They were married pretty quick, and the money from the insurance settlement had bought the house, the aircraft hangar church, the Day-Glo guitar signs, and the pickup. Mr. Harold wondered if there was any money left. He figured they might be pretty well run through it by now.

"Is that the Guys?" the blind man asked as the pickup engine was cut.

"Yeah," said Mr. Harold.

"Maybe we ought to look busy."

"I don't reckon it matters now."

Sonny got out of the pickup and waddled over to the edge of the property and looked at the mauled grass and weeds. He walked over to the aircraft hangar church and took it all in from that angle with his hands on his ample hips. He stuck his fingers under his overall straps and walked alongside the fence with the big black dog running behind it, barking, grabbing at the chicken wire with his teeth.

The minister's wife stood by the pickup. She had a bun of colorless hair stacked on her head. The stack had the general shape of some kind of tropical anthill that might house millions of angry ants. Way she was built, that hair and all, it looked as if the hill had been precariously built on top of a small round rock supported by an irregular-shaped one, the bottom rock wearing a print dress and a pair of black flat-heeled shoes.

The two dumpling kids, one boy and one girl, leaned against the truck's bumper as if they had just felt the effect of some relaxing drug. They both wore jeans, tennis shoes and Disney T-shirts with the Magic Kingdom in the background. Mr. Harold couldn't help but note the whole family had upturned noses, like pigs. It wasn't something that could be ignored.

Sonny Guy shook his head and walked across the lot and over to the blind man. "You sure messed this up. It's gonna cost me more'n I'd have paid you to get it fixed. That crippled nigger never done nothing like this. He run over a sprinkler head once, but that was it. And he paid for it." Sonny turned his attention to Mr. Harold. "You have anything to do with this?"

"I was just tryin' to help," Mr. Harold said.

"I was doin' all right until he come over," said the blind man.

"He started tellin' me how I was messin' up and all and got me nervous, and sure enough, I began to lose my place and my concentration. You can see the results."

"You'd have minded your own business," Sonny said to Mr. Harold, "the man woulda done all right, but you're one of those thinks a handicap can't do some jobs."

"The man's blind," said Mr. Harold. "He can't see to cut grass. Not four acres with a weed-eater. Any moron can see that."

The Reverend Sonny Guy had a pretty fast right hand for a fat man. He caught Mr. Harold a good one over the left eye and staggered him.

The blind man stepped aside so they'd have plenty of room, and Sonny set to punching Mr. Harold quite regularly. It seemed like something the two of them were made for. Sonny to throw punches and Mr. Harold to absorb them.

When Mr. Harold woke up, he was lying on his back in the grass and the shadow of the blind man lay like a slat across him.

"Where is he?" asked Mr. Harold, feeling hot and sick to his stomach.

"When he knocked you down and you didn't get up, he went in the house with his wife," said the blind man. "I think he was thirsty. He told me he wasn't giving me no five dollars. Actually, he said he wasn't giving me jackshit. And him a minister. The kids are still out here though, they're looking at their watches, I think. They had a bet on how long it'd be before you got up. I heard them talking."

Mr. Harold sat up and glanced toward the Dodge club cab. The blind man was right. The kids were still leaning against the truck. When Mr. Harold looked at them, the boy, who was glancing at his watch, lifted one eye and raised his hand quickly and pulled it down, said, "Yesss!" The little girl looked pouty. The little boy said, "This time you blow me."

They went in the house. Mr. Harold stood up. The blind man gave him the weed-eater for support. He said, "Sonny says the crippled nigger will be back next week. I can't believe it. Scooped by a nigger. A crippled nigger."

Mr. Harold pursed his lips and tried to recall a couple of calming Bible verses. When he felt somewhat relaxed, he said, "Why'd you tell him it was my fault?"

"I figured you could handle yourself," the blind man said.

Mr. Harold rubbed one of the knots Sonny had knocked on his head. He considered homicide, but knew there wasn't any future in it. He said, "Tell you what. I'll give you a ride home."

"We could watch some more TV?"

"Nope," said Mr. Harold, probing a split in his lip. "I've got other plans."

Mr. Harold got his son and the three of them drove over to where the blind man said he lived. It was a lot on the far side of town, outside the city limits. It was bordered on either side by trees. It was a trailer lot, scraped down to the red clay. There were a few anemic grass patches here and there and it had a couple of lawn ornaments out front. A cow and a pig with tails that hooked up to hoses and spun around and around and worked as lawn sprinklers.

Behind the sprinklers a heap of wood and metal smoked pleasantly in the sunlight.

They got out of the car and Mr. Harold's son said, "Holy shit."

"Let me ask you something," said Mr. Harold to the blind man.

"Your place got a cow and a pig lawn ornament? Kind that sprinkles the yard?"

The blind man appeared nervous. He sniffed the air. He said, "Is the cow one of those spotted kind?"

"A Holstein?" asked Mr. Harold. "My guess is the pig is a Yorkshire."

"That's them."

"Well, I reckon we're at your place all right, but it's burned down."

"Oh, shit," said the blind man. "I left the beans on."

"They're done now," said the boy.

The blind man sat down in the dirt and began to cry. It was a serious cry. A cat walking along the edge of the woods behind the remains of the trailer stopped to watch in amazement. The cat seemed surprised that any one thing could make such noise.

"Was they pinto beans?" the boy asked.

The blind man sputtered and sobbed and his chest heaved. Mr. Harold went and got the pig sprinkler and turned it on so that the water from its tail splattered on the pile of smoking rubble. When he felt that was going good, he got the cow working. He thought about calling the fire department, but that seemed kind of silly. About all they could do was come out and stir what was left with a stick.

"Is it all gone?" asked the blind man.

"The cow's all right," said Mr. Harold, "but the pig was a little too close to the fire, there's a little paint bubbled up on one of his legs."

Now the blind man really began to cry. "I damn near had it paid for. It wasn't no double-wide, but it was mine."

They stayed that way momentarily, the blind man crying, the water hissing onto the trailer's remains, then the blind man said, "Did the dogs get out?"

Mr. Harold gave the question some deep consideration. "My guess would be no."

"Then I don't guess there's any hope for the parakeet neither," said the blind man.

Reluctantly, Mr. Harold loaded the blind man back in the car with his son, and started home.

It wasn't the way Mr. Harold had hoped the day would turn out. He had been trying to do nothing more than a good deed, and now he couldn't get rid of the blind man. He wondered if this kind of shit ever happened to Jesus. He was always doing good stuff in the Bible. Mr. Harold wondered if he'd ever had an incident misfire on him, something that hadn't been reported in the Testaments.

Once, when Mr. Harold was about eleven, he'd experienced a similar incident, only he hadn't been trying to be a good Samaritan. Still, it was one of those times where you go in with one thing certain and it turns on you.

During recess he'd gotten in a fight with a little kid he thought would be easy to take. He punched the kid when he wasn't looking, and that little dude dropped and got hold of his knee with his arms and wrapped both his legs around him, positioned himself so that his bottom was on Mr. Harold's shoe.

Mr. Harold couldn't shake him. He dragged him across the school yard and even walked him into a puddle of water, but the kid stuck. Mr. Harold got a pretty good sized stick and hit the kid over the head with it, but that hadn't changed conditions. A dog tick couldn't have been fastened any tighter. He had to go back to class with the kid on his leg, pulling that little rascal after him wherever he went, like he had an anvil tied to his foot.

The teacher couldn't get the kid to let go either. They finally had to go to the principal's office and get the principal and the football coach to pry him off, and even they had to work at it. The coach said he'd once wrestled a madman with a butcher knife, and he'd rather do that again than try and get that kid off someone's leg.

The blind man was kind of like that kid. You couldn't lose the sonofabitch.

Near the house, Mr. Harold glanced at his watch and noted it was time for his wife to be home. He was overcome with deep concerns. He'd just thought the blind man pissing on his bathroom wall would be a problem, now he had greater worries. He actually had the gentleman in tow, bringing him to the house at suppertime. Mr. Harold pulled over at a station and got some gas and bought the boy and the blind man a Coke. The blind man seemed to have gotten over the loss of his trailer. Sadness for its contents, the dogs and the parakeet, failed to plague him.

While the boy and the blind man sat on the curb, Mr. Harold went around to a pay booth and called home. On the third ring his wife answered.

"Where in the world are you?" she said.

"I'm out here at a filling station. I got someone with me."

"You better have Marvin with you."

"I do, but I ain't talking about the boy. I got a blind man with me."

"You mean he can't see?"

"Not a lick. He's got a weed-eater. He's the groundskeeper next door. I tried to take him home but his trailer burned up with his dogs and bird in it, and I ain't got no place to take him but home for supper."

A moment of silence passed as Mrs. Harold considered. "Ain't there some kinda home you can put him in?"

"I can't think of any. I suppose I could tie a sign around his neck said 'Blind Man' and leave him on someone's step with his weed-eater."

"Well, that wouldn't be fair to whoever lived in that house, just pushing problems on someone else."

Mr. Harold was nervous. Mrs. Harold seemed awfully polite. Usually she got mad over the littlest thing. He was trying to figure if it was a trap when he realized that something about all this was bound to appeal to her religious nature. She went to church a lot. She read the *Baptist Standard* and watched a couple of Sunday afternoon TV shows with preaching in them. Blind people were loved by Baptists. Them and cripples. They got mentioned in the Bible a lot. Jesus had a special affection for them. Well, he liked lepers too, but Mr. Harold figured that was where even Mrs. Harold's dedicated Baptist beliefs might falter.

A loophole presented itself to Mr. Harold. He said, "I figure it's our Christian charity to take this fella in, honey. He can't see and he's lost his job and his trailer burned down with his pets in it."

"Well, I reckon you ought to bring him on over then. We'll feed him and I'll call around and see what my ladies' charities can do. It'll be my project. Wendy Lee is goin' around gettin' folks to pick up trash on a section of the highway, but I figure helping out a blind man would be Christian. Jesus helped blind people, but I don't never remember him picking up any trash."

When Mr. Harold loaded his son and the blind man back into the car, he was a happier man. He wasn't in trouble. Mrs. Harold thought taking in the blind man was her idea. He figured he could put up with the bastard another couple hours, then he'd find him a place to stay. Some homeless shelter with a cot and some hot soup if he wanted it. Maybe some preaching and breakfast before he had to hit the road.

At the house, Mrs. Harold met them at the door. Her little round body practically bounced. She found the blind man's hand and shook it. She told him how sorry she was, and he dropped his head and looked sad and thanked her. When they were inside, he said, "Is that cornbread I smell?"

"Yes it is," Mrs. Harold said, "and it won't be no time till it's ready. And we're having pinto beans with it. The beans were cooked yesterday and just need heating. They taste best when they've set a night."

"That's what burned his trailer down," the boy said. "He was cooking some pinto beans and forget 'em."

"Oh my," said Mrs. Harold, "I hope the beans won't bring back sad memories."

"No ma'am, them was limas I was cookin'."

"There was dogs in there and a parakeet," said the boy. "They got burned up too. There wasn't nothing left but some burnt wood and a piece of a couch and an old birdcage."

"I have some insurance papers in a deposit box downtown," the blind man said. "I could probably get me a couple of doublewides and have enough left over for a vacation with the money I'll get. I could get me some dogs and a bird easy enough too. I could even name them the same names as the ones burned up."

They sat and visited for a while in the living room while the cornbread cooked and the beans warmed up. The blind man and Mrs. Harold talked about religion. The blind man knew her favorite gospel tunes and sang a couple of them. Not too good, Mr. Harold thought, but Mrs. Harold seemed almost swoony.

The blind man knew her Sunday preaching programs too, and they talked about a few highlighted TV sermons. They debated the parables in the Bible and ended up discussing important and obscure points in the scripture, discovered the two of them saw things a lot alike when it came to interpretation. They had found dire warnings in Deuteronomy that scholars had overlooked.

Mrs. Harold got so lathered up with enthusiasm, she went into the kitchen and started throwing an apple pie together. Mr. Harold became nervous as soon as the pie pans began to rattle. This wasn't like her. She only cooked a pie to take to relatives after someone died or if it was Christmas or Thanksgiving and more than ten people were coming.

While she cooked, the blind man discussed wrestling holds with Mr. Harold's son. When dinner was ready, the blind man was positioned in Mr. Harold's chair, next to Mrs. Harold. They ate, and the blind man and Mrs. Harold further discussed scripture, and from time to time, the blind man would stop the religious talk long enough to give the boy a synopsis of some wrestling match or another. He had a way of cleverly turning the conversation without seeming to. He wasn't nearly as clever about passing the beans or the cornbread. The apple pie remained strategically guarded by his elbow.

After a while, the topic switched from the Bible and wrestling to the blind man's aches and miseries. He was overcome with them. There wasn't a thing that could be wrong with a person he didn't have.

Mrs. Harold used this conversational opportunity to complain about hip problems, hypoglycemia, overactive thyroids, and out-of-control sweat glands.

The blind man had a tip or two on how to make living with each of Mrs. Harold's complaints more congenial. Mrs. Harold said, "Well, sir, there's just not a thing you don't know something about. From wrestling to medicine."

The blind man nodded. "I try to keep up. I read a lot of Braille and listen to the TV and the radio. They criticize the TV, but they shouldn't. I get lots of my education there. I can learn from just about anything or anyone but a nigger."

Mrs. Harold, much to Mr. Harold's chagrin, agreed. This was a side of his wife he had never known. She had opinions and he hadn't known that. Stupid opinions, but opinions.

When Mr. Harold finally left the table, pieless, to hide out in the bathroom, the blind man and Mrs. Harold were discussing a plan for getting all the black folk back to Africa. Something to do with the number of boats necessary and the amount of proper hygiene needed.

And speaking of hygiene, Mr. Harold stood up as his bottom became wet. He had been sitting on the lid of the toilet and dampness had soaked through his pants. The blind man had been in the bathroom last and he'd pissed all over the lowered lid and splattered the wall.

Mr. Harold changed clothes and cleaned up the piss and washed his hands and splashed his face and looked at himself in the mirror. It was still him in there and he was awake.

About ten P.M. Mrs. Harold and the blind man put the boy to bed and the blind man sang the kid a rockabilly song, told him a couple of nigger jokes and one kike joke, and tucked him in.

Mr. Harold went in to see the boy, but he was asleep. The blind man and Mrs. Harold sat on the couch and talked about chicken and dumpling recipes and how to clean squirrels properly for frying. Mr. Harold sat in a chair and listened, hoping for some opening in the conversation into which he could spring. None presented itself.

Finally Mrs. Harold got the blind man some bedclothes and folded out the couch and told him a pleasant good night, touching the blind man's arm as she did. Mr. Harold noted she left her hand there quite a while.

In bed, Mr. Harold, hoping to prove to himself he was still man of the house, rolled over and put his arm around Mrs. Harold's hip. She had gotten dressed and gotten into bed in record time while he was taking a leak, and now she was feigning sleep, but Mr. Harold decided he wasn't going to go for it. He rubbed her ass and tried to work his hand between her legs from behind. He touched what he wanted, but it was as dry as a ditch in the Sahara.

Mrs. Harold pretended to wake up. She was mad. She said he ought to let a woman sleep, and didn't he think about anything else? Mr. Harold admitted that sex was a foremost thought of his, but he knew now nothing he said would matter. Neither humor nor flattery would work. He would not only go pieless this night, he would go assless as well.

Mrs. Harold began to explain how one of her mysterious headaches with back pain had descended on her. Arthritis might be the culprit, she said, though sometimes she suspicioned something more mysterious and deadly. Perhaps something incurable that would eventually involve large leaking sores and a deep coma.

Mr. Harold, frustrated, closed his eyes and tried to go to sleep with a hard-on. He couldn't understand, having had so much experience now, why it was so difficult for him to just forget his boner and go to bed, but it was, as always, a trial.

Finally, after making a trip to the bathroom to work his pistol and plunk its stringy wet bullet into the toilet water, he was able to go back to bed and drift off into an unhappy sleep.

A few hours later he awoke. He heard a noise like girlish laughter. He lay in bed and listened. It was, in fact, laughter, and it was coming from the living room. The blind man must have the TV on. But then he recognized the laughter. It hadn't come to him right away, because it had been ages since he had heard it. He reached for Mrs. Harold and she was gone.

He got out of bed and opened the bedroom door and crept quietly down the hall. There was a soft light on in the living room; it was the lamp on the TV muted by a white towel.

On the couch-bed was the blind man, wearing only his underwear and dark glasses. Mrs. Harold was on the bed too. She was wearing her nightie. The blind man was on top of her and they were pressed close. Mrs. Harold's hand sneaked over the blind's man's back and slid into his underwear and cupped his ass.

Mr. Harold let out his breath, and Mrs. Harold turned her head and saw him. She gave a little cry and rolled out from under the blind man. She laughed hysterically. "Why, honey, you're up."

The blind man explained immediately. They had been practicing a wrestling hold, one of the more complicated and not entirely legal ones, that involved grabbing the back of an opponent's tights. Mrs. Harold admitted that, as of tonight, she had been overcome with a passion for wrestling and was going to watch all the wrestling programs from now on. She thanked the blind man for the wrestling lesson and shook his hand and went past Mr. Harold and back to bed.

Mr. Harold stood looking at the blind man. He was on the couch on all fours looking in Mr. Harold's direction. The muted light from the towel-covered lamp hit the blind man's dark glasses and made them shine like the eyes of a wolf. His bared teeth completed the image.

Mr. Harold went back to bed. Mrs. Harold snuggled close. She wanted to be friendly. She ran her hand over his chest and down his belly and held his equipment, but he was as soft as a sock. She worked him a little and finally he got hard in spite of himself. They rolled together and did what he wanted to do earlier. For the first time in years, Mrs. Harold got off. She came with a squeak and thrust of her hips, and Mr. Harold knew that behind her closed eyes she saw a pale face and dark glasses, not him.

Later, he lay in bed and stared at the ceiling. Mrs. Harold's pussy had been as wet as a fish farm after her encounter with the blind man, wetter than he remembered it in years. What was it about the blind man that excited her? He was a racist cracker asshole who really knew nothing. He didn't have a job. He couldn't even work a weed-eater that good.

Mr. Harold felt fear. What he had here at home wasn't all that good, but he realized now he might lose it, and it was probably the best he could do. Even if his wife's conversation was as dull as the Republican convention and his son was as interesting as needlework, his home life took on a new and desperate importance. Something had to be done.

Next day, Mr. Harold got a break. The blind man made a comment about his love for snow cones. It was made while they were sitting alone in the kitchen. Mrs. Harold was in the shower and the boy was playing Nintendo in the living room. The blind man was rattling on like always. Last night rang no guilty bells for him.

"You know," said Mr. Harold, "I like a good snow cone myself. One of those blue ones."

"Oh yeah, that's coconut," said the blind man.

"What you say you and me go get one?"

"Ain't it gonna be lunch soon? I don't want to spoil my appetite."

"A cone won't spoil nothing. Come on, my treat."

The blind man was a little uncertain, but Mr. Harold could tell the idea of a free snow cone was strong within him. He let Mr. Harold lead him out to the car. Mr. Harold began to tremble with anticipation. He drove toward town, but when he got there, he drove on through.

"I thought you said the stand was close?" said the blind man. "Ain't we been driving a while?"

"Well, it's Sunday, and that one I was thinking of was closed. I know one cross the way stays open seven days a week during the summer."

Mr. Harold drove out into the country. He drove off the main highway and down a red clay road and pulled over to the side near a gap where irresponsibles dumped their garbage. He got out and went around to the blind man's side and took the blind man's arm and led him away from the car toward a pile of garbage. Flies hummed operative notes in the late morning air.

"We're in luck," Mr. Harold said. "Ain't no one here but us."

"Yeah, well it don't smell so good around here. Somethin' dead somewheres?"

"There's a cat hit out there on the highway."

"I'm kinda losin' my appetite for a cone."

"It'll come back soon as you put that cone in your mouth. Besides, we'll eat in the car."

Mr. Harold placed the blind man directly in front of a bag of household garbage. "You stand right here. Tell me what you want and I'll get it."

"I like a strawberry. Double on the juice."

"Strawberry it is."

Mr. Harold walked briskly back to his car, cranked it, and drove by the blind man, who cocked his head as the automobile passed. Mr. Harold drove down a ways, turned around and drove back the way he had come. The blind man still stood by the garbage heap, his cane looped over his wrist, only now he was facing the road.

Mr. Harold honked the horn as he drove past.

Just before reaching the city limits, a big black pickup began to make ominous maneuvers. The pickup was behind him and was riding his bumper. Mr. Harold tried to speed up, but that didn't work. He tried slowing down, but the truck nearly ran up his ass. He decided to pull to the side, but the truck wouldn't pass.

Eventually, Mr. Harold coasted to the emergency lane and stopped, but the truck pulled up behind him and two burly men got out. They looked as if the last bath they'd had was during the last rain, probably caught out in it while pulp wooding someone's posted land.

Mr. Harold assumed it was all some dreadful mistake. He got out of the car so they could see he wasn't who they thought he must be. The biggest one walked up to him and grabbed him behind the head with one hand and hit him with the other. The smaller man, smaller because his head seemed undersized, took his turn and hit Mr. Harold. The two men began to work on him. He couldn't fall down because the car held him up, and for some reason he couldn't pass out. These guys weren't as fast as Sonny Guy, and they weren't knocking him out, but they certainly hurt more.

"What kinda fella are you that would leave a blind man beside the road?" said the bigger man just before he busted Mr. Harold a good one in the nose.

Mr. Harold finally hit the ground. The small-headed man kicked him in the balls and the bigger man kicked him in the mouth, knocking out what was left of his front teeth; the man's fist had already stolen the others. When Mr. Harold was close to passing out, the small-headed man bent down and got hold of Mr. Harold's hair and looked him in the eye and said, "We hadn't been throwing out an old stray dog down that road, that fella might have got lost or hurt."

"He's much more resourceful than you think," Mr. Harold said, realizing who they meant, and then the small-headed man hit him a short chopping blow.

"I'm glad we seen him," said the bigger man, "and I'm glad we caught up with you. You just think you've took a beating. We're just getting started."

But at that moment the blind man appeared above Mr. Harold. He had found his way from the truck to the car, directed by the sound of the beating most likely. "No, boys," said the blind man, "that's good enough. I ain't the kind holds a grudge, even 'gainst a man would do what he did. I've had some theology training and done a little Baptist ministering. Holding a grudge ain't my way."

"Well, you're a good one," said the bigger man. "I ain't like that at all. I was blind and I was told I was gonna get a snow cone and a fella put me out at a garbage dump, I'd want that fella dead, or crippled up at the least."

"I understand," said the blind man. "It's hard to believe there's people like this in the world. But if you'll just drive me home, that'll be enough. I'd like to get on the way if it's no inconvenience. I have a little Bible lesson in Braille I'd like to study."

They went away and left Mr. Harold lying on the highway beside his car. As they drove by, the pickup tires tossed gravel on him and the exhaust enveloped him like a foul cotton sack.

Mr. Harold got up after five minutes and got inside his car and fell across the seat and lay there. He couldn't move. He spat out a tooth. His balls hurt. His face hurt. For that matter, his kneecaps where they'd kicked him didn't feel all that good either.

After an hour or so, Mr. Harold began to come around. An intense hatred for the blind man boiled up in his stomach. He sat up and started the car and headed home.

When he turned on his road, he was nearly sideswiped by a yellow moving van. It came at him so hard and fast he swerved into a ditch filled with sand and got his right rear tire stuck. He couldn't drive the car out. More he worked at it, the deeper the back tire spun in the sand. He got his jack out of the trunk and cranked up the rear end and put debris under the tire. Bad as he felt, it was quite a job. He finally drove out of there, and off the jack, leaving it lying in the dirt.

When he got to his house, certain in his heart the blind man was inside, he parked next to Mrs. Harold's station wagon. The station wagon was stuffed to the gills with boxes and sacks. He wondered what that was all about, but he didn't wonder too hard. He looked around the yard for a weapon. Out by the side of the house was the blind man's weed-eater. That would do. He figured he caught the blind man a couple of licks with that, he could get him down on the ground and finish him, stun him before the sonofabitch applied a wrestling hold.

He went in the house by the back door with the weed-eater cocked, and was astonished to find the room was empty. The kitchen table and chairs were gone. The cabinet doors were open and all the canned goods were missing. Where the stove had set was a greasy spot. Where the refrigerator had set was a wet spot. A couple of roaches, feeling brave and free to roam, scuttled across the kitchen floor as merry as kids on skates.

The living room was empty too. Not only of people, but furniture and roaches. The rest of the house was the same. Dust motes spun in the light. The front door was open.

Outside, Mr. Harold heard a car door slam. He limped out the front door and saw the station wagon. His wife was behind the wheel, and sitting next to her was the boy, and beside him the blind man, his arm hanging out the open window.

Mr. Harold beckoned to them by waving the weed-eater, but they ignored him. Mrs. Harold backed out of the drive quickly. Mr. Harold could hear the blind man talking to the boy about something or another and the boy was laughing. The station wagon turned onto the road and the car picked up speed. Mr. Harold went slack and leaned on the weed-eater for support.

At the moment before the station wagon passed in front of a line of high shrubs, the blind man turned to look out the window, and Mr. Harold saw his own reflection in the blind man's glasses.

Tight Little Stitches in a Dead Man's Back

For Ardath Mayhar

FROM THE JOURNAL OF PAUL MARDER

(Boom!)

That's a little scientist joke, and the proper way to begin this. As for the purpose of my notebook, I'm uncertain. Perhaps to organize my thoughts and not to go insane.

No. Probably so I can read it and feel as if I'm being spoken to. Maybe neither of those reasons. It doesn't matter. I just want to do it, and that is enough.

What's new?

Well, Mr. Journal, after all these years I've taken up martial arts again—or at least the forms and calisthenics of Tae Kwon Do. There is no one to spar with here in the lighthouse, so the forms have to do.

There is Mary, of course, but she keeps all her sparring verbal. And as of late, there is not even that. I long for her to call me a sonofabitch. Anything. Her hatred of me has cured to 100-percent perfection and she no longer finds it necessary to speak. The tight lines around her eyes and mouth, the emotional heat that radiates from her body like a dreadful cold sore looking for a place to lie down is voice enough for her. She lives only for the moment when she (the cold sore) can attach herself to me with her needles, ink and thread. She lives only for the design on my back.

That's all I live for as well. Mary adds to it nightly and I enjoy the pain. The tattoo is of a great, blue mushroom cloud, and in the cloud, etched ghost-like, is the face of our daughter, Rae. Her lips are drawn tight, eyes are closed and there are stitches deeply pulled to simulate the lashes. When I move fast and hard they rip slightly and Rae cries bloody tears.

That's one reason for the martial arts. The hard practice of them helps me to tear the stitches so my daughter can cry. Tears are the only thing I can give her.

Each night I bare my back eagerly to Mary and her needles. She pokes deep and I moan in pain as she moans in ecstasy and hatred. She adds more color to the design, works with brutal precision to bring Rae's face out in sharper relief. After ten minutes she tires and will work no more. She puts the tools away and I go to the full-length mirror on the wall. The lantern on the shelf flickers like a jack-o-lantern in a high wind, but there is enough light for me to look over my shoulder and examine the tattoo. And it is beautiful. Better each night as Rae's face becomes more and more defined.

Rae.

Rae. God, can you forgive me, sweetheart?

But the pain of the needles, wonderful and cleansing as they are, is not enough. So I go sliding, kicking and punching along the walkway around the lighthouse, feeling Rae's red tears running down my spine, gathering in the waistband of my much-stained canvas pants.

Winded, unable to punch and kick anymore, I walk over to the railing and call down into the dark, "Hungry?"

In response to my voice a chorus of moans rises up to greet me.

Later, I lie on my pallet, hands behind my head, examine the ceiling and try to think of something worthy to write in you, Mr. Journal. So seldom is there anything. Nothing seems truly worthwhile.

Bored of this, I roll on my side and look at the great light that once shone out to the ships, but is now forever snuffed. Then I turn the other direction and look at my wife sleeping on her bunk, her naked ass turned toward me. I try to remember what it was like to make love to her, but it is difficult. I only remember that I miss it. For a long moment I stare at my wife's ass as if it is a mean mouth about to open and reveal teeth. Then I roll on my back again, stare at the ceiling, and continue this routine until daybreak.

Mornings I greet the flowers, their bright red and yellow blooms bursting from the heads of long-dead bodies that will not rot. The flowers open wide to reveal their little black brains and their feathery feelers, and they lift their blooms upward and moan. I get a wild pleasure out of this. For one crazed moment I feel like a rock singer appearing before his starry-eyed audience.

When I tire of the game I get the binoculars, Mr. Journal, and examine the eastern plains with them, as if I expect a city to materialize

JOE R. LANSDALE

there. The most interesting thing I have seen on those plains is a herd of large lizards thundering north. For a moment, I considered calling Mary to see them, but I didn't. The sound of my voice, the sight of my face, upsets her. She loves only the tattoo and is interested in nothing more.

When I finish looking at the plains, I walk to the other side. To the west, where the ocean was, there is now nothing but miles and miles of cracked, black sea bottom. Its only resemblance to a great body of water are the occasional dust storms that blow out of the west like dark tidal waves and wash the windows black at mid-day. And the creatures. Mostly mutated whales. Monstrously large, sluggish things. Abundant now where once they were near extinction. (Perhaps the whales should form some sort of Greenpeace organization for humans now. What do you think, Mr. Journal? No need to answer. Just another one of those little scientist jokes.)

These whales crawl across the sea bottom near the lighthouse from time to time, and if the mood strikes them, they rise on their tails and push their heads near the tower and examine it. I keep expecting one to flop down on us, crushing us like bugs. But no such luck. For some unknown reason the whales never leave the cracked seabed to venture onto what we formerly called the shore. It's as if they live in invisible water and are bound by it. A racial memory perhaps. Or maybe there's something in that cracked black soil they need. I don't know.

Besides the whales I suppose I should mention I saw a shark once. It was slithering along at a great distance and the tip of its fin was winking in the sunlight. I've also seen some strange, legged fish and some things I could not put a name to. I'll just call them whale food since I saw one of the whales dragging his bottom jaw along the ground one day, scooping up the creatures as they tried to beat a hasty retreat.

Exciting, huh? Well, that's how I spend my day, Mr. Journal. Roaming about the tower with my glasses, coming in to write in you, waiting anxiously for Mary to take hold of that kit and give me the signal. The mere thought of it excites me to erection. I suppose you could call that our sex act together.

And what was I doing the day they dropped The Big One?

Glad you asked that, Mr. Journal, really I am.

I was doing the usual. Up at six, did the shit, shower and shave routine. Had breakfast. Got dressed. Tied my tie. I remember doing the latter, and not very well, in front of the bedroom mirror, and noticing that I had shaved poorly. A hunk of dark beard decorated my chin like a bruise.

Rushing to the bathroom to remedy that, I opened the door as Rae, naked as the day of her birth, was stepping from the tub.

Surprised, she turned to look at me. An arm went over her breasts, and a hand, like a dove settling into a fiery bush, covered her pubic area.

Embarrassed, I closed the door with an "excuse me" and went about my business—unshaved. It was an innocent thing. An accident. Nothing sexual. But when I think of her now, more often than not, that is the first image that comes to mind. I guess it was the moment I realized my baby had grown into a beautiful woman.

That was also the day she went off to her first day of college and got to see, ever so briefly, the end of the world.

And it was the day the triangle—Mary, Rae and myself—shattered.

If my first memory of Rae alone is that day, naked in the bathroom, my foremost memory of us as a family is when Rae was six. We used to go to the park and she would ride the merry-go-round, swing, teeter-totter, and finally my back. ("I want to piggy, Daddy.") We would gallop about until my legs were rubber, then we would stop at the bench where Mary sat waiting. I would turn my back to the bench so Mary could take Rae down, but always before she did, she would reach around from behind, caressing Rae, pushing her tight against my back, and Mary's hands would touch my chest.

God, but if I could describe those hands. She still has hands like that, after all these years. I feel them fluttering against my back when she works. They are long and sleek and artistic. Naturally soft, like the belly of a baby rabbit. And when she held Rae and me that way, I felt that no matter what happened in the world, we three could stand against it and conquer.

But now the triangle is broken and the geometry gone away.

So the day Rae went off to college and was fucked into oblivion by the dark, pelvic thrust of the bomb, Mary drove me to work. Me, Paul Marder, big shot with The Crew. One of the finest, brightest young minds in the industry. Always teaching, inventing and improving on our nuclear threat, because, as we'd often joke, "We cared enough to send only the very best."

When we arrived at the guard booth, I had out my pass, but there was no one to take it. Beyond the chain-link gate there was a wild melee of people running, screaming, falling down.

I got out of the car and ran to the gate. I called out to a man I knew as he ran by. When he turned his eyes were wild and his lips were flecked with foam. "The missiles are flying," he said, then he was gone, running madly.

I jumped in the car, pushed Mary aside and stomped the gas. The Buick leaped into the fence, knocking it asunder. The car spun, slammed into the edge of a building and went dead. I grabbed Mary's hand, pulled her from the car and we ran toward the great elevators.

We made one just in time. There were others running for it as the door closed, and the elevator went down. I still remember the echo of their fists on the metal just as it began to drop. It was like the rapid heartbeat of something dying.

And so the elevator took us to the world of Down Under and we locked it off. There we were in a five-mile layered city designed not only as a massive office and laboratory, but as an impenetrable shelter. It was our special reward for creating the poisons of war. There was food, water, medical supplies, films, books, you name it. Enough to last two thousand people for a hundred years. Of the two thousand it was designed for, perhaps eleven hundred made it. The others didn't run fast enough from the parking lot or the other buildings, or they were late for work, or maybe they had called in sick.

Perhaps they were the lucky ones. They might have died in their sleep. Or while they were having a morning quickie with the spouse. Or perhaps as they lingered over that last cup of coffee.

Because you see, Mr. Journal, Down Under was no paradise. Before long suicides were epidemic, I considered it myself from time to time. People slashed their throats, drank acid, took pills. It was not unusual to come out of your cubicle in the morning and find people dangling from pipes and rafters like ripe fruit.

There were also the murders. Most of them performed by a crazed group who lived in the deeper recesses of the unit and called themselves the Shit Faces. From time to time they smeared dung on themselves and ran amok, clubbing men, women, and children born down under to death. It was rumored they ate human flesh.

We had a police force of sorts, but it didn't do much. It didn't have much sense of authority. Worse, we all viewed ourselves as deserving victims. Except for Mary, we had all helped to blow up the world.

Mary came to hate me. She came to the conclusion I had killed Rae. It was a realization that grew in her like a drip, growing and growing until it became a gushing flood of hate. She seldom talked to me. She tacked up a picture of Rae and looked at it most of the time.

Topside she had been an artist, and she took that up again. She rigged a kit of tools and inks and became a tattooist. Everyone came to her for a mark. And though each was different, they all seemed to indicate one thing: I fucked up. I blew up the world. Brand me.

Day in and day out she did her tattoos, having less and less to do with me, pushing herself more and more into this work until she was as skilled with skin and needles as she had been Topside with brush and canvas. And one night, as we lay on our separate pallets, feigning sleep, she said to me, "I just want you to know how much I hate you."

"I know," I said.

"You killed Rae."

"I know."

"You say you killed her, you bastard. Say it."

"I killed her," I said, and meant it.

Next day I asked for my tattoo. I told her of this dream that came to me nightly. There would be darkness, and out of this darkness would come a swirl of glowing clouds, and the clouds would melt into a mushroom shape, and out of that—torpedo-shaped, nose pointing skyward, striding on ridiculous cartoon legs—would step The Bomb.

There was a face painted on The Bomb, and it was my face. And suddenly the dream's point of view would change, and I would be looking out of the eyes of that painted face. Before me was my daughter. Naked. Lying on the ground. Her legs wide apart. Her sex glazed like a wet canyon.

And I/The Bomb would dive into her, pulling those silly feet after me, and she would scream. I could hear it echo as I plunged through her belly, finally driving myself out of the top of her head, then blowing to terminal orgasm. And the dream would end where it began. A mushroom cloud. Darkness.

When I told Mary the dream and asked her to interpret it in her art, she said, "Bare your back," and that's how the design began. An inch of work at a time—a painful inch. She made sure of that.

Never once did I complain. She'd send the needles home as hard and deep as she could, and though I might moan or cry out, I never asked her to stop. I could feel those fine hands touching my back and I loved it. The needles. The hands. The needles. The hands.

And if that was so much fun, you ask, why did I come Topside?

You ask such probing questions, Mr. Journal. Really you do, and I'm glad you asked that. My telling will be like a laxative, I hope. Maybe if I just let the shit flow I'll wake up tomorrow and feel a lot better about myself.

Sure. And it will be the dawning of a new Pepsi generation as well. It will have all been a bad dream. The alarm clock will ring. I'll get up, have my bowl of Rice Krispies and tie my tie.

Okay, Mr. Journal. The answer. Twenty years or so after we went Down Under, a fistful of us decided it couldn't be any worse Topside than it was below. We made plans to go see. Simple as that. Mary and I even talked a little. We both entertained the crazed belief Rae might have survived. She would be thirty-eight. We might have been hiding below like vermin for no reason. It could be a brave new world up there.

I remember thinking these things, Mr. Journal, and half-believing them.

We outfitted two sixty-foot crafts that were used as part of our transportation system Down Under, plugged in the half-remembered codes that opened the elevators, and drove the vehicles inside. The elevator lasers cut through the debris above them and before long we were Topside. The doors opened to sunlight muted by gray-green clouds and a desert-like landscape. Immediately I knew there was no brave new world over the horizon. It had all gone to hell in a fiery hand basket, and all that was left of man's millions of years of development were a few pathetic humans living Down Under like worms, and a few others crawling Topside like the same.

We cruised about a week and finally came to what had once been the Pacific Ocean. Only there wasn't any water now, just that cracked blackness.

We drove along the shore for another week and finally saw life. A whale. Jacobs immediately got the idea to shoot one and taste its meat.

Using a high-powered rifle he killed it, and he and seven others cut slabs off it, brought the meat back to cook. They invited all of us to eat, but the meat looked greenish and there wasn't much blood and we warned him against it. But Jacobs and the others ate it anyway. As Jacobs said, "It's something to do."

A little later on Jacobs threw up blood and his intestines boiled out of his mouth, and not long after those who had shared the meat had the same thing happen to them. They died crawling on their bellies like gutted dogs. There wasn't a thing we could do for them. We couldn't even bury them. The ground was too hard. We stacked them like cordwood along the shoreline and moved camp down a way, tried to remember how remorse felt.

And that night, while we slept as best we could, the roses came.

Now, let me admit, Mr. Journal, I do not actually know how the roses survived, but I have an idea. And since you've agreed to hear my story—and even if you haven't, you're going to anyway—I'm going to put logic and fantasy together and hope to arrive at the truth.

These roses lived in the ocean bed, underground, and at night they came out. Up until then they had survived as parasites of reptiles and animals, but a new food had arrived from Down Under. Humans. Their creators, actually. Looking at it that way, you might say we were the gods who conceived them, and their partaking of our flesh and blood was but a new version of wine and wafer.

I can imagine the pulsating brains pushing up through the sea bottom on thick stalks, extending feathery feelers and tasting the air out there beneath the light of the moon—which through those odd clouds gave the impression of a pus-filled boil—and I can imagine them uprooting and dragging their vines across the ground toward the shore where the corpses lay.

Thick vines sprouted little, thorny vines, and these moved up the bank and touched the corpses. Then, with a lashing motion, the thorns tore into the flesh, and the vines, like snakes, slithered through the wounds and inside. Secreting a dissolving fluid that turned the innards to the consistency of watery oatmeal, they slurped up the mess, and the vines grew and grew at amazing speed, moved and coiled throughout the bodies, replacing nerves and shaping into the symmetry of the muscles they had devoured, and lastly they pushed up through the necks, into the skulls, ate tongues and eyeballs and sucked up the mouse-gray brains like soggy gruel. With an explosion of skull shrapnel, the roses bloomed, their tooth-hard petals expanding into beautiful red and yellow flowers, hunks of human heads dangling from them like shattered watermelon rinds.

In the center of these blooms a fresh, black brain pulsed and feathery feelers once again tasted air for food and breeding grounds. Energy waves from the floral brains shot through the miles and miles of vines that were knotted inside the bodies, and as they had replaced nerves, muscles and vital organs, they made the bodies stand. Then those corpses turned their flowered heads toward the tents where we slept, and the blooming corpses (another little scientist joke there if you're into English idiom, Mr. Journal) walked, eager to add the rest of us to their animated bouquet.

I saw my first rose-head while I was taking a leak.

I had left the tent and gone down by the shoreline to relieve myself when I caught sight of it out of the corner of my eye. Because of the bloom I first thought it was Susan Dyers. She wore a thick, woolly Afro that surrounded her head like a lion's mane, and the shape of the thing struck me as her silhouette. But when I zipped and turned, it wasn't an Afro. It was a flower blooming out of Jacobs. I recognized him by his clothes and the hunk of his face that hung off one of the petals like a worn-out hat on a peg.

In the center of the blood-red flower was a pulsating sack, and all around it little wormy things squirmed. Directly below the brain was a thin proboscis. It extended toward me like an erect penis. At its tip, just inside the opening, were a number of large thorns.

A sound like a moan came out of that proboscis, and I stumbled back. Jacobs's body quivered briefly, as if he had been besieged by a sudden chill, and ripping through his flesh and clothes, from neck to foot, was a mass of thorny, wagging vines that shot out to five feet in length.

With an almost invisible motion, they waved from west to east, slashed my clothes, tore my hide, knocked my feet out from beneath me. It was like being hit by a cat-o'-nine-tails.

Dazed, I rolled onto my hands and knees, bear-walked away from it. The vines whipped against my back and butt, cut deep.

Every time I got to my feet, they tripped me. The thorns not only cut, they burned like hot ice picks. I finally twisted away from a net of vines, slammed through one last shoot, and made a break for it.

Without realizing it, I was running back to the tent. My body felt as if I had been lying on a bed of nails and razor blades. My forearm hurt something terrible where I had used it to lash the thorns away from me. I glanced down at it as I ran. It was covered in blood. A strand of vine about two feet in length was coiled around it like a garter snake. A thorn had torn a deep wound in my arm, and the vine was sliding an end into the wound.

Screaming, I held my forearm in front of me like I had just discovered it. The flesh, where the vine had entered, rippled and made a bulge that looked like a junkie's favorite vein. The pain was nauseating. I snatched at the vine, ripped it free. The thorns turned against me—like fishhooks.

The pain was so much I fell to my knees, but I had the vine out of me. It squirmed in my hand, and I felt a thorn gouge my palm. I threw the vine into the dark. Then I was up and running for the tent again.

The roses must have been at work for quite some time before I saw Jacobs, because when I broke back into camp yelling, I saw Susan, Ralph, Casey and some others, and already their heads were blooming, skulls cracking away like broken model kits.

Jane Calloway was facing a rose-possessed corpse, and the dead body had its hands on her shoulders, and the vines were jetting out of the corpse, weaving around her like a web, tearing, sliding inside her, breaking off. The proboscis poked into her mouth and extended down her throat, forced her head back. The scream she started came out a gurgle.

I tried to help her, but when I got close, the vines whipped at me and I had to jump back. I looked for something to grab, to hit the damn thing with, but there was nothing. When next I looked at Jane, vines were stabbing out of her eyes and her tongue, now nothing more than lava-thick blood, was dripping out of her mouth onto her breasts, which, like the rest of her body, were riddled with stabbing vines.

I ran away then. There was nothing I could do for Jane. I saw others embraced by corpse hands and tangles of vines, but now my only thought was Mary. Our tent was to the rear of the campsite, and I ran there as fast as I could.

She was lumbering out of our tent when I arrived. The sound of screams had awakened her. When she saw me running she froze. By the time I got to her, two vine-riddled corpses were coming up on the tent from the left side. Grabbing her hand I half-pulled, half-dragged her away from there. I got to one of the vehicles and pushed her inside.

I locked the doors just as Jacobs, Susan, Jane, and others appeared at the windshield, leaning over the rocket-nose hood, the feelers around the brain sacks vibrating like streamers in a high wind. Hands slid greasily down the windshield. Vines flopped and scratched and cracked against it like thin bicycle chains.

I got the vehicle started, stomped the accelerator, and the rose-heads went flying. One of them, Jacobs, bounced over the hood and splattered into a spray of flesh, ichor and petals.

I had never driven the vehicle, so my maneuvering was rusty. But it didn't matter. There wasn't exactly a traffic rush to worry about.

After an hour or so, I turned to look at Mary. She was staring at me, her eyes like the twin barrels of a double-barreled shotgun. They seemed to say, "More of your doing," and in a way she was right. I drove on.

Daybreak we came to the lighthouse. I don't know how it survived. One of those quirks. Even the glass was unbroken. It looked like a great stone finger shooting us the bird.

The vehicle's tank was near empty, so I assumed here was as good a place to stop as any. At least there was shelter, something we could fortify. Going on until the vehicle was empty of fuel didn't make much sense. There wouldn't be any more fill-ups, and there might not be any more shelter like this.

Mary and I (in our usual silence) unloaded the supplies from the vehicle and put them in the lighthouse. There was enough food, water, chemicals for the chemical toilet, odds and ends, extra clothes to last us a year. There were also some guns. A Colt .45 revolver, two twelve-gauge shotguns and a .38, and enough shells to fight a small war.

When everything was unloaded, I found some old furniture downstairs and, using tools from the vehicle, tried to barricade the bottom door and the one at the top of the stairs. When I finished, I thought of a line from a story I had once read, a line that always disturbed me. It went something like, "Now we're shut in for the night."

Days. Nights. All the same. Shut in with one another, our memories and the fine tattoo.

A few days later I spotted the roses. It was as if they had smelled us out. And maybe they had. From a distance, through the binoculars, they reminded me of old women in bright sun hats.

It took them the rest of the day to reach the lighthouse, and they immediately surrounded it, and when I appeared at the railing they would lift their heads and moan.

And that, Mr. Journal, brings us up to now.

I thought I had written myself out, Mr. Journal. Told the only part of my life story I would ever tell, but now I'm back. You can't keep a good world-destroyer down.

I saw my daughter last night and she's been dead for years. But I saw her, I did, naked, smiling at me, calling to ride piggyback.

Here's what happened.

It was cold last night. Must be getting along winter. I had rolled off my pallet onto the cold floor. Maybe that's what brought me awake. The cold. Or maybe it was just gut instinct.

It had been a particularly wonderful night with the tattoo. The face had been made so clear it seemed to stand out from my back. It had finally become more defined than the mushroom cloud. The needles went in hard and deep, but I've had them in me so much now I barely feel the pain. After looking in the mirror at the beauty of the design, I went to bed happy, or as happy as I can get.

During the night the eyes ripped open. The stitches came out and I didn't know it until I tried to rise from the cold, stone floor and my back puckered against it where the blood had dried.

I pulled myself free and got up. It was dark, but we had a good moonspill that night and I went to the mirror to look. It was bright enough that I could see Rae's reflection clearly, the color of her face, the color of the cloud. The stitches had fallen away and now the wounds were spread wide, and inside the wounds were eyes. Oh God, Rae's blue eyes. Her mouth smiled at me and her teeth were very white.

Oh, I hear you, Mr. Journal. I hear what you're saying. And I thought of that. My first impression was that I was about six bricks shy a load, gone around the old bend. But I know better now. You see, I lit a candle and held it over my shoulder, and with the candle and the moonlight, I could see even more clearly. It was Rae all right, not just a tattoo.

I looked over at my wife on the bunk, her back to me, as always. She had not moved.

I turned back to the reflection. I could hardly see the outline of myself, just Rae's face smiling out of that cloud.

"Rae," I whispered, "is that you?"

"Come on, Daddy," said the mouth in the mirror, "that's a stupid question. Of course it's me."

"But . . . You're . . . you're . . . "

"Dead?"

"Yes . . . Did . . . did it hurt much?"

She cackled so loudly the mirror shook. I could feel the hairs on my neck rising. I thought for sure Mary would wake up, but she slept on.

"It was instantaneous, Daddy, and even then, it was the greatest pain imaginable. Let me show you how it hurt."

The candle blew out and I dropped it. I didn't need it anyway. The mirror grew bright and Rae's smile went from ear to ear—literally—and the flesh on her bones seemed like crepe paper before a powerful fan, and that fan blew the hair off her head, the skin off her skull and melted those beautiful, blue eyes and those shiny white teeth of hers to a putrescent goo the color and consistency of fresh bird shit. Then there was only the skull, and it heaved in half and flew backwards into the dark world of the mirror and there was no reflection now, only the hurtling fragments of a life that once was and was now nothing more than swirling cosmic dust.

I closed my eyes and looked away.

"Daddy?"

I opened them, looked over my shoulder into the mirror. There was Rae again, smiling out of my back.

"Darling," I said, "I'm so sorry."

"So are we," she said, and there were faces floating past her in the mirror. Teenagers, children, men and women, babies, little embryos swirling around her head like planets around the sun. I closed my eyes again, but I could not keep them closed. When I opened them the multitudes of swirling dead, and those who had never had a chance to live, were gone. Only Rae was there.

"Come close to the mirror, Daddy."

I backed up to it. I backed until the hot wounds that were Rae's eyes touched the cold glass and the wounds became hotter and hotter and Rae called out, "Ride me piggy, Daddy," and then I felt her weight on my back, not the weight of a six-year-old child or a teenage girl, but a great weight, like the world was on my shoulders and bearing down.

Leaping away from the mirror I went hopping and whooping about the room, same as I used to in the park. Around and around I went, and as I did, I glanced in the mirror. Astride me was Rae, lithe and naked, her red hair fanning around her as I spun. And when I whirled by the mirror again, I saw that she was six years old. Another spin and there was a skeleton with red hair, one hand held high, the jaws open and yelling, "Ride 'em, cowboy."

"How?" I managed, still bucking and leaping, giving Rae the ride of her life. She bent to my ear and I could feel her warm breath. "You want to know how I'm here, Daddy-dear? I'm here because you created me. Once you laid between Mother's legs and thrust me into existence, the two of you, with all the love there was in you. This time you thrust me into existence with your guilt and Mother's hate. Her thrusting needles, your arching back. And now I've come back for one last ride, Daddy-o. Ride, you bastard, ride."

All the while I had been spinning, and now as I glimpsed the mirror I saw wall to wall faces, weaving in, weaving out, like smiling stars, and all those smiles opened wide and words came out in chorus, "Where were you when they dropped The Big One?"

Each time I spun and saw the mirror again, it was a new scene. Great flaming winds scorching across the world, babies turning to fleshy Jell-O, heaps of charred bones, brains boiling out of the heads of men and women like backed-up toilets overflowing, The Almighty, Glory Hallelujah, Ours Is Bigger Than Yours Bomb hurtling forward, the mirror going mushroom white, then clear, and me, spinning, Rae pressed tight against my back, melting like butter on a griddle, evaporating into the eye wounds on my back, and finally me alone, collapsing to the floor beneath the weight of the world.

Mary never awoke.

The vines outsmarted me.

A single strand found a crack downstairs somewhere and wound up the steps and slipped beneath the door that led into the tower. Mary's bunk was not far from the door, and in the night, while I slept and later while I spun in front of the mirror and lay on the floor before it, it made its way to Mary's bunk, up between her legs, and entered her sex effortlessly.

I suppose I should give the vine credit for doing what I had not been able to do in years, Mr. Journal, and that's enter Mary. Oh God, that's a funny one, Mr. Journal. Real funny. Another little scientist joke. Let's make that a mad scientist joke, what say? Who but a madman would play with the lives of human beings by constantly trying to build the bigger and better boom machine?

So what of Rae, you ask?

I'll tell you. She is inside me. My back feels the weight. She twists in my guts like a corkscrew. I went to the mirror a moment ago, and the tattoo no longer looks like it did. The eyes have turned to crusty sores and the entire face looks like a scab. It's as if the bile that made up my soul, the unthinking nearsightedness, the guilt that I am, has festered from inside and spoiled the picture with pustule bumps, knots and scabs.

To put it in layman's terms, Mr. Journal, my back is infected. Infected with what I am. A blind, senseless fool.

The wife?

Ah, the wife. God, how I loved that woman. I have not really touched her in years, merely felt those wonderful hands on my back as she jabbed the needles home, but I never stopped loving her. It was not a love that glowed anymore, but it was there, though hers for me was long gone and wasted.

This morning when I got up from the floor, the weight of Rae and the world on my back, I saw the vine coming up from beneath the door and stretching over to her. I yelled her name. She did not move. I ran to her and saw it was too late. Before I could put a hand on her, I saw her flesh ripple and bump up, like a den of mice were nesting under a quilt. The vines were at work. (Out go the old guts, in go the new vines.)

There was nothing I could do for her.

I made a torch out of a chair leg and old quilt, set fire to it, burned the vine from between her legs, watched it retreat, smoking, under the door. Then I got a board, nailed it along the bottom, hoping it would keep others out for at least a little while. I got one of the twelve-gauges and loaded it. It's on the desk beside me, Mr. Journal, but even I know I'll never use it. It was just something to do, as Jacobs said when he killed and ate the whale. Something to do.

I can hardly write anymore. My back and shoulders hurt so bad. It's the weight of Rae and the world.

I've just come back from the mirror and there is very little left of the tattoo. Some blue and black ink, a touch of red that was Rae's hair. It looks like an abstract painting now. Collapsed design, running colors. It's real swollen. I look like the hunchback of Notre Dame.

What am I going to do, Mr. Journal?

Well, as always, I'm glad you asked that. You see, I've thought this out.

I could throw Mary's body over the railing before it blooms. I could do that. Then I could doctor my back. It might even heal, though I doubt it. Rae wouldn't let that happen, I can tell you now. And I don't blame her. I'm on her side. I'm just a walking dead man and have been for years.

I could put the shotgun under my chin and work the trigger with my toes, or maybe push it with the very pen I'm using to create you, Mr. Journal. Wouldn't that be neat? Blow my brains to the ceiling and sprinkle you with my blood.

But as I said, I loaded the gun because it was something to do. I'd never use it on myself or Mary.

You see, I want Mary. I want her to hold Rae and me one last time like she used to in the park. And she can. There's a way.

I've drawn all the curtains and made curtains out of blankets for those spots where there aren't any. It'll be sunup soon and I don't want that kind of light in here. I'm writing this by candlelight and it gives the entire room a warm glow. I wish I had wine. I want the atmosphere to be just right.

Over on Mary's bunk she's starting to twitch. Her neck is swollen where the vines have congested and are writhing toward their favorite morsel, the brain. Pretty soon the rose will bloom (I hope she's one of the bright yellow ones, yellow was her favorite color and she wore it well) and Mary will come for me.

When she does, I'll stand with my naked back to her. The vines will whip out and cut me before she reaches me, but I can stand it. I'm used to pain. I'll pretend the thorns are Mary's needles. I'll stand that way until she folds her dead arms around me and her body pushes up against the wound she made in my back, the wound that is our daughter Rae. She'll hold me so the vines and the proboscis can do their work. And while she holds me, I'll grab her fine hands and push them against my chest, and it will be we three again, standing against the world, and I'll close my eyes and delight in her soft, soft hands one last time.

The Big Blow

For Norman Partridge

TUESDAY, SEPTEMBER 4, 1900, 4:00 P.M.

Telegraphed Message from Washington, D.C., Weather Bureau, Central Office, to Issac Cline, Galveston, Texas, Weather Bureau:

Tropical storm disturbance moving northward over Cuba.

6:38 P.M.

On an afternoon hotter than two rats fucking in a wool sock, John McBride, six-foot one-and-a-half inches, 220 pounds, ham-handed, built like a wild boar and of similar disposition, arrived by ferry from mainland Texas to Galveston Island, a six-gun under his coat and a razor in his shoe.

As the ferry docked, McBride set his suitcase down, removed his bowler, took a crisp white handkerchief from inside his coat, wiped the bowler's sweatband with it, used it to mop his forehead, ran it over his thinning black hair, and put the hat back on.

An old Chinese guy in San Francisco told him he was losing his hair because he always wore hats, and McBride decided maybe he was right, but now he wore the hats to hide his baldness. At thirty he felt he was too young to lose his hair. The Chinaman had given him a tonic for his problem at a considerable sum. McBride used it religiously, rubbed it into his scalp. So far, all he could see it had done was shine his bald spot. He ever got back to Frisco, he was gonna look that Chinaman up, maybe knock a few knots on his head.

As McBride picked up his suitcase and stepped off the ferry with the others, he observed the sky. It appeared green as a pool-table cloth. As the sun dipped down to drink from the Gulf, McBride almost expected to see steam rise up from beyond the island. He took in a deep breath of sea air and thought it tasted all right. It made him hungry. That was why he was here. He was hungry. First on the menu was a woman, then a steak, then some rest before the final meal—the thing he had come for. To whip a nigger.

He hired a buggy to take him to a poke house he had been told about by his employers, the fellows who had paid his way from Chicago. According to what they said, there was a redhead there so good and tight she'd make you sing soprano. Way he felt, if she was redheaded, female, and ready, he'd be all right, and to hell with the song. It was on another's tab anyway.

As the coach trotted along, McBride took in Galveston. It was a Southerner's version of New York, with a touch of the tropics. Houses were upraised on stilts—thick support posts actually—against the washing of storm waters, and in the city proper the houses looked to be fresh off Deep South plantations.

City Hall had apparently been designed by an architect with a Moorish background. It was ripe with domes and spirals. The style collided with a magnificent clock housed in the building's highest point, a peaked tower. The clock was like a miniature Big Ben. England meets the Middle East.

Electric streetcars hissed along the streets, and there were a large number of bicycles, carriages, buggies, and pedestrians. McBride even saw one automobile.

The streets themselves were made of buried wooden blocks that McBride identified as ships' ballast. Some of the side streets were made of white shell, and some were hardened sand. He liked what he saw, thought: Maybe, after I do in the nigger, I'll stick around a while. Take in the sun at the beach. Find a way to get my fingers in a little solid graft of some sort.

When McBride finally got to the whorehouse, it was full dark. He gave the black driver a big tip, cocked his bowler, grabbed his suitcase, went through the ornate iron gate, up the steps, and inside to get his tumblers clicked right.

After giving his name to the plump madam, who looked as if she could still grind out a customer or two herself, he was given the royalty treatment. The madam herself took him upstairs, undressed him, bathed him, fondled him a bit.

When he was clean, she dried him off, nestled him in bed, kissed him on the forehead as if he were her little boy, then toddled off. The moment she left, he climbed out of bed, got in front of the mirror on the dresser and combed his hair, trying to push as much as possible over the bald spot. He had just gotten it arranged and gone back to bed when the redhead entered.

She was green-eyed and a little thick-waisted, but not bad to look at. She had fire red hair on her head and a darker fire between her legs, which were white as sheets and smooth as a newborn pig.

He started off by hurting her a little, tweaking her nipples, just to show her who was boss. She pretended to like it. Kind of money his employers were paying, he figured she'd dip a turd in gravel and push it around the floor with her nose and pretend to like it.

McBride roughed her bottom some, then got in the saddle and bucked a few. Later on, when she got a little slow about doing what he wanted, he blacked one of her eyes.

When the representatives of the Galveston Sporting Club showed up, he was lying in bed with the redhead, uncovered, letting a hot wind blow through the open windows and dry his and the redhead's juices.

The madam let the club members in and went away. There were four of them, all dressed in evening wear with top hats in their hands. Two were gray-haired and gray-whiskered. The other two were younger men. One was large, had a face that looked as if it regularly stopped cannonballs. Both eyes were black from a recent encounter. His nose was flat and strayed to the left of his face. He did his breathing through his mouth. He didn't have any top front teeth.

The other young man was slight and a dandy. This, McBride assumed, would be Ronald Beems, the man who had written him on behalf of the Sporting Club.

Everything about Beems annoyed McBride. His suit, unlike the wrinkled and drooping suits of the others, looked fresh-pressed, unresponsive to the afternoon's humidity. He smelled faintly of mothballs and naphtha, and some sort of hair tonic that had ginger as a base. He wore a thin little moustache and the sort of hair McBride wished he had. Black, full, and longish, with muttonchop sideburns. He had perfect features. No fist had ever touched him. He stood stiff, as if he had a hoe handle up his ass.

Beems, like the others, looked at McBride and the redhead with more than a little astonishment. McBride lay with his legs spread and his back propped against a pillow. He looked very big there. His legs and shoulders and arms were thick and twisted with muscle and glazed in sweat. His stomach protruded a bit, but it was hard-looking.

The whore, sweaty, eye blacked, legs spread, breasts slouching from the heat, looked more embarrassed than McBride. She wanted to cover, but she didn't move. Fresh in her memory was that punch to the eye.

"For heaven's sake, man," Beems said. "Cover yourself."

"What the hell you think we've been doin' here?" McBride said. "Playin' checkers?"

"There's no need to be open about it. A man's pleasure is taken in private."

"Certainly you've seen balls before," McBride said, reaching for a cigar that lay on the table next to his revolver and a box of matches. Then he smiled and studied Beems. "Then maybe you ain't . . . And then again, maybe, well, you've seen plenty and close up. You look to me the sort that would rather hear a fat boy fart than a pretty girl sing."

"You disgusting brute," Beems said.

"That's telling me," McBride said. "Now I'm hurt. Cut to the god-damn core." McBride patted the redhead's inner thigh. "You recognize this business, don't you? You don't, I got to tell you about it. We men call it a woman, and that thing between her legs is the ole red snapper."

"We'll not conduct our affairs in this fashion," Beems said.

McBride smiled, took a match from the box, and lit the cigar. He puffed, said, "You dressed-up pieces of dirt brought me all the way down here from Chicago. I didn't ask to come. You offered me a job, and I took it, and I can untake it, it suits me. I got round-trip money from you already. You sent for me, and I came, and you set me up with a paid hair hole, and you're here for a meeting at a whorehouse, and now you're gonna tell me you're too special to look at my balls. Too prudish to look at pussy. Go on out, let me finish what I really want to finish. I'll be out of here come tomorrow, and you can whip your own nigger."

There was a moment of foot shuffling, and one of the elderly men leaned over and whispered to Beems. Beems breathed once, like a fish out of water, said, "Very well. There's not that much needs to be said. We want this nigger whipped, and we want him whipped bad. We understand in your last bout, the man died."

"Yeah," McBride said. "I killed him and dipped my wick in his old lady. Same night."

This was a lie, but McBride liked the sound of it. He liked the way their faces looked when he told it. The woman had actually been the man's half sister, and the man had died three days later from the beating.

"And this was a white man?" Beems said.

"White as snow. Dead as a stone. Talk money."

"We've explained our financial offer."

"Talk it again. I like the sound of money."

"Hundred dollars before you get in the ring with the nigger. Two hundred more if you beat him. A bonus of five hundred if you kill him. This is a short fight. Not forty-five rounds. No prizefighter makes money like that for so little work. Not even John L. Sullivan."

"This must be one hated nigger. Why? He mountin' your dog?"

"That's our business."

"All right. But I'll take half of that money now."

"That wasn't our deal."

"Now it is. And I'll be runnin' me a tab while I'm here, too. Pick it up."

More foot shuffling. Finally, the two elderly men got their heads together, pulled out their wallets. They pooled their money, gave it to Beems. "These gentlemen are our backers," Beems said. "This is Mr.—"

"I don't care who they are," McBride said. "Give me the money."

Beems tossed it on the foot of the bed.

"Pick it up and bring it here," McBride said to Beems.

"I will not."

"Yes, you will, 'cause you want me to beat this nigger. You want me to do it bad. And another reason is this: You don't, I'll get up and whip your dainty little ass all over this room."

Beems shook a little. "But why?"

"Because I can."

Beems, his face red as infection, gathered the bills from the bed, carried them around to McBride. He thrust them at McBride. McBride, fast as a duck on a june bug, grabbed Beems's wrist and pulled him forward, causing him to let go of the money and drop it onto McBride's chest. McBride pulled the cigar from his mouth with his free hand, stuck it against the back of Beems's thumb. Beems let out a squeal, said, "Forrest!"

The big man with no teeth and black eyes started around the bed toward McBride. McBride said, "Step back, Charlie, or you'll have to hire someone to yank this fella out of your ass."

Forrest hesitated, looked as if he might keep coming, then stepped back and hung his head.

McBride pulled Beems's captured hand between his legs and rubbed it over his sweaty balls a few times, then pushed him away. Beems stood with his mouth open, stared at his hand.

"I'm bull of the woods here," McBride said, "and it stays that way from here on out. You treat me with respect. I say, hold my rope while I pee, you hold it. I say, hold my sacks off the sheet while I get a piece, you hold 'em."

Beems said, "You bastard. I could have you killed."

"Then do it. I hate your type. I hate someone I think's your type. I hate someone who likes your type or wants to be your type. I'd kill a dog liked to be with you. I hate all of you expensive bastards with money and no guts. I hate you 'cause you can't whip your own nigger, and I'm glad you can't, 'cause I can. And you'll pay me. So go ahead, send your killers around. See where it gets them. Where it gets you. And I hate your goddamn hair, Beems."

"When this is over," Beems said, "you leave immediately!"

"I will, but not because of you. Because I can't stand you or your little pack of turds."

The big man with missing teeth raised his head, glared at McBride. McBride said, "Nigger whipped your ass, didn't he, Forrest?"

Forrest didn't say anything, but his face said a lot. McBride said, "You can't whip the nigger, so your boss sent for me. I can whip the nigger. So don't think for a moment you can whip me."

"Come on," Beems said. "Let's leave. The man makes me sick."

Beems joined the others, his hand held out to his side. The elderly gentlemen looked as if they had just realized they were lost in the forest. They organized themselves enough to start out the door. Beems followed, turned before exiting, glared at McBride.

McBride said, "Don't wash that hand, Beems. You can say, 'Shake the hand of the man who shook the balls of John McBride.'"

"You go to hell," Beems said.

"Keep me posted," McBride said. Beems left. McBride yelled after him and his crowd, "And gentlemen, enjoyed doing business with you."

JOE R. LANSDALE

9:12 P.M.

Later in the night the redhead displeased him and McBride popped her other eye, stretched her out, lay across her, and slept. While he slept, he dreamed he had a head of hair like Mr. Ronald Beems.

Outside, the wind picked up slightly, blew hot, brine-scented air down Galveston's streets and through the whorehouse window.

9:34 P.M.

Bill Cooper was working outside on the second-floor deck he was building. He had it completed except for a bit of trim work. It had gone dark on him sometime back, and he was trying to finish by lantern light. He was hammering a sidewall board into place when he felt a drop of rain. He stopped hammering and looked up. The night sky had a peculiar appearance, and for a moment it gave him pause. He studied the heavens a moment longer, decided it didn't look all that bad. It was just the starlight that gave it that look. No more drops fell on him.

Bill tossed the hammer on the deck, leaving the nail only partially driven, picked up the lantern, and went inside the house to be with his wife and baby son. He'd had enough for one day.

11:01 P.M.

The waves came in loud against the beach and the air was surprisingly heavy for so late at night. It lay hot and sweaty on "Lil" Arthur John Johnson's bare chest. He breathed in the air and blew it out, pounded the railroad tie with all his might for the hundredth time. His right fist struck it, and the tie moved in the sand. He hooked it with a left, jammed it with a straight right, putting his entire six-foot, two-hundred-pound frame into it. The tie went backwards, came out of the sand, and hit the beach.

Arthur stepped back and held out his broad, black hands and examined them in the moonlight. They were scuffed, but essentially sound. He walked down to the water and squatted and stuck his hands in, let the surf roll over them. The salt didn't even burn. His hands were like leather. He rubbed them together, being sure to coat them completely with seawater. He cupped water in his palms, rubbed it on his face, over his shaved, bullet head.

Along with a number of other pounding exercises, he had been doing this for months, conditioning his hands and face with work and brine. Rumor was, this man he was to fight, this McBride, had fists like razors, fists that cut right through the gloves and tore the flesh.

"Lil" Arthur took another breath, and this one was filled not only with the smell of saltwater and dead fish, but of raw sewage, which was regularly dumped offshore in the Gulf.

He took his shovel and re-dug the hole in the sand and dropped the tie back in, patted it down, went back to work. This time, two socks and it came up. He repeated the washing of his hands and face, then picked up the tie, placed it on a broad shoulder and began to run down the beach. When he had gone a good distance, he switched shoulders and ran back. He didn't even feel winded.

He collected his shovel, and with the tie on one shoulder, started toward his family's shack in the Rats, also known as Nigger Town.

"Lil" Arthur left the tie in front of the shack and put the shovel on the sagging porch. He was about to go inside when he saw a man start across the little excuse of a yard. The man was white. He was wearing dress clothes and a top hat.

When he was near the front porch, he stopped, took off his hat. It was Forrest Thomas, the man "Lil" Arthur had beaten unconscious three weeks back. It had taken only till the middle of the third round.

Even in the cloud-hazy moonlight, "Lil" Arthur could see Forrest looked rough. For a moment, a fleeting moment, he almost felt bad about inflicting so much damage. But then he began to wonder if the man had a gun.

"Arthur," Forrest said. "I come to talk a minute, if'n it's all right."

This was certainly different from the night "Lil" Arthur had climbed into the ring with him. Then, Forrest Thomas had been conceited and full of piss and vinegar and wore the word *nigger* on his lips as firmly as a mole. He was angry he had been reduced by his employer to fighting a black man. To hear him tell it, he deserved no less than John L. Sullivan, who refused to fight a Negro, considering it a debasement to the heavyweight title.

"Yeah," "Lil" Arthur said. "What you want?"

"I ain't got nothing against you," Forrest said.

"Don't matter you do," "Lil" Arthur said.

"You whupped me fair and square."

"I know, and I can do it again."

"I didn't think so before, but I know you can now."

"That's what you come to say? You got all dressed up, just to come talk to a nigger that whupped you?"

"I come to say more."

"Say it. I'm tired."

"McBride's come in."

"That ain't tellin' me nothin'. I reckoned he'd come in sometime. How'm I gonna fight him, he don't come in?"

"You don't know anything about McBride. Not really. He killed a man in the ring, his last fight in Chicago. That's why Beems brought him in, to kill you. Beems and his bunch want you dead 'cause you whipped a white man. They don't care you whipped me. They care you whipped a white man. Beems figures it's an insult to the white race, a white man being beat by a colored. This McBride, he's got a shot at the Championship of the World. He's that good."

"You tellin' me you concerned for me?"

"I'm tellin' you Beems and the members of the Sportin' Club can't take it. They lost a lot of money on bets, too. They got to set it right, see. I ain't no friend of yours, but I figure I owe you that. I come to warn you this McBride is a killer."

"Lil" Arthur listened to the crickets saw their legs a moment, then said, "If that worried me, this man being a killer, and I didn't fight him, that would look pretty good for your boss, wouldn't it? Beems could say the bad nigger didn't show up. That he was scared of a white man."

"You fight this McBride, there's a good chance he'll kill you or cripple you. Boxing bein' against the law, there won't be nobody there legal to keep check on things. Not really. Audience gonna be there ain't gonna say nothin'. They ain't supposed to be there anyway. You died, got hurt bad, you'd end up out there in the Gulf with a block of granite tied to your dick, and that'd be that."

"Sayin' I should run?"'

"You run, it gives Beems face, and you don't take a beatin', maybe get killed. You figure it."

"You ain't doin' nothin' for me. You're just pimpin' for Beems. You tryin' to beat me with your mouth. Well, I ain't gonna take no beatin'. White. Colored. Striped. It don't matter. McBride gets in the ring, I'll knock him down. You go on back to Beems. Tell him I ain't scared, and I ain't gonna run. And ain't none of this workin'.'"

Forrest put his hat on. "Have it your way, nigger." He turned and walked away.

"Lil" Arthur started inside the house, but before he could open the door, his father, Henry, came out. He dragged his left leg behind him as he came, leaned on his cane. He wore a ragged undershirt and work pants. He was sweaty. Tired. Gray. Grayer yet in the muted moonlight.

"You ought not talk to a white man that way," Henry said. "Them Ku Kluxers'll come 'round."

"I ain't afraid of no Ku Kluxers."

"Yeah, well I am, and we be seein' what you say when you swingin' from a rope, a peckerwood cuttin' off yo balls. You ain't lived none yet. You ain't nothin' but twenty-two years. Sit down, boy."

"Papa, you ain't me. I ain't got no bad leg. I ain't scared of nobody."

"I ain't always had no bad leg. Sit down."

"Lil" Arthur sat down beside his father. Henry said, "A colored man, he got to play the game, to win the game. You hear me?"

"I ain't seen you winnin' much."

Henry slapped "Lil" Arthur quickly. It was fast, and "Lil" Arthur realized where he had inherited his hand speed. "You shut yo face," Henry said. "Don't talk to your papa like that."

"Lil" Arthur reached up and touched his cheek, not because it hurt, but because he was still a little amazed. Henry said, "For a colored man, winnin' is stayin' alive to live out the time God give you."

"But how you spend what time you got, Papa, that ain't up to God. I'm gonna be the Heavyweight Champion of the World someday. You'll see."

"There ain't never gonna be no colored Champion of the World, 'Lil' Arthur. And there ain't no talkin' to you. You a fool. I'm gonna be cuttin' you down from a tree some morning, yo neck all stretched out. Help me up. I'm goin' to bed."

"Lil" Arthur helped his father up, and the old man, balanced on his cane, dragged himself inside the shack.

A moment later, "Lil" Arthur's mother, Tina, came out. She was a broad-faced woman, short and stocky, nearly twenty years younger than her husband.

"You don't need talk yo papa that way," she said.

"He don't do nothin', and he don't want me to do nothin'," "Lil" Arthur said.

"He know what he been through, Arthur. He born a slave. He made to fight for white mens like he was some kinda fightin' rooster, and he got his leg paralyzed 'cause he had to fight for them Rebels in the war. You think on that. He in one hell of a fix. Him a colored man out there shootin' at Yankees, 'cause if he don't, they gonna shoot him, and them Rebels gonna shoot him he don't fight the Yankees."

"I ain't all that fond of Yankees myself. They ain't likin' niggers any more than anyone else."

"That's true. But, yo papa, he right about one thing. You ain't lived enough to know nothin' about nothin'. You want to be a white man so bad it hurt you. You is African, boy. You is born of slaves come from slaves come from Africa."

"You sayin' what he's sayin'?"

"Naw, I ain't. I'm sayin', you whup this fella, and you whup him good. Remember when them bullies used to chase you home, and I tell you, you come back without fightin', I'm gonna whup you harder than them?"

"Yes, ma'am."

"And you got so you whupped 'em good, just so I wouldn't whup yo ass?"

"Yes, ma'am."

"Well, these here white men hire out this man against you, threaten you, they're bullies. You go in there, and you whup this fella, and you use what God give you in them hands, and you make your way. But you remember, you ain't gonna have nothin' easy. Only way a white man gonna get respect for you is you knock him down, you hear? And you can knock him down in that ring better than out here, 'cause then you just a bad nigger they gonna hang. But you don't talk to yo papa that way. He better than most. He got him a steady job, and he hold this family together."

"He's a janitor."

"That's more than you is."

"And you hold this family together."

"It a two-person job, son."

"Yes, ma'am."

"Good night, son."

"Lil" Arthur hugged her, kissed her cheek, and she went inside. He followed, but the smallness of the two-room house, all those bodies on pallets—his parents, three sisters, two brothers, and a brother-in-law—made him feel crowded. And the pigeons sickened him. Always the pigeons. They had found a hole in the roof—the one that had been covered with tar paper—and now they were roosting inside on the rafters. Tomorrow, half the house would be covered in bird shit. He needed to get up there and put some fresh tar paper on the roof. He kept meaning to. Papa couldn't do it, and he spent his own time training. He had to do more for the family besides bring in a few dollars from fighting.

"Lil" Arthur got the stick they kept by the door for just such an occasion, used it to rout the pigeons by poking at them. In the long run, it wouldn't matter. They would fly as high as the roof, then gradually creep back down to roost. But the explosion of bird wings, their rise to the sky through the hole in the roof, lifted his spirits.

His brother-in-law, Clement, rose up on an elbow from his pallet, and his wife, "Lil" Arthur's sister Lucy, stirred and rolled over, stretched her arm across Clement's chest, but didn't wake up.

"What you doin', Arthur?" Clement whispered. "You don't know a man's got to sleep? I got work to do 'morrow. Ain't all of us sleep all day."

"Sleep then. And stay out of my sister. Lucy don't need no kids now. We got a house full a folks."

"She my wife. We supposed to do that. And multiply."

"Then get your own place and multiply. We packed tight as turds here."

"You crazy, Arthur."

Arthur cocked the pigeon stick. "Lay down and shut up."

Clement lay down, and Arthur put the stick back and gathered up his pallet and went outside. He inspected the pallet for bird shit, found none, stretched out on the porch, and tried to sleep. He thought about getting his guitar, going back to the beach to strum it, but he was too tired for that. Too tired to do anything, too awake to sleep.

His mother had told him time and again that when he was a baby, an old Negro lady with the second sight had picked up his little hand and said, "This child gonna eat his bread in many countries."

It was something that had always sustained him. But now, he began to wonder. Except for trying to leave Galveston by train once, falling asleep in the boxcar, only to discover it had been making circles in the train yard all night as supplies were unloaded, he'd had no adventures, and was still eating his bread in Galveston.

All night he fought mosquitoes, the heat, and his own ambition. By morning he was exhausted.

JOE R. LANSDALE

Telegraphed Message from Washington, D.C., Weather Bureau, Central Office, to Issac Cline, Galveston, Texas, Weather Bureau:

Disturbance center near Key West moving northwest. Vessels bound for Florida and Cuban ports should exercise caution. Storm likely to become dangerous.

10:23 A.M.

McBride awoke, flicked the redhead, sat up in bed, and cracked his knuckles, said, "I'm going to eat and train, Red. You have your ass here when I get back, and put it on the Sportin' Club's bill. And wash yourself, for heaven's sake."

"Yes, sir, Mr. McBride," she said.

McBride got up, poured water into a washbasin, washed his dick, under his arms, splashed water on his face. Then he sat at the dresser in front of the mirror and spent twenty minutes putting on the Chinaman's remedy and combing his hair. As soon as he had it just right, he put on a cap.

He got dressed in loose pants, a short-sleeved shirt, soft shoes, wrapped his knuckles with gauze, put a little notebook and pencil in his back pocket, then pulled on soft leather gloves. When the redhead wasn't looking, he wrapped his revolver and razor in a washrag, stuffed them between his shirt and his stomach.

Downstairs, making sure no one was about, he removed the rag containing his revolver and razor, stuck them into the drooping greenness of a potted plant, then went away.

He strolled down the street to a cafe and ordered steak and eggs and lots of coffee. He ate with his gloves and hat on. He paid for the meal, but got a receipt.

Comfortably full, he went out to train.

He began at the docks. There were a number of men hard at work. They were loading bags of cottonseed onto a ship. He stood with his hands behind his back and watched. The scent of the sea was strong. The water lapped at the pilings enthusiastically, and the air was as heavy as a cotton sack.

After a while, he strolled over to a large bald man with arms and legs like plantation columns. The man wore faded overalls without a shirt, and his chest was as hairy as a bear's ass. He had on heavy work boots with the sides burst out. McBride could see his bare feet through the openings. McBride hated a man that didn't keep up his appearance, even when he was working. Pride was like a dog. You didn't feed it regularly, it died.

McBride said, "What's your name?"

The man, a bag of cottonseed under each arm, stopped and looked at him, taken aback. "Ketchum," he said. "Warner Ketchum."

"Yeah," McBride said. "Thought so. So, you're the one."

The man glared at him. "One what?"

The other men stopped working, turned to look.

"I just wanted to see you," McBride said. "Yeah, you fit the description. I just never thought there was a white man would stoop to such a thing. Fact is, hard to imagine any man stooping to such a thing."

"What are you talkin' about, fella?"

"Well, word is, Warner Ketchum that works at the dock has been known to suck a little nigger dick in his time."

Ketchum dropped the cottonseed bags. "Who the hell are you? Where you hear that?"

McBride put his gloved hands behind his back and held them. "They say, on a good night, you can do more with a nigger's dick than a cat can with a ball of twine."

The man was fuming. "You got me mixed up with somebody else, you Yankee-talkin' sonofabitch."

"Naw, I ain't got you mixed up. Your name's Warner Ketchum. You look how you was described to me by the nigger whose stick you slicked."

Warner stepped forward with his right foot and swung a right punch so looped it looked like a sickle blade. McBride ducked it without removing his hands from behind his back, slipped inside and twisted his hips as he brought a right uppercut into Warner's midsection.

Warner's air exploded and he wobbled back and McBride was in again, a left hook to the ribs, a straight right to the solar plexus. Warner doubled and went to his knees.

McBride leaned over and kissed him on the ear, said, "Tell me. Them nigger dicks taste like licorice?"

Warner came up then, and he was wild. He threw a right, then a left.

McBride bobbed beneath them. Warner kicked at him. McBride turned sideways, let the kick go by, unloaded a left hand that caught Warner on the jaw, followed it with a right that struck with a sound like the impact of an artillery shell.

Warner dropped to one knee. McBride grabbed him by the head and swung his knee into Warner's face, busting his nose all over the dock. Warner fell face forward, caught himself on his hands, almost got up. Then, very slowly, he collapsed, lay down, and didn't move.

McBride looked at the men who were watching him. He said, "He didn't suck no nigger dicks. I made that up." He got out his paper pad and pencil and wrote: Owed me. Price of one sparring partner, FIVE DOLLARS.

He put the pad and pencil away. Got five dollars out of his wallet, folded it, put it in the man's back pocket. He turned to the other men who stood staring at him as if he were one of Jesus' miracles.

"Frankly, I think you're all a bunch of sorry assholes, and I think, one at a time, I can lick every goddamn one of you Southern white trash pieces of shit. Any takers?"

"Not likely," said a stocky man at the front of the crowd. "You're a ringer." He picked up a sack of cottonseed he had put down, started toward the ship. The other men did the same.

McBride said, "Okay," and walked away.

He thought, maybe, on down the docks he might find another sparring partner.

5:23 P.M.

By the end of the day, near dark, McBride checked his notepad for expenses, saw the Sporting Club owed him forty-five dollars in sparring partners, and a new pair of gloves, as well as breakfast and dinner to come. He added money for a shoeshine. A clumsy sonofabitch had scuffed one of his shoes.

He got the shoeshine and ate a steak, flexed his muscles as he arrived at the whorehouse. He felt loose still, like he could take on another two or three yokels.

He went inside, got his goods out of the potted plant, and climbed the stairs.

Telegraphed Message from Washington, D.C., Weather Bureau, Central Office, to Issac Cline, Galveston, Texas, Weather Bureau:

Storm center just northwest of Key West.

7:30 P.M.

"Lil" Arthur ran down to the Sporting Club that night and stood in front of it, his hands in his pants pockets. The wind was brisk, and the air was just plain sour.

Saturday, he was going to fight a heavyweight crown contender, and though it would not be listed as an official bout, and McBride was just in it to pick up some money, "Lil" Arthur was glad to have the chance to fight a man who might fight for the championship someday. And if he could beat him, even if it didn't affect McBride's record, "Lil" Arthur knew he'd have that, he would have beaten a contender for the Heavyweight Championship of the World.

It was a far cry from the Battle Royales he had first participated in. There was a time when he looked upon those degrading events with favor.

He remembered his first Battle Royale. His friend Ernest had talked him into it. Once a month, sometimes more often, white "sporting men" liked to get a bunch of colored boys and men to come down to the club for a free-for-all. They'd put nine or ten of them in a ring, sometimes make them strip naked and wear Sambo masks. He'd done that once himself.

While the coloreds fought, the whites would toss money and yell for them to kill one another. Sometimes they'd tie two coloreds together by the ankles, let them go at it. Blood flowed thick as molasses on flapjacks. Bones were broken. Muscles torn. For the whites, it was great fun, watching a couple of coons knock each other about.

"Lil" Arthur found he was good at all that fighting, and even knocked Ernest out, effectively ending their friendship. He couldn't help himself. He got in there, got the battling blood up, he would hit whoever came near him.

He started boxing regularly, gained some skill. No more Battle Royales. He got a reputation with the colored boxers, and in time that spread to the whites.

The Sporting Club, plumb out of new white contenders for their champion, Forrest Thomas, gave "Lil" Arthur twenty-five dollars to mix it up with their man, thinking a colored and a white would be a novelty, and the superiority of the white race would be proved in a match of skill and timing.

Right before the fight, "Lil" Arthur said his prayers, and then, considering he was going to be fighting in front of a bunch of angry, mean-spirited whites, and for the first time, white women—sporting women, but women—who wanted to see a black man knocked to jelly, he took gauze and wrapped his dick. He wrapped it so that it was as thick as a blackjack. He figured he'd give them white folks something to look at. The thing they feared the most. A black-as-coal stud nigger.

He whipped Forrest Thomas like he was a redheaded stepchild; whipped him so badly, they stopped the fight so no one would see a colored man knock a white man out.

Against their wishes, the Sporting Club was forced to hand the championship over to "Lil" Arthur John Johnson, and the fact that a colored now held the club's precious boxing crown was like a chicken bone in the club's throat. Primarily Beems's throat. As the current president of the Sporting Club, the match had been Beems's idea, and Forrest Thomas had been Beems's man.

Enter McBride. Beems, on the side, talked a couple of the Sporting Club's more wealthy members into financing a fight. One where a true contender to the heavyweight crown would whip "Lil" Arthur and return the local championship to a white man, even if that white man relinquished the crown when he returned to Chicago, leaving it vacant. In that case, "Lil" Arthur was certain he'd never get another shot at the Sporting Club championship. They wanted him out, by hook or crook.

"Lil" Arthur had never seen McBride. Didn't know how he fought. He'd just heard he was as tough as stone and had balls like a brass monkey. He liked to think he was the same way. He didn't intend to give the championship up. Saturday, he'd find out if he had to.

9:00 P.M.

The redhead, nursing a fat lip, two black eyes, and a bruise on her belly, rolled over gingerly and put her arm across McBride's hairy chest. "You had enough?"

"I'll say when I've had enough."

"I was just thinking, I might go downstairs and get something to eat. Come back in a few minutes."

"You had time to eat before I got back. You didn't eat, you just messed up. I'm paying for this. Or rather the Sportin' Club is."

"An engine's got to have coal, if you want that engine to go."

"Yeah?"

"Yeah." The redhead reached up and ran her fingers through McBride's hair.

McBride reached across his chest and slapped the redhead.

"Don't touch my hair. Stay out of my hair. And shut up. I don't care you want to fuck or not. I want to fuck, we fuck. Got it?"

"Yes, sir."

"Listen here, I'm gonna take a shit. I get back, I want you to wash that goddamn nasty hole of yours. You think I like stickin' my wick in that, it not being clean? You got to get clean."

"It's so hot. I sweat. And you're just gonna mess me up again."

"I don't care. You wash that thing. I went around with my johnson like that, it'd fall off. I get a disease, girl, I'll come back here, kick your ass so hard your butthole will swap places with your cunt."

"I ain't got no disease, Mr. McBride."

"Good."

"Why you got to be so mean?" the redhead asked suddenly, then couldn't believe it had come out of her mouth. She realized, not only would a remark like that anger McBride, but the question was stupid. It was like asking a chicken why it pecked shit. It just did. McBride was mean because he was, and that was that.

But even as the redhead flinched, McBride turned philosophical. "It isn't a matter of mean. It's because I can do what I want, and others can't. You got that, sister?"

"Sure. I didn't mean nothing by it."

"Someone can do to me what I do to them, then all right, that's how it is. Isn't a man, woman, or animal on earth that's worth a damn. You know that?"

"Sure. You're right."

"You bet I am. Only thing pure in this world is a baby. Human or animal, a baby is born hungry and innocent. It can't do a thing for itself. Then it grows up and gets just like everyone else. A baby is all right until it's about two. Then, it ought to just be smothered and save the world the room. My sister, she was all right till she was about two, then it wasn't nothing but her wanting stuff and my mother giving it to her. Later on, Mama didn't have nothing to do with her either, same as me. She got over two years old, she was just trouble. Like I was. Like everybody else is."

"Sure," the redhead said.

"Oh, shut up, you don't know your ass from a pig track."

McBride got up and went to the john. He took his revolver and his wallet and his razor with him. He didn't trust a whore—any woman for that matter—far as he could hurl one.

While he was in the can trying out the new flush toilet, the redhead eased out of bed wearing only a sheet. She slipped out the door, went downstairs and outside, into the streets. She flagged down a man in a buggy, talked him into a ride, for a ride, then she was out of there, destination unimportant.

9:49 P.M.

Later, pissed at the redhead, McBride used the madam herself, blacked both her eyes when she suggested that a lot of sex before a fight might not be a good idea for an athlete.

The madam, lying in bed with McBride's muscular arm across her ample breasts, sighed and watched the glow of the gas streetlights play on the ceiling.

Well, she thought, it's a living.

FRIDAY, SEPTEMBER 7, 10:35 A.M.

Telegraphed Message from Washington, D.C., Weather Bureau, Central Office, to Issac Cline, Galveston, Texas, Weather Bureau:

Storm warning. Galveston, Texas. Take precautions.

Issac Cline, head of the Galveston Weather Bureau, sat at his desk on the third floor of the Levy Building and read the telegram. He went downstairs and outside for a look-see.

The weather was certainly in a stormy mood, but it didn't look like serious hurricane weather. He had been with the Weather Bureau for eight years, and he thought he ought to know a hurricane by now, and this wasn't it. The sky wasn't the right color.

He walked until he got to the beach. By then the wind was picking up, and the sea was swelling. The clouds were like wads of duck down ripped from a pillow: He walked a little farther down the beach, found a turtle wrapped in seaweed, poked it with a stick. It was dead as a stone.

Issac returned to the Levy Building, and by the time he made his way back, the wind had picked up considerably. He climbed the stairs to the roof. The roof barometer was dropping quickly, and the wind was serious. He revised his opinion on how much he knew about storms. He estimated the wind to be blowing at twenty miles an hour, and growing. He pushed against it, made his way to the weather pole, hoisted two flags. The top flag was actually a white pennant. It whipped in the wind like a gossip's tongue. Anyone who saw it knew it meant the wind was coming from the northwest. Beneath it was a red flag with a black center; this flag meant the wind was coming ass over teakettle, and that a seriously violent storm was expected within hours.

The air smelled dank and fishy. For a moment, Cline thought perhaps he had actually touched the dead turtle and brought its stink back with him. But no, it was the wind.

At about this same time, the steamship *Pensacola,* commanded by Captain James Slater, left the port of Galveston from Pier 34, destination Pensacola, Florida.

Slater had read the hurricane reports of the day before, and though the wind was picking up and was oddly steamy, the sky failed to show what he was watching for: A dusty, brick red color, a sure sign of a hurricane. He felt the whole Weather Bureau business was about as much guess and luck as it was anything else. He figured he could do that and be as accurate.

He gave orders to ease the *Pensacola* into the Gulf.

1:06 P.M.

The pigeons fluttered through the opening in the Johnsons' roof. Tar paper lifted, tore, blew away, tumbled through the sky as if they were little black pieces of the structure's soul.

"It's them birds again," his mother said.

"Lil" Arthur stopped doing push-ups, looked to the ceiling. Pigeons were thick on the rafters. So was pigeon shit. The sky was very visible through the roof. And very black. It looked venomous.

"Shit," "Lil" Arthur said.

"It's okay," she said. "Leave 'em be. They scared. So am I."

"Lil" Arthur stood up, said, "Ain't nothin' be scared of. We been through all kinda storms. We're on a rise here. Water don't never get this high."

"I ain't never liked no storm. I be glad when yo daddy and the young'uns gets home."

"Papa's got an old tarp I might can put over that hole. Keep out the rain."

"You think you can, go on."

"I already should'a," "Lil" Arthur said.

"Lil" Arthur went outside, crawled under the upraised porch, and got hold of the old tarp. It was pretty rotten, but it might serve his purpose, at least temporarily. He dragged it into the yard, crawled back under, tugged out the creaking ladder and a rusty hammer. He was about to go inside and get the nails when he heard a kind of odd roaring. He stopped, listened, recognized it.

It was the surf. He had certainly heard it before, but not this loud and this far from the beach. He got the nails and put the ladder against the side of the house and carried the tarp onto the roof. The tarp nearly took to the air when he spread it, almost carried him with it. With considerable effort he got it nailed over the hole, trapping what pigeons didn't flee inside the house.

2:30 P.M.

Inside the whorehouse, the madam, a fat lip added to her black eyes, watched from the bed as McBride, naked, seated in a chair before the dresser mirror, carefully oiled and combed his hair over his bald spot. The windows were closed, and the wind rattled them like dice in a gambler's fist. The air inside the whorehouse was as stuffy as a minister's wife.

"What's that smell?" she asked.

It was the tonic the Chinaman had given him. He said, "You don't want your tits pinched, shut the fuck up."

"All right," she said.

The windows rattled again. Pops of rain flecked the glass.

McBride went to the window, his limp dick resting on the windowsill, almost touching the glass, like a large, wrinkled grub looking for a way out.

"Storm coming," he said.

The madam thought: *No shit.*

McBride opened the window. The wind blew a comb and hairbrush off the dresser. A man, walking along the sandy street, one hand on his hat to save it from the wind, glanced up at McBride. McBride took hold of his dick and wagged it at him. The man turned his head and picked up his pace.

McBride said, "Spread those fat legs, honey-ass, 'cause I'm sailing into port, and I'm ready to drop anchor."

Sighing, the madam rolled onto her back, and McBride mounted her. "Don't mess up my hair this time," he said.

4:30 P.M.

The study smelled of stale cigar smoke and sweat, and faintly of baby oil. The grandfather clock chimed four-thirty. The air was humid and sticky as it shoved through the open windows and fluttered the dark curtains. The sunlight, which was tinted with a green cloud haze, flashed in and out, giving brightness to the false eyes and the yellowed teeth of a dozen mounted animal heads on the walls. Bears. Boar. Deer. Even a wolf.

Beems, the source of much of the sweat smell, thought: It's at least another hour before my wife gets home. Good.

Forrest drove him so hard Beems's forehead slammed into the wall, rocking the head of the wild boar that was mounted there, causing the boar to look as if it had turned its head in response to a distant sound, a peculiar sight.

"It's not because I'm one of them kind I do this," Beems said. "It's just, oh yeah, honey . . . The wife, you know, she don't do nothing for me. I mean, you got to get a little pleasure where you can. A man's got to get his pleasure, don't you think . . . Oh, yes. That's it . . . A man, he's got to get his pleasure, right? Even if there's nothing funny about him?"

Forrest rested his hands on Beems's naked shoulders, pushing him down until his head rested on top of the couch cushion. Forrest cocked his hips, drove forward with teeth clenched, penetrating deep into Beems's ass. He said, "Yeah. Sure."

"You mean that? This don't make me queer?"

"No," Forrest panted. "Never has. Never will. Don't mean nothin'. Not a damn thing. It's all right. You're a man's man. Let me concentrate."

Forrest had to concentrate. He hated this business, but it was part of the job. And, of course, unknown to Beems, he was putting the meat to Beems's wife. So, if he wanted to keep doing that, he had to stay in with the boss. And Mrs. Beems, of course, had no idea he was reaming her husband's dirty ditch, or that her husband had about as much interest in women as a pig does a silver tea service.

What a joke. He was fucking Beems's old lady, doing the dog work for Beems, for a good price, and was reaming Beems's asshole and assuring Beems he wasn't what he was, a fairy. And as an added benefit, he didn't have to fight the nigger tomorrow night. That was a big plus. That sonofabitch hit like a mule kicked. He hoped this McBride would tap him good. The nigger died, he'd make a point of shitting on his grave. Right at the head of it.

Well, maybe, Forrest decided, as he drove his hips forward hard enough to make Beems scream a little, he didn't hate this business after all. Not completely. He took so much crap from Beems, this was kinda nice, having the bastard bent over a couch, dicking him so hard his head slammed the wall. Goddamn, nutless queer, insulting him in public, trying to act tough.

Forrest took the bottle of baby oil off the end table and poured it onto Beems's ass. He put the bottle back and realized he was going soft. He tried to imagine he was plunging into Mrs. Beems, who had the smoothest ass and the brightest blond pubic hair he had ever seen. "I'm almost there," Forrest said.

"Stroke, Forrest! Stroke, man. Stroke!"

In the moment of orgasm, Beems imagined that the dick plunging into his hairy ass belonged to the big nigger, "Lil" Arthur. He thought about "Lil" Arthur all the time. Ever since he had seen him fight naked in a Battle Royale while wearing a Sambo mask for the enjoyment of the crowd.

And the way "Lil" Arthur had whipped Forrest. Oh, God. So thoroughly. So expertly. Forrest had been the man until then, and that made him want Forrest, but now, he wanted the nigger.

Oh God, Beems thought, to have him in me, wearing that mask, that would do it for all time. Just once. Or twice. Jesus, I want it so bad I got to be sure the nigger gets killed. I got to be sure I don't try to pay the nigger money to do this, because he lives after the fight with McBride, I know I'll break down and try. And I break down and he doesn't do it, and word gets around, or he does it, and word gets around, or I get caught . . . I couldn't bear that. This is bad enough. But a nigger . . . ?

Then there was McBride. He thought about him. He had touched McBride's balls and feigned disgust, but he hadn't washed that hand yet, just as McBride suggested.

McBride won the fight with the nigger, better yet, killed him, maybe McBride would do it with him. McBride was a gent that liked money, and he liked to hurt whoever he was fucking. Beems could tell that from the way the redhead was battered. That would be good. That would be all right. McBride was the type who'd fuck anyone or anything, Beems could tell.

He imagined it was McBride at work instead of Forrest. McBride, naked, except for the bowler.

Forrest, in his moment of orgasm, grunted, said, "Oh yeah," and almost called Mrs. Beems's name. He lifted his head as he finished, saw the hard glass eyes of the stuffed wild boar. The eyes were full of sunlight. Then the curtains fluttered and the eyes were full of darkness.

4:45 P.M.

The steamship *Pensacola,* outbound from Galveston, reached the Gulf, and a wind reached the *Pensacola.* Captain Slater felt his heart clench. The sea came high and savage from the east, and the ship rose up and dived back down, and the waves, dark green and shadowed by the thick clouds overhead, reared up on either side of the steamship, hissed, plunged back down, and the *Pensacola* rode up.

Jake Bernard, the pilot commissioner, came onto the bridge looking green as the waves. He was Slater's guest on this voyage, and now he wished he were back home. He couldn't believe how ill he felt. Never, in all his years, had he encountered seas like this, and he had thought himself immune to seasickness.

"I don't know about you, Slater," Bernard said, "but I ain't had this much fun since a bulldog gutted my daddy."

Slater tried to smile, but couldn't make it. He saw that Bernard, in spite of his joshing, didn't look particularly jovial. Slater said, "Look at the glass."

Bernard checked the barometer. It was falling fast.

"Never seen it that low," Bernard said.

"Me either," Slater said. He ordered his crew then. Told them to take in the awning, to batten the hatches, and to prepare for water.

Bernard, who had not left the barometer, said, "God. Look at this, man!"

Slater looked. The barometer read *28.55.*

Bernard said, "Way I heard it, ever gets that low, you're supposed to bend forward, kiss your root, and tell it good-bye."

6:30 P.M.

The Coopers, Bill and Angelique and their eighteen-month-old baby, Teddy, were on their way to dinner at a restaurant by buggy, when their horse, Bess, a beautiful chocolate-colored mare, made a run at the crashing sea.

It was the sea that frightened the horse, but in its moment of fear, it had tried to plunge headlong toward the source of its fright, assuring Bill that horses were, in fact, the most stupid animals in God's creation.

Bill jerked the reins and cussed the horse. Bess wheeled, lurched the buggy so hard Bill thought they might tip, but the buggy bounced on line, and he maneuvered Bess back on track.

Angelique, dark-haired and pretty, said, "I think I soiled my bloomers . . . I smell it . . . No, that's Teddy. Thank goodness."

Bill stopped the buggy outside the restaurant, which was situated on high posts near the beach, and Angelique changed the baby's diaper, put the soiled cloth in the back of the buggy.

When she was finished, they tied up the reins and went in for a steak dinner. They sat by a window where they could see the buggy. The horse bucked and reared and tugged so much, Bill feared she might break the reins and bolt. Above them, they could hear the rocks that covered the flat roof rolling and tumbling about like mice battling over morsels. Teddy sat in a high chair provided by the restaurant, whammed a spoon in a plate of applesauce.

"Had I known the weather was this bad," Angelique said, "we'd have stayed home. I'm sorry, Bill."

"We stay home too much," Bill said, realizing the crash of the surf was causing him to raise his voice. "Building that upper deck on the house isn't doing much for my nerves either. I'm beginning to realize I'm not much of a carpenter."

Angelique widened her dark brown eyes. "No? You, not a carpenter?"

Bill smiled at her.

"I could have told you that, just by listening to all the cussing you were doing. How many times did you hit your thumb, dear?"

"Too many to count."

Angelique grew serious. "Bill. Look."

Many of the restaurant's patrons had abandoned their meals and were standing at the large windows, watching the sea. The tide was high and it was washing up to the restaurant's pilings, splashing against them hard, throwing spray against the glass.

"Goodness," Bill said. "It wasn't this bad just minutes ago."

"Hurricane?" Angelique asked.

"Yeah. It's a hurricane all right. The flags are up. I saw them."

"Why so nervous? We've had hurricanes before."

"I don't know. This feels different, I guess . . . It's all right. I'm just jittery is all."

They ate quickly and drove the buggy home, Bess pulling briskly all the way. The sea crashed behind them and the clouds raced above them like apparitions.

8:00 P.M.

Captain Slater figured the wind was easily eighty knots. A hurricane. The *Pensacola* was jumping like a frog. Crockery was crashing below. A medicine chest so heavy two men couldn't move it leaped up and struck the window of the bridge, went through onto the deck, slid across it, hit the railing, bounced high, and dropped into the boiling sea.

Slater and Bernard bumped heads so hard they nearly knocked each other out. When Slater got off the floor, he got a thick rope out from under a shelf and tossed it around a support post, made a couple of wraps, then used the loose ends to tie bowlines around his and Bernard's waists. That way, he and Bernard could move about the bridge if they had to, but they wouldn't end up following the path of the medicine chest.

Slater tried to think of something to do, but all he knew to do he had done. He'd had the crew drop anchor in the open Gulf, down to a hundred fathoms, and he'd instructed them to find the best shelter possible close to their posts, and to pray.

The *Pensacola* swung to the anchor, struggled like a bull on a leash. Slater could hear the bolts and plates that held the ship together screaming in agony. Those bolts broke, the plates cracked, he didn't need Captain Ahab to tell him they'd go down to Davy Jones's locker so fast they wouldn't have time to take in a lungful of air.

Using the wall for support, Slater edged along to where the bridge glass had been broken by the flying chest. Sea spray slammed against him like needles shot from a cannon. He was concentrating on the foredeck, watching it dip, when he heard Bernard make a noise that was not quite a word, yet more expressive than a grunt.

Slater turned, saw Bernard clutching the latch on one of the bridge windows so tightly he thought he would surely twist it off. Then he saw what Bernard saw.

The sea had turned black as a Dutch oven, the sky the color of gangrene, and between sea and sky there appeared to be something rising out of the water, something huge and oddly shaped, and then Slater realized what it was. It was a great wall of water, many times taller than the ship, and it was moving directly toward and over them.

SATURDAY, SEPTEMBER 8, 3:30 A.M.

Bill Cooper opened his eyes. He had been overwhelmed by a feeling of dread. He rose carefully, so as not to wake Angelique, went into the bedroom across the hall and checked on Teddy. The boy slept soundly, his thumb in his mouth.

Bill smiled at the child, reached down, and gently touched him. The boy was sweaty, and Bill noted that the air in the room smelled foul. He opened a window, stuck his head out, and looked up. The sky had cleared and the moon was bright. Suddenly, he felt silly. Perhaps this storm business, the deck he was building on the upper floor of the house, had made him restless and worried. Certainly, it looked as if the storm had passed them by.

Then his feeling of satisfaction passed. For when he examined the yard, he saw it had turned to molten silver. And then he realized it was moonlight on water. The Gulf had crept all the way up to the house. A small rowboat, loose from its moorings, floated by.

8:06 A.M.

Issac Cline had driven his buggy down the beach, warning residents near the water to evacuate. Some had. Some had not. Most had weathered many storms and felt they could weather another.

Still, many residents and tourists made for the long wooden trestle bridge to mainland Texas. Already, the water was leaping to the bottom of the bridge, slapping at it, testing its strength.

Wagons, buggies, horses, pedestrians were as thick on the bridge as ants on gingerbread. The sky, which had been oddly clear and bright and full of moon early that morning, had now grown gray and it was raining. Of the three railway bridges that led to the mainland, one was already underwater.

3:45 P.M.

Henry Johnson, aided by "Lil" Arthur, climbed up on the wagon beside his wife. Tina held an umbrella over their heads. In the back of the wagon was the rest of the family, protected by upright posts planted in the corners, covered with the tarp that had formerly been on the roof of the house.

All day Henry had debated whether they should leave. But by 2:00, he realized this wasn't going to be just another storm. This was going to be a goddamn, wetassed humdinger. He had organized his family, and now, by hook or crook, he was leaving. He glanced at his shack, the water pouring through the roof like the falls of Niagara. It wasn't much, but it was all he had. He doubted it could stand much of this storm, but he tried not to think about that. He had greater concerns. He said to "Lil" Arthur, "You come on with us."

"I got to fight," "Lil" Arthur said.

"You got to do nothin'. This storm'll wash your ass to sea."

"I got to, Papa."

Tina said, "Maybe yo papa's right, baby. You ought to come."

"You know I can't. Soon as the fight's over, I'll head on out. I promise. In fact, weather's so bad, I'll knock this McBride out early."

"You do that," Tina said.

"Lil" Arthur climbed on the wagon and hugged his mama and shook his father's hand. Henry spoke quickly without looking at "Lil" Arthur, said, "Good luck, son. Knock him out."

"Lil" Arthur nodded. "Thanks, Papa." He climbed down and went around to the back of the wagon and threw up the tarp and hugged his sisters one at a time and shook hands with his brother-in-law, Clement. He pulled Clement close to him, said, "You stay out of my sister, hear?"

"Yeah, Arthur. Sure. But I think maybe we done got a problem. She's already swole up."

"Ah, shit," "Lil" Arthur said.

4:03 P.M.

As Henry Johnson drove the horses onto the wooden bridge that connected Galveston to the mainland, he felt ill. The water was washing over the sides, against the wagon wheels. The horses were nervous, and the line of would-be escapees on the bridge was tremendous. It would take them a long time to cross, maybe hours, and from the look of things, the way the water was rising, wouldn't be long before the bridge was underwater.

He said a private prayer: "Lord, take care of my family. And especially that fool son of mine, 'Lil' Arthur."

It didn't occur to him to include himself in the prayer.

4:37 P.M.

Bill and Angelique Cooper moved everything of value they could carry to the second floor of the house. Already the water was sloshing in the doorway. Rain splattered against the windows violently enough to shake them, and shingles flapped boisterously on the roof.

Bill paused in his work and shuffled through ankle-deep water to a window and looked out. He said, "Angelique, I think we can stop carrying."

"But I haven't carried up the—"

"We're leaving."

"Leaving? It's that bad?"

"Not yet."

Bess was difficult to hook to the buggy. She was wild-eyed and skittish. The barn was leaking badly. Angelique held an umbrella over her head, waiting for the buggy to be fastened. She could feel water rising above her high-button shoes.

Bill paused for a moment to calm the horse, glanced at Angelique, thought she looked oddly beautiful, the water running off the umbrella in streams. She held Teddy close to her. Teddy was asleep, totally unaware of what was going on around him. Any other time, the baby would be squalling, annoyed. The rain and the wind were actually helping him to sleep. At least, thought Bill, I am grateful for that.

By the time the buggy was hooked, they were standing in calf-deep water. Bill opened the barn door with great difficulty, saw that the yard was gone, and so was the street. He would have to guess at directions. Worse yet, it wasn't rainwater running through the street. It was definitely seawater; the water of the Gulf had risen up as if to swallow Galveston the way the ocean was said to have swallowed Atlantis.

Bill helped Angelique and Teddy into the buggy, took hold of the reins, clucked to Bess. Bess jerked and reared, and finally, by reins and voice, Bill calmed her. She began to plod forward through the dark, powerful water.

5:00 P.M.

McBride awoke. The wind was howling. The window glass was rattling violently, even though the windows were raised. The air was cool for a change, but damp. It was dark in the room.

The madam, wrapped in a blanket, sat in a chair pulled up against the far wall. She turned and looked at McBride. She said, "All hell's broken loose."

"Say it has?" McBride got up, walked naked to the windows. The wind was so furious it pushed him. "Damn," he said. "It's dark as midnight. This looks bad."

"Bad?" The madam laughed. "Worst hurricane I've ever seen, and I don't even think it's cranked up good yet."

"You don't think they'll call off the fight, do you?"

"Can you fight in a boat?"

"Hell, honey, I can fight and fuck at the same time on a boat. Come to think of it, I can fight and fuck on a rolling log, I have to. I used to be a lumberjack up north."

"I was you, I'd find a log, and get to crackin'."

A bolt of lightning, white as eternity, split the sky, and when it did, the darkness outside subsided, and in that instant, McBride saw the street was covered in waist-deep water.

"Reckon I better start on over there," he said. "It may take me a while."

The madam thought: Well, honey, go right ahead, and I hope you drown.

5:20 P.M.

"Lil" Arthur was standing on the porch, trying to decide if he should brave the water, which was now up to the lip of the porch, when he saw a loose rowboat drift by.

Suddenly he was in the water, swimming, and the force of the water carried him after the boat, and soon he had hold of it. When he climbed inside, he found the boat was a third filled with water. He found a paddle and a pail half-filled with dirt. The dirt had turned to mud and was beginning to flow over the top of the bucket. A few dead worms swirled in the mess. The world was atumble with wind, water, and darkness.

"Lil" Arthur took the bucket and poured out the mud and the worms and started to bail. Now and then he put the bucket aside and used the boat paddle. Not that he needed it much. The water was carrying him where he wanted to go. Uptown.

5:46 P.M.

Uptown the water was not so deep but it took McBride almost an hour to get to the Sporting Club. He waded through waist-deep water for a block, then knee-deep, and finally ankle-deep. His bowler hat had lost all its shape when he arrived, and his clothes were ruined. The water hadn't done his revolver or his razor any good either.

When he arrived at the building, he was surprised to find a crowd of men had gathered on the steps. Most stood under umbrellas, but many were bareheaded. There were a few women among them. Whores mostly. Decent women didn't go to prizefights.

McBride went up the steps, and the crowd blocked him. He said, "Look here. I'm McBride. I'm to fight the nigger."

The crowd parted, and McBride, with words of encouragement and pats on the back, was allowed indoors. Inside, the wind could still be heard, but it sounded distant. The rain was just a hum.

Beems, Forrest, and the two oldsters were standing in the foyer, looking tense as fat hens at noontime. As soon as they saw McBride, their faces relaxed, and the elderly gentlemen went away. Beems said, "We were afraid you wouldn't make it."

"Worried about your investment?"

"I suppose."

"I'd have come if I had to swim."

"The nigger doesn't show, the title and the money's yours."

"I don't want it like that," McBride said. "I want to hit him. Course, he don't show, I'll take the money. You seen it this bad before?"

"No," Beems said.

"I didn't expect nobody to be here."

"Gamblers always show," Forrest said. "They gamble their money, they gamble their lives."

"Go find something to do, Forrest," Beems said. "I'll show Mr. McBride the dressing room."

Forrest looked at Beems, grinned a little, showed Beems he knew what he had in mind. Beems fumed. Forrest went away. Beems took hold of McBride's elbow and began to guide him.

"I ain't no dog got to be led," McBride said.

"Very well," Beems said, and McBride followed him through a side door and down into a locker room. The room had two inches of water in it.

"My God," Beems said. "We've sprung a leak somewhere."

"Water like this," McBride said. "The force . . . it's washing out the mortar in the bricks, seeping through the chinks in the wall . . . Hell, it's all right for what I got to do."

"There's shorts and boots in the locker there," Beems said. "You could go ahead and change."

McBride sloshed water, sat on a bench and pulled off his shoes and socks with his feet resting on the bench. Beems stood where he was, watching the water rise.

McBride took the razor out of the side of one of the shoes, held it up for Beems to see, said, "Mexican boxing glove."

Beems grinned. He watched as McBride removed his bowler, coat and shirt. He watched carefully as he removed his pants and shorts. McBride reached into the locker Beems had recommended, paused, turned, stared at Beems.

"You're liking what you're seein', ain't you, buddy?" Beems didn't say anything. His heart was in his throat.

McBride grinned at him. "I knew first time I seen you, you was an Alice."

"No," Beems said. "Nothing like that. It's not like that at all."

McBride smiled. He looked very gentle in that moment. He said, "It's all right. Come here. I don't mind that."

"Well . . ."

"Naw. Really. It's just, you know, you got to be careful. Not let everyone know. Not everyone understands, see."

Beems, almost licking his lips, went over to McBride. When he was close, McBride's smile widened, and he unloaded a right uppercut into Beems's stomach. He hit him so hard Beems dropped to his knees in the water, nodded forward, and banged his head on the bench. His top hat came off, hit the water, sailed along the row of lockers, made a right turn near the wall, flowed out of sight behind a bench.

McBride picked Beems up by the hair and pulled his head close to his dick, said, "Look at it a minute, 'cause that's all you're gonna do."

Then McBride pulled Beems to his feet by his pretty hair and went to work on him. Lefts and rights. Nothing too hard. But more than Beems had ever gotten. When he finished, he left Beems lying in the water next to the bench, coughing.

McBride said, "Next time you piss, you'll piss blood, Alice." McBride got a towel out of the locker and sat on the bench and put his feet up and dried them. He put on the boxing shorts. There was a mirror on the inside of the locker, and McBride was upset to see his hair. It was a mess. He spent several minutes putting it in place. When he finished, he glanced down at Beems, who was pretending to be dead.

McBride said, "Get up, fairy-ass. Show me where I'm gonna fight."

"Don't tell anybody," Beems said. "I got a wife. A reputation. Don't tell anybody."

"I'll make you a promise," McBride said, closing the locker door. "That goddamn nigger beats me, I'll fuck you. Shit, I'll let you fuck me. But don't get your butthole all apucker. I ain't losin' nothin'. Tonight, way I feel, I could knock John L. Sullivan on his ass."

McBride started out of the locker room, carrying his socks and the boxing shoes with him. Beems lay in the water, giving him plenty of head start.

6:00 P.M.

Henry couldn't believe how slow the line was moving. Hundreds of people, crawling for hours. When the Johnsons were near the end of the bridge, almost to the mainland, the water rushed in a dark brown wave and washed the buggy in front of them off the bridge. The Johnsons' wagon felt the wave too, but only slid to the railing. But the buggy hit the railing, bounced, went over, pulling the horse into the railing after it. For a moment the horse hung there, its back legs slipping through, pulling with its front legs, then the railing cracked and the whole kit and kaboodle went over.

"Oh Jesus," Tina said.

"Hang on," Henry said. He knew he had to hurry, before another wave washed in, because if it was bigger, or caught them near the gap the buggy had made, they, too, were gone.

Behind them the Johnsons could hear screams of people fleeing the storm. The water was rising rapidly over the bridge, and those to the middle and the rear realized if they didn't get across quickly, they weren't going to make it. As they fought to move forward, the bridge cracked and moaned as if with a human voice.

The wind ripped at the tarp over the wagon and tore it away. "Shit," said Clement. "Ain't that something?"

A horse bearing a man and a woman, the woman wearing a great straw hat that drooped down on each side of her head, raced by the Johnsons. The bridge was too slick and the horse was moving too fast. Its legs splayed and it went down and started sliding. Slid right through the opening the buggy had made. Disappeared immediately beneath the water. When Henry ventured a look in that direction, he saw the woman's straw hat come up once, then blend with the water.

When Henry's wagon was even with the gap, a fresh brown wave came over the bridge, higher and harder this time. It hit his horses and the wagon broadside. The sound of it, the impact of it, reminded Henry of when he was in the Civil War and a wagon he was riding in was hit by Yankee cannon fire. The impact had knocked him spinning, and when he tried to get up, his leg had been ruined. He thought he would never be that frightened again. But now, he was even more afraid.

The wagon drifted sideways, hit the gap, but was too wide for it. It hung on the ragged railing, the sideboards cracking with the impact. Henry's family screamed and lay down flat in the wagon as the water came down on them like a heavy hand. The pressure of the water snapped the wagon's wheels off the axle, slammed the bottom of the wagon against the bridge, but the sideboards held together.

"Everybody out!" Henry said.

Henry, his weak leg failing to respond, tumbled out of the wagon onto the bridge, which was now under a foot of water. He got hold of a sideboard and pulled himself up, helped Tina down, reached up, and snatched his cane off the seat.

Clement and the others jumped down, started hustling toward the end of the bridge on foot. As they came even with Henry, he said, "Go on, hurry. Don't worry none about me."

Tina clutched his arm. "Go on, woman," he said. "You got young'uns to care about. I got to free these horses." He patted her hand. She moved on with the others.

Henry pulled out his pocketknife and set to cutting the horses free of the harness. As soon as they were loose, both fool animals bolted directly into the railing. One of them bounced off of it, pivoted, made for the end of the bridge at a splashing gallop, but the other horse hit with such impact it flipped over, turning its feet to the sky. It pierced the water and was gone.

Henry turned to look for his family. They were no longer visible. Surely, they had made the mainland by now.

Others had come along to fill their place; people in wagons, and buggies, on horseback and on foot. People who seemed to be scrambling on top of water, since the bridge was now completely below sea level.

Then Henry heard a roar. He turned to the east side of the bridge. There was a heavy sheet of water cocked high above him, and it was coming down, like a monstrous wet fly swatter. And when it struck Henry and the bridge, and all those on it, it smashed them flat and drove them into the churning belly of the sea.

6:14 P.M.

Bill and Angelique Cooper, their buggy half-submerged in water, saw the bridge through the driving rain, then suddenly they saw it no more. The bridge and the people were wadded together and washed down.

The bridge rose up on the waves a moment later, like a writhing spinal column. People still clung to it. It leaped forward into the water, the end of it lashing the air, then it was gone and the people with it.

"God have mercy on their souls," Angelique said.

Bill said, "That's it then."

He turned the buggy around in the water with difficulty, headed home. All around him, shingles and rocks from the roofs of structures flew like shrapnel.

7:39 P.M.

"Lil" Arthur, as he floated toward town, realized it was less deep here. It was just as well, the rain was pounding his boat and filling it with water. He couldn't bail and paddle as fast as it went in. He climbed over the side and let the current carry the boat away.

The water surprised him with its force. He was almost swept away, but it was shallow enough to get a foothold and push against the flow. He waded to the Sporting Club, went around back to the colored entrance. When he got there, an elderly black man known as Uncle Cooter let him in, said, "Man, I'd been you, I'd stayed home."

"What," "Lil" Arthur said, "and missed a boat ride?"

"A boat ride?"

"Lil" Arthur told him how he had gotten this far.

"Damnation," Uncle Cooter said. "God gonna put this island underwater 'cause it's so evil. Like that Sodom and Gomorrah place."

"What have you and me done to God?"

Uncle Cooter smiled. "Why, we is the only good children God's got. He gonna watch after us. Well, me anyway. You done gonna get in with this Mr. McBride, and he's some bad stuff, 'Lil' Arthur. God ain't gonna help you there. And this Mr. McBride, he ain't got no sense neither. He done beat up Mr. Beems, and Mr. Beems the one settin' this up, gonna pay him money."

"Why'd he beat him up?"

"Hell, you can't figure white people. They all fucked up. But Mr. Beems damn sure look like a raccoon now. Both his eyes all black, his lip pouched out."

"Where do I change?"

"Janitor's closet. They done put your shorts and shoes in there. And there's some gauze for your hands."

"Lil" Arthur found the shorts. They were old and faded. The boxing shoes weren't too good either. He found some soiled rags and used those to dry himself. He used the gauze to wrap his hands, then his dick. He figured, once you start a custom, you ought to stick with it.

7:45 P.M.

When Bill and Angelique and Teddy arrived at their house, they saw that the water had pushed against the front door so violently, it had come open. Water was flowing into the hall and onto the bottom step of the stairs. Bill looked up and saw a lamp burning upstairs. They had left so quickly, they had forgotten to extinguish it.

With a snort, Bess bolted. The buggy jerked forward, hit a curb, and the harness snapped so abruptly Bill and his family were not thrown from their seat, but merely whipped forward and back against the seat. The reins popped through Bill's hands so swiftly, the leather cut his palms.

Bess rushed across the yard and through the open doorway of the house, and slowly and carefully, began to climb the stairs.

Angelique said, "My lands."

Bill, a little stunned, climbed down, went around, and helped Angelique and the baby out of the buggy. The baby was wet and crying, and Angelique tried to cover him with the umbrella, but now the wind and rain seemed to come from all directions. The umbrella was little more than a wad of cloth.

They waded inside the house, tried to close the door, but the water was too much for them. They gave it up.

Bess had reached the top landing and disappeared. They followed her up. The bedroom door was open and the horse had gone in there. She stood near the table bearing the kerosene lamp. Shaking.

"Poor thing," Angelique said, gathering some towels from a chifforobe. "She's more terrified than we are."

Bill removed the harness that remained on Bess, stroked her, tried to soothe her. When he went to the window and looked out, the horse went with him. The world had not miraculously dried up. The water was obviously rising.

"Maybe we'll be all right here," Angelique said. She was drying Teddy, who was crying violently because he was cold and wet. "Water can't get this high, can it?"

Bill idly stroked Bess's mane, thought of the bridge. The way it had snapped like a wooden toy. He said, "Of course not."

8:15 P.M.

The fight had started late, right after two one-legged colored boys had gone a couple of rounds, hopping about, trying to club each other senseless with oversize boxing gloves.

The crowd was sparse but vocal. Loud enough that "Lil" Arthur forgot the raging storm outside. The crowd kept yelling, "Kill the nigger," and had struck up a chorus of "All coons look alike to me"—a catchy little number that "Lil" Arthur liked in spite of himself.

The yelling, the song, was meant to drop his spirits, but he found it fired him up. He liked being the underdog. He liked to make assholes eat their words. Besides, he was the Galveston Champion, not McBride, no matter what the crowd wanted. He was the one who would step through the ropes tonight the victor. And he had made a change. He would no longer allow himself to be introduced as "Lil" Arthur. When his name had been called, and he had been reluctantly named Galveston Sporting Club Champion by the announcer, the announcer had done as he had asked. He had called him by the name he preferred from here on. Not "Lil" Arthur Johnson. Not Arthur John Johnson, but the name he called him, the name he called himself. Jack Johnson.

So far, however, the fight wasn't going either way, and he had to hand it to McBride, the fella could hit. He had a way of throwing short, sharp punches to the ribs, punches that felt like knife stabs.

Before the fight, Jack, as McBride had surely done, had used his thumbs to rearrange as much of the cotton in his gloves as possible. Arrange it so that his knuckles would be against the leather and would make good contact with McBride's flesh. But so far McBride had avoided most of his blows. The man was a master of slipping and sliding the punches. Jack had never seen anything like that before. McBride could also pick off shots with a flick of his forearms. It was very professional and enlightening.

Even so, Jack found he was managing to take the punches pretty well, and he'd discovered something astonishing. The few times he'd hit McBride was when he got excited, leaned forward, went flat-footed, and threw the uppercut. This was not a thing he had trained for much, and when he had, he usually threw the uppercut by coming up on his toes, twisting his body, the prescribed way to throw it. But he found, against all logic, he could throw it flat-footed and leaning forward, and he could throw it hard.

He thought he had seen a bit of surprise on McBride's face when he'd hit him with it. He knew that he'd certainly surprised himself.

It went like that until the beginning of the fourth round, then when McBride came out, he said, "I've carried you enough, nigger. Now you got to fight."

Then Jack saw stuff he'd never seen before. The way this guy moved, it was something. Bounced around like a cat; like the way he'd heard

Gentleman Jim fought, and the guy was fast with those hands. Tossed bullets, and the bullets stunned a whole lot worse than before. Jack realized McBride had been holding back, trying to make the fight interesting. And he realized something else. Something important about himself. He didn't know as much about boxing as he thought.

He tried hooking McBride, but McBride turned the hooks away with his arms, and Jack tried his surprise weapon, the uppercut, found he could catch McBride a little with that, in the stomach, but not enough to send McBride to the canvas.

When the fifth round came up, Jack was scared. And hurt. And the referee—a skinny bastard with a handlebar moustache—wasn't helping. Anytime he tied McBride up, the referee separated them. McBride tied him up, thumbed him in the eye, butted him, the referee grinned like he was eating jelly.

Jack was thinking maybe of taking a dive. Just going down and lying there, getting himself out of this misery next time McBride threw one of those short ones that connected solid, but then the bell rang and he sat on his bench, and Uncle Cooter, who was the only man in his corner, sprayed water in his mouth and let him spit blood in a bucket.

Uncle Cooter said, "I was you, son, I'd play possum. Just hit that goddamn canvas and lay there like you axed. You don't, this shithead gonna cut you to pieces. This way, you get a little payday and you don't die. Paydays is all right. Dyin' ain't nothin' to rush."

"Jesus, he's good. How can I beat him?"

Uncle Cooter rubbed Jack's shoulders. "You can't. Play dead."

"There's got to be a way."

"Yeah," Uncle Cooter said. "He might die on you. That's the only way you gonna beat him. He got to just die."

"Thanks, Cooter. You're a lot of help."

"You welcome."

Jack feared the sound of the bell. He looked in McBride's corner, and McBride was sitting on his stool as if he were lounging, drinking from a bottle of beer, chatting with a man in the audience. He was asking the man to go get him a sandwich.

Forrest Thomas was in McBride's corner, holding a folded towel over his arm, in case McBride might need it, which, considering he needed to break a good sweat first, wasn't likely.

Forrest looked at Jack, pointed a finger, and lowered his thumb like it was the hammer of a revolver. Jack could see a word on Forrest's lips. The word was: POW!

The referee wandered over to McBride's corner, leaned on the ring post, had a laugh with McBride over something.

The bell rang. McBride gave the bottle of beer to Forrest and came out. Jack rose, saw Beems, eyes blacked, looking rough, sitting in the front row. Rough or not, Beems seemed happy. He looked at Jack and smiled like a gravedigger.

This time out, Jack took a severe pounding. He just couldn't stop those short little hooks of McBride's, and he couldn't seem to hit McBride any kind of blow but the uppercut, and that not hard enough. McBride was getting better as he went along, getting warmed up. If he had another beer and a sandwich, hell, he might go ahead and knock Jack out so he could have coffee and pie.

Jack decided to quit trying to hit the head and the ribs, and just go in and pound McBride on the arms. That way, he could at least hit something. He did, and was amazed at the end of the round to find McBride lowering his guard.

Jack went back to his corner and Uncle Cooter said, "Keep hittin' him on the arms. That's gettin' to him. You wreckin' his tools."

"I figured that much. Thanks a lot."

"You welcome."

Jack examined the crowd in the Sporting Club bleachers. They were not watching the ring. They had turned their heads toward the east wall, and for good reason. It was vibrating. Water was seeping in, and it had filled the floor beneath the ring six inches deep. The people occupying the bottom row of bleachers, all around the ring, had been forced to lift their feet. Above him, Jack heard a noise that sounded like something big and mean peeling skin off an elephant's head.

By the time the bell rang and Jack shuffled out, he noticed that the water had gone up another two inches.

8:46 P.M.

Bill held the lantern in front of him at arm's length as he crouched at the top of the stairs. The water was halfway up the steps. The house was shaking like a fat man's ass on a bucking bronco. He could hear shingles ripping loose, blowing away.

He went back to the bedroom. The wind was screaming. The windows were vibrating; panes had blown out of a couple of them. The baby was crying. Angelique sat in the middle of the bed, trying to nurse the child, but Teddy wouldn't have any of that. Bess was facing a corner of the room, had her head pushed against the wall. The horse lashed her tail back and forth nervously, made nickering noises.

Bill went around and opened all the windows to help take away some of the force of the wind. Something he knew he should have done long ago, but he was trying to spare the baby the howl of the wind, the dampness.

The wind charged through the open windows and the rain charged with it. Bill could hardly stand before them, they were so powerful.

Fifteen minutes later, he heard the furniture below thumping on the ceiling, floating against the floor on which he stood.

9:00 P.M.

My God, thought Jack, how many rounds this thing gonna go? His head ached and his ribs ached worse and his insides felt as if he had swallowed hot tacks and was trying to regurgitate them. His legs, though strong, were beginning to feel the wear. He had thought this was a fifteen-round affair, but realized now it was twenty, and if he wasn't losing by then, he might get word it would go twenty-five.

Jack slammed a glove against McBride's left elbow, saw McBride grimace, drop the arm. Jack followed with the uppercut, and this time he not only hit McBride, he hit him solid. McBride took the shot so hard, he farted. The sandwich he'd eaten between rounds probably didn't seem like such a good idea now.

Next time Jack threw the combination, he connected with the uppercut again. McBride moved back, and Jack followed, hitting him on the arms, slipping in the uppercut now and then, even starting to make contact with hooks and straight rights.

Then every light in the building went out as the walls came apart and the bleachers soared up on a great surge of water and dumped the boxing patrons into the wet darkness. The ring itself began to move, to rise to the ceiling, but before it tilted out from under Jack, McBride hit him a blow so hard Jack thought he felt past lives cease to exist; ancestors fresh from the slime rocked from that blow, and the reverberations of it rippled back to the present and into the future, and back again. The ceiling went away on a torrent of wind, Jack reached out and got hold of something and clung for dear life.

"You stupid sonofabitch," Uncle Cooter said, "you got me by the goddamn head."

Captain Slater thought they would be at the bottom of the Gulf by now, and was greatly surprised they were not. A great wave of water had hit them so hard the night before it had snapped the anchor chain. The ship was driven down, way down, and then all the water in the world washed over them and there was total darkness and horror, and then, what seemed like hours later but could only have been seconds, the water broke and the *Pensacola* flew high up as if shot from a cannon, came down again, leaned starboard so far it took water, then, miraculously, corrected itself. The sea had been choppy and wild ever since.

Slater shook shit and seawater out of his pants legs and followed the rope around his waist to the support post. He got hold of the post, felt for the rest of the rope. In the darkness, he cried out, "Bernard. You there?"

"I think so," came Bernard's voice from the darkness. And then they heard a couple of bolts pop free, fire off like rifle blasts. Then: "Oh, Jesus," Bernard said. "Feel that swell? Here it comes again."

Slater turned his head and looked out. There was nothing but a great wall of blackness moving toward them. It made the first wave seem like a mere rise; this one was bigger than the Great Wall of China.

10:00 P.M.

Bill and Angelique lay on the bed with Teddy. The water was washing over the edges of the feather mattress, blowing wet, cold wind over them. They had started the Edison and a gospel record had been playing, but the wind and rain had finally gotten into the mechanism and killed it.

As it went dead, the far wall cracked and leaned in and a ripple of cracking lumber went across the floor and the ceiling sagged and so did the bed. Bess suddenly disappeared through a hole in the floor. One moment she was there, the next she was gone, beneath the water.

Bill grabbed Angelique by the arm, pulled her to her feet in the knee-deep water. She held Teddy close to her. He pulled them across the room as the floor shifted, pulled them through the door that led onto the unfinished deck, stumbled over a hammer that lay beneath the water, but managed to keep his feet.

Bill couldn't help but think of all the work he had put in on this deck. Now it would never be finished. He hated to leave anything unfinished. He hated worse that it was starting to lean.

There was one central post that seemed to stand well enough, and they took position behind that. The post was one of several that the house was built around; a support post to lift the house above the normal rise of water. It connected bedroom to deck.

Bill tried to look through the driving rain. All he could see was water. Galveston was covered by the sea. It had risen up and swallowed the city and the island.

The house began to shake violently. They heard lumber splintering, felt it shimmying. The deck swayed more dynamically.

"We're not going to make it, are we, Bill?" Angelique said.

"No, darling. We aren't."

"I love you."

"I love you."

He held her and kissed her. She said, "It doesn't matter, you and I. But Teddy. He doesn't know. He doesn't understand. God, why Teddy? He's only a baby . . . How do I drown, darling?"

"One deep breath and it's over. Just one deep pull of the water, and don't fight it."

Angelique started to cry. Bill squatted, ran his hand under the water and over the deck. He found the hammer. It was lodged in its spot because it was caught in a gap in the unfinished deck. Bill brought the hammer out. There was a big nail sticking out of the main support post. He had driven it there the day before, to find it easily enough. It was his last big nail and it was his intent to save it.

He used the claw of the hammer to pull it out. He looked at Angelique. "We can give Teddy a chance."

Angelique couldn't see Bill well in the darkness, but she somehow felt what his face was saying. "Oh, Bill."

"It's a chance."

"But . . ."

"We can't stand against this, but the support post—"

"Oh Lord, Bill," and Angelique sagged, holding Teddy close to her chest. Bill grabbed her shoulders, said, "Give me my son."

Angelique sobbed, then the house slouched far to the right—except for the support post. All the other supports were washing loose, but so far, this one hadn't budged.

Angelique gave Teddy to Bill. Bill kissed the child, lifted him as high on the post as he could, pushed the child's back against the wood, and lifted its arm. Angelique was suddenly there, supporting the baby. Bill kissed her. He took the hammer and the nail, and placing the nail squarely against Teddy's little wrist, drove it through the child's flesh with one swift blow.

Then the storm blew more furious and the deck turned to gelatin. Bill clutched Angelique, and Angelique almost managed to say, "Teddy," then all the powers of nature took them and the flimsy house away.

High above it all, water lapping around the post, Teddy, wet and cold, squalled with pain.

Bess surfaced among lumber and junk. She began to paddle her legs furiously, snorting water. A nail on a board cut across her muzzle, opening a deep gash. The horse nickered, thrashed her legs violently, lifted her head, trying to stay afloat.

SUNDAY, SEPTEMBER 9, 4:00 A.M.

The mechanism that revolved the Bolivar lighthouse beam had stopped working. The stairs that led up to the lighthouse had gradually filled with people fleeing the storm, and as the water rose, so did the people. One man with a young boy had come in last, and therefore was on the constantly rising bottom rung. He kept saying, "Move up. Move up, lessen' you want to see a man and his boy drown." And everyone would move up. And then the man would soon repeat his refrain as the water rose.

The lighthouse was becoming congested. The lighthouse tower had begun to sway. The lighthouse operator, Jim Marlin, and his wife, Elizabeth, lit the kerosene lamp and placed it in the center of the circular, magnifying lens, and tried to turn the beam by hand. They wanted someone to know there was shelter here, even though it was overcrowded, and might soon cease to exist. The best thing to do was to douse the light and hope they could save those who were already there, and save themselves. But Jim and Elizabeth couldn't do that. Elizabeth said, "Way I see it, Jim. It's all or nothing, and the good Lord would want it that way. I want it that way."

All night long they had heard screams and cries for help, and once, when the lighthouse beam was operating, they had seen a young man clinging to a timber. When the light swung back to where the young man had been, he had vanished.

Now, as they tried to turn the light by hand, they found it was too much of a chore. Finally, they let it shine in one direction, and there in the light they saw a couple of bodies being dragged by a large patch of canvas from which dangled ropes, like jellyfish tentacles. The ropes had grouped and twisted around the pair, and the canvas seemed to operate with design, folded and opened like a pair of great wings, as if it were an exotic sea creature bearing them off to a secret lair where they could be eaten in privacy.

Neither Jim nor Elizabeth Marlin knew the bloated men tangled in the ropes together; had no idea they were named Ronald Beems and Forrest Thomas.

5:00 A.M.

A crack of light. Dawn. Jim and Elizabeth had fallen asleep leaning against the base of the great light, and at the first ray of sunshine, they awoke, saw a ship's bow at the lighthouse window, and standing at the bow, looking in at them, was a bedraggled man in uniform, and he was crying savagely.

Jim went to the window. The ship had been lifted up on great piles of sand and lumber. Across the bow he could see the letters PENSA-COLA. The man was leaning against the glass. He wore a captain's hat. He held out his hand, palm first. Jim put his hand to the glass, trying to match the span of the crying captain's hand.

Behind the captain a number of wet men appeared. When they saw the lighthouse they fell to their knees and lifted their heads to the heavens in prayer, having forgotten that it was in fact the heavens that had devastated them.

6:00 A.M.

The day broke above the shining water, and the water began to go down, rapidly, and John McBride sat comfortably on the great hour hand of what was left of the City Hall clock. He sat there with his arms wrapped around debris that dangled from the clock. In the night, a huge spring mechanism had jumped from the face of the clock and hit him a glancing blow in the head, and for a moment, McBride had thought he was still battling the nigger. He wasn't sure which was worse to fight. The hurricane or the nigger. But through the night, he had become grateful for the spring to hold on to.

Below him he saw much of what was left of the Sporting Club, including the lockers where he had put his belongings. The whole damn place had washed up beneath the clock tower.

McBride used his teeth to work off the binds of his boxing gloves and slip his hands free. All through the night the gloves had been a burden. He feared his lack of grip would cause him to fall. It felt good to have his hands out of the tight, wet leather.

McBride ventured to take hold of the minute hand of the clock, swing on it a little, and cause it to lower him onto a pile of rubble. He climbed over lumber and junk and found a mass of bloated bodies, men, women, and children, most of them sporting shingles that had cut into their heads and bodies. He searched their pockets for money and found none, but one of the women—he could tell it was a woman by her hair and dress only, her features were lost in the fleshy swelling of her face—had a ring. He tried to pull it off her finger, but it wouldn't come off. The water had swollen her flesh all around it.

He sloshed his way to the pile of lockers. He searched through them until he found the one where he had put his clothes. They were so filthy with mud, he left them. But he got the razor and the revolver. The revolver was full of grit. He took out the shells and shook them and put them back.

He stuck the gun in his soaked boxing trunks. He opened the razor and shook out the silt and went over to the woman and used the razor to cut off her finger. The blade cut easily through the flesh, and he whacked through the bone. He pushed the ring on his little finger, closed the razor, and slipped it into the waistband of his trunks, next to his revolver.

This was a hell of a thing to happen. He had hidden his money back at the whorehouse, and he figured it and the plump madam were probably far at sea, the madam possibly full of harpoon wounds.

And the shitasses who were to pay him were now all choked, including the main one, the queer Beems. And if they weren't, they were certainly no longer men of means.

This had been one shitty trip. No clothes. No money. No whipped nigger. And no more pussy. He'd come with more than he was leaving with.

What the hell else could go wrong?

He decided to wade toward the whorehouse, see if it was possibly standing, maybe find some bodies along the way to loot—something to make up for his losses.

86 |

As he started in that direction, he saw a dog on top of a doghouse float by. The dog was chained to the house and the chain had gotten tangled around some floating rubble and it had pulled the dog flat against the roof. It lifted its eyes and saw McBride, barked wearily for help. McBride determined it was well within pistol shot.

McBride lifted the revolver and pulled the trigger. It clicked, but nothing happened. He tried again, hoping against hope. It fired this time and the dog took a blast in the skull and rolled off the house, and hung by the chain, then sailed out of sight.

McBride said, "Poor thing."

7:03 A.M.

The water was falling away rapidly, returning to the sea, leaving in its wake thousands of bodies and the debris that had once been Galveston. The stench was awful. Jack and Cooter, who had spent the night in a child's tree house, awoke, amazed they were alive.

The huge oak tree they were in was stripped of leaves and limbs, but the tree house was unharmed. It was remarkable. They had washed right up to it, just climbed off the lumber to which they had been clinging, and went inside. It was dry in there, and they found three hard biscuits in a tin and three hot bottles of that good ole Waco, Texas, drink, Dr Pepper. There was a phone on the wall, but it was a fake, made of lumber and tin cans. Jack had the urge to try it, as if it might be a line to God, for surely, it was God who had brought them here.

Cooter had helped Jack remove his gloves, then they ate the biscuits, drank a bottle of Dr Pepper apiece, then split the last bottle and slept.

When it was good and light, they decided to climb down. The ladder, a series of boards nailed to the tree, had washed away, but they made it to the ground by sliding down like firemen on a pole.

When they reached the earth, they started walking, sloshing through the mud and water that had rolled back to ankle-deep. The world they had known was gone. Galveston was a wet mulch of bloated bodies—humans, dogs, mules, and horses—and mashed lumber. In the distance they saw a bedraggled family walking along like ducks in a row. Jack recognized them. He had seen them around town. They were Issac Cline, his brother Joseph, Issac's wife and children. He wondered if they knew where they were going, or were they like him and Cooter, just out there? He decided on the latter.

Jack and Cooter decided to head for higher ground, back uptown. Soon they could see the tower of City Hall, in sad shape but still standing, the clock having sprung a great spring. It poked from the face of the mechanism like a twisted, metal tongue.

They hadn't gone too far toward the tower when they encountered a man coming toward them. He was wearing shorts and shoes like Jack and was riding a chocolate-brown mare bareback. He had looped a piece of frayed rope around the horse's muzzle and was using that as a primitive bridle. His hair was combed to perfection. It was McBride.

"Shit," Cooter said. "Ain't this somethin'? Well, Jack, you take care, I gonna be seein' you."

"Asshole," Jack said.

Cooter put his hands in his pockets and turned right, headed over piles of junk and bodies on his way to who knew where.

McBride spotted Jack, yelled, "You somethin', nigger. A hurricane can't even drown you."

"You neither," Jack said. They were within twenty feet of one another now. Jack could see the revolver and the razor in McBride's waistband. The horse, a beautiful animal with a deep cut on its muzzle, suddenly buckled and lay down with its legs folded beneath it, dropped its head into the mud.

McBride stepped off the animal, said, "Can you believe that? God-damn horse survived all this and it can't carry me no ways at all."

McBride pulled his pistol and shot the horse through the head. It rolled over gently, lay on its side without so much as one last heave of its belly. McBride turned back to Jack. The revolver lay loose in his hand. He said, "Had it misfired, I'd have had to beat that horse to death with a board. I don't believe in animals suffering. Gun's been underwater, and it's worked two out of three. Can you believe that?"

"That horse would have been all right," Jack said.

"Nah, it wouldn't," McBride said. "Why don't you shake it, see if it'll come around?" McBride pushed the revolver into the waistband of his shorts. "How's about you and me? Want to finish where we left off?"

"You got to be jokin'," Jack said.

"You hear me laughin'?"

"I don't know about you, peckerwood, but I feel like I been in a hurricane, then swam a few miles in boxing gloves, then slept all night in a tree house and had biscuits and Dr Pepper for breakfast."

"I ain't even had no breakfast, nigger. Listen here. I can't go home not knowing I can whip you or not. Hell, I might never get home. I want to know I can take you. You want to know."

"Yeah. I do. But I don't want to fight no pistol and razor."

McBride removed the pistol and razor from his trunks, found a dry spot and put them there. He said, "Come on."

"Where?"

"Here's all we got."

Jack turned and looked. He could see a slight rise of dirt beyond the piles of wreckage. A house had stood there. One of its great support poles was still visible.

"Over there," Jack said.

They went over there and found a spot about the size of a boxing ring. Down below them on each side were heaps of bodies and heaps of gulls on the bodies, scrambling for soft flesh and eyeballs. McBride studied the bodies, what was left of Galveston, turned to Jack, said, "Fuck the rules."

They waded into each other, bare knuckle. It was obvious after only moments that they were exhausted. They were throwing hammers, not punches, and the sounds of their strikes mixed with the caws and cries of the gulls. McBride ducked his head beneath Jack's chin, drove it up. Jack locked his hands behind McBride's neck, kneed him in the groin.

They rolled on the ground and in the mud, then came apart. They regained their feet and went at it again. Then the sounds of their blows and the shrieks of the gulls were overwhelmed by a cry so unique and savage, they ceased punching.

"Time," Jack said.

"What in hell is that?" McBride said.

They walked toward the sound of the cry, leaned on the great support post. Once a fine house had stood here, and now, there was only this. McBride said, "I don't know about you, nigger, but I'm one tired sonofabitch."

The cry came again. Above him. He looked up. A baby was nailed near the top of the support. Its upraised, nailed arm was covered in caked blood. Gulls were flapping around its head, making a kind of halo.

"I'll be goddamned," Jack said. "Boost me, McBride."

"What?"

"Boost me."

"You got to be kidding."

Jack lifted his leg. McBride sighed, made a stirrup with his cupped hands, and Jack stood, got hold of the post and worked his way painfully up. At the bottom, McBride picked up garbage and hurled it at the gulls.

"You gonna hit the baby, you jackass," Jack said.

When he got up there, Jack found the nail was sticking out of the baby's wrist by an inch or so. He wrapped his legs tight around the post, held on with one arm while he took hold of the nail and tried to work it free with his fingers. It wouldn't budge.

"Can't get it loose," Jack yelled down. He was about to drop; his legs and arms had turned to butter.

"Hang on," McBride said, and went away.

It seemed like forever before he came back. He had the revolver with him. He looked up at Jack and the baby. He looked at them for a long moment. Jack watched him, didn't move. McBride said, "Listen up, nigger. Catch this, use it to work out the nail."

McBride emptied the remaining cartridges from the revolver and tossed it up. Jack caught it on the third try. He used the trigger guard to snag the nail, but mostly mashed the baby's wrist. The baby had stopped crying. It was making a kind of mewing sound, like a dying goat.

The nail came loose, and Jack nearly didn't grab the baby in time, and when he did, he got hold of its nailed arm and he felt and heard its shoulder snap out of place. He was weakening, and he knew he was about to fall.

"McBride," he said, "catch."

The baby dropped and so did the revolver. McBride reached out and grabbed the child. It screamed when he caught it, and McBride raised it over his head and laughed.

He laid the baby on top of a pile of wide lumber and looked at it.

Jack was about halfway down the post when he fell, landing on his back, knocking the wind out of him. By the time he got it together enough to get up and find the revolver and wobble over to McBride, McBride had worked the child's shoulder back into place and was cooing to him.

Jack said, "He ain't gonna make it. He's lost lots of blood."

McBride stood up with the baby on his shoulder. He said, "Naw. He's tough as a warthog. Worst this little shit will have is a scar. Elastic as he is, there ain't no real damage. And he didn't bleed out bad neither. He gets some milk in him, fifteen, sixteen years from now, he'll be chasin' pussy. Course, best thing is, come around when he's about two and go on and kill him. He'll just grow up to be men like us."

McBride held the child out and away from him, looked him over. The baby's penis lifted and the child peed all over him. McBride laughed uproariously.

"Well, shit, nigger. I reckon today ain't my day, and it ain't the day you and me gonna find out who's the best. Here. I don't know no one here. Take 'im."

Jack took the child, gave McBride his revolver, said, "I don't know there's anyone I know anymore."

"I tell you, you're one lucky nigger," McBride said. "I'm gonna forgo you a beating, maybe a killing."

"That right?"

"Uh-huh. Someone's got to tote this kid to safety, and if'n I kept him, I might get tired of him in an hour. Put his little head underwater."

"You would, wouldn't you?"

"I might. And you know, you're a fool to give me back my gun."

"Naw. I broke it gettin' that nail loose."

McBride grinned, tossed the gun in the mud, shaded his eyes, and looked at the sky. "Can you beat that? Looks like it's gonna be a nice day."

Jack nodded. The baby sucked on his shoulder. He decided McBride was right. This was one tough kid. It was snuggled against him as if nothing had happened, trying to get milk. Jack wondered about the child's family. Wondered about his own. Where were they? Were they alive?

McBride grinned, said, "Nigger, you got a hell of an uppercut." Then he turned and walked away.

Jack patted the baby's back, watched McBride find his razor, then walk on. Jack watched him until he disappeared behind a swell of lumber and bodies, and he never saw him again.

The Magic Wagon

An excerpt

The preacher got there first, which is often the case, and we told him he could make a little talk when the crowd was big enough, but we'd appreciate it if he didn't try to get folks into a round of gospel singing.

We had everything set up. The mules had been pulled off the wagon, fed and watered, and were tied out next to the woods. We had the clearing fixed up for Billy Bob's shooting show, and we had the ring built for Rot Toe to wrestle in. The ring was six tall poles buried deep in the ground and a wide-hole netting pulled around it and over the top. This way, Rot Toe couldn't get out and scare folks, and the fellas he wrestled with couldn't get away. It kept Rot Toe from doing another thing which wasn't popular with the crowd, and that was throwing his wrestling partners at them. Albert said that back when they first got Rot Toe and come up with the wrestling bit, they used a common roped-in ring, but Rot Toe threw his partners out pretty regular like. This kept Albert busy picking up folks and brushing them off, and when men who had planned to wrestle the ape saw two-hundred-pound men, and sometimes bigger, flying through the air and smashing against the ground right smart, it made them look off in other directions and push their two-bits wrestling fee deeper into their pockets.

We had the side of the wagon facing the woods unhinged at the top and pulled down with supports under it to make a stage. Where the wall had been we pulled a blanket curtain across to keep Billy Bob and the stuff in the wagon hid. That way he could make his entrance out from behind the blanket. He just loved that kind of thing, and I have to admit, when he was duded up and ready to give a show, there was something almost magic about him, and even more so since we'd gotten that body in the box. He'd have probably done good in something like Buffalo Bill's Wild West Show, and I wished from time to time that he'd run off and join it.

Finally enough crowd got there for the preacher to preach to, and by the time he finished others had showed up and it looked as if we were going to have quite a gathering. The thing now was to entertain them good, then come on with the Cure-All and hope to sell a couple cases at the worst.

I looked out at the crowd to see if Texas Jack was out there, but didn't see him, which gave me some relief. I figured if Jack showed and saw Billy Bob's shooting, he'd want to shoot too, and in the end Billy Bob would find out he was the fella out of some of his dime novels, the one who was supposed to have backed down his hero, Wild Bill Hickok, and that could mean a killing. Billy Bob was just looking for an excuse to use those guns of his, and defending the honor of Wild Bill would be just the thing.

When the crowd was good-sized, Albert gave me the high sign and I climbed up on the stage. I had on my city-slicker suit with the derby and I felt about as natural as a pig in boots, but it comforted people to see a boy dressed up.

"Ladies and gentlemen," I said, "tonight, we got a special treat for you. We're going to show you some shooting the likes of which you've never seen. We're going to show you some magic. We're going to let any man who thinks he's man enough to wrestle with Rot Toe, the chimpanzee from Africa. And there's even more. But to introduce the events and demonstrate the manly art of six guns and bullets, I give you our star, the one, and the only, Billy Bob Daniels."

Nobody clapped. They were waiting to see if there was anything to clap about.

A moment later Billy Bob stepped out from behind the curtain and the clapping began.

I'll tell you, he did look good. He had something about him, and it was stronger and richer than ever before. He was wearing a wide-brimmed, tan hat with a band of rattlesnake hide around it, and his shirt and pants were fringed buckskins the color of butternut, and the buttons on his shirt were ivory-colored bone. Around his waist was a blood-red sash and there was a big Bowie knife stuck in the left side of it, and stuffed more to the front were his revolvers, butts out.

His revolvers were just like the ones Hickok's corpse had. Cartridge-converted Colt .60s. They were sightless, so as not to snag on the draw, and the gun metal was almost blue. The grips were magnolia white.

On his feet were moccasin-styled boots with heels, which put another two inches on his height. The boots were the same color as his hat and they had fancy bead and quill work that started at the top and ran down to the toe point.

Billy Bob held up his hand and the clapping stopped. He walked out to the edge of the stage, took a moment to look over the crowd and smile. It was the smile he used when he was winning over the gals.

"My name is Billy Bob Daniels," he said. "I am the son of Wild Bill Hickok."

He let that soak in before he went on.

"Yes, I know what you're thinking. You're thinking I'm saying that for effect, that it's part of the act. But the truth is I am James Butler Hickok's illegitimate son. My mother was a fallen woman of Deadwood, and that is where I was conceived, shortly before that coward Jack McCall snuck up behind Wild Bill and shot him through the back of the head. Even so, my father's hand, out of pure reflex alone, had half drawn his pistol before he fell forward on his cards. Aces and eights, ladies and gentlemen. The cards that from that day forth have been known as the dead man's hand.

"Well, my mother didn't want me. That's the sad truth. I was given up to a family named Daniels and raised by them and it wasn't until I was a grown man that I knew the truth, knew that I was actually a Hickok."

Billy Bob had a way of getting a little trill in his throat when he talked about Hickok, and I'll tell you, it was darn near enough to make you believe that Hickok was his papa, even if like me, you knew it wasn't so. Or reckoned it wasn't so. Albert told me it wasn't true, and that was enough for me.

"When we were in Deadwood some time ago," Billy Bob said, "I met a kindly old medicine man, and he told me a secret. He told me this because he recognized me as the son of Wild Bill. He said he knew it instantly. He came forward, and you know what he told me? He told me the body of Wild Bill was not in its grave. That's correct, ladies and gentlemen, not in his grave. This old Indian, whose life my father had saved on countless occasions, had stolen it, out of respect, mind you, and with herbs and spices known only to Indians, he had petrified the body and kept it in a cave where he bowed down before it twice a day to give thanks to Wild Bill for having saved his life.

"But you know what he did? He took me to that body, and because

I'm Wild Bill's son, he gave it to me. And, ladies and gentlemen, that body is here today for you to see."

Albert had slipped into the back of the wagon, and now he came out from behind the curtain rolling the box on a hand truck, and when he stopped dead center of the stage, Billy Bob stepped over, grabbed the lid, and swung it back.

Hickok's body had been set up so that his arms were lifted and the revolver barrels were resting on what was left of his shoulders, and when the lid came off, the arms fell forward, locked on the hinges Billy Bob had built into the elbows, and two wires attached to the back of the box and the revolver hammers grew taut and the hammers cocked. That sudden movement of the arms, those hammers cocking loudly, always made the crowd jump back and there was usually at least one woman in the crowd that would squeal. This time darn near everybody jumped and squealed. I just loved that part.

When the crowd settled down, Billy Bob said, "Ladies and gentlemen, I present to you Wild Bill Hickok, preserved and holding the very revolvers that sent many a man to hell on his shadow."

Billy Bob used his finger to point out the hole in Hickok's head where McCall's bullet had come out, then backtracked into a story about how Hickok had saved the medicine man's life, and how when the Indian preserved the body he blessed it. Well, it was a good story and all, but it wasn't the truth. I remembered how we came by that box clear as if it were yesterday, and the only thing about Billy Bob's story that was right was that there had been an Indian medicine man, and it happened in Deadwood. Or at least it got started there.

It was a rainy night in Deadwood and things had not gone well. Earlier that day we had given the show, but it was raining then too, and hardly nobody came, and them that did were soon run off by the rain, except for a couple of drunks, and Billy Bob nearly got in a fight with them. From then on Billy Bob's mood went from sour to mean. I think it had something to do with him expecting more from Deadwood, as it was the death place of his hero. But even the graveyard where Wild Bill was buried seemed to disappoint Billy Bob. I reckon he thought standing near the grave would be a spiritual experience or something, but I think all he got out of it was what me and Albert got out of it, and that was wet and cold.

So it was night and we had pulled out to the edge of Deadwood and were about to throw up a windblind for the mules and get bedded down, when this string-bean fellow in a black-and-orange-check suit wearing a derby hat showed up. He got off his horse and came smiling up to us, the rain running off his derby like a waterfall.

I recognized him on account of that suit. He had been at the show that day, but like the others, the rain had run him off. I remembered that he had bad teeth, except for the front two. They were so big and thick-looking you could have tied either one of them on a stick and used it for a hoe.

"What's it we can do for you?" Billy Bob asked the fellow, and I seen his hand dip into his coat pocket, and for once I was glad Billy Bob had a pistol in there and knew how to use it. Something about the fellow in the checkerboard suit made me nervous.

"Mister," he says to Billy Bob, "I heard what you said about being the son of Wild Bill Hickok today, and I come to talk to you."

"That's about all you heard," Billy Bob said. "You left kind of early."

"Well, sir, I wouldn't have, but the rain put a damper on the festivities."

"You didn't mind coming out here in it."

"No, sir, I didn't. And that's because I got something to tell you, might be of interest."

"Well, tell me, I'm wanting to get out of this rain."

"I know where the body of your father, Wild Bill Hickok, is."

"Well, don't bandy it around you idiot, only everyone in these United States and the territories knows that. He's in Deadwood cemetery, you hollow-headed fool. I was up there today to look at his grave."

"No, sir, he ain't there. But let me explain myself now. I'm Bob Chauncey, but folks call me Checkers on account of my suit." And he smiled real big.

Well now, I'll tell you. A man that wears the same suit enough to be named after it ain't high on my list of would-be partners. I ain't the best for cleanliness myself sometimes, but I don't live in the same suit neither. I have been known to put on a clean shirt once in a while. And I wasn't one to believe old Checkers washed out his coat and pants nightly and dried it. He wasn't the type. I think the fact that he had what my mama used to call an unsavory habit led me to figure him as something of a messy person. He was a nose picker, and about the best I've ever seen at it. He didn't do it like a lady will do, like she ain't really doing it but just scratching, and her finger will shoot in and scoop out the prize and she'll flick it away before you can say, "Hey, ain't that a booger?"

He didn't even do it like some men do, which is honest, but not impolite. They'll turn sort of to the side and get in there after it in a businesslike manner, but you didn't actually have to witness the work or what come of it.

No, Checkers Chauncey, who I think of as Nose Picker Chauncey, must have once been a miner or a mule whacker, as they're the nastiest, and the most mannerless, creatures on earth. There ain't a thing they won't do in front of man, child, or lady. They just don't give a damn. Chauncey went about his digging front-on and open, using his finger so hard it rose a mound on his nostrils, like a busy groundhog throwing up dirt. And when he got what he was looking for, he always held it in front of him just to see, I guess, if he'd accidently found something other than what he expected, and when he thumped it away you had to be kind of fast on your feet, because he didn't care who or what it stuck to.

"Well, Checkers, if you think you can tell me where he is," Billy Bob said, "I'm all ears, and watch where you're thumping them things, will you?"

"Well, he ain't in no cemetery. That sign on his grave is just to fool folks. He used to be up there, but he ain't now. Few years ago they moved the cemetery and he got dug up. They were expanding the town, you see, needed the room. Didn't want a bunch of rots and bloaters in the middle of the main street. So when they dug old Bill up, they opened his box and found he was in pretty good shape for a dead man. Had petrified like an old tree. If you could have tore his arm off, it would have been hard enough I reckon to beat a good-sized pig to death."

"How come you know all this, Checkers?" Billy Bob asked.

"I was there when they dug him up. Was just a kid here in Deadwood when he got his brains blowed out. Missed that, which grieves me, since it was history in the making. Had a job emptying out the spittoons, and Mann's number ten was next on my route, but I didn't get there soon enough."

"So you're saying you saw him dug up and the body was taken then?"

"Nope, ain't saying that. Not right then. They reburied Bill, but that night a couple of fellas I knowed came and dug him back up, and they sold him to an old Sioux medicine man for the whereabouts of a mine up in the hills, as there was considerable gold digging going on then."

"Sold Wild Bill Hickok to an Indian?" Billy Bob said. "Yep. And he wasn't just any old Indian. Hickok had killed his oldest son in some shindig once, and he had vowed to get Hickok's body someday. Those two miners remembered that, and they knew he knew these hills like a chicken knows an egg, so they made a swap with him."

"My God," Billy Bob said, "that ain't white."

"This old Indian made him a box out of some sacred trees, and he put that body in it. He figured the spirits in the trees would keep Hickok's dead spirit from getting out and doing something to him. Hickok was so good with them pistols of his, lot of folks, especially Indians, thought he had some magic in him, or in those guns. That box was the Indian's way of holding that magic back, get me?"

"I get you, but you still ain't told me where the body is."

"This old Indian liked to open the box up a couple times a day, lift up his breechcloth and expose himself to old Bill's corpse."

"That's disgusting," Billy Bob said.

"Showing your privates like that is a kind of Indian joke. An insult."

"All right, enough about the damned savages and their jokes, where is this old Indian that has the body?"

"The old Indian don't have it no more."

Billy Bob was starting to fidget, and I thought any minute he was going to jerk out that pistol and start beating Nose Picker about the head and ears with it, which would have been all right with me. I could see this was leading to no good, and I was cold and wet and getting wetter. Albert was leaning against the wagon, watching and listening. He didn't look any happier than I felt.

"I swear you are the windiest gas bag I ever did see. If he ain't with the old Indian, then where is he?"

"With the old Indian's son. He's a medicine man too. You see, the old man died and the young fella sort of inherited Wild Bill. He's been living back East getting him a white education, but he had to come back on account of he got caught cheating somebody in Yankee land. He has the body now and wants to sell it, get him some seed money. Get out of the cave he's living in. Maybe go back East when things cool down on what he done."

"And what's your cut in all this, Checkers?" Billy Bob said.

Checkers smiled. I wished he hadn't. I didn't like them teeth. "Finders fee. Indian said he'd give me a cut of the money, and then there's just the plain, simple fact that I'd like to see a family brought back together again, even if one of them is dead."

"That's right touching of you," Billy Bob said.

"Always did have me a sentimental streak. It's a kind of sweetness that runs through me. You interested or not?"

"I'm interested. And Checkers?"

"Yeah?"

"You wouldn't lie to an ole Southern boy, would you?"

"No. I wouldn't. I'm partial to Southern boys, actually."

"I hope you are. How much this Indian wanting for the body, provided I see it and want it?"

"Twenty dollars."

"Twenty dollars!"

"That's right. And twenty for me taking you to it."

"Hell, man, ain't nobody got no forty dollars to be giving away."

"Well now, I figure since he's your pa, you'll want the body. And another thing, maybe an even more important thing, is you have that body and you're going to make a ton of money. I mean, you can't kid Checkers. You carry that old boy around with you and it's going to sell more of that watered-down liquor you call Cure-All. And that's going to make you lots of money, I know."

"When do I see the body?" Billy Bob asked.

"Has to be tonight."

"That's a mite hasty, ain't it, considering the weather?"

"I'm leaving the Hills tomorrow. Don't know if I'm coming back. Hell, for all I know, that Indian might have already cut loose of it. He was big to sell."

So there we were, it pitch black and raining bad enough to strangle a duck, and Billy Bob wanted to go into the Black Hills with a total stranger who couldn't stop picking his nose, and look at a rotting body in a box. A body that might, or might not, be Wild Bill Hickok. Then he'd probably buy that rascal with the wages he owed me and Albert.

Billy Bob put the wagon in storage, put our old mules in the livery, and rented us some horses, including one for Chauncey, and one mule for carrying the box out should he buy it, which seemed like a foregone conclusion to me. Provided there was a body in a box.

We put Rot Toe over to one of the whorehouses, and I told one of the fat ladies to take good care of him, and if anything happened to us, which was damn likely, he was partial to fruit and would touch a bite of meat now and then if that's all there was.

By the time we were all squared away it was pretty late and raining worse than ever. I just couldn't see any sense in this thing we were doing, but I reckon I can't complain too loudly, because there wasn't much sense in me either. I went along and I could have deserted right then and there, lit out and never had to look at Billy Bob again. But I didn't, and I like to think it wasn't so much a dose of the stupids as it was the fact that I didn't want to leave Albert. You see, I knew, for whatever reason, he was going to stick with Billy Bob. And Billy Bob was one of them kind that once he got his mind set on a thing, he was going to do it, and there wasn't no swaying him. Way he was acting, you'd think Wild Bill really was his pap.

Nose Picker worried me too. He was too eager to my way of think-ing. Even twenty dollars and the cut of another twenty didn't seem worth what he was doing. I figured soon as we were up in the Hills, bunch of his cutthroat partners would come out of the rocks, kill us, steal the rented horses, and take everything we had on us, right down to our underwear, and them too if they were in the right sizes.

In spite of all this, Billy Bob wasn't a total fool. He had put pistols in both his buffalo-coat pockets and he had another little one in his belt. He fixed me up with a .38 Smith-and-Wesson and gave Albert a big .45. Chauncey didn't see any of this, as he waited outside the wagon while we got a few things, and him not knowing about the guns was at least some sort of comfort.

As we rode I could see from the way Albert was looking all around, one of his hands inside his coat near the .45, that he felt like I did. He was worried.

I kept my hand away from the Smith-and-Wesson because I was afraid of guns, and figured if it came down to me using it, I'd most likely try to pull it and end up shooting off my kneecap, or some other part of my body I was even more proud of.

Billy Bob, on the other hand, looked like he was on a picnic, or like he had just ridden out of one of them dime novels he liked to read. The rain didn't even bother him. He sat straight in the saddle, face forward. He was wearing a big, wide-brimmed, black hat, that buffalo coat, dark blue pants with a yellow military stripe, and black, fur-lined boots.

Chauncey slouched in the saddle, smiling to himself, singing some ditty or another, picking his nose all the while. I couldn't tell if he was naturally happy, stupid, or thinking on what he was going to do with his share of the clothes and such he was going to help steal from us later.

Whatever, there we were, right smack dab out in the middle of what used to be called Red Cloud's Big Open, and any minute I expected to get my brains blowed out by robbers in cahoots with Nose Picker Chauncey, or maybe by some Indians that didn't know, or didn't care, that we had won the Indian wars.

But none of that happened.

After we'd ridden for quite a few hours and I'd begun to feel like my butt had growed to the saddle, we came on a bad section of rocks and the trail narrowed. Lightning flashed, and when it did I seen at the top of the trail that there were a series of small caves, and those caves looked like open mouths begging us to step inside and get chewed.

When the lightning flashed again, Chauncey pointed at one of the caves, and we got the general idea which one it was, and that that was where the Indian lived.

We started along the narrow trail that led up there, and I could hear pebbles tumbling off the edge and down to the depths below. When the lightning flashed again, I looked down and wished I hadn't. If me and my horse went over, there wouldn't never be no way to sort out which of us was which.

Finally we come to a spot about halfway to the caves and stopped. Chauncey got down and had us do the same.

"We got to walk the rest of the way," Chauncey said, and he had to yell for us to understand him because the wind was whipping away his words. "We can leave our mounts here. Get the nigger to hold them."

Though it would have been smarter for Billy Bob to have left me holding the mules, since I didn't know slick mud from fresh honey, he went along with Chauncey, seeing how Albert was colored. He damn sure didn't want no white man to know he'd feel safer with a colored by his side instead of one of his own kind.

"Let's go then," Billy Bob said.

I handed Albert the rein to my horse.

"You watch yourself, hear?" Albert said.

"I will."

So the three of us, Chauncey, Billy Bob, and me, went up. It was a rough walk and the higher it got the less there was to walk on. Rocks slid out from under our feet and cut at our legs and the gorge loomed just to our left, and when the lightning flashed it looked deep enough for you to fall all the way down to the pits of hell.

After the jumble of rocks we came to a clear spot and the cave. There was a torch just inside against the wall, lodged in some rocks, and Chauncey lit it, which was quite a chore as he had to take a finger out of his nose to hold the torch in one hand and the match in the other.

When the torch was lit, we went deeper inside the cave. Bats flapped above us, and their leavings were all over the floor and smelt right smart. I didn't like bats, no kind of way. They always looked to me like rats with wings, and I don't like rats either. Especially ones that can fly.

Finally it got lighter ahead of us, and we crunched through some old bones lying about, and Chauncey showed us that a lot of them were human. He said this cave had once belonged to a grizzly and that now and then some folks had come in and met him, and he hadn't been such a good host. I know I was glad when he lifted that torch and I didn't have to stare at those bones, particularly one skull with its entire right side crushed in, like a big paw had swatted it.

The light around the bend was from a campfire, and it was right cozy in there. There were a few handmade chairs, a bed, and a table, and over on the right-hand side of the wall, leaning up against it, was a rough-cut box with a lid on it.

But the thing that really got my attention was the young Indian. He wasn't all that young, I reckon. Maybe thirty-five. It's hard to tell with Indians. They seem to me to either age real fast or not at all.

He had on a dusty black suit with a yellowish shirt that was once white and he was wearing an Abraham Lincoln hat. He was a friendly looking fellow and he was smiling at us while he held one hand in his coat pocket.

I figured he had his hand on a pistol and was just smiling either out of habit, or to get us off guard. When he seen that Checkers was with us, he relaxed a mite and spoke.

"Checkers, my good comrade. I thought that I might not see you again. It was my suspicion that you had been caught for some nefarious deed, like horse thievery, but I see that this was not the case. And better yet, you have brought friends to cheer my fire."

"Why's he talk like that?" Billy Bob half whispered to Checkers.

"That damned education stuff," Checkers said. "But he's all right."

"Come," said the Indian, "please come and warm yourself by my meager fire. Take a load off your feet and your mind, and I will see to some liquid refreshment."

What he did for liquid refreshment was reach into his other pocket and take out a pint flask, which he sat on a rock by the fire.

We got over near the fire and warmed our hands, but nobody sat yet.

The Indian found four cups and brought them over, then he poured us all a little splash from the bottle and we drank it.

"Please, please," he said, pouring us some more. "Sit, please do sit. There is no need to stand on parade here. My home is your home. Or to take two lines from the opera *Clari, the Maid of Milan*: 'Mid pleasures and palaces though we may roam, be it ever so humble, there's no place like home; a charm from the skies seems to hallow us there, which sought through the world is ne'er met with elsewhere.'"

Billy Bob wasn't so quiet this time. "What in hell is he talking about?"

"Just more of that education stuff," Chauncey said. "An opry is where folks yell at each other to music."

"Ah, Checkers," said the Indian, "you have no heart. An opera is the heart, the soul, the very wing tips of a bird. It soars through the breast and mind and fills the soul."

"How about we do less soaring," Billy Bob said, "and talk about this body I come to look at."

"Yes," the Indian said, "the body of the Great White Warrior, the Pistoleer Prince of the Plains, the one and only, the indescribable Wild Bill Hickok."

"That's him," Billy Bob said.

"Now you remember that deal you made me about bringing a buyer here?" Checkers said to the Indian.

"It has been a month, my good friend. But I remember."

The Indian smiled. "What if you had brought them here and I had sold the body?"

"Chance I took," Checkers said. "Besides, I didn't figure you'd sold it. You don't like going down into town so much."

The Indian opened his arms wide. "Isn't that polite? That is Mr. Checkers's way of saying that I am a wanted man in Deadwood."

"What for?" Billy Bob said. "I thought it was back East where you was wanted."

The Indian sighed. "There too. But I can hide better here. As for Deadwood, well, I'm wanted for a slight altercation with a young gentleman who had some rather foul comments about my ancestry. I was forced in a moment of passion, perhaps a moment fired by devil rum, to place the full length of a Bowie knife between his top two ribs, and therefore, let the soul fly out of him."

"What?" Billy Bob said, glancing at Checkers.

"He stabbed the sonofabitch to death," Checkers said.

"And I hope, dear friend," said the Indian, "that you have been better able to quiet your tongue on that matter below than you have here this night."

"You told them, you silly bastard," Checkers said. "I was just explaining."

"So you were, so you were," the Indian said.

The Indian and Checkers grinned at each other. The way they were doing it, I figured it was hurting their lips.

"Can we just get on with what I come here for?" Billy Bob said.

"Of course," said the Indian, "but first let me introduce myself. I'm Elijah Bigshield, Oglala medicine man, retired." He held out his hand.

Billy Bob's face worked to the left, then to the right. "I don't shake hands with niggers or Indians," he said.

"You don't say?" the Indian said.

"I do say. Now let's get on with it."

Checkers cleared his throat. "This here boy has got a special interest in the body. Hickok was his daddy. Some whore in Deadwood was his mother."

"You don't say?" Elijah Bigshield said, but the honey in his voice had gone considerably sour. "Isn't that nice. Why you even look like him, now that it is mentioned. 'As a little childe riding behind his father, said simply unto him, Father, when you are dead, I shall ride in the Saddle.' Stefan Guazzo, *Civile Conversation*. And now that saddle has been passed to you, and you may ride in the tracks of Hickok the killer."

I was beginning to feel a mite uncomfortable, but Billy Bob didn't show a sign of it. "I don't want to hear no more of your education," he said. "An Indian or a nigger with an education ain't nothing more than a bird that can talk. It sounds like it knows something, but any fool knows it don't. It just mocks."

"I find you most unpleasant, sir," Elijah said.

"You're going to find me leaning over your ugly face, beating you upside the head with my fist, if you don't show me this body Checkers has been carping about. And there better be a body in that damn box, that's what I'm trying to tell you."

"Anything to please the young gentleman," Elijah said snidely. He walked over to the box and rubbed a hand against it. "I'm asking twenty dollars for it, sir."

We followed him over, with Checkers standing back a bit, and Elijah opened the lid. That was the first time I seen the body, and I knew in my heart that it was none other than who they said it was, Wild Bill Hickok.

"The body possesses magical properties, sir," Elijah said, stepping to the side to let Billy Bob see. "Hickok's ability with his guns was most phenomenal. And he himself said on more than one occasion that his hands were guided by spirits."

"How come you know so much about it, you being an Indian?" Billy Bob asked.

"Even the mouse must learn the ways of the hawk if he wishes to survive. That body, sir, is so full of magic, that it is said that if you put it at the foot of your bed at night, Hickok's skill with the pistols will enter into you and allow you to shoot as fast and straight and true as this man-killer ever did."

"Is that a fact?" Billy Bob said. "Who's done it to know?"

"No one. My father told me this, and he was one to know. He tried to steal the magic from the corpse and put it in a pot, but the magic was too strong to be stolen. When he died, my father's soul joined those in the wood that surround the white man-killer."

"The spirits in the wood, huh?"

Elijah nodded. The firelight flickered across his copper face, and even in that silly suit and hat, he looked very, very Indian. The smile lines around his eyes and mouth had fallen off like dead leaves.

"That is correct. The spirits in the wood are old as the world, and they collect to them new spirits when they die, providing those spirits are worthy to become the protectors of the Oglala."

"You don't say?" Billy Bob sneered.

"Oh, I do say. It is the spirits in the wood that keep the black magic of Hickok inside him, lest it be passed on to the whites. The whites have enough magic, without the gun magic of Hickok."

"And why don't you, or why didn't your father, let Wild Bill's magic pass on to you Indians?"

"White man's magic. It cannot be used by Indians, and Indians don't want it. We have our own magic."

"Lot of good it's done you," Billy Bob said.

"That is quite correct, sir," Elijah said, "quite correct." But his voice had an edge to it, and I was beginning to get spooked. I looked at the body in the box and it seemed strangely alive. It wasn't that I expected it to get out of that box and walk or nothing. It was more like what that medicine man was saying about spirits and all, and there was something about that body, maybe the way the firelight glinted off the bone in those empty eye sockets, that made you think there was a powerful and ugly thing inside it. I somehow felt whatever spirits might have been in Hickok were bad. Maybe Hickok wasn't all bad his ownself, but those spirits were, and now they were all that was left of him. I felt better knowing he was between them boards full of Indian magic.

"You tell a good story, Indian," Billy Bob said, smiling one of his nasty smiles, "but it ain't nothing to me but spook talk."

Elijah smiled slowly, so slowly you could almost count his teeth one at a time as his lips folded back. "Yes, you white men certainly have it over us ignorant savages."

Billy Bob nodded to that. "How do I know this here is Wild Bill Hickok, and not just some drunk you've pickled?"

Elijah stepped forward, put a finger on the body's head. "Bend close and look at that hole. Is that not an exit wound from a bullet? Was not Wild Bill shot from behind and the bullet came out the front of his head?"

"That's so," Billy Bob said, leaning forward for a look. In spite of myself, I leaned too, but I couldn't look into those empty sockets. Billy Bob was what I was looking at, and his eyes seemed to have fallen out of his head and down those sockets like two marbles tumbling down mine shafts. His face tightened for a moment, and then suddenly he turned.

Elijah, after pointing out that bullet hole, had stepped back and pulled what was in his coat pocket out. A Bowie knife. And even as Billy Bob turned, and I turned with him, that knife came flying through the air. To this day I don't know how it missed Billy Bob. I couldn't believe he could move that fast. His left hand came out of his coat pocket, and it was full of Colt .60. The Colt jumped and roared and Elijah's lips were parted by the bullet. The gun roared again, and this time the slug hit Elijah square between the eyes. The shots were so close together, they almost sounded like one.

Before Elijah hit the ground, Billy Bob flicked his wrist to the left and had Checkers covered. Checkers had one hand to his nose and the other inside his coat.

"Don't shoot me, fella," Checkers said. "I was trying to go for the Indian. I seen what he was about to do and I tried to go for him. I swear, it was the Indian I was after. It's just you're so blooming fast . . . Grief, but you just might be the son of old Wild Bill. That was the fastest damned draw I ever did see."

Slowly Checkers went ahead and brought his gun hand out. There was a little pistol in it. He lowered his arm down by his side and let it dangle.

"I swear," Checkers said, "I wouldn't throw in with no Indian against a white man."

"Put the gun up," Billy Bob said, "and see if he's dead."

Checkers did as he was told. While he did I smelt something burning, and glancing at the fire, I seen it was Elijah's stovepipe hat. The first shot had knocked it off his head and it had rolled into the fire. It was just a black wisp now.

Checkers bent over the body, then stood. "He's dead. Course he's dead. He's got two holes in his head. I could have told you that from over there."

Billy Bob turned to look at where the Bowie had gone. It was stuck just to the right of Hickok's head. Billy Bob reached and pulled it out of the wood, and the knife squeaked free of it like a mouse that had had its back stepped on. Billy Bob stuck it in the belt around his coat.

"Too bad he wasn't white," Billy Bob said. "Would have been my first kill. Hickok didn't count no Indians or niggers, and I don't aim to neither."

"Didn't count spicks neither," Checkers said.

"That's right," Billy Bob said, "no spicks neither."

Billy Bob reloaded his pistol and dipped it back into his left coat pocket.

"Checkers," he said, "you look that body over for money. He got anything you give it to me. I ain't so sure you didn't lead us up here to cheat and kill us, so you don't get nothing out of the deal, not even the twenty for the trip."

Checkers's face went red and he forgot to put his finger in his nose. "That ain't fair."

"Didn't say it was," Billy Bob said. "Don't feel like being fair right now."

"I brought you up here in the rain, it storming—"

"Shut up and do as I say," Billy Bob said. He opened and closed his hands above his coat pockets where the butts of his pistols showed.

Checkers moved his jaw back and forth a few times, then he bent to searching Elijah.

"Don't palm nothing," Billy Bob said. "I would find that disagreeable."

Checkers brought over a pocket watch, a derringer, and a little bag full of bones, dirt, and beads.

Billy Bob put the watch in his inside shirt pocket. "Indians are hell for trinkets," he said, "but what they need to know time for?" He poured what was in the bag into his hand and then back into the bag. "What's this?"

"His medicine bag," Checkers said. "Has his powers in it."

"Did him a lot of good, didn't it?" Billy Bob said, and tossed it into the fire. He flung the derringer as far as he could to the back of the cave. "Whore's gun," he said. "That and tin horns."

Billy Bob put the lid on the box, and we went out of there, back down to where Albert waited, me and Checkers carrying the box with Wild Bill in it. It was pretty heavy.

I didn't tell Albert right then all that happened. I figured he knew a lot of the story from the way I looked at him, and I thought maybe he'd heard the shots, though later he said he hadn't. With the storm like it was, and us being deep inside the cave, he hadn't heard a thing.

We strapped the box on the side of the mule, and Billy Bob took to leading it behind his mount. Me and Checkers rode behind him, almost side by side, and behind us was Albert.

We'd gone a mile or so when the storm got so bad every little bit of the sky lit up with forks of blue-white lightning and the thunder roared like there was a cannon war going on.

About the time all this storm business got built up, Checkers made his play. Maybe he and the Indian had planned such a thing all along and it hadn't gone good. I don't know. Maybe Checkers planned to rob us after we had the body and the Indian's money, that way he could make double. And maybe he hadn't planned nothing at all and was just mad because he hadn't made his share like he thought he should.

Doesn't matter now. With Billy Bob in front of him, he had the perfect chance to do to him what Jack McCall had done to Hickok.

I seen him go for his gun, and I tried to yell, but with the thunder and lightning like it was, I didn't know if Billy Bob could hear me. But he did, or maybe he'd just been waiting for Checkers to make his play all along. Billy Bob swiveled, on his critter, and as he did, I seen there was a smile on his face, like he was about to get a present he'd been waiting a long time for.

The way Billy Bob's hand moved was too fast to be real. I figured it was a trick of the lightning or something. One second his hand was on his knee and the next it was full of pistol and the pistol was cocked.

Only he didn't get to kill Checkers. The lightning did it. It was faster even than Billy Bob, and it reached down out of the sky and hit Checkers's little pistol and there was the sound like a giant whip cracking, then Checkers and his horse exploded and I was wearing some of him and some of his suit and some of his horse.

Billy Bob, with a wail, threw himself off his horse onto the ground and started pounding his hand against the ground, screaming, "I had him beat. My first white man. I had him beat," then he began to cry.

I just sort of sat there, dumbfounded, wearing Checkers, his suit, and his horse. Finally I got down off my horse, led him over a piece, got down on my knees, and threw up.

When I was able to get up, I looked over and seen Albert was helping Billy Bob to his feet. Billy Bob was saying over and over, "I had him beat. My first white man."

Albert helped Billy Bob over to his horse and put him in the saddle. He patted him on the knee. "There's just a whole bunch of white men, Mister Billy Bob. Don't you fret. There'll be others."

"I had him, Albert. I had him whipped fair and square, didn't I?"

"Couldn't have been no fairer or squarer," Albert said, like he was talking to a little kid.

"It ain't right. I had him beat."

"Plumb beat," Albert said.

"By the time Wild Bill was my age he's done a lot of his killing already," Billy Bob said.

"Things were different then," Albert said. "Folks was more for killing in them times. Got up with it on their minds. They had more niggers to do their work, and there was lots of free time for shooting folks."

"I had him," Billy Bob said, shaking his head. "I had him."

Actually, I had a lot of him. I got a handkerchief and cleaned off what I could and got sick some more.

When I was feeling some better, I went over and stood with Albert and he put his arm around my shoulder. We looked at what was left of Nose Picker Chauncey and his horse. It wasn't much. Just a heap of bones, smoking meat, some saddle leather, and a hunk of checkered suit.

Maybe I should have felt some worse about old Checkers, but to tell it true, I couldn't work up a lot of enthusiasm for feeling bad. I figured after he killed Billy Bob he planned to finish off me and Albert, not knowing we had guns on us and seeing us as easy pickings, which I reckon I would have been. And besides, I just couldn't warm myself to a man that spent the largest part of his life with a finger up his nose, even if he did end up sad like, being cooked with a horse and a checkered suit.

It seemed like it took forever to get out of the hills, what with the storm being like it was and Billy Bob sort of pouting along, stopping now and then to shake his fists at the heavens and to cuss God and the lightning, calling them some of the meanest, foulest names I've ever heard a mouth utter. The way that thunder rumbled and that lightning sizzled blue-white around Billy Bob, framing him now and then like a bright-colored picture, I half felt it was cussing and threatening him back.

By the middle of the next morning we got down out of the hills and back to Deadwood. The sun hadn't come out.

We collected the wagon, the mules, and Rot Toe, who smelled mighty sweet from all them women petting him, and we got out of town lickety-split, started heading Southwest, which was a direction that suited me fine.

We hadn't gone a day out of that storm when Billy Bob decided to fix up some cracked sideboards in the wagon.

He'd been putting it off for a month and there didn't seem any sense in it right then, but I think he did it to make light of what that medicine man had told him about them boards in Wild Bill's box being made out of sacred trees. He knew I'd told Albert the story, and he knew that Albert believed it, and I about half believed it, so he wanted to show us what fools we were.

Like I said, we'd gotten ahead of the rain for a while, and had all been sitting on top of the wagon, trying to get us some sun, and suddenly Billy Bob had us pull over.

Usually, any work to be done, me and Albert did it, but this time Billy Bob took it on himself. He dragged the box with Wild Bill outside the wagon, propped the body against it, knocked out those old sideboards he wanted to replace, and put in some boards from Wild Bill's box.

It took about half a day for him to get that done, as Billy Bob wasn't no joiner to speak of, and by the time he was finished and we were on our way, thunder was right behind us, rumbling loud, and when I turned to look back I got the willies, cause them dark storm clouds that were following us looked to have come together in the shape of Elijah's stovepipe hat.

That was the day that storm started pushing for us, and it stayed after us from then on.

A week or so later, we stopped in a little town to do our act, and Billy Bob had a joiner make a new box for Wild Bill. When that was done, he took the guns that were in Wild Bill's rotting sash out, cleaned them up, and put them in the corpse's bony hands, rigged up those hinges in the elbows and those wires that cocked the guns.

And that's the true story of how we came by that body in the box, not the one Billy Bob was telling the crowd about a noble red man giving it to him because he was Hickok's son. I mean, his tale was a good story, all right, but it was nothing more than a damned lie.

To get back to this time in Mud Creek, Billy Bob told his story, then he went out to the clearing with everyone tagging along behind, and he did some shooting.

And I mean shooting. I want to witness that I hadn't never seen him as good as he was that day. He split playing cards edgewise, like always, but now he was doing it from farther away. The same for when he held the mirror with one hand and shot over his shoulder with the other. And he hit nickels tossed in the air with either hand. Before he'd only done that kind of shooting with his right hand.

To put it simply, the man could not miss.

He even went as far as to strike a match with a shot, and I'd heard that was just an old wives' tale and couldn't be done. But he done it, and neatly.

When next I looked out at the crowd, I seen Skinny had joined us. He still had on his apron. He was eating from a bag of peppermints, drooling it down his chin. His eyes looked like a couple of dark holes. It was kind of good to see the old boy.

Then I seen something that made me considerably less happy.

Blue Hat and Texas Jack.

Dirt Devils

The Ford came into town full of men and wrapped in a cloud of dust and through the dust the late afternoon sun looked like a cheap lamp shining through wraps of gauze. The cloud glided for a great distance, slowed when the car stopped moving forward, spun and finally faded out and down on all sides until the car could clearly be seen coated in a sheet of white powder. It took a moment to realize that beneath the grime the car was as black as tar. The wind that had been blowing stopped and shifted and the dust wound itself up into a big dust devil that twirled and gritted its way down the rutted street and tore out between two wind-squeaked abandoned buildings toward a gray tree line in the distance.

Outside of the car there wasn't much of the town to see, just a few ramshackle buildings wiped clean by the sandstorms that chewed wood and scraped paint and bleached the color out of clothes hung on wash lines. The dust was everywhere, coating windows and porch steps and rooftops. Sometimes, in just the right light, the dust looked like snow and one half expected polar bears and bewildered Eskimos to appear. The infernal sand seeped under cracks no matter how well blocked or rag stuffed, and it crept into closed cars and through nailed-down windows. The world belonged to sand.

The street was slightly less sandy in spots since tire wheels and foot-steps kept it worn down, but you had to stay in the ruts if you drove a car, and the Ford had done just that before parking in front of a little store with a single gas pump with the gas visible in a big dust-covered bulb on top.

The car parked and a man on the passenger side got out. He had a hat in his hand and he put it on. He wore a nice blue suit and fine black shoes and he looked almost clean, the dust having only touched his outfit and hat like glitter tossed at him by The Great Depression Fairy. He leaned left and then leaned right, stretching himself. The other doors opened and three men got out. They all wore suits. One of the men wearing a brown pinstripe suit and two-tone shoes came over and put his foot on the back of the car and wiped at his shoes with a handkerchief that he refolded and put in his inside coat pocket. He said to the man in the blue suit, "You want I should get some Co-colas or somethin', Ralph?"

"Yeah, that'll be all right. But don't come back with all manner of shit like you do. We ain't havin' a picnic. Get some drinks, a few things to nibble on, and that's it."

As the man in the pinstripe suit went into the store, an old man came out to the pump. He looked as if he had once been wadded and was now starting to slowly unfold. His hair was as white as the sand and floated when he walked. "I help you fellas?"

"Yeah," said Ralph. "Filler up."

The old man took the hose and removed the car's gas cap and started filling the tank. He looked at the car window, and then he looked away and looked back at the store. He swallowed once, hard, like he had an apple hung in his throat.

Ralph leaned against the car and took off his hat and ran his hand through his oiled hair and put it back on. He stared at the old man a long time. "Much hunting around here?" he asked the old man.

"Lot of hunting, but not much catching. Depression must be gettin' better though, only seen one man chasin' a rabbit the other day."

It was a tired joke, but Ralph grinned.

"This used to be a town," the old man said. "Wasn't never nothing much, but it was a town. Now most of the folks done moved off and what's here is worn out and gritted over. Hell, you get up in the morning you find sand in the crack of your ass."

Ralph nodded. "Everything's gritted over, and just about everybody too. I think I'm gonna go to California."

"Lots done have. But there ain't no work out there."

"My kind of work, I can find something."

The old man hesitated, and when he asked the question, it was like the words were sneaking out of the corner of his mouth: "What do you do?"

"I work with banks."

"Oh," the old man said. "Well, banking didn't do so good either."

"I work a special division."

"I see . . . Well, it's gonna be another bad night with lots of wind and plenty of dust."

"How can you tell?"

"'Cause it always is. And when it ain't, I can tell before it comes about. I can sniff it. I used to farm some before the winds came, before the dust. Then I bought this and it ain't no better than farming because people 'round here are farmers and they ain't got no money 'cause they ain't got no farms so I ain't got no money. I don't make hardly nothin'."

"Nothin', huh?"

"What you're givin' me for this here gas and the like, that's all I've made all day."

"That does sound like a problem."

"Tell me about it."

"So if I was to rob you, I'd just be keepin' my own money."

"You would . . . You boys staying in town long?"

"Where's to stay?"

"You got that right. Thirty, forty more feet, you're out of town. There ain't nothing here and ain't nobody got nothin'."

"That right?"

"Nothing to be had."

Ralph said, "My daddy, he had a store like this in Kansas. He ain't got nothin' now. He got droughted out and blown out. He died last spring. You remind me somethin' of him."

The other two men who had been loitering on the other side of the car came around to join Ralph and the old man, and when Ralph said what he said about his old man, one of the men, brown suited, glanced at Ralph, then glanced away.

"Me, I'm just hanging in by the skin of my teeth, and I just got a half dozen of 'em left." The old man smiled at Ralph so he would know it was true. "I'm just about done here."

"You a Bible reader?" Ralph asked the old man.

"Everyday."

"I figured that much. My old man was a Bible reader. He could quote chapter and verse."

"I can quote some chapters and some verses."

"You done any preachin'?"

"No. I don't preach."

"My old man did. He ran a store and preached and had too many children. I was the last of 'em."

The old man looked at the tank. "You was bone dry, son, but I about got you filled now."

In the store the man in the brown suit with pinstripes, whose name was Emory, saw a little Negro boy sitting on a stool wearing a thick cloth cap that looked as if it had been used to catch baseballs. The boy had a little pocketknife and was whittlin' on a stick without much energy.

Emory looked at the boy. The boy latched his eyes on Emory.

"What you lookin' at, boy?"

"Nuthin'."

"Nuthin', sir."

"Yes, suh."

Emory wandered around the store and found some candies and some canned peaches. He got some Co-colas out of the ice box and set them dripping wet on the counter with the canned peaches and the candies.

Emory turned and looked at the boy. "You help out here, nigger?"

"Just a little."

"Well, why don't you do just a little? Get over here behind the counter and get me some of them long cigars there, and a couple packs of smokes."

"I don't do that kind of thing," the boy said. "That there is Mr. Grady's job. I just run errands and such. I ain't supposed to go behind the counter."

"Yeah. I guess that make sense. And them errands. What's a nigger get for that kind of work?"

"A nickel sometimes."

"Per errand?"

"Naw, suh. Per day."

"That's a little better. There's white men workin' in the fields ain't making a dollar a day."

"Yes, suh. They's colored men too."

"Yeah. Well, how hard are they workin'?"

"They workin' plenty hard."

"Say they are," Emory said, and took a hard look at the boy. The boy's eyes were still locked on his and the boy had his hands on his knees. The boy's face was kind of stiff like he was thinking hard on something but one eye sagged slightly to the left and there was a scar above and below it. He had one large foot and a very worn-looking oversized shoe about the size of a cinder block.

"What happened to your eye?"

"I had a saw jump back on me. I was cuttin' some wood and it got stuck and I yanked and it come back on me. I can still see though."

"I can tell that. What's wrong with your foot?"

"It's a club foot."

"What club does it belong to?"

"What's that?"

"You ain't so smart, are you?"

"Smart enough, I reckon."

"So, with that foot, you don't really run errands, you walk 'em."

The boy finally quit looking at Emory. "Ain't that right," Emory said when the boy didn't answer.

"I s'pose so," the boy said. "That a gun you got under your coat?"

"You a nosey little nigger, ain't ya? Yeah, that's a gun. You know what I call it?"

The boy shook his head.

"My nigger shooter. You know what I shoot with it?"

The boy jumped up. It caused the stool to turn over. The boy dropped the stick and the pocketknife and moved as fast as his foot would allow toward the door, turned and went right along the side of the store, giving Emory a glance at him through the dusty glass, and then there was just wall and the boy was gone from view.

Emory laughed. "Bet that's the fastest he ever run," he said aloud. "Bet that's some kind of club-footed nigger record."

———

The old man was topping off the pump as the boy ran by and around the edge of the building and out of sight. By the time the old man called out "Joshua," it was too late and from the way the boy was moving, unlikely to stop anyway.

"What the hell has got into him?" the old man said.

"Ain't no way to figure a colored boy," Ralph said.

"He's all right," the old man said. "He's a good boy."

The other two men were standing next to the pump, and Ralph looked at them. He said, "John, why don't you and Billy go in there and see you can help Emory?"

"He don't need no help," Billy said. He was a small man in an oversized black suit and no hat and he had enough hair for himself and a small dog, all of it greasy and nested on top of his head, the sides of his skull shaved to the skin over the ears so that he gave the impression of some large leafy vegetable ready to be pulled from the ground.

"Well," Ralph said, "you go help him anyway."

The old man was hanging up the gas nozzle. He said, "That's gonna be a dollar."

"Damn," Ralph said. "You run some of that out on the ground?"

"Things gone up," the old man said. "In this town, we got to charge off of what the suppliers charge us. You know that, your daddy owned a store."

Ralph pondered that. He buttoned and unbuttoned his coat. "Yeah, I know it. Just don't like it. Hell, I'm gonna go in the store too. A minute out of this sun ain't gonna hurt me, that's for sure."

Ralph and the old man went into the store side by side until they came to the door, and Ralph let the old man go in first.

The old man went behind the counter and Ralph said, "You sure look a lot like my old man."

"Don't reckon I'm him, though," the old man said, and showed his scattered teeth again, but the smile waved a bit, like the lips might fall off.

"No," Ralph said. "You ain't him, that's for sure. He's good and dead."

"Well, I'm almost dead," the old man said. "Here until God calls me."

"He don't call some," Ralph said. "Some he yanks."

The old man didn't know what to say to that. Ralph noticed that there were pops of sweat on the old man's forehead.

"You look hot," Ralph said.

"I ain't so hot," the old man said.

"You sweatin' good," Billy said.

"Ain't nobody talkin' to you," Ralph said. "Go on over there and sit on that stool and shut up."

Billy didn't pick up and sit on the stool, but he went quiet.

"I guess maybe I am a little hot," the old man said, straightening the items on the counter. "We got the gas, and we got these goods. Canned peaches, some candies, and Co-colas. That's be about a dollar fifty for all that, and then the gas."

"That dollar tank of gas," Ralph said.

"Yes, sir. That'll be two-fifty."

"You got all manner of stuff, didn't you, Emory?" Ralph said. "I told you not to get all that stuff."

"I got carried away," Emory said, and turned to the old man. "You give any stamps or any kind of shit like that with a purchase?"

The men had gathered together near the counter, except for Billy, who was standing off to the side with hurt feelings and some of his hair in his eyes.

The old man shook his head. "No. Nothing like that."

"That don't seem right," Emory said. "Some stores do that."

"Do they?" the old man said.

"Some give dishes," Emory said.

"Shut up," Ralph said. "You wouldn't know what to do with a dish you had it. You'd shit in a bowl and sling the plates. Just get things together and let's go."

The old man was sacking up the groceries, but he left the Co-colas on the counter. "You gonna carry those separate?" he asked.

"That'll be all right," Ralph said. "You even got hands like my old man. That's somethin'."

"Yes, sir," the old man said, "I s'pose it is."

Ralph looked around and saw that the others were staring at him. When he looked at them they looked away. Ralph turned back to the old man.

"You got a phone here?"

"No. No phone."

Ralph nodded. "Total it. I'm goin' on out to the car. Emory, you or John take care of it."

Ralph walked around to the front of the car and got out his cigarettes and pulled one loose of the pack with his lips, put the pack away and lit up with a wooden kitchen match he struck on the bottom of his shoe. As he smoked, he looked through the front window of the car. He walked around to the side of the car and looked in. The tommy gun he had told Billy to put up lay on the backseat in plain view.

He walked around to the other side of the car where the gas pump was and looked in through the side window. You could see it real good from that angle, about where the old man stood to put the gas in.

He walked back around to the front of the car and started to lean against it but saw it was covered in dust, so didn't. He just stood there smoking and thinking.

After a bit, there was a sharp snapping sound from inside the store. Ralph tossed the cigarette and went inside. Emory was putting away his gun.

"What you done?" Ralph said, and he walked to the edge of the counter and took a look. The old man lay on the floor. His eyes were open and his head was turned toward Ralph. The old man had one arm propped on his elbow, and his hand stuck up in the air and his fingers were spread like he was waving hello. On his forehead was what looked like a cherry blossom and it grew darker and the petals fell off and splashed down the old man's face and dripped on the floor in red explosions and then a pool of the same spread out at the back of his head and coated the floor thick as spilled paint.

Ralph turned and looked at Emory. "Why'd you do that?"

"You told me to," Emory said.

Ralph came out from behind the counter and hit Emory hard enough with the flat of his hand to knock Emory's hat off. "I meant pay the man, not shoot him." Emory put a hand to the side of his face.

"We all thought that it's what you wanted," Billy said, and Ralph turned and kicked Billy in the balls. Billy went to his knees.

"I didn't say kill nobody."

"You know he seen that gun in the car," Emory said, backing up. "We all knowed it. We was twenty feet down the road, he was gonna go somewhere and find a phone."

Ralph looked at John. John held both hands up. "Hey, I didn't say to do nothing. It was over before I knew it was happening."

Emory picked up his hat. Billy lay on the floor with his hands between his legs. John didn't move. Ralph took a deep breath, said, "You think nobody noticed a gun shot? You think that little nigger ain't gonna remember you, 'cause I know you run him out. Grab that shit and let's go. And help that retard Billy up."

John drove and Ralph set up front on the passenger side. Billy was behind him, and across from Billy was Emory, his hands still tucked between his legs, holding what made him a gentleman.

"I thought you meant kill him, Ralph," Emory said. "I figured on account of what you said, him like your father and all, and considering what you—"

"Shut up! Shut the hell up!"

Emory shut up.

Ralph said to John: "You better find some back roads. I know some out this way, but it's been awhile. There's one that a car can travel on down by the river."

They took the road when Ralph pointed it out. It wound down amongst some ragged cottonwood trees. The trees had few leaves and what leaves it had were brown with sand stripping and the limbs were covered in sand the color of cigarette ash. The car dipped over a rise and there were some rare green trees below that hadn't been stripped. The trees stood by the river where it was low down and the wind was cut by the hills. The river was thin on water and there were drifts of sand all around it. They drove down there and turned along the edge of the river and went that way awhile till Ralph told John to stop.

They got out and Ralph went over by the bank and looked at the remains of the river. Emory came over. He said, "I didn't mean to make you mad." "I thought you wanted me to do what I did."

Ralph didn't say anything. Emory unbuttoned his fly and started peeing in the water. "I just thought it was one way and it was another," he said while he peed. "I didn't understand."

Ralph reached inside his coat. He didn't do it fast, just with certainty. He turned and had a .45 in his hand. He shot Emory in the mouth when he turned his head toward him, while he was trying to explain something. Emory's head went back so hard it seemed as if it would fly off his neck and parts of it went down the bank and a piece slid into the chalky-colored water and the water turned rusty. Emory lay on his side, still holding his pecker with his right hand. He was still peeing, but in a dribble, and he had clenched himself so hard between thumb and forefinger it looked like he was trying to pinch it off.

"Goddamn!" Billy said. "Goddamn."

He came over and went down the bank and bent over Emory and looked at what was left of his head and saw pieces of Emory's skull on the ground and in the dark water. "Goddamn. You killed him."

"I should think so," Ralph said.

Billy stood up straight and looked at Ralph, who had the gun down by his side. "Wasn't no cause for that. He did what he thought you wanted on account of you saying he looked like your old man. Goddamn it, Ralph."

Ralph lifted the .45 a little and John came over and put his hand on Ralph's arm, said, "It's all right, Ralph. You done done it. Billy ain't thinking. He and Emory were cousins. He don't know how things are. He's grieving. You understand that. We all been there."

"Double cousins," Billy said. "Goddamn it."

"Shut up, Billy," John said, and he kept his hand on Ralph's arm.

Billy looked at Ralph's face, and some of his spirit drained away. Billy said, "All right. All right."

"Why don't you put the gun up?" John asked Ralph.

Ralph slowly put the gun in the shoulder holster under his coat. "That fellow looked so much like my old man."

"I know," John said.

"He had the same hands."

"I know."

"Emory shouldn't have done that. Now the town will turn out. They'll have the law all over us. That little nigger will remember Emory's face."

"That won't be a problem. He ain't got a face no more. I don't think he seen the rest of us that good."

"It don't matter," Ralph said, taking off his hat. "They'll know who we are."

"They got to catch us first," John said.

Ralph took off his hat and ran his hand through his oily hair. There was dust on his fingers and some of it came off in his hair. He put the hat back on. "Goddamn, Emory. Goddamn him." He looked over at Billy.

Billy was sitting on the bank looking at Emory's body. Flies had already collected on it.

Ralph started over that way. John touched his arm, but Ralph gently pulled it away. Ralph stood over Billy. "You get to thinking what you ought not, it could go bad for you."

Billy turned his head and looked up at Ralph. "Only thing I'm thinking is my cousin's dead."

"And he ain't comin' back. No matter how much you look at him or shake him, he ain't gonna come around and his head ain't gonna go back together. And I want you to know, I don't feel bad for doin' it. I tell you to do somethin', you don't figure what I mean, you got to know what I mean, not guess. I run this outfit."

Billy ran his hands over his knees, lifting his fingers so that they stood up like white tarantulas. "Yeah. Yeah."

"Give me your gun," Ralph said.

Billy looked at him so hard his eyes teared up. "I'm over it," he said.

"Give me your gun."

Billy reached inside his coat and took hold of a .38 revolver and pulled it out and when he did, Ralph pulled out his .45. "I'll just hold it for you," Ralph said. "While you grieve."

Billy gave Ralph the .38. It was small enough Ralph put it in his coat pocket. "Sometimes, we're upset, we do things we shouldn't."

"That's what you did," Billy said.

"It wasn't something I shouldn't have done. I don't feel bad at all. Ain't no one kills no one unless I say so."

Billy seemed about to say something, but didn't.

Ralph said, "Build up a fire. I don't think anyone will see the smoke much down here, and we'll just have it for a while."

"Why?" Billy said.

"We'll get right on it," John said, came over and took hold of Billy's arm and pulled him up and pushed him toward the woods. He called back to Ralph. "We'll get some wood right away."

While they were gathering wood, Billy said, "He killed him for nothing. He killed him while he was holding his dick in his hand. He didn't have to do that, didn't have to kill him that way."

"He killed him because the old man reminded him of his old man. He'd be just as dead if he hadn't been holding his dick."

"His old man . . . That can't be it. You know what he done."

"I know, but there ain't no way to figure it straight, because what he did wasn't straight. It's just his way."

"Just his way? Jesus. That was my cousin."

"Yeah, and he ain't gonna get no deader, and he ain't gonna get alive not even a little bit, so you got to let it go. I've had to let a lot of things go. Drop it."

"I don't know I want to keep doing this."

"We split up the money, then we can go the ways we want. But you don't want to make Ralph nervous. You make him nervous, only so much I'm gonna do. Me, I plan to make Thanksgiving at home this year. I don't want to end up on the creek bank with part of me in the water and flies all over me. So I'm doin' the last of what I'm doin' for you, you savvy, because I'm more worried about me and I want my share of money. Look at it this way, more money split three ways than four. That's a thing to think about. You savvy?"

"More split two ways than three," Billy said.

"I wouldn't think that. You think that, you'll think yourself into the dirt with your head blown off."

They stacked up the wood like Ralph said and then they sat on a hill above the bank for a while and then Ralph said, "John, you go look in the turtle hull and get out the hose and the jug there, siphon out a bit of gas. Maybe about half a jug full. And bring me back a can of them peaches."

"Sure," John said, and got up to go do it.

Billy made to get up too, but Ralph said, "You stay here and keep me company."

Billy sat back down. Ralph said: "Listen here, now, boy. Your cousin talked too much and didn't listen to me good. John should have stopped him. He should have known better. You're just a dumb kid. But you ain't gonna get to be any older or any smarter you don't start payin' attention. You get me?"

"Yeah," Billy said.

"I don't think you get me."

"I do."

"Not really."

"No. I do."

"We'll see. You go down there and get your cousin, don't have to bring up his brains and stuff, just drag his body up here and you put him face down on that pile of sticks you got together, and then you fold his hands up so that they're under his face."

"Why would I do that?"

"See there, boy, you don't get me. You don't understand a thing I tell you and you always got a question. Now, I told you to go down there and get him."

Billy got up and went down the bank. Ralph didn't move. He lipped out a cigarette and lit it with one of his kitchen matches. After a while, Billy come up the hill tugging at Emory by the heels. He got the body over by the sticks about the time John come back with the clear jug half full of gasoline and the can of peaches. He gave Ralph the peaches.

"Take that gasoline," Ralph said, "and put about half on that pile of sticks, sprinkle it around, and pour the rest on Emory's hands and face. That way, ain't nobody gonna recognize him and he ain't gonna have no fingerprints. Take off his clothes first."

Billy had quit pulling on Emory. He said, "They'll know who we are anyway. You said yourself that little nigger seen us. And Emory hasn't got much of a face left."

"We're just making it harder for them," Ralph said.

"I think you're just making it meaner," Billy said. "I think you're teaching me a lesson."

Ralph turned his head to one side curiously. "That what you think? You think you ain't already got a hole God's gonna put you in? A slot."

"That ain't your call?" Billy said.

"It sure was with Emory. I helped God fit him to his slot. I sent him where he was goin' and I didn't choose his place, just his time, and that there, it was preordained, my old man taught me that. And the place Emory went, I don't figure him nor any of us is going to a place we'd like to go, do you?"

"Ain't mine to think about."

"Oh, Billy, sure it is."

"Not if it's done planned."

"Billy," John said. "I'll help you."

"I ain't gonna put him on that fire."

"You don't, it'll still get done," Ralph said, "and maybe I get John to siphon out some more gas, get some more sticks. You get where the wind is ablowin' on that?"

Billy was breathing heavy. John said, "Billy, let's just do it. Okay?"

Billy looked at John. John's face was pleading. "All right," Billy said.

Billy and John got hold of Emory and rolled him over. They took off his clothes except for his shorts, which were full of shit. Billy got a stick and worked Emory's dick back into the slit in his underwear. John started to pour gasoline on Emory's open-eyed face. The top of Emory's head looked like it had been worked open with a dull can opener.

"No," Ralph said. "Have Billy do that." John handed Billy the jug. Billy looked at John, but there was no help there. He took the jug and poured gas on Emory's head.

"Now put him face down on the sticks and put his hands under his head," Ralph said. He had used his pocketknife to open the can of peaches and he was poking them with the knife and gobbling them down, some of the peach juice running down his chin.

Billy and John did as they were asked and then Ralph gave John a kitchen match. John set the sticks on fire. The stench of Emory's burning body filled the air.

"Let's go," Billy said. "I don't want to see this, smell it neither."

"No," Ralph said, eating more peaches, "you just find you a seat. We'll kinder pretend we're at the movies."

The three of them sat on the hill but Billy sat with his face away from the fire. The fire licked at Emory and pretty soon the head and hands were burned up and so were the feet and parts of the rest of his body.

"Close enough," Ralph said. He had long finished the peaches and had tossed the can down the bank toward the water, but it didn't go that far. "Spread them sticks out and kill the fire so we don't burn half the county down. What's left of him won't matter. Dogs and such will have them a cooked meal tonight."

When they went out to the car, Ralph fell back and said to John, "Any kind of noise goes off, you just hold steady, you hear?"

"Yeah," John said, and then he walked briskly away from Ralph toward the driver's side. Billy was about to get in the backseat when Ralph said, "You sit up front, Billy."

Billy turned and looked at Ralph. He studied him for a long hard moment. He said, "That's okay. I don't mind the back."

"You sit up front," Ralph said.

"You always ride up front," Billy said.

"Not today."

"I don't mind."

"You sit in my seat."

Ralph sat behind Billy in the back, and John drove. They drove out of the trail and out of the woods and onto the main road. It was starting to get dark. John pulled on the lights.

John glanced at Billy. Billy's face was beaded up with sweat. "I been thinking," Billy said. "Everything you was talking about was right, Ralph. I was just upset."

"Yeah," Ralph said.

"Yeah. I mean, I wasn't thinking."

Billy turned halfway around and put his arm on the seat. Ralph was looking right at him. In the early evening he was only slightly better defined than a shadow. He had his hat pulled down tight.

"Turn around, Billy," Ralph said.

Billy turned. He looked at John. John said, "I done told you."

Billy said, "He's my cousin, so of course I was upset. I ain't gonna say nothing about it to no one. Not even his mama."

"That's good," Ralph said, and reached in his pocket and took Billy's revolver out of it and rested it on his knee, his hand resting gently on top of it like a man caressing a pet.

"You know we all done done the sins that's gonna send us to hell,"

Ralph said. "It's just a matter of when now, but we're all goin'. There ain't a thing we can do to change things. For some of us when it comes, it'll come quick and with a pop."

"Sure we can," Billy said. "We can all do better."

"I don't think so," Ralph said.

"It's like you said, I ain't nothin' but a kid. I ain't thinkin' things through. But I'll get better. We all thought you wanted that old man done."

"Leave me out of this," John said. "I ain't part of that we."

Billy was talking fast. "You sayin' he looked like your daddy, and us knowing what you did."

"Don't mention my old man again," Ralph said. "Ever."

"Sure," Billy said. "Sure. But I've learned my lesson. I've learned a lot."

"Sure you have," Ralph said, and then there was a long silence, and then Billy heard the revolver cock.

The Pit

Six months earlier they had captured him. Tonight Harry went into the pit. He and Big George, right after the bull terriers got through tearing the guts out of one another. When that was over, he and George would go down and do the business. The loser would stay there and be fed to the dogs, each of which had been starved for the occasion.

When the dogs finished eating, the loser's head would go up on a pole. Already a dozen poles circled the pit. On each rested a head, or skull, depending on how long it had been exposed to the elements, ambitious pole-climbing ants and hungry birds. And of course how much flesh the terriers ripped off before it was erected.

Twelve poles. Twelve heads.

Tonight a new pole and a new head went up.

Harry looked about at the congregation. All sixty or so of them. They were a sight. Like mad creatures out of Lewis Carroll. Only they didn't have long rabbit ears or tall silly hats. They were just backwoods rednecks, not too unlike himself. With one major difference. They were as loony as waltzing mice. Or maybe they weren't crazy and he was. Sometimes he felt as if he had stepped into an alternate universe where the old laws of nature and what was right and wrong did not apply. Just like Alice plunging down the rabbit hole into Wonderland.

The crowd about the pit had been mumbling and talking, but now they grew silent. Out into the glow of the neon lamps stepped a man dressed in a black suit and hat. A massive rattlesnake was coiled about his right arm. It was wriggling from shoulder to wrist. About his left wrist a smaller snake was wrapped, a copperhead. The man held a Bible in his right hand. He was called Preacher.

Draping the monstrous rattlesnake around his neck, Preacher let it hang there. It dangled that way as if drugged. Its tongue would flash out from time to time. It gave Harry the willies. He hated snakes. They always seemed to be smiling. Nothing was that fucking funny, not all the time.

Preacher opened his Bible and read:

"Behold, I give unto you the power to tread on serpents and scorpions, and over all the power of the enemy: and nothing will by any means hurt you."

Preacher paused and looked at the sky. "So God," he said, "we want to thank you for a pretty good potato crop, though you've done better, and we want to thank you for the terriers, even though we had to raise and feed them ourselves, and we want to thank you for sending these outsiders our way, thank you for Harry Joe Stinton and Big George, the nigger."

Preacher paused and looked about the congregation. He lifted the hand with the copperhead in it high above his head. Slowly he lowered it and pointed the snake-filled fist at George. "Three times this here nigger has gone into the pit, and three times he has come out victorious. Couple times against whites, once against another nigger. Some of us think he's cheating.

"Tonight, we bring you another white feller, one of your chosen people, though you might not know it on account of the way you been letting the nigger win here, and we're hoping for a good fight with the nigger being killed at the end. We hope this here business pleases you. We worship you and the snakes in the way we ought to. Amen."

Big George looked over at Harry. "Be ready, sucker. I'm gonna take you apart like a gingerbread man."

Harry didn't say anything. He couldn't understand it. George was a prisoner just as he was. A man degraded and made to lift huge rocks and pull carts and jog miles on miles every day. And just so they could get in shape for this—to go down into that pit and try and beat each other to death for the amusement of these crazies.

And it had to be worse for George. Being black, he was seldom called anything other than "the nigger" by these psychos. Furthermore, no secret had been made of the fact that they wanted George to lose, and for him to win. The idea of a black pit champion was eating their little honkey hearts out.

Yet, Big George had developed a sort of perverse pride in being the longest-lived pit fighter yet.

"It's something I can do right," George had once said. "On the outside I wasn't nothing but a nigger, an uneducated nigger working in rose fields, mowing big lawns for rich white folks. Here I'm still the nigger, but I'm THE NIGGER, the badass nigger, and no matter what these peckerwoods call me, they know it, and they know I'm the best at what I do. I'm the king here. And they may hate me for it, keep me in a cell and make me run and lift stuff, but for that time in the pit, they know I'm the one that can do what they can't do, and they're afraid of me. I like it."

Glancing at George, Harry saw that the big man was not nervous. Or at least not showing it. He looked as if he were ready to go on holiday. Nothing to it. He was about to go down into that pit and try and beat a man to death with his fists and it was nothing. All in a day's work. A job well done for an odd sort of respect that beat what he had had on the outside.

The outside. It was strange how much he and Big George used that term. *The outside.* As if they were enclosed in some small bubble-like cosmos that perched on the edge of the world they had known; a cosmos invisible to *the outsiders,* a spectral place with new mathematics and nebulous laws of mind and physics.

Maybe he was in hell. Perhaps he had been wiped out on the highway and had gone to the dark place. Just maybe his memory of how he had arrived here was a false dream inspired by demonic powers. The whole thing about him taking a wrong turn through Big Thicket country and having his truck break down just outside of Morganstown was an illusion, and stepping onto the main street of Morganstown, population 66, was his crossing the River Styx and landing smack dab in the middle of a hell designed for good old boys.

God, had it been six months ago?

He had been on his way to visit his mother in Woodville, and he had taken a shortcut through the Thicket. Or so he thought. But he soon realized that he had looked at the map wrong. The shortcut listed on the paper was not the one he had taken. He had mistaken that road for the one he wanted. This one had not been marked. And then he had reached Morganstown and his truck had broken down. He had been forced into six months' hard labor alongside George, the champion pit fighter, and now the moment for which he had been groomed had arrived.

They were bringing the terriers out now. One, the champion, was named Old Codger. He was getting on in years. He had won many a pit fight. Tonight, win or lose, this would be his last battle. The other dog, Muncher, was young and inexperienced, but he was strong and eager for blood.

A ramp was lowered into the pit. Preacher and two men, the owners of the dogs, went down into the pit with Codger and Muncher. When they reached the bottom a dozen bright spotlights were thrown on them. They seemed to wade through the light.

The bleachers arranged about the pit began to fill. People mumbled and passed popcorn. Bets were placed and a little fat man wearing a bowler hat copied them down in a note pad as fast as they were shouted. The ramp was removed.

In the pit, the men took hold of their dogs by the scruff of the neck and removed their collars. They turned the dogs so they were facing the walls of the pit and could not see one another. The terriers were about six feet apart, butts facing.

Preacher said, "A living dog is better than a dead lion."

Harry wasn't sure what that had to do with anything.

"Ready yourselves," Preacher said. "Gentlemen, face your dogs."

The owners slapped their dogs across the muzzle and whirled them to face one another. They immediately began to leap and strain at their masters' grips.

"Gentlemen, release your dogs."

The dogs did not bark. For some reason, that was what Harry noted the most. They did not even growl. They were quick little engines of silence.

Their first lunge was a miss and they snapped air. But the second time they hit head on with the impact of .45 slugs. Codger was knocked on his back and Muncher dove for his throat. But the experienced dog popped up its head and grabbed Muncher by the nose. Codger's teeth met through Muncher's flesh.

Bets were called from the bleachers.

The little man in the bowler was writing furiously.

Muncher, the challenger, was dragging Codger, the champion, around the pit, trying to make the old dog let go of his nose. Finally, by shaking his head violently and relinquishing a hunk of his muzzle, he succeeded.

Codger rolled to his feet and jumped Muncher. Muncher turned his head just out of the path of Codger's jaws. The older dog's teeth snapped together like a spring-loaded bear trap, saliva popped out of his mouth in a fine spray.

Muncher grabbed Codger by the right ear. The grip was strong and Codger was shook like a used condom about to be tied and tossed. Muncher bit the champ's ear completely off.

Harry felt sick. He thought he was going to throw up. He saw that Big George was looking at him. "You think this is bad, motherfucker," George said, "this ain't nothing but a cakewalk. Wait till I get you in that pit."

"You sure run hot and cold, don't you?" Harry said.

"Nothing personal," George said sharply and turned back to look at the fight in the pit.

Nothing personal, Harry thought. God, what could be more personal? Just yesterday, as they trained, jogged along together, a pickup loaded with gun-bearing crazies driving alongside of them, he had felt close to George. They had shared many personal things these six months, and he knew that George liked him. But when it came to the pit, George was a different man. The concept of friendship became alien to him. When Harry had tried to talk to hint about it yesterday, he had said much the same thing. "Ain't nothing personal, Harry my man, but when we get in that pit don't look to me for nothing besides pain, 'cause I got plenty of that to give you, a lifetime of it, and I'll just keep it coming."

Down in the pit Codger screamed. It could be described no other way. Muncher had him on his back and was biting him on the belly. Codger was trying to double forward and get hold of Muncher's head, but his tired jaws kept slipping off of the sweaty neck fur. Blood was starting to pump out of Codger's belly.

"Bite him, boy," someone yelled from the bleachers, "tear his ass up, son."

Harry noted that every man, woman and child was leaning forward in their seat, straining for a view. Their faces were full of lust, like lovers approaching vicious climax. For a few moments they were in that pit and they were the dogs. Vicarious thrills without the pain.

Codger's leg began to flap.

"Kill him! Kill him!" the crowd began to chant.

Codger had quit moving. Muncher was burrowing his muzzle deeper into the old dog's guts. Preacher called for a pickup. Muncher's owner pried the dog's jaws loose of Codger's guts. Muncher's muzzle looked as if it had been dipped in red ink.

"This sonofabitch is still alive," Muncher's owner said to Codger.

Codger's owner walked over to the dog and said, "You little fucker!" He pulled a Saturday Night Special from his coat pocket and shot Codger twice in the head. Codger didn't even kick. He just evacuated his bowels right there.

Muncher came over and sniffed Codger's corpse, then, lifting his leg, he took a leak on the dead dog's head. The stream of piss was bright red.

The ramp was lowered. The dead dog was dragged out and tossed behind the bleachers. Muncher walked up the ramp beside his owner. The little dog strutted like he had just been crowned King of Creation. Codger's owner walked out last. He was not a happy man. Preacher stayed in the pit. A big man known as Sheriff Jimmy went down the ramp to join him. Sheriff Jimmy had a big pistol on his hip and a toy badge on his chest. The badge looked like the sort of thing that had come in a plastic bag with a capgun and whistle. But it was his sign of office and his word was iron.

A man next to Harry prodded him with the barrel of a shotgun. Walking close behind George, Harry went down the ramp and into the pit. The man with the shotgun went back up. In the bleachers the betting had started again, the little fat man with the bowler was busy.

Preacher's rattlesnake was still lying serenely about his neck, and the little copperhead had been placed in Preacher's coat pocket. It poked its head out from time to time and looked around.

Harry glanced up. The heads and skulls on the poles—in spite of the fact they were all eyeless, and due to the strong light nothing but bulbous shapes on shafts—seemed to look down, taking as much amusement in the situation as the crowd on the bleachers.

Preacher had his Bible out again. He was reading a verse. ". . . when thou walkest through the fire, thou shalt not be burned; neither shall the flame kindle upon thee . . ."

Harry had no idea what that or the snake had to do with anything. Certainly he could not see the relationship with the pit. These people's minds seemed to click and grind to a different set of internal gears than those on *the outside.*

The reality of the situation settled on Harry like a heavy woolen coat. He was about to kill or be killed, right here in this dog-smelling pit, and there was nothing he could do that would change that.

He thought perhaps his life should flash before his eyes or something, but it did not. Maybe he should try to think of something wonderful, a last fine thought of what used to be. First he summoned up the image of his wife. That did nothing for him. Though his wife had once been pretty and bright, he could not remember her that way. The image that came to mind was quite different. A dumpy, lazy woman with constant back pains and her hair pulled up into an eternal topknot of greasy brown hair. There was never a smile on her face or a word of encouragement for him. He always felt that she expected him to entertain her and that he was not doing a very good job of it. There was not even a moment of sexual ecstasy that he could recall. After their daughter had been born she had given up screwing as a wasted exercise. Why waste energy on sex when she could spend it complaining?

He flipped his mental card file to his daughter. What he saw was an ugly, potato-nosed girl of twelve. She had no personality. Her mother was Miss Congeniality compared to her. Potato Nose spent all of her time pining over thin, blond heartthrobs on television. It wasn't bad enough that they glared at Harry via the tube, they were also pinned to her walls and hiding in magazines she had cast throughout the house.

These were the last thoughts of a man about to face death?

There was just nothing there.

His job had sucked. His wife hadn't.

He clutched at straws. There had been Melva, a fine-looking little cheerleader from high school. She had had the brain of a dried black-eyed pea, but God-All-Mighty, did she know how to hide a weenie. And there had always been that strange smell about her, like bananas. It was especially strong about her thatch, which was thick enough for a bald eagle to nest in.

But thinking about her didn't provide much pleasure either. She had gotten hit by a drunk in a Mack truck while parked offside of a dark road with that Pulver boy.

Damn that Pulver. At least he had died in ecstasy. Had never known what hit him. When that Mack went up his ass he probably thought for a split second he was having the greatest orgasm of his life.

Damn that Melva. What had she seen in Pulver anyway?

He was skinny and stupid and had a face like a peanut pattie.

God, he was beat at every turn. Frustrated at every corner. No good thoughts or beautiful visions before the moment of truth. Only blackness, a life of dull, planned movements as consistent and boring as a bran-conscious geriatric's bowel movement. For a moment he thought he might cry.

Sheriff Jimmy took out his revolver. Unlike the badge it was not a toy. "Find your corner, boys."

George turned and strode to one side of the pit, took off his shirt and leaned against the wall. His body shined like wet licorice in the spotlights.

After a moment, Harry made his legs work. He walked to a place opposite George and took off his shirt. He could feel the months of hard work rippling beneath his flesh. His mind was suddenly blank. There wasn't even a god he believed in. No one to pray to. Nothing to do but the inevitable.

Sheriff Jimmy walked to the middle of the pit. He yelled out for the crowd to shut up.

Silence reigned.

"In this corner," he said, waving the revolver at Harry, "we have Harry Joe Stinton, family man and pretty good feller for an outsider. He's six two and weighs two hundred and thirty-eight pounds, give or take a pound since my bathroom scales ain't exactly on the money." A cheer went up.

"Over here," Sheriff Jimmy said, waving the revolver at George, "standing six four tall and weighing two hundred and forty-two pounds, we got the nigger, present champion of this here sport."

No one cheered. Someone made a loud sound with his mouth that sounded like a fart, the greasy kind that goes on and on and on.

George appeared unfazed. He looked like a statue. He knew who he was and what he was. The Champion Of The Pit.

"First off," Sheriff Jimmy said, "you boys come forward and show your hands."

Harry and George walked to the center of the pit, held out their hands, fingers spread wide apart, so that the crowd could see that they were empty.

"Turn and walk to your corners and don't turn around," Sheriff Jimmy said.

George and Harry did as they were told. Sheriff Jimmy followed Harry and put an arm around his shoulders. "I got four hogs riding on you," he said. "And I'll tell you what, you beat the nigger and I'll do you a favor. Elvira, who works over at the cafe, has already agreed. You win and you can have her. How's that sound?"

Harry was too numb with the insanity of it all to answer. Sheriff Jimmy was offering him a piece of ass if he won, as if this would be greater incentive than coming out of the pit alive. With this bunch there was just no way to anticipate what might come next. Nothing was static.

"She can do more tricks with a six-inch dick than a monkey can with a hundred foot of grapevine, boy. When the going gets rough in there, you remember that. Okay?"

Harry didn't answer. He just looked at the pit wall.

"You ain't gonna get nowhere in life being sullen like that," Sheriff Jimmy said. "Now, you go get him and plow a rut in his black ass."

Sheriff Jimmy grabbed Harry by the shoulders and whirled him around, slapped him hard across the face in the same way the dogs had been slapped. George had been done the same way by the preacher. Now George and Harry were facing one another. Harry thought George looked like an ebony gargoyle fresh escaped from hell. His bald, bullet-like head gleamed in the harsh lights and his body looked as rough and ragged as stone.

Harry and George raised their hands in classic boxer stance and began to circle one another.

From above someone yelled, "Don't hit the nigger in the head, it'll break your hand. Go for the lips, they got soft lips."

The smell of sweat, dog blood and Old Codger's shit was thick in the air. The lust of the crowd seemed to have an aroma as well. Harry even thought he could smell Preacher's snakes. Once, when a boy, he had been fishing down by the creek bed and had smelled an odor like that, and a water moccasin had wriggled out beneath his legs and splashed in the water. It was as if everything he feared in the world had been put in this pit. The idea of being put deep down in the ground. Irrational people for whom logic did not exist. Rotting skulls on poles about the pit. Living skulls attached to hunched-forward bodies that yelled for blood. Snakes. The stench of death—blood and shit. And every white man's fear, racist or not—a big, black man with a lifetime of hatred in his eyes.

The circle tightened. They could almost touch one another now.

Suddenly George's lips began to tremble. His eyes poked out of his head, seemed to be looking at something just behind and to the right of Harry.

"Sss . . . snake!" George screamed.

God, thought Harry, one of Preacher's snakes has escaped. Harry jerked his head for a look.

And George stepped in and knocked him on his ass and kicked him full in the chest. Harry began scuttling along the ground on his hands and knees, George following along kicking him in the ribs. Harry thought he felt something snap inside, a cracked rib maybe. He finally scuttled to his feet and bicycled around the pit. Goddamn, he thought, I fell for the oldest, silliest trick in the book. Here I am fighting for my life and I fell for it.

"Way to go, stupid fuck!" A voice screamed from the bleachers. "Hey nigger, why don't you try 'hey, your shoe's untied,' he'll go for it."

"Get off the goddamned bicycle," someone else yelled. "Fight."

"You better run," George said. "I catch you I'm gonna punch you so hard in the mouth, gonna knock your fucking teeth out your asshole . . ."

Harry felt dizzy. His head was like a yo-yo doing the Around the World trick. Blood ran down his forehead, dribbled off the tip of his nose and gathered on his upper lip. George was closing the gap again.

I'm going to die right here in this pit, thought Harry. I'm going to die just because my truck broke down outside of town and no one knows where I am. That's why I'm going to die. It's as simple as that.

Popcorn rained down on Harry and a tossed cup of ice hit him in the back. "Wanted to see a fucking foot race," a voice called, "I'd have gone to the fucking racetrack."

"Ten on the nigger," another voice said.

"Five bucks the nigger kills him in five minutes."

When Harry backpedaled past Preacher, the snake man leaned forward and snapped, "You asshole, I got a sawbuck riding on you."

Preacher was holding the big rattler again. He had the snake gripped just below the head, and he was so upset over how the fight had gone so far, he was unconsciously squeezing the snake in a vice-like grip. The rattler was squirming and twisting and flapping about, but Preacher didn't seem to notice. The snake's forked tongue was outside its mouth and it was really working, slapping about like a thin strip of rubber come loose on a whirling tire. The copperhead in Preacher's pocket was still looking out, as if along with Preacher he might have a bet on the outcome of the fight as well. As Harry danced away the rattler opened its mouth so wide its jaws came unhinged. It looked as if it were trying to yell for help.

Harry and George came together again in the center of the pit. Fists like black ball bearings slammed the sides of Harry's head. The pit was like a whirlpool, the walls threatening to close in and suck Harry down into oblivion.

Kneeing with all his might, Harry caught George solidly in the groin. George grunted, stumbled back, half-bent over.

The crowd went wild.

Harry brought cupped hands down on George's neck, knocked him to his knees. Harry used the opportunity to knock out one of the big man's teeth with the toe of his shoe.

He was about to kick him again when George reached up and clutched the crotch of Harry's khakis, taking a crushing grip on Harry's testicles.

"Got you by the balls," George growled.

Harry bellowed and began to hammer wildly on top of George's head with both fists. He realized with horror that George was pulling him forward. *By God, George was going to bite him on the balls.*

Jerking up his knee he caught George in the nose and broke his grip. He bounded free, skipped and whipped about the pit like an Indian dancing for rain.

He skipped and whooped by Preacher. Preacher's rattler had quit twisting. It hung loosely from Preacher's tight fist. Its eyes were bulging out of its head like the humped backs of grub worms. Its mouth was closed and its forked tongue hung limply from the edge of it.

The copperhead was still watching the show from the safety of Preacher's pocket, its tongue zipping out from time to time to taste the air. The little snake didn't seem to have a care in the world.

George was on his feet again, and Harry could tell that already he was feeling better. Feeling good enough to make Harry feel real bad.

Preacher abruptly realized that his rattler had gone limp.

"No, God no!" he cried. He stretched the huge rattler between his hands. "Baby, baby," he bawled, "breathe for me, Sapphire, breathe for me." Preacher shook the snake viciously, trying to jar some life into it, but the snake did not move.

The pain in Harry's groin had subsided and he could think again. George was moving in on him, and there just didn't seem any reason to run. George would catch him, and when he did, it would just be worse because he would be even more tired from all that running. It had to be done. The mating dance was over, now all that was left was the intercourse of violence.

A black fist turned the flesh and cartilage of Harry's nose into smoldering putty. Harry ducked his head and caught another blow to the chin. The stars he had not been able to see above him because of the lights, he could now see below him, spinning constellations on the floor of the pit.

It came to him again, the fact that he was going to die right here without one good, last thought. But then maybe there was one. He envisioned his wife, dumpy and sullen and denying him sex. George became her and she became George and Harry did what he had wanted to do for so long, he hit her in the mouth. Not once, but twice and a third time. He battered her nose and he pounded her ribs. And by God, but she could hit back. He felt something crack in the center of his chest and his left cheekbone collapsed into his face. But Harry did not stop battering her. He looped and punched and pounded her dumpy face until it was George's black face and George's black face turned back to her face and he thought of her now on the bed, naked, on her back, battered, and he was naked and mounted her, and the blows of his fists were the sexual thrusts of his cock and he was pounding her until—George screamed. He had fallen to his knees. His right eye was hanging out on the tendons. One of Harry's straight rights had struck George's cheekbone with such power it had shattered it and pressured the eye out of its socket.

Blood ran down Harry's knuckles. Some of it was George's. Much of it was his own. His knuckle bones showed through the rent flesh of his hands, but they did not hurt. They were past hurting.

George wobbled to his feet. The two men stood facing one another, neither moving. The crowd was silent. The only sound in the pit was the harsh breathing of the two fighters, and Preacher, who had stretched Sapphire out on the ground on her back and was trying to blow air into her mouth. Occasionally he'd lift his head and say in tearful supplication, "Breathe for me, Sapphire, breathe for me."

Each time Preacher blew a blast into the snake, its white underbelly would swell and then settle down, like a leaky balloon that just wouldn't hold air.

George and Harry came together. Softly. They had their arms on each other's shoulders and they leaned against one another, breathed each other's breath.

Above, the silence of the crowd was broken when a heckler yelled, "Start some music, the fuckers want to dance."

"It's nothing personal," George said.

"Not at all," Harry said.

They managed to separate, reluctantly, like two lovers who had just copulated to the greatest orgasm of their lives.

George bent slightly and put up his hands. The eye dangling on his cheek looked like some kind of tentacled creature trying to crawl up and into George's socket. Harry knew that he would have to work on that eye.

Preacher screamed. Harry afforded him a sideways glance. Sapphire was awake. And now she was dangling from Preacher's face. She had bitten through his top lip and was hung there by her fangs. Preacher was saying something about the power to tread on serpents and stumbling about the pit. Finally his back struck the pit wall and he slid down to his butt and just sat there, legs sticking out in front of him, Sapphire dangling off his lip like some sort of malignant growth. Gradually, building momentum, the snake began to thrash.

Harry and George met again in the center of the pit. A second wind had washed in on them and they were ready. Harry hurt wonderfully. He was no longer afraid. Both men were smiling, showing the teeth they had left. They began to hit each other.

Harry worked on the eye. Twice he felt it beneath his fists, a grapelike thing that cushioned his knuckles and made them wet. Harry's entire body felt on fire—twin fires, ecstasy and pain.

George and Harry collapsed together, held each other, waltzed about.

"You done good," George said, "make it quick."

The black man's legs went out from under him and he fell to his knees, his head between. Harry took the man's head in his hands and kneed him in the face with all his might. George went limp. Harry grasped George's chin and the back of his head and gave a violent twist. The neck bone snapped and George fell back, dead.

The copperhead, which had been poking its head out of Preacher's pocket, took this moment to slither away into a crack in the pit's wall.

Out of nowhere came weakness. Harry fell to his knees. He touched George's ruined face with his fingers.

Suddenly hands had him. The ramp was lowered. The crowd cheered. Preacher—Sapphire dislodged from his lip—came forward to help Sheriff Jimmy with him. They lifted him up.

Harry looked at Preacher. His lip was greenish. His head looked like a sun-swollen watermelon, yet, he seemed well enough. Sapphire was wrapped around his neck again. They were still buddies. The snake looked tired. Harry no longer felt afraid of it. He reached out and touched its head. It did not try to bite him. He felt its feathery tongue brush his bloody hand.

They carried him up the ramp and the crowd took him, lifted him up high above their heads. He could see the moon and the stars now. For some odd reason they did not look familiar. Even the nature of the sky seemed different.

He turned and looked down. The terriers were being herded into the pit. They ran down the ramp like rats. Below, he could hear them begin to feed, to fight for choice morsels. But there were so many dogs, and they were so hungry, this only went on for a few minutes. After a while they came back up the ramp followed by Sheriff Jimmy closing a big lock-bladed knife, and by Preacher, who held George's head in his outstretched hands. George's eyes were gone. Little of the face remained. Only that slick, bald pate had been left undamaged by the terriers.

A pole came out of the crowd and the head was pushed onto its sharpened end and the pole was dropped into a deep hole in the ground. The pole, like a long neck, rocked its trophy for a moment, then went still. Dirt was kicked into the hole and George joined the others, all those beautiful, wonderful heads and skulls.

They began to carry Harry away. Tomorrow he would have Elvira, who could do more tricks with a six-inch dick than a monkey could with a hundred foot of grapevine, then he would heal and a new outsider would come through and they would train together and then they would mate in blood and sweat in the depths of the pit.

The crowd was moving toward the forest trail, toward town. The smell of pines was sweet in the air. And as they carried him away, Harry turned his head so he could look back and see the pit, its maw closing in shadow as the lights were cut, and just before the last one went out Harry saw the heads on the poles, and dead center of his vision was the shiny, bald pate of his good friend George.

Night They Missed the Horror Show

For Lew Shiner, a story that doesn't flinch

If they'd gone to the drive-in like they'd planned, none of this would have happened. But Leonard didn't like drive-ins when he didn't have a date, and he'd heard about *Night of the Living Dead,* and he knew a nigger starred in it. He didn't want to see no movie with a nigger star. Niggers chopped cotton, fixed flats, and pimped nigger girls, but he'd never heard of one that killed zombies. And he'd heard too that there was a white girl in the movie that let the nigger touch her, and that peeved him. Any white gal that would let a nigger touch her must be the lowest trash in the world. Probably from Hollywood, New York, or Waco, some god-forsaken place like that.

Now Steve McQueen would have been all right for zombie killing and girl handling. He would have been the ticket. But a nigger? No sir.

Boy, that Steve McQueen was one cool head. Way he said stuff in them pictures was so good you couldn't help but think someone had written it down for him. He could sure think fast on his feet to come up with the things he said, and he had that real cool, mean look.

Leonard wished he could be Steve McQueen, or Paul Newman even. Someone like that always knew what to say, and he figured they got plenty of bush too. Certainly they didn't get as bored as he did. He was so bored he felt as if he were going to die from it before the night was out. Bored, bored, bored. Just wasn't nothing exciting about being in the Dairy Queen parking lot leaning on the front of his '64 Impala looking out at the highway. He figured maybe old crazy Harry who janitored at the high school might be right about them flying saucers. Harry was always seeing something. Bigfoot, six-legged weasels, all manner of things. But maybe he was right about the saucers. He'd said he'd seen one a couple nights back hovering over Mud Creek and it was shooting down these rays that looked like wet peppermint sticks. Leonard figured if Harry really had seen the saucers and the rays, then those rays were boredom rays. It would be a way for space critters to get at earth folks, boring them to death. Getting melted down by heat rays would have been better. That was at least quick, but being bored to death was sort of like being nibbled to death by ducks.

Leonard continued looking at the highway, trying to imagine flying saucers and boredom rays, but he couldn't keep his mind on it. He finally focused on something in the highway. A dead dog.

Not just a dead dog. But a DEAD DOG. The mutt had been hit by a semi at least, maybe several. It looked as if it had rained dog. There were pieces of that pooch all over the concrete and one leg was lying on the curbing on the opposite side, stuck up in such a way that it seemed to be waving hello. Doctor Frankenstein with a grant from Johns Hopkins and assistance from NASA couldn't have put that sucker together again.

Leonard leaned over to his faithful, drunk companion, Billy— known among the gang as Farto, because he was fart-lighting champion of Mud Creek—and said, "See that dog there?"

Farto looked where Leonard was pointing. He hadn't noticed the dog before, and he wasn't nearly as casual about it as Leonard. The puzzle-piece hound brought back memories. It reminded him of a dog he'd had when he was thirteen. A big, fine German shepherd that loved him better than his Mama.

Sonofabitch dog tangled its chain through and over a barbed wire fence somehow and hung itself. When Farto found the dog its tongue looked like a stuffed, black sock and he could see where its claws had just been able to scrape the ground, but not quite enough to get a toe hold.

It looked as if the dog had been scratching out some sort of a coded message in the dirt. When Farto told his old man about it later, crying as he did, his old man laughed and said, "Probably a goddamn suicide note."

Now, as he looked out at the highway, and his whiskey-laced Coke collected warmly in his gut, he felt a tear form in his eyes. Last time he'd felt that sappy was when he'd won the fart-lighting championship with a four-inch burner that singed the hairs of his ass and the gang awarded him with a pair of colored boxing shorts. Brown and yellow ones so he could wear them without having to change them too often.

So there they were, Leonard and Farto, parked outside the DQ, leaning on the hood of Leonard's Impala, sipping Coke and whiskey, feeling bored and blue and horny, looking at a dead dog and having nothing to do but go to a show with a nigger starring in it. Which, to be up front, wouldn't have been so bad if they'd had dates. Dates could make up for a lot of sins, or help make a few good ones, depending on one's outlook.

But the night was criminal. Dates they didn't have. Worse yet, wasn't a girl in the entire high school would date them. Not even Marylou Flowers, and she had some kind of disease.

All this nagged Leonard something awful. He could see what the problem was with Farto. He was ugly. Had the kind of face that attracted flies. And though being fart-lighting champion of Mud Creek had a certain prestige among the gang, it lacked a certain something when it came to charming the gals.

But for the life of him, Leonard couldn't figure his own problem. He was handsome, had some good clothes, and his car ran good when he didn't buy that old cheap gas. He even had a few bucks in his jeans from breaking into washaterias. Yet his right arm had damn near grown to the size of his thigh from all the whacking off he did. Last time he'd been out with a girl had been a month ago, and as he'd been out with her along with nine other guys, he wasn't rightly sure he could call that a date. He wondered about it so much, he'd asked Farto if he thought it qualified as a date. Farto, who had been fifth in line, said he didn't think so, but if Leonard wanted to call it one, wasn't no skin off his back.

But Leonard didn't want to call it a date. It just didn't have the feel of one, lacked that something special. There was no romance to it.

True, Big Red had called him Honey when he put the mule in the barn, but she called everyone Honey—except Stoney. Stoney was Possum Sweets, and he was the one who talked her into wearing the grocery bag with the mouth and eye holes. Stoney was like that. He could sweet talk the camel out from under a sand nigger. When he got through chatting Big Red down, she was plumb proud to wear that bag.

When finally it came his turn to do Big Red, Leonard had let her take the bag off as a gesture of goodwill. That was a mistake. He just hadn't known a good thing when he had it. Stoney had had the right idea. The bag coming off spoiled everything. With it on, it was sort of like balling the Lone Hippo or some such thing, but with the bag off, you were absolutely certain what you were getting, and it wasn't pretty.

Even closing his eyes hadn't helped. He found that the ugliness of that face had branded itself on the back of his eyeballs. He couldn't even imagine the sack back over her head. All he could think about was that puffy, too-painted face with the sort of bad complexion that began at the bone.

He'd gotten so disappointed, he'd had to fake an orgasm and get off before his hooter shriveled up and his Trojan fell off and was lost in the vacuum.

Thinking back on it, Leonard sighed. It would certainly be nice for a change to go with a girl that didn't pull the train or have a hole between her legs that looked like a manhole cover ought to be on it. Sometimes he wished he could be like Farto, who was as happy as if he had good sense. Anything thrilled him. Give him a can of Wolf Brand Chili, a big moon pie, Coke and whiskey and he could spend the rest of his life fucking Big Red and lighting the gas out of his asshole.

God, but this was no way to live. No women and no fun. Bored, bored, bored. Leonard found himself looking overhead for spaceships and peppermint-colored boredom rays, but he saw only a few moths fluttering drunkenly through the beams of the DQ's lights.

Lowering his eyes back to the highway and the dog, Leonard had a sudden flash. "Why don't we get the chain out of the back and hook it up to Rex there? Take him for a ride?"

"You mean drag his dead ass around?" Farto asked.

Leonard nodded.

"Beats stepping on a tack," Farto said.

They drove the Impala into the middle of the highway at a safe moment and got out for a look. Up close the mutt was a lot worse. Its innards had been mashed out of its mouth and asshole and it stunk something awful. The dog was wearing a thick, metal-studded collar and they fastened one end of their fifteen-foot chain to that and the other to the rear bumper.

Bob, the Dairy Queen manager, noticed them through the window, came outside and yelled, "What are you fucking morons doing?"

"Taking this doggie to the vet," Leonard said. "We think this sumbitch looks a might peeked. He may have been hit by a car."

"That's so fucking funny I'm about to piss myself," Bob said.

"Old folks have that problem," Leonard said.

Leonard got behind the wheel and Farto climbed in on the passenger side. They maneuvered the car and dog around and out of the path of a tractor-trailer truck just in time. As they drove off, Bob screamed after them, "I hope you two no-dicks wrap that Chevy piece of shit around a goddamn pole."

As they roared along, parts of the dog, like crumbs from a flaky loaf of bread, came off. A tooth here. Some hair there. A string of guts. A dew claw. And some unidentifiable pink stuff. The metal-studded collar and chain threw up sparks now and then like fiery crickets. Finally they hit seventy-five and the dog was swinging wider and wider on the chain, like it was looking for an opportunity to pass.

Farto poured him and Leonard up Cokes and whiskey as they drove along. He handed Leonard his paper cup and Leonard knocked it back, a lot happier now than he had been a moment ago. Maybe this night wasn't going to turn out so bad after all.

They drove by a crowd at the side of the road, a tan station wagon and a wreck of a Ford up on a jack. At a glance they could see that there was a nigger in the middle of the crowd and he wasn't witnessing to the white boys. He was hopping around like a pig with a hotshot up his ass, trying to find a break in the white boys so he could make a run for it. But there wasn't any break to be found and there were too many to fight. Nine white boys were knocking him around like he was a pinball and they were a malicious machine.

"Ain't that one of our niggers?" Farto asked. "And ain't that some of the White Tree football players that's trying to kill him?"

"Scott," Leonard said, and the name was dogshit in his mouth. It had been Scott who had outdone him for the position of quarterback on the team. That damn jig could put together a play more tangled than a can of fishing worms, but it damn near always worked. And he could run like a spotted-ass ape.

As they passed, Farto said, "We'll read about him tomorrow in the papers."

But Leonard drove only a short way before slamming on the brakes and whipping the Impala around. Rex swung way out and clipped off some tall, dried sunflowers at the edge of the road like a scythe.

"We gonna go back and watch?" Farto asked. "I don't think them White Tree boys would bother us none if that's all we was gonna do, watch."

"He may be a nigger," Leonard said, not liking himself, "but he's our nigger and we can't let them do that. They kill him, they'll beat us in football."

Farto saw the truth of this immediately. "Damn right. They can't do that to our nigger."

Leonard crossed the road again and went straight for the White Tree boys, hit down hard on the horn. The White Tree boys abandoned beating their prey and jumped in all directions. Bullfrogs couldn't have done any better.

Scott stood startled and weak where he was, his knees bent in and touching one another, his eyes as big as pizza pans. He had never noticed how big grillwork was. It looked like teeth there in the night and the headlights looked like eyes. He felt like a stupid fish about to be eaten by a shark.

Leonard braked hard, but off the highway in the dirt it wasn't enough to keep from bumping Scott, sending him flying over the hood and against the glass where his face mashed to it then rolled away, his shirt snagging one of the windshield wipers and pulling it off.

Leonard opened the car door and called to Scott, who lay on the ground, "It's now or never."

A White Tree boy made for the car, and Leonard pulled the taped hammer handle out from beneath the seat and stepped out of the car and hit him with it. The White Tree boy went down to his knees and said something that sounded like French but wasn't. Leonard grabbed Scott by the back of the shirt and pulled him up and guided him around and threw him into the open door. Scott scrambled over the front seat and into the back. Leonard threw the hammer handle at one of the White Tree boys and stepped back, whirled into the car behind the wheel. He put the car in gear again and stepped on the gas. The Impala lurched forward, and with one hand on the door Leonard flipped it wider and clipped a White Tree boy with it as if he were flexing a wing. The car bumped back on the highway and the chain swung out and Rex cut the feet out from under two White Tree boys as neatly as he had taken down the dried sunflowers.

Leonard looked in his rear-view mirror and saw two White Tree boys carrying the one he had clubbed with the hammer handle to the station wagon. The others he and the dog had knocked down were getting up. One had kicked the jack out from under Scott's car and was using it to smash the headlights and windshield.

"Hope you got insurance on that thing," Leonard said.

"I borrowed it," Scott said, peeling the windshield wiper out of his T-shirt. "Here, you might want this." He dropped the wiper over the seat and between Leonard and Farto.

"That's a borrowed car?" Farto said. "That's worse."

"Nah," Scott said. "Owner don't know I borrowed it. I'd have had that flat changed if that sucker had had him a spare tire, but I got back there and wasn't nothing but the rim, man. Say, thanks for not letting me get killed, else we couldn't have run that ole pig together no more. Course, you almost run over me. My chest hurts."

Leonard checked the rear-view again. The White Tree boys were coming fast. "You complaining?" Leonard said.

"Nah," Scott said, and turned to look through the back glass. He could see the dog swinging in short arcs and pieces of it going wide and far. "Hope you didn't go off and forget your dog tied to the bumper."

"Goddamn," said Farto, "and him registered too."

"This ain't so funny," Leonard said. "Them White Tree boys are gaining."

"Well, speed it up," Scott said.

Leonard gnashed his teeth. "I could always get rid of some excess baggage, you know."

"Throwing that windshield wiper out ain't gonna help," Scott said.

Leonard looked in his mirror and saw the grinning nigger in the backseat. Nothing worse than a comic coon. He didn't even look grateful. Leonard had a sudden horrid vision of being overtaken by the White Tree boys. What if he were killed with the nigger? Getting killed was bad enough, but what if tomorrow they found him in a ditch with Farto and the nigger? Or maybe them White Tree boys would make him do something awful with the nigger before they killed them. Like making him suck the nigger's dick or some such thing. Leonard held his foot all the way to the floor; as they passed the Dairy Queen he took a hard left and the car just made it and Rex swung out and slammed a light pole then popped back in line behind them.

The White Tree boys couldn't make the corner in the station wagon and they didn't even try. They screeched into a car lot down a piece, turned around and came back. By that time the tail lights of the Impala were moving away from them rapidly, looking like two inflamed hemorrhoids in a dark asshole.

"Take the next right coming up," Scott said, "then you'll see a little road off to the left. Kill your lights and take that."

Leonard hated taking orders from Scott on the field, but this was worse. Insulting. Still, Scott called good plays on the field, and the habit of following instructions from the quarterback died hard.

Leonard made the right and Rex made it with them after taking a dip in a water-filled bar ditch.

Leonard saw the little road and killed his lights and took it. It carried them down between several rows of large tin storage buildings, and Leonard pulled between two of them and drove down a little alley lined with more. He stopped the car and they waited and listened. After about five minutes, Farto said, "I think we skunked those father rapers."

"Ain't we a team?" Scott said.

In spite of himself, Leonard felt good. It was like when the nigger called a play that worked and they were all patting each other on the ass and not minding what color the other was because they were just creatures in football suits.

"Let's have a drink," Leonard said.

Farto got a paper cup off the floorboard for Scott and poured him up some warm Coke and whiskey. Last time they had gone to Longview, he had peed in that paper cup so they wouldn't have to stop, but that had long since been poured out, and besides, it was for a nigger. He poured Leonard and himself drinks in their same cups.

Scott took a sip and said, "Shit, man, that tastes kind of rank."

"Like piss," Farto said.

Leonard held up his cup. "To the Mud Creek Wildcats and fuck them White Tree boys."

"You fuck 'em," Scott said. They touched their cups, and at that moment the car filled with light.

Cups upraised, the Three Musketeers turned blinking toward it. The light was coming from an open storage-building door and there was a fat man standing in the center of the glow like a bloated fly on a lemon wedge. Behind him was a big screen made of a sheet and there was some kind of movie playing on it. And though the light was bright and fading out the movie, Leonard, who was in the best position to see, got a look at it. What he could make out looked like a gal down on her knees sucking this fat guy's dick (the man was visible only from the belly down) and the guy had a short, black revolver pressed to her forehead. She pulled her mouth off of him for an instant and the man came in her face then fired the revolver. The woman's head snapped out of frame and the sheet seemed to drip blood, like dark condensation on a window pane. Then Leonard couldn't see anymore because another man had appeared in the doorway, and like the first he was fat. Both looked like huge bowling balls that had been set on top of shoes.

More men appeared behind these two, but one of the fat men turned and held up his hand and the others moved out of sight. The two fat guys stepped outside and one pulled the door almost shut, except for a thin band of light that fell across the front seat of the Impala.

Fat Man Number One went over to the car and opened Farto's door and said, "You fucks and the nigger get out." It was the voice of doom. They had only thought the White Tree boys were dangerous. They realized now they had been kidding themselves. This was the real article. This guy would have eaten the hammer handle and shit a two-by-four.

They got out of the car and the fat man waved them around and lined them up on Farto's side and looked at them. The boys still had their drinks in their hands, and sparing that, they looked like cons in a lineup.

Fat Man Number Two came over and looked at the trio and smiled. It was obvious the fatties were twins. They had the same bad features in the same fat faces. They wore Hawaiian shirts that varied only in profiles and color of parrots and had on white socks and too-short black slacks and black, shiny, Italian shoes with toes sharp enough to thread needles.

Fat Man Number One took the cup away from Scott and sniffed it. "A nigger with liquor," he said. "That's like a cunt with brains. It don't go together. Guess you was getting tanked up so you could put the old black snake to some chocolate pudding after a while. Or maybe you was wantin' some vanilla and these boys were gonna set it up."

"I'm not wanting anything but to go home," Scott said. Fat Man Number Two looked at Fat Man Number One and said, "So he can fuck his mother."

The fatties looked at Scott to see what he'd say but he didn't say anything. They could say he screwed dogs and that was all right with him. Hell, bring one on and he'd fuck it now if they'd let him go afterwards.

Fat Man Number One said, "You boys running around with a jungle bunny makes me sick."

"He's just a nigger from school," Farto said. "We don't like him none. We just picked him up because some White Tree boys were beating on him and we didn't want him to get wrecked on account of he's our quarterback."

"Ah," Fat Man Number One said, "I see. Personally, me and Vinnie don't cotton to niggers in sports. They start taking showers with white boys the next thing they want is to take white girls to bed. It's just one step from one to the other."

"We don't have nothing to do with him playing," Leonard said. "We didn't integrate the schools."

"No," Fat Man Number One said, "that was ole Big Ears Johnson, but you're running around with him and drinking with him."

"His cup's been peed in," Farto said. "That was kind of a joke on him, you see. He ain't our friend, I swear it. He's just a nigger that plays football."

"Peed in his cup, huh?" said the one called Vinnie. "I like that, Pork, don't you? Peed in his fucking cup."

Pork dropped Scott's cup on the ground and smiled at him. "Come here, nigger. I got something to tell you."

Scott looked at Farto and Leonard. No help there. They had suddenly become interested in the toes of their shoes; they examined them as if they were true marvels of the world.

Scott moved toward Pork, and Pork, still smiling, put his arm around Scott's shoulders and walked him toward the big storage building. Scott said, "What are we doing?"

Pork turned Scott around so they were facing Leonard and Farto, who still stood holding their drinks and contemplating their shoes. "I didn't want to get it on the new gravel drive," Pork said and pulled Scott's head in close to his own and with his free hand reached back and under his Hawaiian shirt and brought out a short, black revolver and put it to Scott's temple and pulled the trigger. There was a snap like a bad knee going out and Scott's feet lifted in unison and went to the side and something dark squirted from his head and his feet swung back toward Pork and his shoes shuffled, snapped, and twisted on the concrete in front of the building.

"Ain't that somethin'," Pork said as Scott went limp and dangled from the thick crook of his arm. "The rhythm is the last thing to go."

Leonard couldn't make a sound. His guts were in his throat. He wanted to melt and run under the car. Scott was dead and the brains that had made plays twisted as fishing worms and commanded his feet on down the football field were scrambled like breakfast eggs.

Farto said, "Holy shit."

Pork let go of Scott and Scott's legs split and he sat down and his head went forward and clapped on the cement between his knees. A dark pool formed under his face.

"He's better off, boys," Vinnie said. "Nigger was begat by Cain and the ape and he ain't quite monkey and he ain't quite man. He's got no place in this world 'cept as a beast of burden. You start trying to train them to do things like drive cars and run with footballs it ain't nothing but grief to them and the whites too. Get any on your shirt, Pork?"

"Nary a drop."

Vinnie went inside the building and said something to the men there that could be heard but not understood, then he came back with some crumpled newspapers. He went over to Scott and wrapped them around the bloody head and let it drop back on the cement. "You try hosing down that shit when it's dried, Pork, and you wouldn't worry none about that gravel. The gravel ain't nothing."

Then Vinnie said to Farto, "Open the back door of that car." Farto nearly twisted an ankle doing it. Vinnie picked Scott up by the back of the neck and the seat of his pants and threw him onto the floorboard of the Impala.

Pork used the short barrel of his revolver to scratch his nuts, then put the gun behind him, under his Hawaiian shirt. "You boys are gonna go to the river bottoms with us and help us get shed of this nigger."

"Yes, sir," Farto said. "We'll toss his ass in the Sabine for you."

"How about you?" Pork asked Leonard. "You trying to go weak, sister?"

"No," Leonard croaked, "I'm with you."

"That's good," Pork said. "Vinnie, you take the truck and lead the way."

Vinnie took a key from his pocket and unlocked the building door next to the one with the light, went inside, and backed out a sharp-looking gold Dodge pickup. He backed it in front of the Impala and sat there with the motor running.

"You boys keep your place," Pork said. He went inside the lighted building for a moment. They heard him say to the men inside, "Go on and watch the movies. And save some of them beers for us. We'll be back." Then the light went out and Pork came out, shutting the door. He looked at Leonard and Farto and said, "Drink up, boys."

Leonard and Farto tossed off their warm Coke and whiskey and dropped the cups on the ground.

"Now," Pork said, "you get in the back with the nigger, I'll ride with the driver."

Farto got in the back and put his feet on Scott's knees. He tried not to look at the head wrapped in newspaper, but he couldn't help it. When Pork opened the front door and the overhead light came on Farto saw there was a split in the paper and Scott's eye was visible behind it. Across the forehead the wrapping had turned dark. Down by the mouth and chin was an ad for a fish sale.

Leonard got behind the wheel and started the car. Pork reached over and honked the horn. Vinnie rolled the pickup forward and Leonard followed him to the river bottoms. No one spoke. Leonard found himself wishing with all his heart that he had gone to the outdoor picture show to see the movie with the nigger starring in it.

The river bottoms were steamy and hot from the closeness of the trees and the under and overgrowth. As Leonard wound the Impala down the narrow, red clay roads amidst the dense foliage, he felt as if his car were a crab crawling about in a pubic thatch. He could feel from the way the steering wheel handled that the dog and the chain were catching brush and limbs here and there. He had forgotten all about the dog and now being reminded of it worried him. What if the dog got tangled and he had to stop? He didn't think Pork would take kindly to stopping, not with the dead burrhead on the floorboards and him wanting to get rid of the body.

Finally they came to where the woods cleared out a spell and they drove along the edge of the Sabine River. Leonard hated water and always had. In the moonlight the river looked like poisoned coffee flowing there. Leonard knew there were alligators and gars big as little alligators and water moccasins by the thousands swimming underneath the water, and just the thought of all those slick, darting bodies made him queasy.

They came to what was known as Broken Bridge. It was an old worn-out bridge that had fallen apart in the middle and it was connected to the land on this side only. People sometimes fished off of it. There was no one fishing tonight.

Vinnie stopped the pickup and Leonard pulled up beside it, the nose of the Chevy pointing at the mouth of the bridge. They all got out and Pork made Farto pull Scott out by the feet. Some of the newspapers came loose from Scott's head, exposing an ear and part of the face. Farto patted the newspaper back into place.

"Fuck that," Vinnie said. "It don't hurt if he stains the fucking ground. You two idgits find some stuff to weight this coon down so we can sink him."

Farto and Leonard started scurrying about like squirrels, looking for rocks or big, heavy logs. Suddenly they heard Vinnie cry out. "Godamighty, fucking A. Pork. Come look at this."

　　　　　　　　　　　　　　　　　　　JOE R. LANSDALE

Leonard looked over and saw that Vinnie had discovered Rex. He was standing looking down with his hands on his hips. Pork went over to stand by him, then Pork turned around and looked at them. "Hey, you fucks, come here."

Leonard and Farto joined them in looking at the dog. There was mostly just a head now, with a little bit of meat and fur hanging off a spine and some broken ribs.

"That's the sickest fucking thing I've ever fucking seen," Pork said.

"Godamighty," Vinnie said.

"Doing a dog like that. Shit, don't you got no heart? A dog. Man's best fucking goddamn friend and you two killed him like this."

"We didn't kill him," Farto said.

"You trying to fucking tell me he done this to himself? Had a bad fucking day and done this."

"Godamighty," Vinnie said.

"No, sir," Leonard said. "We chained him on there after he was dead."

"I believe that," Vinnie said. "That's some rich shit. You guys murdered this dog. Godamighty."

"Just thinking about him trying to keep up and you fucks driving faster and faster makes me mad as a wasp," Pork said.

"No," Farto said. "It wasn't like that. He was dead and we were drunk and we didn't have anything to do, so we—"

"Shut the fuck up," Pork said, sticking a finger hard against Farto's forehead. "You just shut the fuck up. We can see what the fuck you fucks did. You drug this here dog around until all his goddamn hide came off . . . What kind of mothers you boys got anyhow that they didn't tell you better about animals?"

"Godamighty," Vinnie said.

Everyone grew silent, stood looking at the dog. Finally Farto said, "You want us to go back to getting some stuff to hold the nigger down?"

Pork looked at Farto as if he had just grown up whole from the ground. "You fucks are worse than niggers, doing a dog like that. Get on back over to the car."

Leonard and Farto went over to the Impala and stood looking down at Scott's body in much the same way they had stared at the dog. There, in the dim moonlight shadowed by trees, the paper wrapped around Scott's head made him look like a giant papier-mâché doll. Pork came up and kicked Scott in the face with a swift motion that sent newspapers flying and sent a thonking sound across the water that made frogs jump.

"Forget the nigger," Pork said. "Give me your car keys, ball sweat." Leonard took out his keys and gave them to Pork and Pork went around to the trunk and opened it. "Drag the nigger over here."

Leonard took one of Scott's arms and Farto took the other and they pulled him over to the back of the car.

"Put him in the trunk," Pork said.

"What for?" Leonard asked.

"'Cause I fucking said so," Pork said.

Leonard and Farto heaved Scott into the trunk. He looked pathetic lying there next to the spare tire, his face partially covered with newspaper. Leonard thought, if only the nigger had stolen a car with a spare he might not be here tonight. He could have gotten that flat changed and driven on before the White Tree boys even came along.

"All right, you get in there with him," Pork said, gesturing to Farto.

"Me?" Farto said.

"Nah, not fucking you, the fucking elephant on your fucking shoulder. Yeah, you, get in the trunk. I ain't got all night."

"Jesus, we didn't do anything to that dog, mister. We told you that. I swear. Me and Leonard hooked him up after he was dead . . . It was Leonard's idea."

Pork didn't say a word. He just stood there with one hand on the trunk lid looking at Farto. Farto looked at Pork, then the trunk, then back to Pork. Lastly he looked at Leonard, then climbed into the trunk, his back to Scott.

"Like spoons," Pork said, and closed the lid. "Now you, whatsit, Leonard? You come over here." But Pork didn't wait for Leonard to move. He scooped the back of Leonard's neck with a chubby hand and pushed him over to where Rex lay at the end of the chain with Vinnie still looking down at him.

"What you think, Vinnie?" Pork asked. "You got what I got in mind?"

Vinnie nodded. He bent down and took the collar off the dog. He fastened it on Leonard. Leonard could smell the odor of the dead dog in his nostrils. He bent his head and puked.

"There goes my shoeshine," Vinnie said, and he hit Leonard a short one in the stomach. Leonard went to his knees and puked some more of the hot Coke and whiskey.

"You fucks are the lowest pieces of shit on this earth, doing a dog like that," Vinnie said. "A nigger ain't no lower."

Vinnie got some strong fishing line out of the back of the truck and they tied Leonard's hands behind his back. Leonard began to cry.

"Oh shut up," Pork said. "It ain't that bad. Ain't nothing that bad."

But Leonard couldn't shut up. He was caterwauling now and it was echoing through the trees. He closed his eyes and tried to pretend he had gone to the show with the nigger starring in it and had fallen asleep in his car and was having a bad dream, but he couldn't imagine that. He thought about Harry the janitor's flying saucers with the peppermint rays, and he knew if there were any saucers shooting rays down, they weren't boredom rays after all. He wasn't a bit bored.

Pork pulled off Leonard's shoes and pushed him back flat on the ground and pulled off the socks and stuck them in Leonard's mouth so tight he couldn't spit them out. It wasn't that Pork thought anyone was going to hear Leonard, he just didn't like the noise. It hurt his ears.

Leonard lay on the ground in the vomit next to the dog and cried silently. Pork and Vinnie went over to the Impala and opened the doors and stood so they could get a grip on the car to push. Vinnie reached in and moved the gear from park to neutral and he and Pork began to shove the car forward. It moved slowly at first, but as it made the slight incline that led down to the old bridge, it picked up speed. From inside the trunk, Farto hammered lightly at the lid as if he didn't really mean it. The chain took up slack and Leonard felt it jerk and pop his neck. He began to slide along the ground like a snake.

Vinnie and Pork jumped out of the way and watched the car make the bridge and go over the edge and disappear into the water with amazing quietness. Leonard, pulled by the weight of the car, rustled past them. When he hit the bridge, splinters tugged at his clothes so hard they ripped his pants and underwear down almost to his knees.

The chain swung out once toward the edge of the bridge and the rotten railing, and Leonard tried to hook a leg around an upright board there, but that proved wasted. The weight of the car just pulled his knee out of joint and jerked the board out of place with a screech of nails and lumber.

Leonard picked up speed and the chain rattled over the edge of the bridge, into the water and out of sight, pulling its connection after it like a pull toy. The last sight of Leonard was the soles of his bare feet, white as the bellies of fish.

"It's deep there," Vinnie said. "I caught an old channel cat there once, remember? Big sucker. I bet it's over fifty-feet deep down there."

They got in the truck and Vinnie cranked it.

"I think we did them boys a favor," Pork said. "Them running around with niggers and what they did to that dog and all. They weren't worth a thing."

"I know it," Vinnie said. "We should have filmed this, Pork, it would have been good. Where the car and that nigger lover went off in the water was choice."

"Nah, there wasn't any women."

"Point," Vinnie said, and he backed around and drove onto the trail that wound its way out of the bottoms.

Bubba Ho-Tep

For Chet Williamson

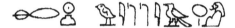

Elvis dreamed he had his dick out, checking to see if the bump on the head of it had filled with pus again. If it had, he was going to name the bump Priscilla, after his ex-wife, and bust it by jacking off. Or he liked to think that's what he'd do. Dreams let you think like that. The truth was, he hadn't had a hard-on in years.

That bitch, Priscilla. Gets a new hairdo and she's gone, just because she caught him fucking a big-tittied gospel singer. It wasn't like the singer had mattered. Priscilla ought to have understood that, so what was with her making a big deal out of it?

Was it because she couldn't hit a high note same and as good as the singer when she came?

When had that happened anyway, Priscilla leaving?

Yesterday? Last year? Ten years ago?

Oh God, it came to him instantly as he slipped out of sleep like a soft turd squeezed free of a loose asshole—for he could hardly think of himself or life in any context other than sewage, since so often he was too tired to do anything other than let it all fly in his sleep, wake up in an ocean of piss or shit, waiting for the nurses or the aides to come in and wipe his ass. But now it came to him. Suddenly he realized it had been years ago that he had supposedly died, and longer years than that since Priscilla left, and how old was she anyway? Sixty-five? Seventy?

And how old was he?

Christ! He was almost convinced he was too old to be alive, and had to be dead, but he wasn't convinced enough, unfortunately. He knew where he was now, and in that moment of realization, he sincerely wished he were dead. This was worse than death.

From across the room, his roommate, Bull Thomas, bellowed and coughed and moaned and fell back into painful sleep, the cancer gnawing at his insides like a rat plugged up inside a watermelon.

Bull's bellow of pain and anger and indignation at growing old and diseased was the only thing bullish about him now, though Elvis had seen photographs of him when he was younger, and Bull had been very bullish indeed. Thick-chested, slab-faced and tall. Probably thought he'd live forever, and happily. A boozing, pill-popping, swinging dick until the end of time.

Now Bull was shrunk down, was little more than a wrinkled sheet-white husk that throbbed with occasional pulses of blood while the carcinoma fed.

Elvis took hold of the bed's lift button, eased himself upright. He glanced at Bull. Bull was breathing heavily and his bony knees rose up and down like he was pedaling a bicycle; his kneecaps punched feebly at the sheet, making pup tents that rose up and collapsed, rose up and collapsed.

Elvis looked down at the sheet stretched over his own bony knees. He thought: *My God, how long have I been here? Am I really awake now, or am I dreaming I'm awake? How could my plans have gone so wrong? When are they going to serve lunch, and considering what they serve, why do I care? And if Priscilla discovered I was alive, would she come see me, would she want to see me, and would we still want to fuck, or would we have to merely talk about it? Is there finally, and really, anything to life other than food and shit and sex?*

Elvis pushed the sheet down to do what he had done in the dream. He pulled up his gown, leaned forward, and examined his dick. It was wrinkled and small. It didn't look like something that had dive-bombed movie starlet pussies or filled their mouths like a big zucchini or pumped forth a load of sperm frothy as cake icing. The healthiest thing about his pecker was the big red bump with the black ring around it and the pus-filled white center. Fact was, that bump kept growing, he was going to have to pull a chair up beside his bed and put a pillow in it so the bump would have some place to sleep at night. There was more pus in that damn bump than there was cum in his loins. Yep. The old diddlebopper was no longer a flesh cannon loaded for bare ass. It was a peanut too small to harvest; wasting away on the vine. His nuts were a couple of darkening, about-to-rot grapes, too limp to produce juice for life's wine. His legs were stick and paper things with over-large, vein-swollen feet on the ends. His belly was such a bloat, it was a pain for him to lean forward and scrutinize his dick and balls.

Pulling his gown down and the sheet back over himself, Elvis leaned back and wished he had a peanut butter and banana sandwich fried in butter. There had been a time when he and his crew would board his private jet and fly clean across country just to have a special-made fried peanut butter and 'nanner sandwich. He could still taste the damn things.

Elvis closed his eyes and thought he would awake from a bad dream, but didn't. He opened his eyes again, slowly, and saw that he was still where he had been, and things were no better. He reached over and opened his dresser drawer and got out a little round mirror and looked at himself.

He was horrified. His hair was white as salt and had receded dramatically. He had wrinkles deep enough to conceal outstretched earthworms, the big ones, the night crawlers. His pouty mouth no longer appeared pouty. It looked like the dropping waddles of a bulldog, seeming more that way because he was slobbering a mite. He dragged his tired tongue across his lips to daub the slobber, revealed to himself in the mirror that he was missing a lot of teeth.

Goddamn it! How had he gone from King of Rock and Roll to this? Old guy in a rest home in East Texas with a growth on his dick?

And what was that growth? Cancer? No one was talking. No one seemed to know. Perhaps the bump was a manifestation of the mistakes of his life, so many of them made with his dick.

He considered on that. Did he ask himself this question every day, or just now and then? Time sort of ran together when the last moment and the immediate moment and the moment forthcoming were all alike.

Shit, when was lunchtime? Had he slept through it?

Was it about time for his main nurse again? The good-looking one with the smooth chocolate skin and tits like grapefruits? The one who came in and sponge bathed him and held his pitiful little pecker in her gloved hands and put salve on his canker with all the enthusiasm of a mechanic oiling a defective part?

He hoped not. That was the worst of it. A doll like that handling him without warmth or emotion. Twenty years ago, just twenty, he could have made with the curled-lip smile and had her eating out of his asshole. Where had his youth gone? Why hadn't fame sustained old age and death, and why had he left his fame in the first place, and did he want it back, and could he have it back, and if he could, would it make any difference?

And finally, when he was evacuated from the bowels of life into the toilet bowl of the beyond and was flushed, would the great sewer pipe flow him to the other side where God would—in the guise of a great all-seeing turd with corn kernel eyes—be waiting with open turd arms, and would there be amongst the sewage his mother (bless her fat little heart) and father and friends, waiting with fried peanut butter and 'nanner sandwiches and ice cream cones, predigested, of course?

He was reflecting on this, pondering the afterlife, when Bull gave out with a hell of a scream, pouched his eyes damn near out of his head, arched his back, grease-farted like a blast from Gabriel's trumpet, and checked his tired old soul out of the Mud Creek Shady Rest Convalescent Home; flushed it on out and across the great shitty beyond.

Later that day, Elvis lay sleeping, his lips fluttering the bad taste of lunch—steamed zucchini and boiled peas—out of his belly. He awoke to a noise, rolled over to see a young attractive woman cleaning out Bull's dresser drawer. The curtains over the window next to Bull's bed were pulled wide open, and the sunlight was cutting through it and showing her to great advantage. She was blonde and Nordic-featured and her long hair was tied back with a big red bow and she wore big gold hoop earrings that shimmered in the sunlight. She was dressed in a white blouse and a short black skirt and dark hose and high heels. The heels made her ass ride up beneath her skirt like soft bald baby heads under a thin blanket.

She had a big yellow plastic trashcan and she had one of Bull's dresser drawers pulled out, and she was picking through it, like a magpie looking for bright things. She found a few—coins, a pocketknife, a cheap watch. These were plucked free and laid on the dresser top, then the remaining contents of the drawer—Bull's photographs of himself when young, a rotten pack of rubbers (wishful thinking never deserted Bull), a bronze star and a purple heart from his performance in the Vietnam War—were dumped into the trashcan with a bang and a flutter.

Elvis got hold of his bed lift button and raised himself for a better look. The woman had her back to him now, and didn't notice. She was replacing the dresser drawer and pulling out another. It was full of clothes. She took out the few shirts and pants and socks and underwear, and laid them on Bull's bed— remade now, and minus Bull, who had been toted off to be taxidermied, embalmed, burned up, whatever.

"You're gonna toss that stuff," Elvis said. "Could I have one of them pictures of Bull? Maybe that purple heart? He was proud of it."

The young woman turned and looked at him. "I suppose," she said. She went to the trashcan and bent over it and showed her black panties to Elvis as she rummaged. He knew the revealing of her panties was neither intentional nor unintentional. She just didn't give a damn. She saw him as so physically and sexually non-threatening, she didn't mind if he got a bird's-eye view of her; it was the same to her as a house cat sneaking a peek.

Elvis observed the thin panties straining and slipping into the caverns of her ass cheeks and felt his pecker flutter once, like a bird having a heart attack, then it laid down and remained limp and still.

Well, these days, even a flutter was kind of reassuring.

The woman surfaced from the trashcan with a photo and the purple heart, went over to Elvis's bed and handed them to him.

Elvis dangled the ribbon that held the purple heart between his fingers, said, "Bull your kin?"

"My daddy," she said.

"I haven't seen you here before."

"Only been here once before," she said. "When I checked him in."

"Oh," Elvis said. "That was three years ago, wasn't it?"

"Yeah. Were you and him friends?"

Elvis considered the question. He didn't know the real answer. All he knew was Bull listened to him when he said he was Elvis Presley and seemed to believe him. If he didn't believe him, he at least had the courtesy not to patronize. Bull always called him Elvis, and before Bull grew too ill, he always played cards and checkers with him.

"Just roommates," Elvis said. "He didn't feel good enough to say much. I just sort of hated to see what was left of him go away so easy. He was an all-right guy. He mentioned you a lot. You're Callie, right?"

"Yeah," she said. "Well, he was all right."

"Not enough you came and saw him though."

"Don't try to put some guilt trip on me, Mister. I did what I could. Hadn't been for Medicaid, Medicare, whatever that stuff was, he'd have been in a ditch somewhere. I didn't have the money to take care of him."

Elvis thought of his own daughter, lost long ago to him. If she knew he lived, would she come to see him? Would she care? He feared knowing the answer.

"You could have come and seen him," Elvis said.

"I was busy. Mind your own business. Hear?"

The chocolate-skin nurse with the grapefruit tits came in. Her white uniform crackled like cards being shuffled. Her little white nurse hat was tilted on her head in a way that said she loved mankind and made good money and was getting regular dick. She smiled at Callie and then at Elvis. "How are you this morning, Mr. Haff?"

"All right," Elvis said. "But I prefer Mr. Presley. Or Elvis. I keep telling you that. I don't go by Sebastian Haff anymore. I don't try to hide anymore."

"Why, of course," said the pretty nurse. "I knew that. I forgot. Good morning, Elvis."

Her voice dripped with sorghum syrup. Elvis wanted to hit her with his bedpan.

The nurse said to Callie: "Did you know we have a celebrity here, Miss Thomas? Elvis Presley. You know, the rock and roll singer?"

"I've heard of him," Callie said. "I thought he was dead."

Callie went back to the dresser and squatted and set to work on the bottom drawer. The nurse looked at Elvis and smiled again, only she spoke to Callie. "Well, actually, Elvis is dead, and Mr. Haff knows that, don't you, Mr. Haff?"

"Hell no," said Elvis. "I'm right here. I ain't dead, yet."

"Now, Mr. Haff, I don't mind calling you Elvis, but you're a little confused, or like to play sometimes. You were an Elvis impersonator. Remember? You fell off a stage and broke your hip. What was it . . . Twenty years ago? It got infected and you went into a coma for a few years. You came out with a few problems."

"I was impersonating myself," Elvis said. "I couldn't do nothing else. I haven't got any problems. You're trying to say my brain is messed up, aren't you?"

Callie quit cleaning out the bottom drawer of the dresser. She was interested now, and though it was no use, Elvis couldn't help but try and explain who he was, just one more time. The explaining had become a habit, like wanting to smoke a cigar long after the enjoyment of it was gone.

"I got tired of it all," he said. "I got on drugs, you know. I wanted out. Fella named Sebastian Haff, an Elvis imitator, the best of them. He took my place. He had a bad heart and he liked drugs too. It was him died, not me. I took his place."

"Why would you want to leave all that fame," Callie said, "all that money?" and she looked at the nurse, like "Let's humor the old fart for a lark."

"'Cause it got old. Woman I loved, Priscilla, she was gone. Rest of the women . . . were just women. The music wasn't mine anymore. *I* wasn't even me anymore. I was this thing they made up. Friends were sucking me dry. I got away and liked it, left all the money with Sebastian, except for enough to sustain me if things got bad. We had a deal, me and Sebastian. When I wanted to come back, he'd let me. It was all written up in a contract in case he wanted to give me a hard time, got to liking my life too good. Thing was, copy of the contract I had got lost in a trailer fire. I was living simple. Way Haff had been. Going from town to town doing the Elvis act. Only I felt like I was really me again. Can you dig that?"

"We're digging it, Mr. Haff . . . Mr. Presley," said the pretty nurse.

"I was singing the old way. Doing some new songs. Stuff I wrote. I was getting attention on a small but good scale. Women throwing themselves at me, 'cause they could imagine I was Elvis, only I was Elvis, playing Sebastian Haff playing Elvis. . . . It was all pretty good. I didn't mind the contract being burned up. I didn't even try to go back and convince anybody. Then I had the accident. Like I was saying, I'd laid up a little money in case of illness, stuff like that. That's what's paying for here. These nice facilities. Ha!"

"Now, Elvis," the nurse said. "Don't carry it too far. You may just get way out there and not come back."

"Oh, fuck you," Elvis said.

The nurse giggled.

Shit, Elvis thought. *Get old, you can't even cuss somebody and have it bother them. Everything you do is either worthless or sadly amusing.*

"You know, Elvis," said the pretty nurse, "we have a Mr. Dillinger here too. And a President Kennedy. He says the bullet only wounded him and his brain is in a fruit jar at the White House, hooked up to some wires and a battery, and as long as the battery works, he can walk around without it. His brain, that is. You know, he says everyone was in on trying to assassinate him. Even Elvis Presley."

"You're an asshole," Elvis said.

"I'm not trying to hurt your feelings, Mr. Haff," the nurse said. "I'm merely trying to give you a reality check."

"You can shove that reality check right up your pretty black ass," Elvis said.

The nurse made a sad little snicking sound. "Mr. Haff, Mr. Haff. Such language."

"What happened to get you here?" said Callie. "Say you fell off a stage?"

"I was gyrating," Elvis said. "Doing 'Blue Moon,' but my hip went out. I'd been having trouble with it." Which was quite true. He'd sprained it making love to a blue-haired old lady with ELVIS tattooed on her fat ass. He couldn't help himself from wanting to fuck her. She looked like his mother, Gladys.

"You swiveled right off the stage?" Callie said. "Now that's sexy."

Elvis looked at her. She was smiling. This was great fun for her, listening to some nut tell a tale. She hadn't had this much fun since she put her old man in the rest home.

"Oh, leave me the hell alone," Elvis said.

The women smiled at one another, passing a private joke. Callie said to the nurse: "I've got what I want." She scraped the bright things off the top of Bull's dresser into her purse. "The clothes can go to Goodwill or the Salvation Army."

The pretty nurse nodded to Callie. "Very well. And I'm very sorry about your father. He was a nice man."

"Yeah," said Callie, and she started out of there. She paused at the foot of Elvis's bed. "Nice to meet you, Mr. Presley."

"Get the hell out," Elvis said.

"Now, now," said the pretty nurse, patting his foot through the covers, as if it were a little cantankerous dog. "I'll be back later to do that . . . little thing that has to be done. You know?"

"I know," Elvis said, not liking the words "little thing."

Callie and the nurse started away then, punishing him with the clean lines of their faces and the sheen of their hair, the jiggle of their asses and tits. When they were out of sight, Elvis heard them laugh about something in the hall, then they were gone, and Elvis felt as if he were on the far side of Pluto without a jacket. He picked up the ribbon with the purple heart and looked at it.

Poor Bull. In the end, did anything really matter?

Meanwhile . . .

The Earth swirled around the sun like a spinning turd in the toilet bowl (to keep up with Elvis's metaphors) and the good old abused Earth clicked about on its axis and the hole in the ozone spread slightly wider, like a shy lady fingering open her vagina, and the South American trees that had stood for centuries were visited by the dozer, the chainsaw, and the match, and they rose up in burned black puffs that expanded and dissipated into minuscule wisps, and while the puffs of smoke dissolved, there were IRA bombings in London, and there was more war in the Mid-East. Blacks died in Africa of famine, the HIV virus infected a million more, the Dallas Cowboys lost again, and that Ole Blue Moon that Elvis and Patsy Cline sang so well about swung around the Earth and came in close and rose over the Shady Rest Convalescent Home, shone its bittersweet, silver-blue rays down on the joint like a flashlight beam shining through a blue-haired lady's do, and inside the rest home, evil waddled about like a duck looking for a spot to squat, and Elvis rolled over in his sleep and awoke with the intense desire to pee.

All right, thought Elvis. *This time I make it.* No more piss or crap in the bed. (Famous last words.)

Elvis sat up and hung his feet over the side of the bed and the bed swung far to the left and around the ceiling and back, and then it wasn't moving at all. The dizziness passed.

Elvis looked at his walker and sighed, leaned forward, took hold of the grips and eased himself off the bed and clumped the rubber-padded tips forward, made for the toilet.

He was in the process of milking his bump-swollen weasel when he heard something in the hallway. A kind of scrambling, like a big spider scuttling about in a box of gravel.

There was always some sound in the hallway, people coming and going, yelling in pain or confusion, but this time of night, three A.M., was normally quite dead.

It shouldn't have concerned him, but the truth of the matter was, now that he was up and had successfully pissed in the pot, he was no longer sleepy; he was still thinking about that bimbo, Callie, and the nurse (what the hell was her name?) with the tits like grapefruits, and all they had said.

Elvis stumped his walker backwards out of the bathroom, turned it, made his way forward into the hall. The hall was semi-dark, with every other light cut, and the lights that were on were dimmed to a watery egg-yolk yellow. The black and white tile floor looked like a great chessboard, waxed and buffed for the next game of life, and here he was, a semi-crippled pawn, ready to go.

Off in the far wing of the home, Old Lady McGee, better known in the home as The Blue Yodeler, broke into one of her famous yodels (she claimed to have sung with a Country and Western band in her youth) then ceased abruptly. Elvis swung the walker forward and moved on. He hadn't been out of his room in ages, and he hadn't been out of his bed much either. Tonight, he felt invigorated because he hadn't pissed his bed, and he'd heard the sound again, the spider in the box of gravel. (Big spider. Big box. Lots of gravel.) And following the sound gave him something to do.

Elvis rounded the corner, beads of sweat popping out on his fore-head like heat blisters. Jesus. He wasn't invigorated now. Thinking about how invigorated he was had bushed him. Still, going back to his room to lie on his bed and wait for morning so he could wait for noon, then afternoon and night, didn't appeal to him.

He went by Jack McLaughlin's room, the fellow who was convinced he was John F. Kennedy, and that his brain was in the White House running on batteries. The door to Jack's room was open. Elvis peeked in as he moved by, knowing full well that Jack might not want to see him. Sometimes he accepted Elvis as the real Elvis, and when he did, he got scared, saying it was Elvis who had been behind the assassination.

Actually, Elvis hoped he felt that way tonight. It would at least be some acknowledgment that he was who he was, even if the acknowl-edgment was a fearful shriek from a nut.

Course, Elvis thought, *maybe I'm nuts too. Maybe I am Sebastian Haff and I fell off the stage and broke more than my hip, cracked some part of my brain that lost my old self and made me think I'm Elvis.*

No. He couldn't believe that. That's the way they wanted him to think. They wanted him to believe he was nuts and he wasn't Elvis, just some sad old fart who had once lived out part of another man's life because he had none of his own.

He wouldn't accept that. He wasn't Sebastian Haff. He was Elvis Goddamn Aaron Fucking Presley with a boil on his dick.

Course, he believed that, maybe he ought to believe Jack was John F. Kennedy, and Mums Delay, another patient here at Shady Rest, was Dillinger. Then again, maybe not. They were kind of scanty on evidence. He at least looked like Elvis gone old and sick. Jack was black—he claimed The Powers That Be had dyed him that color to keep him hidden—and Mums was a woman who claimed she'd had a sex-change operation.

Jesus, was this a rest home or a nuthouse?

Jack's room was one of the special kind. He didn't have to share. He had money from somewhere. The room was packed with books and little luxuries. And though Jack could walk well, he even had a fancy electric wheelchair that he rode about in sometimes. Once, Elvis had seen him riding it around the outside circular drive, popping wheelies and spinning doughnuts.

When Elvis looked into Jack's room, he saw him lying on the floor. Jack's gown was pulled up around his neck, and his bony black ass appeared to be made of licorice in the dim light. Elvis figured Jack had been on his way to the shitter, or was coming back from it, and had collapsed. His heart, maybe.

"Jack," Elvis said.

Elvis clumped into the room, positioned his walker next to Jack, took a deep breath and stepped out of it, supporting himself with one side of it. He got down on his knees beside Jack, hoping he'd be able to get up again. God, but his knees and back hurt.

Jack was breathing hard. Elvis noted the scar at Jack's hairline, a long scar that made Jack's skin lighter there, almost gray. ("That's where they took the brain out," Jack always explained, "put it in that fucking jar. I got a little bag of sand up there now.")

Elvis touched the old man's shoulder. "Jack. Man, you okay?"

No response.

Elvis tried again. "Mr. Kennedy?"

"Uh," said Jack (Mr. Kennedy).

"Hey, man. You're on the floor," Elvis said.

"No shit? Who are you?"

Elvis hesitated. This wasn't the time to get Jack worked up.

"Sebastian," he said. "Sebastian Haff."

Elvis took hold of Jack's shoulder and rolled him over. It was about as difficult as rolling a jelly roll. Jack lay on his back now. He strayed an eyeball at Elvis. He started to speak, hesitated. Elvis took hold of Jack's nightgown and managed to work it down around Jack's knees, trying to give the old fart some dignity.

Jack finally got his breath. "Did you see him go by in the hall? He scuttled like."

"Who?"

"Someone they sent."

"Who's they?"

"You know. Lyndon Johnson. Castro. They've sent someone to finish me. I think maybe it was Johnson himself. Real ugly. Real goddamn ugly."

"Johnson's dead," Elvis said.

"That won't stop him," Jack said.

Later that morning, sunlight shooting into Elvis's room through venetian blinds, Elvis put his hands behind his head and considered the night before while the pretty black nurse with the grapefruit tits salved his dick. He had reported Jack's fall and the aides had come to help Jack back in bed, and him back on his walker. He had clumped back to his room (after being scolded for being out there that time of night) feeling that an air of strangeness had blown into the rest home, an air that wasn't there as short as the day before. It was at low ebb now, but certainly still present, humming in the background like some kind of generator ready to buzz up to a higher notch at a moment's notice.

And he was certain it wasn't just his imagination. The scuttling sound he'd heard last night, Jack had heard it too. What was that all about? It wasn't the sound of a walker, or a crip dragging their foot, or a wheelchair creeping along, it was something else, and now that he thought about it, it wasn't exactly spider legs in gravel, more like a roll of barbed wire tumbling across tile.

Elvis was so wrapped up in these considerations, he lost awareness of the nurse until she said, "Mr. Haff!"

"What . . . " and he saw that she was smiling and looking down at her hands. He looked too. There, nestled in one of her gloved palms, was a massive, blue-veined hooter with a pus-filled bump on it the size of a pecan. It was *his* hooter and *his* pus-filled bump.

"You ole rascal," she said, and gently lowered his dick between his legs. "I think you better take a cold shower, Mr. Haff."

Elvis was amazed. That was the first time in years he'd had a boner like that. What gave here?

Then he realized what gave. He wasn't thinking about not being able to do it. He was thinking about something that interested him, and now, with something clicking around inside his head besides old memories and confusions, concerns about his next meal and going to the crapper, he had been given a dose of life again. He grinned his gums and what teeth were in them at the nurse.

"You get in there with me," he said, "and I'll take that shower."

"You silly thing," she said, and pulled his nightgown down and stood and removed her plastic gloves and dropped them in the trashcan beside his bed.

"Why don't you pull on it a little?" Elvis said.

"You ought to be ashamed," the nurse said, but she smiled when she said it.

She left the room door open after she left. This concerned Elvis a little, but he felt his bed was at such an angle no one could look in, and if they did, tough luck. He wasn't going to look a gift hard-on in the pee-hole. He pulled the sheet over him and pushed his hands beneath the sheets and got his gown pulled up over his belly. He took hold of his snake and began to choke it with one hand, running his thumb over the pus-filled bump. With his other hand, he fondled his balls. He thought of Priscilla and the pretty black nurse and Bull's daughter and even the blue-haired fat lady with ELVIS tattooed on her butt, and he stroked harder and faster, and goddamn but he got stiffer and stiffer, and the bump on his cock gave up its load first, exploded hot pus down his thighs, and then his balls, which he thought forever empty, filled up with juice and electricity, and finally he threw the switch. The dam broke and the juice flew. He heard himself scream happily and felt hot wetness jetting down his legs, splattering as far as his big toes.

"Oh God," he said softly. "I like that. I like that."

He closed his eyes and slept. And for the first time in a long time, not fitfully.

Lunchtime. The Shady Rest lunch room.

Elvis sat with a plate of steamed carrots and broccoli and flaky roast beef in front of him. A dry roll, a pat of butter and a short glass of milk soldiered on the side. It was not inspiring.

Next to him, The Blue Yodeler was stuffing a carrot up her nose while she expounded on the sins of God, The Heavenly Father, for knocking up that nice Mary in her sleep, slipping up her ungreased poontang while she snored, and—bless her little heart—not even knowing it, or getting a clit throb from it, but waking up with a belly full of baby and no memory of action.

Elvis had heard it all before. It used to offend him, this talk of God as rapist, but he'd heard it so much now he didn't care. She rattled on.

Across the way, an old man who wore a black mask and sometimes a white Stetson, known to residents and staff alike as Kemosabe, snapped one of his two capless cap pistols at the floor and called for an invisible Tonto to bend over so he could drive him home.

At the far end of the table, Dillinger was talking about how much whisky he used to drink, and how many cigars he used to smoke before he got his dick cut off at the stump and split so he could become a she and hide out as a woman. Now she said she no longer thought of banks and machine guns, women and fine cigars. She now thought about spots on dishes, the colors of curtains and drapes as coordinated with carpets and walls.

Even as the depression of his surroundings settled over him again, Elvis deliberated last night, and glanced down the length of the table at Jack (Mr. Kennedy), who headed its far end. He saw the old man was looking at him, as if they shared a secret.

Elvis's ill mood dropped a notch; a real mystery was at work here, and come nightfall, he was going to investigate.

Swing the Shady Rest Convalescent Home's side of the Earth away from the sun again, and swing the moon in close and blue again. Blow some gauzy clouds across the nasty, black sky. Now ease on into 3 A.M.

Elvis awoke with a start and turned his head toward the intrusion. Jack stood next to the bed looking down at him. Jack was wearing a suit coat over his nightgown and he had on thick glasses. He said, "Sebastian. It's loose."

Elvis collected his thoughts, pasted them together into a not-too-scattered collage. "What's loose?"

"It," said Sebastian. "Listen."

Elvis listened. Out in the hall he heard the scuttling sound of the night before. Tonight, it reminded him of great locust-wings beating frantically inside a small cardboard box, the tips of them scratching at the cardboard, cutting it, ripping it apart.

"Jesus Christ, what is it?" Elvis said.

"I thought it was Lyndon Johnson, but it isn't. I've come across new evidence that suggests another assassin."

"Assassin?"

Jack cocked an ear. The sound had gone away, moved distant, then ceased.

"It's got another target tonight," said Jack. "Come on. I want to show you something. I don't think it's safe if you go back to sleep."

"For Christ sake," Elvis said. "Tell the administrators."

"The suits and the white starches," Jack said. "No thanks. I trusted them back when I was in Dallas, and look where that got my brain and me. I'm thinking with sand here, maybe picking up a few waves from my brain. Someday, who's to say they won't just disconnect the battery at the White House?"

"That's something to worry about, all right," Elvis said.

"Listen here," Jack said. "I know you're Elvis, and there were rumors, you know . . . about how you hated me, but I've thought it over. You hated me, you could have finished me the other night. All I want from you is to look me in the eye and assure me you had nothing to do with that day in Dallas, and that you never knew Lee Harvey Oswald or Jack Ruby."

Elvis stared at him as sincerely as possible. "I had nothing to do with Dallas, and I knew neither Lee Harvey Oswald or Jack Ruby."

"Good," said Jack. "May I call you Elvis instead of Sebastian?"

"You may."

"Excellent. You wear glasses to read?"

"I wear glasses when I really want to see," Elvis said. Get 'em and come on."

Elvis swung his walker along easily, not feeling as if he needed it too much tonight. He was excited. Jack was a nut, and maybe he himself was nuts, but there was an adventure going on.

They came to the hall restroom. The one reserved for male visitors. "In here," Jack said.

"Now wait a minute," Elvis said. "You're not going to get me in there and try and play with my pecker, are you?"

Jack stared at him. "Man, I made love to Jackie and Marilyn and a ton of others, and you think I want to play with your nasty ole dick?"

"Good point," said Elvis.

They went into the restroom. It was large, with several stalls and urinals.

"Over here," said Jack. He went over to one of the stalls and pushed open the door and stood back by the commode to make room for Elvis's walker. Elvis eased inside and looked at what Jack was now pointing to.

Graffiti.

"That's it?" Elvis said. "We're investigating a scuttling in the hall, trying to discover who attacked you last night, and you bring me in here to show me stick pictures on the shit house wall?"

"Look close," Jack said.

Elvis leaned forward. His eyes weren't what they used to be, and his glasses probably needed to be upgraded, but he could see that instead of writing, the graffiti was a series of simple pictorials.

A thrill, like a shot of good booze, ran through Elvis. He had once been a fanatic reader of ancient and esoteric lore, like *The Egyptian Book of the Dead* and *The Complete Works of H. P. Lovecraft,* and straight away he recognized what he was staring at. "Egyptian hieroglyphics," he said.

"Right-a-reen-O," Jack said. "Hey, you're not as stupid as some folks made you out."

"Thanks," Elvis said.

Jack reached into his suit coat pocket and took out a folded piece of paper and unfolded it. He pressed it to the wall. Elvis saw that it was covered with the same sort of figures that were on the wall of the stall.

"I copied this down yesterday. I came in here to shit because they hadn't cleaned up my bathroom. I saw this on the wall, went back to my room and looked it up in my books and wrote it all down. The top line translates something like: *Pharaoh gobbles donkey goober.* And the bottom line is: *Cleopatra does the dirty.*"

"What?"

"Well, pretty much," Jack said.

Elvis was mystified. "All right," he said. "One of the nuts here, present company excluded, thinks he's Tutankhamun or something, and he writes on the wall in hieroglyphics. So what? I mean, what's the connection? Why are we hanging out in a toilet?"

"I don't know how they connect exactly," Jack said. "Not yet. But this . . . thing, it caught me asleep last night, and I came awake just in time to . . . well, he had me on the floor and had his mouth over my asshole."

"A shit eater?" Elvis said.

"I don't think so," Jack said. "He was after my soul. You can get that out of any of the major orifices in a person's body. I've read about it."

"Where?" Elvis asked. *"Hustler?"*

"The Everyday Man or Woman's Book of the Soul, by David Webb. It has some pretty good movie reviews about stolen soul movies in the back too."

"Oh, that sounds trustworthy," Elvis said.

They went back to Jack's room and sat on his bed and looked through his many books on astrology, the Kennedy assassination, and a number of esoteric tomes, including the philosophy book, *The Everyday Man or Woman's Book of the Soul.*

Elvis found that book fascinating in particular; it indicated that not only did humans have a soul, but that the soul could be stolen, and there was a section concerning vampires and ghouls and incubi and succubi, as well as related soul suckers. Bottom line was, one of those dudes was around, you had to watch your holes. Mouth hole. Nose hole. Asshole. If you were a woman, you needed to watch a different hole. Dick pee-holes and ear holes—male or female—didn't matter. The soul didn't hang out there. They weren't considered major orifices for some reason.

In the back of the book was a list of items, related and not related to the book, that you could buy. Little plastic pyramids. Hats you could wear while channeling. Subliminal tapes that would help you learn Arabic. Postage was paid.

"Every kind of soul eater is in that book except politicians and science-fiction fans," Jack said. "And I think that's what we got here in Shady Rest. A soul eater. Turn to the Egyptian section."

Elvis did. The chapter was prefaced by a movie still from *The Ten Commandments* with Yul Brynner playing Pharaoh. He was standing up in his chariot looking serious, which seemed a fair enough expression, considering the Red Sea, which had been parted by Moses, was about to come back together and drown him and his army.

Elvis read the article slowly while Jack heated hot water with his plug-in heater and made cups of instant coffee. "I get my niece to smuggle this stuff in," said Jack. "Or she claims to be my niece. She's a black woman. I never saw her before I was shot that day in Dallas and they took my brain out. She's part of the new identity they've given me. She's got a great ass."

"Damn," said Elvis. "What it says here, is that you can bury some dude, and if he gets the right tanna leaves and spells said over him and such bullshit, he can come back to life some thousands of years later, and to stay alive, he has to suck on the souls of the living, and that if the souls are small, his life force doesn't last long. Small. What's that mean?"

"Read on . . . No, never mind, I'll tell you." Jack handed Elvis his cup of coffee and sat down on the bed next to him. "Before I do, want a Ding Dong? Not mine. The chocolate kind. Well, I guess mine is chocolate, now that I've been dyed."

"You got Ding Dongs?" Elvis asked.

"Couple of Pay Days and Baby Ruth too," Jack said. "Which will it be? Let's get decadent."

Elvis licked his lips. "I'll have a Ding Dong."

While Elvis savored the Ding Dong, gumming it sloppily, sipping his coffee between bites, Jack, coffee cup balanced on his knee, a Baby Ruth in one mitt, expounded.

"Small souls means those without much fire for life," Jack said. "You know a place like that?"

"If souls were fires," Elvis said, "they couldn't burn much lower without being out than here. Only thing we got going in this joint is the pilot light."

"Exactamundo," Jack said. "What we got here in Shady Rest is an Egyptian soul sucker of some sort. A mummy hiding out, coming in here to feed on the sleeping. It's perfect, you see. The souls are little, and don't provide him with much. If this thing comes back two or three times in a row to wrap his lips around some elder's asshole, that elder is going to die pretty soon, and who's the wiser? Our mummy may not be getting much energy out of this, way he would with big souls, but the prey is easy. A mummy couldn't be too strong, really. Mostly just husk. But we're pretty much that way ourselves. We're not too far off being mummies."

"And with new people coming in all the time," Elvis said, "he can keep this up forever, this soul robbing."

"That's right. Because that's what we're brought here for. To get us out of the way until we die. And the ones don't die first of disease, or just plain old age, he gets."

Elvis considered all that. "That's why he doesn't bother the nurses and aides and administrators? He can go unsuspected."

"That, and they're not asleep. He has to get you when you're sleeping or unconscious."

"All right, but the thing throws me, Jack, is how does an ancient Egyptian end up in an East Texas rest home, and why is he writing on shit house walls?"

"He went to take a crap, got bored, and wrote on the wall. He probably wrote on pyramid walls, centuries ago."

"What would he crap?" Elvis said. "It's not like he'd eat, is it?"

"He eats souls," Jack said, "so I assume, he craps soul residue. And what that means to me is, you die by his mouth, you don't go to the other side, or wherever souls go. He digests the souls till they don't exist anymore—"

"And you're just so much toilet water decoration," Elvis said.

"That's the way I've got it worked out," Jack said. "He's just like anyone else when he wants to take a dump. He likes a nice clean place with a flush. They didn't have that in his time, and I'm sure he finds it handy. The writing on the walls is just habit. Maybe, to him, Pharaoh and Cleopatra were just yesterday."

Elvis finished off the Ding Dong and sipped his coffee. He felt a rush from the sugar and he loved it. He wanted to ask Jack for the Pay Day he had mentioned, but restrained himself. Sweets, fried foods, late nights and drugs had been the beginning of his original downhill spiral. He had to keep himself collected this time. He had to be ready to battle the Egyptian soul-sucking menace.

Soul-sucking menace?

God. He *was* really bored. It was time for him to go back to his room and to bed so he could shit on himself, get back to normal.

But Jesus and Ra, this was different from what had been going on up until now! It might all be bullshit, but considering what was going on in his life right now, it was absorbing bullshit. It might be worth playing the game to the hilt, even if he was playing it with a black guy who thought he was John F. Kennedy and believed an Egyptian mummy was stalking the corridors of Shady Rest Convalescent Home, writing graffiti on toilet stalls, sucking people's souls out through their assholes, digesting them, and crapping them down the visitors' toilet.

Suddenly Elvis was pulled out of his considerations. There came from the hall the noise again. The sound that each time he heard it reminded him of something different. This time it was dried corn husks being rattled in a high wind. He felt goose bumps travel up his spine and the hairs on the back of his neck and arms stood up. He leaned forward and put his hands on his walker and pulled himself upright.

"Don't go in the hall," Jack said.

"I'm not asleep."

"That doesn't mean *it* won't hurt you."

"*It*, my ass, there isn't any mummy from Egypt."

"Nice knowing you, Elvis."

Elvis inched the walker forward. He was halfway to the open door when he spied the figure in the hallway.

As the thing came even with the doorway, the hall lights went dim and sputtered. Twisting about the apparition, like pet crows, were flutters of shadows. The thing walked and stumbled, shuffled and flowed. Its legs moved like Elvis's own, meaning not too good, and yet, there was something about its locomotion that was impossible to identify. Stiff, but ghostly smooth. It was dressed in nasty-looking jeans, a black shirt, a black cowboy hat that came down so low it covered where the thing's eyebrows should be. It wore large cowboy boots with the toes curled up, and there came from the thing a kind of mixed-stench: a compost pile of mud, rotting leaves, resin, spoiled fruit, dry dust, and gassy sewage.

Elvis found that he couldn't scoot ahead another inch. He froze. The thing stopped and cautiously turned its head on its apple-stem neck and looked at Elvis with empty eye sockets, revealing that it was, in fact, uglier than Lyndon Johnson.

Surprisingly, Elvis found he was surging forward as if on a zooming camera dolly, and that he was plunging into the thing's right eye socket, which swelled speedily to the dimensions of a vast canyon bottomed by blackness.

Down Elvis went, spinning and spinning, and out of the emptiness rushed resin-scented memories of pyramids and boats on a river, hot blue skies, and a great silver bus lashed hard by black rain, a crumbling bridge and a charge of dusky water and a gleam of silver. Then there was a darkness so caliginous it was beyond being called dark, and Elvis could feel and taste mud in his mouth and a sensation of claustrophobia beyond expression. And he could perceive the thing's hunger, a hunger that prodded him like hot pins, and then—

—there came a *popping* sound in rapid succession, and Elvis felt himself whirling even faster, spinning backwards out of that deep memory canyon of the dusty head, and now he stood once again within the framework of his walker, and the mummy—for Elvis no longer denied to himself that it was such—turned its head away and began to move again, to shuffle, to flow, to stumble, to glide, down the hall, its pet shadows screeching with rusty throats around its head. *Pop! Pop! Pop!*

As the thing moved on Elvis compelled himself to lift his walker and advance into the hall. Jack slipped up beside him, and they saw the mummy in cowboy clothes traveling toward the exit door at the back of the home. When it came to the locked door, it leaned against where the door met the jamb and twisted and writhed, squeezed through the invisible crack where the two connected. Its shadows pursued it, as if sucked through by a vacuum cleaner.

The popping sound went on, and Elvis turned his head in that direction, and there, in his mask, his double concho-studded holster belted around his waist, was Kemosabe, a silver Fanner Fifty in either hand. He was popping caps rapidly at where the mummy had departed, the black-spotted red rolls flowing out from behind the hammers of his revolvers in smoky relay.

"Asshole!" Kemosabe said. "Asshole!"

And then Kemosabe quivered, dropped both hands, popped a cap from each gun toward the ground, stiffened, collapsed.

Elvis knew he was dead of a ruptured heart before he hit the black and white tile; gone down and out with both guns blazing, soul intact.

The hall lights trembled back to normal.

The administrators, the nurses and the aides came then. They rolled Kemosabe over and drove their palms against his chest, but he didn't breathe again. No more Hi-Yo-Silver. They sighed over him and clucked their tongues, and finally an aide reached over and lifted Kemosabe's mask, pulled it off his head and dropped it on the floor, nonchalantly, and without respect, revealed his identity.

It was no one anyone really knew.

Once again, Elvis got scolded, and this time he got quizzed about what had happened to Kemosabe, and so did Jack, but neither told the truth. Who was going to believe a couple of nuts? Elvis and Jack Kennedy explaining that Kemosabe was gunning for a mummy in cowboy duds, a Bubba Ho-Tep with a flock of shadows roiling about his cowboy-hatted head?

So, what they did was lie.

"He came snapping caps and then he fell," Elvis said, and Jack corroborated his story, and when Kemosabe had been carried off, Elvis, with some difficulty, using his walker for support, got down on his knee and picked up the discarded mask and carried it away with him.

He had wanted the guns, but an aide had taken those for her four-year-old son.

Later, he and Jack learned through the grapevine that Kemosabe's roommate, an eighty-year-old man who had been in a semi-comatose condition for several years, had been found dead on the floor of his room. It was assumed Kemosabe had lost it and dragged him off his bed and onto the floor and the eighty-year-old man had kicked the bucket during the fall. As for Kemosabe, they figured he had then gone nuts when he realized what he had done, and had wandered out in the hall firing, and had a heart attack.

Elvis knew different. The mummy had come and Kemosabe had tried to protect his roommate in the only way he knew how. But instead of silver bullets, his gun smoked sulfur. Elvis felt a rush of pride in the old fart.

He and Jack got together later, talked about what they had seen, and then there was nothing left to say.

Night went away and the sun came up, and Elvis, who had slept not a wink, came up with it and put on khaki pants and a khaki shirt and used his walker to go outside. It had been ages since he had been out, and it seemed strange out there, all that sunlight and the smells of flowers and the Texas sky so high and the clouds so white.

It was hard to believe he had spent so much time in his bed. Just the use of his legs with the walker these last few days had tightened the muscles, and he found he could get around better.

The pretty nurse with the grapefruit tits came outside and said: "Mr. Presley, you look so much stronger. But you shouldn't stay out too long. It's almost time for a nap and for us, to, you know . . ."

"Fuck off, you patronizing bitch," said Elvis. "I'm tired of your shit. I'll lube my own transmission. You treat me like a baby again, I'll wrap this goddamn walker around your head."

The pretty nurse stood stunned, then went away quietly.

Elvis inched his way with the walker around the great circular drive that surrounded the home. It was a half hour later when he reached the back of the home and the door through which the mummy had departed. It was still locked, and he stood and looked at it amazed. How in hell had the mummy done that, slipping through an indiscernible chink between door and frame?

Elvis looked down at the concrete that lay at the back of the door.

No clues there. He used the walker to travel toward the growth of trees out back, a growth of pin-oaks and sweet gums and hickory nut trees that shouldered on either side of the large creek that flowed behind the home.

The ground tipped sharply there, and for a moment he hesitated, then reconsidered. *Well, what the fuck?* he thought.

He planted the walker and started going forward, the ground sloping ever more dramatically. By the time he reached the bank of the creek and came to a gap in the trees, he was exhausted. He had the urge to start yelling for help, but didn't want to belittle himself, not after his performance with the nurse. He knew that he had regained some of his former confidence. His cursing and abuse had not seemed cute to her that time. The words had bitten her, if only slightly, Truth was, he was going to miss her greasing his pecker.

He looked over the bank of the creek. It was quite a drop there. The creek itself was narrow, and on either side of it was a gravel-littered six feet of shore. To his left, where the creek ran beneath a bridge, he could see where a mass of weeds and mud had gathered over time, and he could see something shiny in their midst.

Elvis eased to the ground inside his walker and sat there and looked at the water churning along. A huge woodpecker laughed in a tree nearby and a jay yelled at a smaller bird to leave his territory.

Where had ole Bubba Ho-Tep gone? Where did he come from? How in hell did he get here?

He recalled what he had seen inside the mummy's mind. The silver bus, the rain, the shattered bridge, the wash of water and mud.

Well, now, wait a minute, he thought. Here we have water and mud and a bridge, though it's not broken, and there's something shiny in the midst of all those leaves and limbs and collected debris. All these items were elements of what he had seen in Bubba Ho-Tep's head. Obviously there was a connection.

But what was it?

When he got his strength back, Elvis pulled himself up and got the walker turned, and worked his way back to the home. He was covered in sweat and stiff as wire by the time he reached his room and tugged himself into bed. The blister on his dick throbbed and he unfastened his pants and eased down his underwear. The blister had refilled with pus, and it looked nastier than usual.

It's a cancer, he determined. He made the conclusion in a certain final rush. They're keeping it from me because I'm old and to them it doesn't matter. They think age will kill me first, and they are probably right.

Well, fuck them. I know what it is, and if it isn't, it might as well be.

He got the salve and doctored the pus-filled lesion, and put the salve away, and pulled up his underwear and pants, and fastened his belt.

Elvis got his TV remote off the dresser and clicked it on while he waited for lunch. As he ran the channels, he hit upon an advertisement for Elvis Presley week. It startled him. It wasn't the first time it had happened, but at the moment it struck him hard. It showed clips from his movies, *Clambake, Roustabout,* several others. All shit movies. Here he was complaining about loss of pride and how life had treated him, and now he realized he'd never had any pride and much of how life had treated him had been quite good, and the bulk of the bad had been his own fault. He wished now he'd fired his manager, Colonel Parker, about the time he got into films. The old fart had been a fool, and he had been a bigger fool for following him. He wished too he had treated Priscilla right. He wished he could tell his daughter he loved her.

Always the questions. Never the answers. Always the hopes. Never the fulfillments.

Elvis clicked off the set and dropped the remote on the dresser just as Jack came into the room. He had a folder under his arm. He looked like he was ready for a briefing at the White House.

"I had the woman who calls herself my niece come get me," he said. "She took me downtown to the newspaper morgue. She's been helping me do some research."

"On what?" Elvis said.

"On our mummy."

"You know something about him?" Elvis asked.

"I know plenty."

Jack pulled a chair up next to the bed, and Elvis used the bed's lift button to raise his back and head so he could see what was in Jack's folder.

Jack opened the folder, took out some clippings, and laid them on the bed. Elvis looked at them as Jack talked.

"One of the lesser mummies, on loan from the Egyptian government, was being circulated across the United States. You know, museums, that kind of stuff. It wasn't a major exhibit, like the King Tut exhibit some years back, but it was of interest. The mummy was flown or carried by train from state to state. When it got to Texas, it was stolen.

"Evidence points to the fact that it was stolen at night by a couple of guys in a silver bus. There was a witness. Some guy walking his dog or something. Anyway, the thieves broke in the museum and stole it, hoping to get a ransom probably. But in came the worst storm in East Texas history. Tornadoes. Rain. Hail. You name it. Creeks and rivers overflowed. Mobile homes were washed away. Livestock drowned. Maybe you remember it. . . . No matter. It was one hell of a flood.

"These guys got away, and nothing was ever heard from them. After you told me what you saw inside the mummy's head—the silver bus, the storm, the bridge, all that—I came up with a more interesting, and I believe, considerably more accurate scenario."

"Let me guess. The bus got washed away. I think I saw it today. Right out back in the creek. It must have washed up there years ago."

"That confirms it. The bridge you saw breaking, that's how the bus got in the water, which would have been as deep then as a raging river. The bus was carried downstream. It lodged somewhere nearby, and the mummy was imprisoned by debris, and recently it worked its way loose."

"But how did it come alive?" Elvis asked. "And how did I end up inside its memories?"

"The speculation is broader here, but from what I've read, sometimes mummies were buried without their names, a curse put on their sarcophagus, or coffin, if you will. My guess is our guy was one of those. While he was in the coffin, he was a drying corpse. But when the bus was washed off the road, the coffin was overturned, or broken open, and our boy was freed of coffin and curse. Or more likely, it rotted open in time, and the holding spell was broken. And think about him down there all that time, waiting for freedom, alive, but not alive. Hungry, and no way to feed. I said he was free of his curse, but that's not entirely true. He's free of his imprisonment, but he still needs souls.

"And now, he's free to have them, and he'll keep feeding unless he's finally destroyed. . . . You know, I think there's a part of him, oddly enough, that wants to fit in. To be human again. He doesn't entirely know what he's become. He responds to some old desires and the new desires of his condition. That's why he's taken on the illusion of clothes, probably copying the dress of one of his victims.

"The souls give him strength. Increase his spectral powers. One of which was to hypnotize you, kinda, draw you inside his head. He couldn't steal your soul that way, you have to be unconscious to have that done to you, but he could weaken you, distract you."

"And those shadows around him?"

"His guardians. They warn him. They have some limited powers of their own. I've read about them in the *Everyday Man or Woman's Book of the Soul*."

"What do we do?" Elvis said.

"I think changing rest homes would be a good idea," Jack said. "I can't think of much else. I will say this. Our mummy is a nighttime kind of guy. 3 A.M., actually. So, I'm going to sleep now, and again after lunch. Set my alarm for before dark so I can fix myself a couple cups of coffee. He comes tonight, I don't want him slapping his lips over my asshole again. I think he heard you coming down the hall about the time he got started on me the other night, and he ran. Not because he was scared, but because he didn't want anyone to find out he's around. Consider it. He has the proverbial bird's nest on the ground here."

After Jack left, Elvis decided he should follow Jack's lead and nap. Of course, at his age, he napped a lot anyway, and could fall asleep at any time, or toss restlessly for hours. There was no rhyme or reason to it.

He nestled his head into his pillow and tried to sleep, but sleep wouldn't come. Instead, he thought about things. Like, what did he really have left in life but this place? It wasn't much of a home, but it was all he had, and he'd be damned if he'd let a foreign, graffiti-writing, soul-sucking sonofabitch in an oversized hat and cowboy boots (with elf toes) take away his family members' souls and shit them down the visitors' toilet.

In the movies he had always played heroic types. But when the stage lights went out, it was time for drugs and stupidity and the coveting of women. Now it was time to be a little of what he had always fantasized being.

A hero.

Elvis leaned over and got hold of his telephone and dialed Jack's room. "Mr. Kennedy," Elvis said when Jack answered. "Ask not what your rest home can do for you. Ask what you can do for your rest home."

"Hey, you're copping my best lines," Jack said.

"Well, then, to paraphrase one of my own, 'Let's take care of business.'"

"What are you getting at?"

"You know what I'm getting at. We're gonna kill a mummy."

The sun, like a boil on the bright blue ass of day, rolled gradually forward and spread its legs wide to reveal the pubic thatch of night, a hairy darkness in which stars crawled like lice, and the moon crabbed slowly upward like an albino dog tick thriving for the anal gulch.

During this slow-rolling transition, Elvis and Jack discussed their plans, then they slept a little, ate their lunch of boiled cabbage and meatloaf, slept some more, ate a supper of white bread and asparagus and a helping of shit on a shingle without the shingle, slept again, awoke about the time the pubic thatch appeared and those starry lice began to crawl.

And even then, with night about them, they had to wait until midnight to do what they had to do.

Jack squinted through his glasses and examined his list. "Two bottles of rubbing alcohol?" Jack said.

"Check," said Elvis. "And we won't have to toss it. Look here." Elvis held up a paint sprayer. "I found this in the storage room."

"I thought they kept it locked," Jack said.

"They do. But I stole a hairpin from Dillinger and picked the lock."

"Great!" Jack said. "Matches?"

"Check. I also scrounged a cigarette lighter."

"Good. Uniforms?"

Elvis held up his white suit, slightly grayed in spots with a chili stain on the front. A white silk scarf and the big gold and silver and ruby-studded belt that went with the outfit lay on the bed. There were zippered boots from K-Mart. "Check."

Jack held up a gray business suit on a hanger. "I've got some nice shoes and a tie to go with it in my room."

"Check," Elvis said.

"Scissors?"

"Check."

"I've got my motorized wheelchair oiled and ready to roll," Jack said, "and I've looked up a few words of power in one of my magic books. I don't know if they'll stop a mummy, but they're supposed to ward off evil. I wrote them down on a piece of paper."

"We use what we got," Elvis said. "Well, then. Two forty-five out back of the place."

"Considering our rate of travel, better start moving about two-thirty," Jack said.

"Jack," Elvis asked. "Do we know what we're doing?"

"No, but they say fire cleanses evil. Let's hope they, whoever they are, is right."

"Check on that too," said Elvis. "Synchronize watches."

They did, and Elvis added: "Remember. The key words for tonight are Caution and Flammable. And Watch Your Ass."

The front door had an alarm system, but it was easily manipulated from the inside. Once Elvis had the wires cut with the scissors, they pushed the compression lever on the door, and Jack shoved his wheelchair outside, and held the door while Elvis worked his walker through. Elvis tossed the scissors into the shrubbery, and Jack jammed a paperback book between the doors to allow them re-entry, should re-entry be an option at a later date.

Elvis was wearing a large pair of glasses with multicolored gem-studded chocolate frames and his stained white jumpsuit with scarf and belt and zippered boots. The suit was open at the front and hung loose on him, except at the belly. To make it even tighter there, Elvis had made up a medicine bag of sorts, and stuffed it inside his jump-suit. The bag contained Kemosabe's mask, Bull's purple heart, and the newspaper clipping where he had first read of his alleged death.

Jack had on his gray business suit with a black-and-red-striped tie knotted carefully at the throat, sensible black shoes, and black nylon socks. The suit fit him well. He looked like a former president.

In the seat of the wheelchair was the paint sprayer, filled with rub-bing alcohol, and beside it, a cigarette lighter and a paper folder of matches. Jack handed Elvis the paint sprayer. A strap made of a strip of torn sheet had been added to the device. Elvis hung the sprayer over his shoulder, reached inside his belt and got out a flattened, half-smoked stogie he had been saving for a special occasion. An occasion he had begun to think would never arrive. He clenched the cigar between his teeth, picked the matches from the seat of the wheelchair, and lit his cigar. It tasted like a dog turd, but he puffed it anyway. He tossed the folder of matches back on the chair and looked at Jack, said, "Let's do it, amigo."

Jack put the matches and the lighter in his suit pocket. He sat down in the wheelchair, kicked the foot stanchions into place and rested his feet on them. He leaned back slightly and flicked a switch on the arm rest. The electric motor hummed, the chair eased forward.

"Meet you there," said Jack. He rolled down the concrete ramp, on out to the circular drive, and disappeared around the edge of the building.

Elvis looked at his watch. It was nearly two forty-five. He had to hump it. He clenched both hands on the walker and started truckin'.

Fifteen exhaustive minutes later, out back, Elvis settled in against the door, the place where Bubba Ho-Tep had been entering and exiting. The shadows fell over him like an umbrella. He propped the paint gun across the walker and used his scarf to wipe the sweat off his forehead.

In the old days, after a performance, he'd wipe his face with it and toss it to some woman in the crowd, watch as she creamed on herself. Panties and hotel keys would fly onto the stage at that point, bouquets of roses.

Tonight, he hoped Bubba Ho-Tep didn't use the scarf to wipe his ass after shitting him down the crapper.

Elvis looked where the circular concrete drive rose up slightly to the right, and there, seated in the wheelchair, very patient and still, was Jack. The moonlight spread over Jack and made him look like a concrete yard gnome.

Apprehension spread over Elvis like a dose of the measles. He thought: *Bubba Ho-Tep comes out of that creek bed, he's going to come out hungry and pissed, and when I try to stop him, he's going to jam this paint gun up my ass, then jam me and that wheelchair up Jack's ass.*

He puffed his cigar so fast it made him dizzy. He looked out at the creek bank, and where the trees gaped wide, a figure rose up like a cloud of termites, scrabbled like a crab, flowed like water, chunked and chinked like a mass of oilfield tools tumbling downhill.

Its eyeless sockets trapped the moonlight and held it momentarily before permitting it to pass through and out the back of its head in irregular gold beams. The figure that simultaneously gave the impression of shambling and gliding appeared one moment as nothing more than a shadow surrounded by more active shadows, then it was a heap of twisted brown sticks and dried mud molded into the shape of a human being, and in another moment, it was a cowboy-hatted, booted thing taking each step as if it were its last.

Halfway to the rest home it spotted Elvis, standing in the dark framework of the door. Elvis felt his bowels go loose, but he determined not to shit his only good stage suit. His knees clacked together like stalks of ribbon cane rattling in a high wind. The dog-turd cigar fell from his lips.

He picked up the paint gun and made sure it was ready to spray. He pushed the butt of it into his hip and waited.

Bubba Ho-Tep didn't move. He had ceased to come forward. Elvis began to sweat more than before. His face and chest and balls were soaked. If Bubba Ho-Tep didn't come forward, their plan was fucked. They had to get him in range of the paint sprayer. The idea was he'd soak him with the alcohol, and Jack would come wheeling down from behind, flipping matches or the lighter at Bubba, catching him on fire.

Elvis said softly, "Come and get it, you dead piece of shit."

Jack had nodded off for a moment, but now he came awake. His flesh was tingling. It felt as if tiny ball bearings were being rolled beneath his skin. He looked up and saw Bubba Ho-Tep paused between the creek bank, himself, and Elvis at the door.

Jack took a deep breath. This was not the way they had planned it. The mummy was supposed to go for Elvis because he was blocking the door. But, no soap.

Jack got the matches and the cigarette lighter out of his coat pocket and put them between his legs on the seat of the chair. He put his hand on the gear box of the wheelchair, gunned it forward. He had to make things happen; had to get Bubba Ho-Tep to follow him, come within range of Elvis's spray gun.

Bubba Ho-Tep stuck out his arm and clotheslined Jack Kennedy. There was a sound like a rifle crack (no question, Warren Commission, this blow was from the front), and over went the chair, and out went Jack, flipping and sliding across the driveway, the cement tearing his suit knees open, gnawing into his hide. The chair, minus its rider, tumbled over and came upright, and still rolling, veered downhill toward Elvis in the doorway, leaning on his walker, spray gun in hand.

The wheelchair hit Elvis's walker. Elvis bounced against the door, popped forward, grabbed the walker just in time, but dropped his spray gun.

He glanced up to see Bubba Ho-Tep leaning over the unconscious Jack. Bubba Ho-Tep's mouth went wide, and wider yet, and became a black toothless vacuum that throbbed pink as a raw wound in the moonlight; then Bubba Ho-Tep turned his head and the pink was not visible. Bubba Ho-Tep's mouth went down over Jack's face, and as

Bubba Ho-Tep sucked, the shadows about it thrashed and gobbled like turkeys.

Elvis used the walker to allow him to bend down and get hold of the paint gun. When he came up with it, he tossed the walker aside, eased himself around, and into the wheelchair. He found the matches and the lighter there. Jack had done what he had done to distract Bubba Ho-Tep, to try and bring him down closer to the door. But he had failed. Yet by accident, he had provided Elvis with the instruments of mummy destruction, and now it was up to him to do what he and Jack had hoped to do together. Elvis put the matches inside his open-chested outfit, pushed the lighter tight under his ass.

Elvis let his hand play over the wheelchair switches, as nimbly as he had once played with studio keyboards. He roared the wheelchair up the incline toward Bubba Ho-Tep, terrified but determined, and as he rolled, in a voice cracking, but certainly reminiscent of him at his best, he began to sing "Don't Be Cruel," and within instants, he was on Bubba Ho-Tep and his busy shadows.

Bubba Ho-Tep looked up as Elvis roared into range, singing. Bubba Ho-Tep's open mouth irised to normal size, and teeth, formerly non-existent, rose up in his gums like little black stumps. Electric locusts crackled and hopped in his empty sockets. He yelled something in Egyptian. Elvis saw the words jump out of Bubba Ho-Tep's mouth in visible hieroglyphics like dark beetles and sticks.

Elvis bore down on Bubba Ho-Tep. When he was in range, he ceased singing, and gave the paint sprayer trigger a squeeze. Rubbing alcohol squirted from the sprayer and struck Bubba Ho-Tep in the face.

Elvis swerved, screeched around Bubba Ho-Tep in a sweeping circle, came back, the lighter in his hand. As he neared Bubba, the shadows swarming around the mummy's head separated and flew high up above him like startled bats.

The black hat Bubba wore wobbled and sprouted wings and flapped away from his head, becoming what it had always been, a living shadow. The shadows came down in a rush, screeching like harpies. They swarmed over Elvis's face, giving him the sensation of skinned animal pelts—blood-side in—being dragged over his flesh.

---

* *"By the unwinking eye of Ra!"*

Bubba bent forward at the waist like a collapsed puppet, bopped his head against the cement drive. His black bat hat came down out of the dark in a swoop, expanding rapidly and falling over Bubba's body, splattering it like spilled ink. Bubba blob-flowed rapidly under the wheels of Elvis's mount and rose up in a dark swell beneath the chair and through the spokes of the wheels and billowed over the front of the chair and loomed upwards, jabbing his ravaged, ever-changing face through the flittering shadows, poking it right at Elvis.

Elvis, through gaps in the shadows, saw a face like an old jack-o'-lantern gone black and to rot, with jagged eyes, nose and mouth. And that mouth spread tunnel wide, and down that tunnel-mouth Elvis could see the dark and awful forever that was Bubba's lot, and Elvis clicked the lighter to flame, and the flame jumped, and the alcohol lit Bubba's face, and Bubba's head turned baby-eye blue, flowed jet-quick away, splashed upward like a black wave carrying a blazing oil slick. Then Bubba came down in a shuffle of blazing sticks and dark mud, a tar baby on fire, fleeing across the concrete drive toward the creek. The guardian shadows flapped after it, fearful of being abandoned.

Elvis wheeled over to Jack, leaned forward and whispered: "Mr. Kennedy."

Jack's eyelids fluttered. He could barely move his head, and something grated in his neck when he did. "The President is soon dead," he said, and his clenched fist throbbed and opened, and out fell a wad of paper. "You got to get him."

Jack's body went loose and his head rolled back on his damaged neck and the moon showed double in his eyes. Elvis swallowed and saluted Jack. "Mr. President," he said.

Well, at least he had kept Bubba Ho-Tep from taking Jack's soul. Elvis leaned forward, picked up the paper Jack had dropped. He read it aloud to himself in the moonlight: "You nasty thing from beyond the dead. No matter what you think and do, good things will never come to you. If evil is your black design, you can bet the goodness of the Light Ones will kick your bad behind."

That's it? thought Elvis. *That's the chant against evil from the* Book of Souls? *Yeah, right, boss. And what kind of decoder ring does that come with? Shit, it doesn't even rhyme well.*

Elvis looked up. Bubba Ho-Tep had fallen down in a blue blaze, but he was rising up again, preparing to go over the lip of the creek, down to wherever his sanctuary was.

Elvis pulled around Jack and gave the wheelchair full throttle. He gave out with a rebel cry. His white scarf fluttered in the wind as he thundered forward.

Bubba Ho-Tep's flames had gone out. He was on his feet. His head was hissing gray smoke into the crisp night air. He turned completely to face Elvis, stood defiant, raised an arm and shook a fist. He yelled, and once again Elvis saw the hieroglyphics leap out of his mouth. The characters danced in a row, briefly—and vanished.

Elvis let go of the protective paper. It was dog shit. What was needed here was action.

When Bubba Ho-Tep saw Elvis was coming, chair geared to high, holding the paint sprayer in one hand, he turned to bolt, but Elvis was on him.

Elvis stuck out a foot and hit Bubba Ho-Tep in the back, and his foot went right through Bubba. The mummy squirmed, spitted on Elvis's leg. Elvis fired the paint sprayer, as Bubba Ho-Tep, himself, and chair went over the creek bank in a flash of moonlight and a tumble of shadows.

Elvis screamed as the hard ground and sharp stones snapped his body like a piñata. He made the trip with Bubba Ho-Tep still on his leg, and when he quit sliding, he ended up close to the creek.

Bubba Ho-Tep, as if made of rubber, twisted around on Elvis's leg, and looked at him.

Elvis still had the paint sprayer. He had clung to it as if it were a life preserver. He gave Bubba another dose. Bubba's right arm flopped way out and ran along the ground and found a hunk of wood that had washed up on the edge of the creek, gripped it, and swung the long arm back. The arm came around and hit Elvis on the side of the head with the wood.

Elvis fell backwards. The paint sprayer flew from his hands. Bubba Ho-Tep was leaning over him. He hit Elvis again with the wood. Elvis

---

* *"Eat the dog dick of Anubis, you ass-wipe!"*

felt himself going out. He knew if he did, not only was he a dead sono-fabitch, but so was his soul. He would be just so much crap; no afterlife for him; no reincarnation; no angels with harps. Whatever lay beyond would not be known to him. It would all end right here for Elvis Presley. Nothing left but a quick flush.

Bubba Ho-Tep's mouth loomed over Elvis's face. It looked like an open manhole. Sewage fumes came out of it.

Elvis reached inside his open jumpsuit and got hold of the folder of matches. Laying back, pretending to nod out so as to bring Bubba Ho-Tep's ripe mouth closer, he thumbed back the flap on the matches, thumbed down one of the paper sticks, and pushed the sulfurous head of the match across the black strip.

Just as Elvis felt the cloying mouth of Bubba Ho-Tep falling down on his kisser like a Venus Flytrap, the entire folder of matches ignited in Elvis's hand, burned him and made him yell.

The alcohol on Bubba's body called the flames to it, and Bubba burst into a stalk of blue flame, singeing the hair off Elvis's head, scorching his eyebrows down to nubs, blinding him until he could see nothing more than a scalding white light.

Elvis realized that Bubba Ho-Tep was no longer on or over him, and the white light became a stained white light, then a gray light, and eventually, the world, like a Polaroid negative developing, came into view, greenish at first, then full of the night's colors.

Elvis rolled on his side and saw the moon floating in the water. He saw too a scarecrow floating in the water, the straw separating from it, the current carrying it away.

No, not a scarecrow. Bubba Ho-Tep. For all his dark magic and ability to shift, or to appear to shift, fire had done him in, or had it been the stupid words from Jack's book on souls? Or both?

It didn't matter. Elvis got up on one elbow and looked at the corpse. The water was dissolving it more rapidly and the current was carrying it away.

Elvis fell over on his back. He felt something inside him grate against something soft. He felt like a water balloon with a hole poked in it.

He was going down for the last count, and he knew it.

But I've still got my soul, he thought. Still mine. All mine. And the folks in Shady Rest, Dillinger, The Blue Yodeler, all of them, they have theirs, and they'll keep 'em.

Elvis stared up at the stars between the forked and twisted boughs of an oak. He could see a lot of those beautiful stars, and he realized now that the constellations looked a little like the outlines of great hieroglyphics. He turned away from where he was looking, and to his right, seeming to sit on the edge of the bank, were more stars, more hieroglyphics.

He rolled his head back to the figures above him, rolled to the right and looked at those. Put them together in his mind.

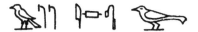

He smiled. Suddenly, he thought he could read hieroglyphics after all, and what they spelled out against the dark beautiful night was simple, and yet profound.

ALL IS WELL.

Elvis closed his eyes and did not open them again.

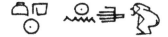

THE END

Thanks to

(Mark Nelson) for translating East Texas "Egyptian" Hieroglyphics.

The Fat Man and the Elephant

For Pat LoBrutto

The signs were set in relay and went on for miles. The closer you got to the place the bigger they became. They were so enthusiastic in size and brightness of paint it might be thought you were driving to heaven and God had posted a sure route so you wouldn't miss it. They read:

WORLD'S LARGEST GOPHER!
ODDITIES!
SEE THE SNAKES! SEE THE ELEPHANT!
SOUVENIRS!
BUTCH'S HIGHWAY MUSEUM AND EMPORIUM!

But Sonny knew he wasn't driving to heaven. Butch's was far from heaven and he didn't want to see anything but the elephant. He had been to the Museum and Emporium many times, and the first time was enough for the sights—because there weren't any.

The World's Largest Gopher was six feet tall and inside a fenced-in enclosure. It cost you two dollars on top of the dollar admission fee to get in there and have a peek at it and feel like a jackass. The gopher was a statue, and it wasn't even a good statue. It looked more like a dog standing on its haunches than a gopher. It had a strained, constipated look on its homely face, and one of its two front teeth had been chipped off by a disappointed visitor with a rock.

The snake show wasn't any better. Couple of dead, stuffed rattlers with the rib bones sticking through their taxidermied hides, and one live, but about to go, cottonmouth who didn't have any fangs and looked a lot like a deflated bicycle tire when it was coiled and asleep. Which was most of the time. You couldn't wake the sonofabitch if you beat on the glass with a rubber hose and yelled FIRE!

There were two main souvenirs. One was the armadillo purses, and the other was a miniature statue of the gopher with a little plaque on it that read: SAW THE WORLD'S LARGEST GOPHER AT BUTCH'S HIGHWAY MUSEUM AND EMPORIUM OFF HIGHWAY 59. And the letters were so crowded on there you had to draw mental slashes between the words. They sold for a dollar fifty apiece and they moved right smart. In fact, Butch made more money on those (75¢ profit per statue) than he did on anything else, except the cold drinks, which he marked up a quarter. When you were hot from a long drive and irritated about actually seeing the World's Largest Gopher, you tended to spend money foolishly on soda waters and gopher statues.

Or armadillo purses. The armadillos came from Hank's Armadillo Farm and Hank was the one that killed them and scooped their guts out and made purses from them. He lacquered the bodies and painted them gold and tossed glitter in the paint before it dried. The 'dillos were quite bright and had little zippers fixed into their bellies and a rope handle attached to their necks and tails so you could carry them upside down with their sad little feet pointing skyward.

Butch's wife had owned several of the purses. One Fourth of July she and the week's receipts had turned up missing along with one of her 'dillo bags. She and the purse and the receipts were never seen again. Elrod down at the Gulf station disappeared too. Astute observers said there was a connection.

But Sonny came to see the elephant, not buy souvenirs or look at dead snakes and statues. The elephant was different from the rest of Butch's stuff. It was special.

It wasn't that it was beautiful, because it wasn't. It was in bad shape. It could hardly even stand up. But the first time Sonny had seen it, he had fallen in love with it. Not in the romantic sense, but in the sense of two great souls encountering one another. Sonny came back time after time to see it when he needed inspiration, which of late, with the money dwindling and his preaching services not bringing in the kind of offerings he thought they should, was quite often.

Sonny wheeled his red Chevy pickup with the GOD LOVES EVEN FOOLS LIKE ME sticker on the back windshield through the gate of Butch's and paid his dollar for admission, plus two dollars to see the elephant.

Butch was sitting at the window of the little ticket house as usual. He was toothless and also wore a greasy, black work cap, though Sonny couldn't figure where the grease came from. He had never known

Butch to do any kind of work, let alone something greasy—unless you counted the serious eating of fried chicken. Butch just sat there in the window of the little house in his zip-up coveralls (summer or winter) and let Levis Garrett snuff drip down his chin while he played with a pencil or watched a fly dive bomb a jelly doughnut. He seldom talked, unless it was to argue about money. He didn't even like to tell you how much admission was. It was like it was some secret you were supposed to know, and when he did finally reveal it, it was as if he had given up part of his heart.

Sonny drove his pickup over to the big barn where the elephant stayed, got out and went inside.

Candy, the ancient clean-up nigger, was shoving some dirt around with a push broom, stirring up dust mostly. When Candy saw Sonny wobble in, his eyes lit up.

"Hello there, Mr. Sonny. You done come to see your elephant, ain't you?"

"Yeah, I have," Sonny said.

"That's good, that's good." Candy looked over Sonny's shoulder at the entrance, then glanced at the back of the barn. "That's good, and you right on time too, like you always is."

Candy held out his hand.

Sonny slipped a five into it and Candy folded it carefully and put it in the front pocket of his faded khakis, gave it a pat like a good dog, then swept up the length of the barn. When he got to the open door, he stood there watching, waiting for Mr. Butch to go to lunch, like he did every day at eleven-thirty sharp.

And sure enough, there he went in his black Ford pickup out the gate of Butch's Museum and Emporium. Then came the sound of the truck stopping and the gate being locked. Butch closed the whole thing down every day for lunch rather than leave it open for the nigger to tend. Anyone inside the Emporium at that time was just shit out of luck. They were trapped there until Butch came back from lunch thirty minutes later, unless they wanted to go over the top or ram the gate with their vehicle.

It wasn't a real problem, however. Customers seldom showed up mid-day, dead of summer. They didn't seem to want to see the World's Largest Gopher at lunchtime.

Which was why Sonny liked to come when he did. He and Candy had an arrangement.

When Candy heard Butch's truck clattering up the highway, he dropped the broom, came back and led Sonny over to the elephant stall.

"He in this one today, Mr. Sonny."

Candy took out a key and unlocked the chain-link gate that led inside the stall and Sonny stepped inside and Candy said what he always said. "I ain't supposed to do this now. You supposed to do all your looking through this gate." Then, without waiting for a reply, he closed the gate behind Sonny and leaned on it.

The elephant was lying on its knees and it stirred slightly. Its skin creaked like tight shoes and its breathing was heavy.

"You wants the usual, Mr. Sonny?"

"Does it have to be so hot this time? Ain't it hot enough in here already?"

"It can be any way you wants it, Mr. Sonny, but if you wants to do it right, it's got to be hot. You know I'm telling the truth now, don't you?"

"Yeah . . . but it's so hot."

"Don't do no good if it ain't, Mr. Sonny. Now we got to get these things done before Mr. Butch comes back. He ain't one for spir'tual things. That Mr. Butch ain't like you and me. He just wants that dollar. You get that stool and sit yourself down, and I'll be back dreckly, Mr. Sonny."

Sonny sat the stool upright and perched his ample butt on it, smelled the elephant shit and studied the old pachyderm. The critter didn't look as if it had a lot of time left, and Sonny wanted to get all the wisdom from it he could.

The elephant's skin was mottled grey and more wrinkled than a bloodhound's. Its tusks had been cut off short years before and they had turned a ripe lemon yellow, except for the jagged tips and they were the color of dung. Its eyes were scummy and it seldom stood anymore, not even to shit. Therefore, its flanks were caked with it. Flies had collected in the mess like raisins spread thickly on rank chocolate icing. When the old boy made a feeble attempt to slap at them with his tail, they rose up en masse like bad omens.

Candy changed the hay the elephant lay on now and then, but not often enough to rid the stall of the stink. With the heat like it was, and the barn being made of tin and old oak, it clung to the structure and the elephant even when the bedding was fresh and the beast had been hosed down. But that was all right with Sonny. He had come to associate the stench with God.

The elephant was God's special animal—shit smell and all. God had created the creature in the same way he had created everything else—with a wave of his majestic hand. (Sonny always imagined the hand bejeweled with rings.) But God had given the elephant something special—which seemed fair to Sonny, since he had put the poor creature in the land of crocodiles and niggers—and that special something was wisdom.

Sonny had learned of this from Candy. He figured since Candy was born of niggers who came from Africa, he knew about elephants. Sonny reasoned that elephant love was just the sort of information niggers would pass down to one another over the years. They probably passed along other stuff that wasn't of importance too, like the best bones for your nose and how to make wooden dishes you could put inside your lips so you could flap them like Donald Duck. But the stuff on the elephants would be the good stuff.

He was even more certain of this when Candy told him on his first visit to see the elephant that the critter was most likely his totem. Candy had taken one look at him and said that. It surprised Sonny a bit that Candy would even consider such things. He seemed like a plain old clean-up nigger to him. In fact, he had hired Candy to work for him before. The sort of work you wanted a nigger to do, hot and dirty. He'd found Candy to be slow and lazy and at the end of the day he had almost denied him the two dollars he'd promised. He could hardly see that he'd earned it. In fact, he'd gotten the distinct impression that Candy was getting uppity in his old age and thought he deserved a white man's wages.

But, lazy or not, Candy did have wisdom—least when it came to elephants. When Candy told him he thought the elephant was his totem, Sonny asked how he had come by that, and Candy said, "You big and the elephant is big, and you both tough-hided and just wise as Old Methus'la. And you can attract them gals just like an ole bull elephant can attract them elephant females, now can't you? Don't lie to Candy now, you know you can."

This was true. All of it. And the only way Candy could have known about it was to know he was like the elephant and the elephant was his totem. And the last thing about attracting the women, well, that was the thing above all that convinced him that the nigger knew his business.

Course, even though he had this ability to attract the women, he had never put it to bad use. That wouldn't be God's way. Some preachers, men of God or not, would have taken advantage of such a gift, but not him. That wouldn't be right.

It did make him wonder about Louise though. Since the Lord had seen fit to give him this gift, why in the world had he ended up with her? What was God's master plan there? She was a right nice Christian woman on the inside, but the outside looked like a four-car pileup. She could use some work.

He couldn't remember what it was that had attracted him to her in the first place. He had even gone so far as to look at old pictures of them together to see if she had gotten ugly slowly. But no, she'd always been that way. He finally had to blame his choice on being a drinking man in them days and a sinner. But now, having lost his liquor store business, and having sobered to God's will and gotten a little money (though that was dwindling), he could see her for what she was.

Fat and ugly.

There, he'd thought it clearly. But he did like her. He knew that. There was something so wonderfully Christian about her. She could recite from heart dozens of Bible verses, and he'd heard her give good argument against them that thought white man came from monkey, and a better argument that the nigger did. But he wished God had packaged her a little better. Like in the body of his next-door neighbor's wife for instance. Now there was a Godly piece of work.

It seemed to him, a man like himself, destined for great things in God's arena, ought to at least have a wife who could turn heads toward her instead of away from her. A woman like that could help a man go far.

There wasn't any denying that Louise had been a big help. When he married her she had all that insurance money, most of which they'd used to buy their place and build a church on it. But the settlement was almost run through now, and thinking on it, he couldn't help but think Louise had gotten cheated.

Seemed to him that if your first husband got kicked to death by a wild lunatic that the nuthouse let out that very afternoon calling him cured, they ought to have to fork up enough money to take care of the man's widow for the rest of her life. And anyone she might remarry, especially if that person had some medical problems, like a trick back, and couldn't get regular work anymore.

Still, they had managed what she had well; had gotten some real mileage out of the four hundred thousand. There was the land and the house and the church and the four hundred red-jacketed, leatherette

Bibles that read in gold, gilt letters on the front: THE MASTER'S OWN BAPTIST MINISTRIES INC., SONNY GUY OFFICIATING. And there were some little odds and ends here and there he couldn't quite recall. But he felt certain not a penny had been wasted. Well, maybe those seven thousand bumper stickers they bought that said GO JESUS on them was a mistake. They should have made certain that the people who made them were going to put glue on the backs so they'd stick to something. Most folks just wouldn't go to the trouble to tape them on the bumpers and back glasses of their automobiles, and therefore weren't willing to put out four-fifty per sticker.

But that was all right. Mistakes were to be expected in a big enterprise. Even if it was for God, The Holy Ghost, and The Lord Jesus Crucified.

Yet, things weren't going right, least not until he started visiting the elephant. Now he had him some guidance and there was this feeling he had that told him it was all going to pay off. That through this creature of the Lord he was about to learn God's *grand-doise plan* for his future. And when he did learn it, he was going to start seeing those offering plates (a bunch of used hubcaps bought cheap from the wrecking yard) fill up with some serious jack.

Candy came back with the electric heater, extension cord and tarp. He had a paper bag in one back pocket, his harmonica in the other. He looked toward the entrance, just in case Butch should decide for the first time in his life to come back early.

But no Butch.

Candy smiled and opened the stall's gate.

"Here we go, Mr. Sonny, you ready to get right with God and the elephant?"

Sonny took hold of the tarp and pulled it over his head and Candy came in and found places to attach all four corners to the fence near the ground and draped it over the old elephant, who squeaked its skin and turned its head ever so slightly and rolled its goo-filled eyes.

"Now you just keep you seat, Mr. Bull Elephant," Candy said, "and we all gonna be happy and ain't none of us gonna get trampled."

Candy stooped back past Sonny on his stool and crawled out from under the tarp and let it fall down Sonny's back to the ground. He got the electric heater and pushed it under the tarp next to Sonny's stool, then he took the extension cord and went around and plugged it into one of the barn's deadly-looking wall sockets. He went back to the tarp and lifted it up and said to Sonny, "You can turn it on now, Mr. Sonny. It's all set up."

Sonny sighed and turned the heater on. The grillwork went pink, then red, and the fan in the machine began to whirl, blowing the heat at him.

Candy, who still had his face under the tarp, said, "You got to lean over it now to get the full effects, Mr. Sonny. Get that heat on you good. Get just as hot as a nigger field hand."

"I know," Sonny said. "I remember how to do it."

"I knows you do, Mr. Sonny. You great for remembering, like an elephant. It heating up in there good?"

"Yeah."

"Real hot?"

"Yeah."

"That's good. Make you wonder how anyone wouldn't want to do good and stay out of hell, don't it, Mr. Sonny? I mean it's hotter under here than when I used to work out in that hot sun for folks like you, and I bet when I drop this here tarp it just gonna get hotter, and then that heat and that stink gonna build up in there and things gonna get right for you . . . Here's you paper bag."

Candy took the bag out of his back pocket and gave it to Sonny. "Remember now," Candy said, "when you get good and full of that shit-smell and that heat, you put this bag over you face and you start blowing like you trying to push a grapefruit through a straw. That gonna get you right for the ole elephant spirit to get inside you and do some talking at you 'cause it's gonna be hot as Africa and you gonna be out of breath just like niggers dancing to drums, and that's how it's got to be."

"Ain't I done this enough to know, Candy?"

"Yes, suh, you have. Just like to earns my five dollars and see a good man get right with God."

Candy's head disappeared from beneath the tarp and when the tarp hit the ground it went dark in there except for the little red lines of the heater grate, and for a moment all Sonny could see was the lumpy shape of the elephant and the smaller lumps of his own knees. He could hear the elephant's labored breathing and his own labored breathing. Outside, Candy began to play nigger music on the harmonica. It filtered into the hot tent and the notes were fire ants crawling over his skin and under his overalls. The sweat rolled down him like goat berries.

After a moment, Candy began to punctuate the harmonica notes with singing. "Sho gonna hate it when the elephant dies. Hot in here, worse than outside, and I'm sho gonna hate it when the elephant dies." A few notes on the harmonica. "Yes, suh, gonna be bad when the pachyderm's dead, ain't gonna have five dollars to buy Coalie's bed." More notes. "Come on brother can you feel the heat. I'm calling to you Jesus, cross my street."

Sonny put the bag over his face and began to blow viciously. He was blowing so hard he thought he would knock the bottom out of the bag, but that didn't happen. He grew dizzy, very dizzy, felt stranger than the times before. The harmonica notes and singing were far away and he felt like a huge hunk of ice cream melting on a hot stone. Then he didn't feel the heat anymore. He was flying. Below him the ribs of the heater were little rivers of molten lava and he was falling toward them from a great height. Then the rivers were gone. There was only darkness and the smell of elephant shit, and finally that went away and he sat on his stool on a sunny landscape covered in tall grass. But he and his stool were taller than the grass, tall as an elephant itself. He could see scrubby trees in the distance and mountains and to the left of him was a blue-green line of jungle from which came the constant and numerous sounds of animals. Birds soared overhead in a sky bluer than a jay's feathers. The air was as fresh as a baby's first breath.

There was a dot in the direction of the mountains and the dot grew and became silver-grey and there was a wink of white on either side of it. The dot became an elephant and the closer it came the more magnificent it looked, its skin tight and grey and its tusks huge and long and porcelain-white. A fire sprang up before the elephant and the grass blazed in a long, hot line from the beast to the stool where Sonny sat. The elephant didn't slow. It kept coming. The fire didn't bother it. The blaze wrapped around its massive legs and licked at its belly like a lover's tongue. Then the elephant stood before him and they were eye to eye; the tusks extended over Sonny's shoulders. The trunk reached out and touched his cheek; it was as soft as a woman's lips.

The smell of elephant shit filled the air and the light went dark and another smell intruded, the smell of burning flesh. Sonny felt pain. He let out a whoop. He had fallen off the stool on top of the heater and the heater had burned his chest above the bib of his overalls.

There was light again. Candy had ripped off the tarp and was pulling him up and sitting him on the stool and righting the electric heater. "Now there, Mr. Sonny, you ain't on fire no more. You get home you get you some shaving cream and put on them burns, that'll make you feel right smart again. Did you have a good trip?"

"Africa again, Candy," Sonny said, the hot day air feeling cool to him after the rancid heat beneath the tarp. "And this time I saw the whole thing. It was all clearer than before and the elephant came all the way up to me."

"Say he did?" Candy said, looking toward the barn door.

"Yeah, and I had a revelation."

"That's good you did, Mr. Sonny. I was afraid you wasn't gonna have it before Mr. Butch come back. You gonna have to get out of here now. You know how Mr. Butch is, 'specially since his wife done run off with that ole 'diller purse and the money that time. Ain't been a fit man to take a shit next to since."

Candy helped Sonny to his feet and guided him out of the stall and leaned him against it.

"A firewalking elephant," Sonny said. "Soon as I seen it, it come to me what it all meant."

"I'm sho glad of that, Mr. Sonny."

Candy looked toward the open door to watch for Butch. He then stepped quickly into the stall, jammed the paper bag in his back pocket and folded up the tarp and put it under his arm and picked the heater up by the handle and carried it out, the cord dragging behind it. He sat the tarp and the heater down and closed the gate and locked it. He looked at the elephant. Except for a slight nodding of its head it looked dead.

Candy got hold of the tarp and the heater again and put them in their place. He had no more than finished when he heard Butch's truck pulling up to the gate. He went over to Sonny and took him by the arm and smiled at him and said, "It sho been a pleasure having you, and the elephant done went and gave you one of them rav'lations too. And the best one yet, you say?"

"It was a sign from God," Sonny said.

"God's big on them signs. He's always sending someone a sign or a bush on fire or a flood or some such thing, ain't he, Mr. Sonny?"

"He's given me a dream to figure on, and in that dream he's done told me some other things he ain't never told any them other preachers."

"That's nice of him, Mr. Sonny. He don't talk to just everyone. It's the elephant connection does it."

Butch drove through the open gate and parked his truck in the usual spot and started for the ticket booth. He had the same forward trudge he always had, like he was pushing against a great wind and not thinking it was worth it.

"The Lord has told me to expand the minds of Baptists," Sonny said.

"That's a job he's given you, Mr. Sonny."

"There is another path from the one we've been taking. Oh, some of the Baptist talk is all right, but God has shown me that firewalking is the correct way to get right with the holy spirit."

"Like walking on coals and stuff?"

"That's what I mean."

"You gonna walk on coals, Mr. Sonny?"

"I am."

"I'd sho like to see that, Mr. Sonny, I really would."

Candy led Sonny out to the pickup and Sonny opened the door and climbed in, visions of firewalking Baptists trucking through his head.

"You gonna do this with no shoes on?" Candy asked, closing the pickup door for Sonny.

"It wouldn't be right to wear shoes. That would be cheating. It wouldn't have a purpose."

"Do you feet a mite better."

Sonny wasn't listening. He found the keys in his overalls and touched the red furrows on his chest that the heater had made. He was proud of them. They were a sign from God. They were like the trenches of fire he would build for his Baptists. He would teach them to walk the trenches and open their hearts and souls and trust their feet to Jesus. And not mind putting a little something extra in the offering plate. People would get so excited he could move those red leatherette Bibles.

"Lord be praised," Sonny said.

"Ain't that the truth," Candy said.

Sonny backed the truck around and drove out of the gate onto the highway. He felt like Moses must have felt when he was chosen to lead the Jews out of the wilderness. But he had been chosen instead to lead the Baptists into a new way of Salvation by forming a firewalking branch of the Baptist church. He smiled and leaned over the steering wheel, letting it touch the hot wounds on his chest. Rows of rich converts somewhere beyond the horizon of his mind stepped briskly through trenches of hot coals, smiling.

A Fine Dark Line

An excerpt

We rode swiftly beneath the light of the partial moon. The shadows of the pine trees fell silent across the road in front of us in dark arrowhead shapes. The air was cool and bats circled overhead diving at bugs. The only sound was the whistling of bicycle tires on concrete, the grind of our chains rolling on their sprockets as we pedaled.

When we came to the abandoned sawmill, we stopped and looked at it. In the moonlight it seemed formidable. I half expected the machinery to start up. Every shadow I saw was, for an instant, a ghostly sawmill worker moving about his job.

"All the sawmill workers I ever knowed was missin' a finger," Richard said. "My daddy's worked sawmill some, and he's missin' a finger on his left hand. Since he whips my ass with the belt in his right, it ain't been a real hindrance to him. 'Sides, a missing piece of finger don't matter if you can make a fist."

"I came to see a ghost," Callie said. "If there is such a thing. I don't want to hear about fingers cut off in sawmills."

"Place where it is is on the other side of the sawmill," Richard said. "Through the woods, down by the tracks. I can't guarantee you'll see anything. But that's where it's supposed to be."

"Through the woods?" Callie said.

"That's right." Richard looked at me. "That's why I didn't want you to bring a girl."

"What's that mean?" Callie asked.

"You sound all frighty. Ooooh, the woods. You might get a bramble in your hair."

"I didn't say I couldn't do it. Wouldn't do it. I merely asked where the ghost was. I'm here to see a ghost, aren't I? You think an old sawmill and some trees are going to stop me?"

"Did Stanley tell you this ghost hasn't got a head?"

"If you're trying to scare me, save it. I assume if I'm frightened by this ghost, if there is a ghost, I'll be just as scared if it has a head or doesn't."

"We'll leave our bikes by the sawmill," Richard said.

We pushed our bikes into the brush by the mill, leaned them against the rotting posts that held up the back wall. Richard looked at Callie, said, "Stanley tell you there's a little dead nigger boy under all that sawdust?"

"Do what?"

Richard paused to tell her the story. I realized in his own damaged way, he was flirting with Callie, trying to impress her.

"I don't believe that story at all," she said. "And I'd rather you not use that word in my presence."

"What word?"

"What you call Negroes."

"Niggers?"

"That's the word."

"Nigger, nigger, nigger."

Callie gave Richard a look that made him move back slightly. In the dark I could feel that look, and I wasn't even the target.

"Let's just go see the ghost," Callie said.

Richard's mouth formed the beginnings of one more smart remark, but he saved it. I thought that a wise decision.

The moonlight lay only on the trail in front of us, the rest of it was sucked up by the darkness between the trees. A night bird called, and a possum, surprised by our presence as we rounded the trail, hissed loudly at us, then scampered away and blended into the woods.

"I almost dirtied my pants," Callie said.

"I even jumped a little," Richard said.

"You jumped a lot," Callie said. "I thought you were going to jump up in my arms."

Before Richard could argue, we heard a sound, like sobbing, then the crunch of something followed by a whacking noise, then more crunching. All of this overlaid with the sobbing.

Richard, who was in front of us, held up his hand, and we stopped. "Step off the path," he said. His voice gave little more sound than the beating of a butterfly's wings.

We hunkered down by a big tree.

"What is that?" Callie asked. "An animal?"

"If it is, it ain't no animal I know of," Richard said. "And I'm in these woods all the time."

"Maybe this animal hasn't been in the woods when you're in them," Callie said. "Until now."

We listened some more. Definitely sobbing. A crunching sound. Then a sound like something smacking at the dirt.

"It's off up in the woods to the right," Richard said.

"It could be the ghost."

"I thought she was by the railroad tracks," I said.

"Maybe she got tired of the railroad tracks."

"That sounds like a man crying," Callie said.

"There's a little trail over on that side of the path," Richard said. "If we're real quiet, we can come out close enough to see what's making the noise."

"Are we sure we want to?" I said.

"We came to see the ghost, didn't we?" Richard said.

"I don't believe it's a ghost," Callie said.

"If we ain't afraid of a ghost," Richard said, "then we ought not be afraid of someone cryin', should we?"

"I suppose not," Callie said.

We got back on the path, went up a ways. Richard led us onto a side trail that was overlapped with brush. We had to bend low to pass along it. It eventually widened, the brush disappeared, and there were just pines planted in a row, awaiting the saw.

Through them we could see something moving. We eased up, staying close to trees. When we finally stopped and squatted down, we saw it was a man. He had his back to us. He was wearing a hat, and he was digging in the dirt. Beside him, on the ground, lay something large wrapped in a blanket. The man was sobbing as he dug.

"It's my daddy," Richard said. "I can tell."

"Why's he crying?" I asked.

"How would I know . . . I ain't never known him to cry. About nothin'."

"You think he's burying money?"

"What money? I can't believe this. I ain't never seen him cry like that."

"Everybody cries," Callie said.

"I ain't never seen my daddy cry," Richard said.

"Now you have," Callie said.

We continued to squat there, whispering, then finally fell silent. Mr. Chapman ceased digging with his shovel, dropped it on the ground, picked up an axe and went to chopping. After a moment, he put the axe down, grabbed the shovel, went back to digging. Finally he tossed the shovel down and dragged the blanket-wrapped object into the hole and started covering it with dirt.

After a time, he patted the ground with the shovel, said a soft prayer, then, with tools in hand, went through the woods sobbing.

"I want to see what it is," Richard said.

"Maybe we ought not," I said.

"If my daddy is cryin' over it," Richard said, "I want to see what it is."

"What do you think, Callie?" I asked.

"It don't matter what neither of you think," Richard said. "I'm gonna have me a look."

We moved cautiously over to the fresh diggings. Richard got down on his knees, began raking back the dirt. We joined him. Obviously, the digging had been hard, marred by all the roots, and that's what the axe had been for; there were pieces of chopped root mixed with the dirt.

There was a wide place above us with no tree limbs and the moonlight came through and landed right on the hole. It showed us what Mr. Chapman had put there. A patchwork quilt.

"That's one of my mother's quilts," Richard said.

"It's very pretty," Callie said. Then looked at me, like: What am I saying?

Richard took hold of the quilt, tugged, but nothing happened. He pulled harder. The blanket moved. A head rolled free, and moonlight fell into its visible, dirt-specked eye.

It was a large dog's head. At first, I thought the head had been severed, but it was merely rolling loosely on the neck.

"It's Butch," Richard said.

"Why is he burying a dog?" Callie asked. "Besides it being dead, of course."

"It's his dog," I said.

"Daddy was cryin' over the dog," Richard said. "He loved Butch. Damn. I didn't know he was dead. He was pretty old. I guess he just keeled over . . . Damn, cryin'."

I noticed Richard was crying as well. His tears in the moonlight looked like balls of amber that had heated up and come loose. They rolled down his face and over his chin. I thought at the time he was crying for Butch. Later I thought different.

"I wouldn't have thought he would have cried for anything. But Butch . . . I'll be damned."

"Maybe we should cover him back up," Callie said.

Richard pulled the quilt around Butch. We shoved the dirt back into the hole, finished by scraping pine straw over the grave with our feet.

"Tomorrow, I'll bring some rocks out here, put them on top," Richard said. "It'll keep the varmints from diggin' him up."

"You want to just go on home?" I said.

Richard shook his head. "No. I guess if I go home Daddy will see me. He may already know I'm gone. If I'm gonna take a beatin', I ought to take it for somethin' I did completely. He wouldn't want to know I seen him cryin', and I damn sure don't want him to know."

A breeze made the pines sigh, as if standing tall made them tired. When we reached the trail the breeze picked up, tossed leaves about, hurtled them past and against us like blinded birds.

As we went, I had the uncanny feeling that someone was following us. That sensation you get of dagger points in the back of your head. When I turned there was nothing but the trees bending and flapping and leaves flying. I wondered if it could be Mr. Chapman out there, watching, or the ghost, or an animal. Or Bubba Joe. Or my imagination.

The trail emptied into a field scraped flat and pocked with gravel. There was a little railway shed there with a big padlock on the door. A little farther out were the rails, glowing like silver ribbons in the moonlight. Even before we were close, you could smell the creosote on the railroad ties. It was strong enough to make your eyes water.

"Where's the ghost?" Callie asked.

"I didn't say she'd be standin' here waitin' on us," Richard said. "'Sides, this ain't where they found her body. It's up a ways. There ain't no guarantee you'll see anything."

We walked to the tracks, crossed, sauntered up to where the woods crept close to the tracks and there was only a bit of a gravel path next to the rails.

"I can't believe I'm out here doing this," Callie said. "I must be crazy."

"I didn't make you come," I said.

"I couldn't let you go by yourself. Jeez Louise, what was I thinking. I could end up never leaving the house again. Daddy just set me free, and here I am again, acting like an idiot. Well, actually, I didn't really do anything the first time."

"You sure have this time," I said.

"Why don't you shut your holes," Richard said. "If we come on the ghost, y'all gonna scare it away."

"If we can scare it, it isn't much of a ghost," Callie said.

I don't know how far we went, but in the woods you could see swampy water and hear huge bullfrogs calling as if through megaphones. The way they splashed in the water, they sounded big as dogs.

"I knowed this colored woman once told me there's a King of Bullfrogs," Richard said.

"A king?" Callie said.

"A great big bullfrog. Said he was once this old nig—colored man, and he got this spell put on him, and he turned into this big black bullfrog. He rules over all the frogs and snakes and swimmin' things."

"Isn't he lucky," Callie said.

"Why'd he get turned into a frog?" I asked.

"He messed with women, and his wife was a witch and she done it 'cause he wouldn't do right."

"Good for her," Callie said.

"He's supposed to steal kids, take them back to the swamp for the frogs to eat."

"Frogs don't have teeth," Callie said.

"They still eat."

"Well, they aren't big enough to eat children," she said.

"Mostly the King Frog eats them. He's got a crown on his head: He looks like a big colored man that squats like a frog. He ain't exactly a man or a frog, but kinda both."

"Maybe Chester would make a nice white frog to complement the black one," Callie said. "He could be the Queen Frog . . . Think you could get me that frog recipe, Richard?"

"I thought you didn't like Chester," I said.

"I don't. I liked him, you think I'd want him to be a frog?"

"Colored man's wife turned him into a frog," Richard said. "Didn't she like him?"

"Not after she turned him into a frog," Callie said.

"Ssshhhhhh," Richard said. "That's her house."

"Whose house?" I asked.

"Hers. Margret's. The girl got her head run over. The one that's a ghost."

A chill went over me. It was strange to think that I was perhaps walking ground she had walked.

Visible through the trees, beyond a stand of slick, slimy water, we could see a small, white clapboard house. The moonlight leaned on it like a thug and made it very bright.

In the distance were other small houses. It was what some called a clapboard community.

"Her mother still lives there. Daddy says she shacks up with a nigger . . . a colored man. She's a whore is what I hear."

"You hear a lot," Callie said.

"What's that mean?"

"It means you hear all kinds of things, but that doesn't mean all, or any of it, is true."

"I tell you, that's the house. That's where Margret lived. Her body with the head cut off was found right around here somewheres. She wasn't that far from home."

"What's that?" I said.

Down the tracks where they bent around the trees and the swampland, I could see something bright. It didn't have a definite color. Sometimes it seemed green, sometimes gold. It moved toward us bobbing up and down, as if it were being dribbled. Then it moved from side to side. Disappeared. Popped back into view and started moving toward us again.

"Someone coming down the tracks," Callie said.

"Where's the someone?" Richard said. "It's the ghost. It's Margret's ghost."

"With a flashlight," Callie said.

The light nodded up and down, crossed over the tracks, floated up a bit, then veered into the woods, hung over the slimy water, came back to the edge of the tracks and moved toward us.

"If it's a flashlight," I said, "whoever is carrying it is very busy. And very acrobatic. And he can walk on water."

The hairs on my neck and arms crawled, and I could feel my scalp constrict.

The light danced along the tracks, went past us.

"What is that?" Callie asked.

"I told you," Richard said. "That's her. The headless ghost. She's out here with a light, looking for her head."

"Where do ghosts get lights?" Callie said. "They go to a store and ask for a light? They buy ghostly flashlights?"

I looked at Callie. She talked cool, but I knew her well enough to know she had been startled.

We watched the light move down the tracks, pop into the woods, dance among the trees and on top of the water. Then, suddenly, it was gone.

I realized I had been holding my breath.

"I don't know if that was a ghost," I said. "But whatever it was, I've had enough. Let's go home."

"Let's stay on this side of the tracks," Callie said. "Maybe we'll see it again."

"I don't want to see it again," Richard said.

"Me neither," I said.

"Oh, don't be such Nellies. Come on."

As we walked it became apparent that in the woods next to us, near the water, something was moving. We all heard it, we stopped to listen, and what was moving stopped as well. I looked at the trees and the glimmer of water between them, but I couldn't see anyone.

We looked at one another, and without so much as a word, started moving again. As we did, the stepping alongside us started up, and this time I saw someone amongst the trees, moving quickly and carefully, darting from tree to tree. If that wasn't enough, to my right, I heard a humming sound.

I turned, glanced. Nothing. But I knew what it was.

The rails. They were humming because a train was approaching.

Callie gave me a look that showed she was finally, and truly, frightened. "Walk faster," she said.

We did. Much faster. So did our companion in the woods. And he was moving close to the edge of the trees, nearer to us. The train's headlight flashed behind us, filled the night with a glow like a second moon. The whistle sounded and I nearly jumped out of my skin.

"Run," Callie said. We broke and ran all out. Whoever, or whatever, was in the woods beside us began running as well; the harder we ran, the harder it ran.

I peered over my shoulder, saw a man lurch out of the woods, start sprinting behind us. I knew in a glance it must be Bubba Joe. His bulk was framed in the light of the train. His hat brim blew back and his coat trailed behind him like the rags of a wraith.

The train was chugging and puffing, popping sparks, blowing its whistle, telling anyone up the way that might listen it was coming fast and would soon cross the trestle bridge.

JOE R. LANSDALE

When it was almost on us, Callie, who was breathing heavy, said, "We got to cross the tracks. We don't, he'll catch us."

She crossed, her long legs flying like those of a grasshopper. I went after her. Richard followed as the train passed and the wind of it blew up the back of my shirt and ruffled my hair. The train charged on, clanked and sparked the rails, filled our nostrils with the stench of charred oil and hot scraped metal.

Our pursuer was left on the other side of the track.

I looked down the track, observed it was a long train awinding. It would be coming for some time before it passed us. I bent over and gulped air and felt as if I were going to throw up. We had missed death by only a few feet. I wanted to grab Callie and start hitting her, and I wanted to grab her and kiss her, because if we hadn't crossed, Bubba Joe, or whoever that was, would have caught us. I don't know what he would have done with us, but he would have caught us.

I said, "I think that was Bubba Joe."

"Could have just been some hobo," Callie said, taking a deep breath.

"I don't care who it was," Richard said. "I'm goin' home, and I don't care if Daddy does catch me and give me a beatin'."

We started walking away, then started running, and pretty soon we were on the wooded trail and the wind and the blowing leaves followed us all the way back to the sawmill. We paused there to get our breath. I looked up at the hanging metal ladder that led up to the upper level of what was left of the mill, heard the chute shift and creak in the breeze.

We got our bikes. Richard rode home. Me and Callie did the same.

Quietly, we put our bikes away, snuck into the house, talked briefly in my room about what we had done and seen. Callie finally wore out and went to bed.

All night I lay awake to look out the crack between the window and water fan, watching to see if Bubba Joe was there. I never saw him, and as the sun crept up, I became too tired to watch and fell asleep.

It was an uneasy sleep, full of the tall dark mill and its creaking sawdust chute. The dancing light that might have been Margret. The black Frog King who should have left other women alone. Bubba Joe. The dead dog in the patchwork quilt. Richard's daddy sobbing, saying a prayer.

Finally, there was the snaky black train, its bright light and shrill whistle, the chill wind from the engine and boxcars as they passed us by.

White Mule, Spotted Pig

Frank's papa, the summer of nineteen hundred and nine, told him right before he died that he had a good chance to win the annual Camp Rapture mule race. He told Frank this 'cause he needed money to keep getting drunk, and he wasn't about to ride no mule himself, fat as he was. If the old man had known he was about to die, Frank figured he would have saved his breath on the race talk and asked for whisky instead, maybe a chaw. But as it was, he said it, and it planted in Frank's head the desire to ride and win.

Frank hated that about himself. Once a thing got into his head he couldn't derail it. He was on the track then, and had to see it to the end. Course, that could be a good trait, but problem was, and Frank knew it, the only things that normally caught up in his head like that and pushed him were bad ideas. Even if he could sense their badness, he couldn't seem to stop their running forward and dragging him with them. He also thought his mama had been right when she told him once that their family was like shit on shoes, the stink of it followed them wherever they went.

But this idea. Winning a mule race. Well, that had some good sides to it. Mainly money.

He thought about what his papa said, and how he said it, and then how, within a few moments, the old man grabbed the bed sheets, moaned once, dribbled some drool, and was gone to wherever it was he was supposed to go, probably a stool next to the devil at fireside.

He didn't leave Frank nothing but an old rundown place with a bit of dried-out corn crop, a mule, a horse with one foot in the grave and the other on a slick spot. And his very own shit to clean out of the sheets, 'cause when the old man let go and departed, he left Frank that present, which was the only kind he had ever given. Something dirty. Something painful. Something shitty.

Frank had to burn the mattress and set fire to the bedclothes, so there really wasn't any real cleaning about it. Then he dug a big hole, and cut roots to do it. Next he had to wrap the old man's naked body in a dirty canvas and put him down and cover him up. It took some work, 'cause the old man must have weighed three hundred pounds, and he wasn't one inch taller than five three if he was wearing boots with dried cow shit on the heels and paper tucked inside them to jack his height. Dragging him along on his dead ass from the house had damn near caused one of Frank's balls to swell up and pop out.

Finished with the burying, Frank leaned against a sickly sweet gum tree and rolled himself a smoke, and thought: Shit, I should have dragged the old man over here on the tarp. Or maybe hitched him up to the mule and dragged his naked ass face down through the dirt. That would have been the way to go, not pulling his guts out.

But, it was done now, and as always, he had used his brain late in the game.

Frank scratched a match on a thumbnail and lit a rolled cigarette and leaned on a sickly sweet gum and smoked and considered. It wasn't that he was all that fond of his old man, but damn if he still didn't in some way want to make him proud, or rather be proud to his memory. He thought: Funny, him not being worth a damn, and me still wanting to please him. Funnier yet, considering the old man used to beat him like a Tom-Tom. Frank had seen him knock mama down once and put his foot on the back of her neck and use his belt to beat her ass while he cussed her for having burned the cornbread. It wasn't the only beating she got, but it was damn sure the champion.

It was shortly after that she decamped with the good horse, a bag of cornmeal, some dried meat and a butcher knife. She also managed, with what Frank thought must have been incredible aim, to piss in one of his old man's liquor jugs. This was discovered by the old man after he took a good strong bolt of the liquor. Cheap as the stuff was he drank, Frank was surprised he could tell the difference, that he had turned out to be such a fine judge of shit liquor.

Papa had ridden out after her on the mule but hadn't found her, which wasn't a surprise, because the only thing Papa had been good at tracking was a whisky bottle or some whore, provided she was practically tied down and didn't cost much. He probably tracked the whores he messed with by the stench.

Back from the hunt, drunk and pissed and empty-handed, Papa had said it was bad enough Frank's mama was a horse and meal thief, but at least she hadn't taken the mule, and frankly, she wasn't that good a cook anyhow.

The mule's name was Rupert, and he could run like his tail was on fire. Papa had actually thought about the mule as a contender for a while, and had put out a little money to have him trained by Leroy, who though short in many departments, and known for having been caught fucking a goat by a half dozen hunters, was pretty good with mules and horses. Perhaps, it could be said he had a way with goats as well. One thing was certain, none of Leroy's stock had testified to the contrary, and only the nanny goats were known to be nervous.

The night after Frank buried his pa, he got in some corn squeezings, and got drunk enough to imagine weasels crawling out from under the floorboards. To clear his head and to relieve his bladder, he went out to do something on his father's grave that would never pass for flowers. He stood there watering, thinking about the prize money and what he would do with it. He looked at the house and the barn and the lot, out to where he could see the dead corn standing in rows like dehydrated soldiers. The house leaned to the left, and one of the windowsills was near on the ground. When he slept at night, he slept on a bed with one side jacked up with flat rocks so that it was high enough and even enough he wouldn't roll out of bed. The barn had one side missing and the land was all rutted from runoff, and had never been terraced.

With the exception of the hill where they grazed their bit of stock, the place was void of grass, and all it brought to mind was brown things and dead things, though there were a few bedraggled chickens who wandered the yard like wild Indians, taking what they could find, even eating one another should one of them keel over dead from starvation or exhaustion. Frank had seen a half dozen chickens go at a weak one lying on the ground, tearing him apart with the chicken still cawing, kicking a leg. It hadn't lasted long. About like a dozen miners at a free lunch table.

Frank smoked his cigarette and thought if he could win that race, he would move away from this shit pile. Sell it to some fool. Move into town and get a job that would keep him. Never again would he look up a mule's ass or fit his hands around the handles on a plow. He was thinking on this while looking up the hill at his mule, Rupert.

The hill was surrounded by a rickety rail fence within which the mule resided primarily on the honor system. At the top of the hill was a bunch of oaks and pines and assorted survivor trees. As Frank watched the sun fall down behind the hill, it seemed as if the limbs of the trees wadded together into a crawling shadow, way the wind blew them and mixed them up. Rupert was clearly outlined near a pathetic persimmon tree from which the mule had stripped the persimmons and much of the leaves.

Frank thought Rupert looked quite noble up there, his mule ears standing high in outline against the redness of the sun behind the dark trees. The world seemed strange and beautiful, as if just created. In that moment Frank felt much older than his years and not so fresh as the world seemed, but ancient and worn like the old Indian pottery he had found while plowing through what had once been great Indian mounds. And now, even as he watched, he noted the sun seemed to darken, as if it were a hot wound turning black from infection. The wind cooled and began to whistle. Frank turned his head to the north and watched as clouds pushed across the fading sky. In instants, all the light was gone and there were just shadows, spitting and twisting in the heavens and filling the hard-blowing wind with the aroma of wet dirt.

When Frank turned again to note Rupert, the mule was still there, but was now little more than a peculiar shape next to the ragged persimmon tree. Had Frank not known it was the mule, he might well have mistaken it for a peculiar rise in the terrain, or a fallen tree lying at an odd angle.

The storm was from the north and blowing west. Thunder boomed and lightning cracked in the dirty sky like snap beans, popped and fizzled like a pissed-on campfire. In that moment, the shadow Frank knew to be Rupert lifted its head, and pointed its dark snout toward the sky, as if in defiance. A bolt of lightning, crooked as a dog's hind leg, and accompanied by a bass-drum blow of thunder, jumped from the heavens and dove for the mule, striking him a perfect white-hot blow on the tip of his nose, making him glow, causing Frank to think that he had in fact seen the inside of the mule light up with all its bones in a row. Then Rupert's head exploded, his body blazed, the persimmon leaped to flames, and the mule fell over in a swirl of heavenly fire and a cannon shot of flying mule shit. The corpse caught a patch of dried grass ablaze. The flames burned in a perfect circle around the corpse and blinked out, leaving a circle of smoke rising skyward.

"Goddamn," Frank said. "Shit."

The cloud split open, let loose of its bladder, pissed all over the hillside and the mule, and not a drop, not one goddamn drop, was thrown away from the hill. The rain just covered that spot, put out the mule and the persimmon tree with a sizzling sound, then passed on, taking darkness, rain, and cool wind with it.

Frank stood there for a long time, looking up the hill, watching his hundred dollars crackle and smoke. Pretty soon the smell from the grilled mule floated down the hill and filled his nostrils.

"Shit," Frank said. "Shit. Shit. Shit."

Late morning, when Frank could finally drag himself out of bed, he went out and caught up the horse, Dobbin, hitched him to a single-tree and some chains, drove him out to where the mule lay. He hooked one of the mule's hind legs to the rigging, and Dobbin dragged the corpse up the hill, between the trees, to the other side. Frank figured he'd just let the body rot there, and being on the other side of the hill, there was less chance of the wind carrying down the smell.

After that, he moped around for a few days, drank enough to see weasels again, and then had an idea. His idea was to seek out Leroy, who had been used to train Rupert. See if he could work a deal with him.

Frank rode Dobbin over to Leroy's place, which was as nasty as his own. More so, due to the yard being full not only of chickens and goats, but children. He had five of them, and when Frank rode up, he saw them right away, running about, raising hell in the yard, one of them minus pants, his little johnson flopping about like a grub worm on a hot griddle. He could see Leroy's old lady on the porch, fat and nasty with her hair tied up. She was yelling at the kids and telling them how she was going to kill them and feed them to the chickens. One of the boys, the ten-year-old, ran by the porch whooping, and the Mrs., moving deftly for such a big woman, scrambled to the edge of the porch, stuck her foot out, caught him one just above the waist and sent him tumbling. He went down hard. She laughed like a lunatic. The boy got up with a bloody nose and ran off across the yard and into the woods, screaming.

Frank climbed down from Dobbin and went over to Leroy, who was sitting on a bucket in the front yard whittling a green limb with a knife big enough to sword fight. Leroy was watching his son retreat into the greenery. As Frank came up, leading Dobbin, Leroy said, "Does that all the time. Sometimes, though, she'll throw something at him. Good thing wasn't nothing lying about. She's got a pretty good throwin' arm on her. Seen her hit a seed salesman with a tossed frying pan from the porch there to about where the road meets the property. Knocked him down and knocked his hat off. Scattered his seed samples, which the chickens ate. Must have laid there for an hour afore he got up and wandered off. Forgot his hat. Got it on my head right now, though I had to put me some newspaper in the band to make it fit."

Wasn't nothing Frank could say to that, so he said, "Leroy, Rupert got hit by lightning. Right in the head."

"The head?"

"Wouldn't have mattered had it been the ass. It killed him deader than a post and burned him up."

"Damn. That there is a shame," Leroy said, and stopped whittling. He pushed the seed salesman's hat up on his forehead to reveal some forks of greasy brown hair. Leroy studied Frank. "Is there something I can do for you? Or you come around to visit?"

"I'm thinking you might could help me get a mule and get back in the race."

"Mules cost."

"I know. Thought we might could come up with something. And if we could, and we won, I'd give you a quarter of the prize money."

"I get a quarter for grooming folks' critters in town."

"I mean a quarter of a hundred. Twenty-five dollars."

"I see. Well, I am your man for animals. I got a knack. I can talk to them like I was one of them. Except for chickens. Ain't no one can talk to chickens."

"They're birds."

"That there is the problem. They ain't animal enough."

Frank thought about Leroy and the fucked goat. Wondered what Leroy had said to the goat as way of wooing it. Had he told her something special? I think you got a good-looking face? I love the way your tail wiggles when you walk? It was a mystery that Frank actually wasn't all that anxious to unravel.

"I know you run in the circles of them that own or know about mules," Frank said. "Why I thought you maybe could help me."

Leroy took off the seed salesman's hat, put it on his knee, threw his knife in the dirt, let the whittling stick fall from his hand. "I could sneak up on an idea or two. Old man Torrence, he's got a mule he's looking to sell. And by his claim, it's a runner. He ain't never ridden it himself, but he's had it ridden. Says it can run."

"There's that buying stuff again. I ain't got no real money."

"Takes money to make money."

"Takes money to have money."

Leroy put the seed salesman's hat back on. "You know, we might could ask him if he'd rent out his mule. Race is a ways off yet, so we could get some good practice in. You being about a hundred and twenty-five pounds, you'd make a good rider."

"I've ridden a lot. I was ready on Rupert, reckon I can get ready on another mule."

"Deal we might have to make is, we won the race, we bought the mule afterwards. That might be the way he'd do it."

"Buy the mule?"

"At a fair price."

"How fair?"

"Say twenty-five dollars."

"That's a big slice of the prize money. And a mule for twenty-five, that's cheap."

"I know Torrence got the mule cheap. Fella that owed him made a deal. Besides, times is hard. So they're selling cheap. Cost more, we can make extra money on side bets. Bet on ourselves. Or if we don't think we got a chance, we bet against ourselves."

"I don't know. We lose, it could be said we did it on purpose."

"I can get someone to bet for us."

"Only if we bet to win. I ain't never won nothing or done nothing right in my life, and I figure this here might be my chance."

"You gettin' Jesus?"

"I'm gettin' tired," Frank said.

There are no real mountains in East Texas, and only a few hills of consequence, but Old Man Torrence lived at the top of a big hill that was called with a kind of braggart's lie, Barrow Dog Mountain. Frank had no idea who Barrow or Dog were, but that was what the big hill had been called for as long as he remembered, probably well before he was born. There was a ridge at the top of it that overlooked the road below. Frank found it an impressive sight as he and Leroy rode in on Dobbin, he at the reins, Leroy behind him.

It was pretty on top of the hill too. The air smelled good, and flowers grew all about in red, blue and yellow blooms, and the cloudless sky was so blue you felt as if a great lake were falling down from the heavens. Trees fanned out bright green on either side of the path, and near the top, on a flat section, was Old Man Torrence's place. It was made of cured logs, and he had a fine chicken coop that was built straight and true. There were hog pens and a nice barn of thick cured logs with a roof that had all of its roofing slats. There was a sizable garden that rolled along the top of the hill, full of tall bright green cornstalks, so tall they shaded the rows between them. There was no grass between the rows, and the dirt there looked freshly laid by. Squash and all manner of vegetables exploded out of the ground alongside the corn, and there were little clumps of beans and peas growing in long pretty rows.

In a large pen next to the barn was a fifteen-hands-high chocolate-colored mule, prettiest thing Frank had ever seen in the mule-flesh department. Its ears stood up straight, and it gave Frank and Leroy a snort as they rode in.

"He's a big one," Leroy said.

"Won't he be slow, being that big?" Frank asked.

"Big mule's also got big muscles, he's worked right. And he looks to have been worked right. Got enough muscles, he can haul some freight. Might be fast as Rupert."

"Sure faster right now," Frank said.

As they rode up, they saw Old Man Torrence on the front porch with his wife and three kids, two boys and a girl. Torrence was a fat, ruddy-faced man. His wife was a little plump, but pretty. His kids were all nice looking and they had their hair combed and, unlike Leroy's kids, looked clean. As if they might bathe daily. As they got closer, Frank could see that none of the kids looked whacked on. They seemed to be laughing at something the mother was saying. It certainly was different than from his own upbringing, different from Leroy's place. Wasn't anyone tripping anyone, cussing, tossing frying pans, threatening to cripple one another or put out an eye. Thinking on this, Frank felt something twist around inside of him like some kind of serpent looking for a rock to slide under. He and Leroy got off Dobbin and tied him to a little hitching post that was built out front of the house, took off their hats, and walked up to the steps.

After being offered lemonade, which they turned down, Old Man Torrence came off the porch, ruffling one of his kids' hair as he did. He smiled back at his wife, and then walked with Frank and Leroy out toward the mule pen, Leroy explaining what they had in mind.

"You want to rent my mule? What if I wanted to run him?"

"Well, I don't know," Leroy said. "It hadn't occurred to me you might. You ain't never before, though I heard tell he was a mule could be run."

"It's a good mule," Torrence said. "Real fast."

"You've ridden him?" Frank asked.

"No. I haven't had the pleasure. But my brother and his boys have. They borrow him from time to time, and they thought on running him this year. Nothing serious. Just a thought. They say he can really cover ground."

"Frank here," Leroy said, "he plans on entering, and we would rent your mule. If we win, we could give you a bit of the prize money. What say we rent him for ten, and if he wins, we give you another fifteen. That way you pick up twenty-five dollars."

Frank was listening to all this, thinking: and then I owe Leroy his share; this purse I haven't won is getting smaller and smaller.

"And what if you don't win?" Torrence said.

"You've made ten dollars," Leroy said.

"And I got to take the chance my mule might go lame or get hurt or some such. I don't know. Ten dollars, that's not a lot of money for what you're asking. It ain't even your mule."

"Which is why we're offering the ten dollars," Leroy said.

They went over and leaned on the fence and looked at the great mule, watched his muscles roll beneath his chocolate flesh as he trotted nervously about the pen.

"He looks excitable," Frank said.

"Robert E. Lee has just got a lot of energy is all," Torrence said.

"He's named Robert E. Lee?" Frank asked.

"Best damn general ever lived. Tell you boys what. You give me twenty-five, and another twenty-five if he wins, and you got a deal."

"But I give you that, and Leroy his share, I don't have nothing hardly left."

"You ain't got nothing at all right now," Torrence said.

"How's about," Leroy said, "we do it this way. We give you fifteen, and another fifteen if he wins. That's thirty. Now that's fair for a rented mule. Hell, we might could go shopping, buy a mule for twenty-five, and even if he don't win, we got a mule. He don't race worth a damn, we could put him to plow."

Old Man Torrence pursed his lips. "That sounds good. All right," he said, sticking out his hand, "deal."

"Well, now," Frank said, not taking the hand. "Before I shake on that, I'd like to make sure he can run. Let me ride him."

Old Man Torrence withdrew his hand and wiped it on his pants as if something had gotten on his palm. "I reckon I could do that, but seeing how we don't have a deal yet, and ain't no fifteen dollars has changed hands, how's about I ride him for you. So you can see."

Frank and Leroy agreed, and watched from the fence as Torrence got the equipment and saddled up Robert E. Lee. Torrence walked Robert E. Lee out of the lot, and onto a pasture atop the hill, where the overhang was. The pasture was huge and the grass was as green as Ireland. It was all fenced in with barbed wire strung tight between deeply planted posts.

"I'll ride him around in a loop. Once slow, and then real fast toward the edge of the overhang there, then cut back before we get there. I ain't got a pocket watch, so you'll have to be your own judge."

Torrence swung into the saddle. "You boys ready?"

"Let'er rip," Leroy said.

Old Man Torrence gave Robert E. Lee his heels. The mule shot off so fast that Old Man Torrence's hat flew off, and Leroy, in sympathy, took hold of the brim of the seed salesman's hat, as if Robert E. Lee's lunge might blow it off his head.

"Goddamn," Leroy said. "Look how low that mule is to the ground. He's gonna have the grass touching his belly."

And so the mule ran, and as it neared the barbed-wire fence, Old Man Torrence gave him a tug, to turn him. But, Robert E. Lee wasn't having any. His speed picked up, and the barbed-wire fence came closer.

Leroy said, "Uh-oh."

Robert E. Lee hit the fence hard. So hard it caused his head to dip over the top wire and his ass to rise up as if he might be planning a headstand. Over the mule flipped, tearing loose the fence, causing a strand of wire to snap and strike Old Man Torrence, and then Torrence was thrown ahead of the tumbling mule. Over the overhang. Out of sight. The mule did in fact do a headstand, landed hard that way, its hind legs high in the air, wiggling. For a moment, it seemed as if he might hang there, and then, Robert E. Lee lost his headstand and went over after his owner.

"Damn," Leroy said.

"Damn," Frank said.

They both ran toward the broken fence. When they got there Frank hesitated, not able to look. He glanced away, back across the bright green field.

Leroy scooted up to the cliff's edge and took a gander, studied what he saw for a long time.

"Well?" Frank said, finally turning his head back to Leroy.

"Robert E. Lee just met his Gettysburg. And Old Man Torrence is somewhere between Gettysburg and Robert E. Lee. Actually, you can't tell which is which. Mule, Gettysburg, or Old Man Torrence. It's all kind of bunched up."

When Frank and Leroy got down there, which took some considerable time, as they worked their way down a little trail on foot, they discovered that Old Man Torrence had been lucky in a fashion. He had landed in sand, and the force of Robert E. Lee's body had driven him down deep into it, his nose poking up and out enough to take in air. Robert E. Lee was as dead as a three-penny nail, and his tail was stuck up in the air and bent over like a flag that had been broken at the staff. The wind moved the hairs on it a little.

Frank and Leroy went about digging Old Man Torrence out, starting first with his head so he could really breathe well. When Torrence spat enough sand out of his mouth, he looked up and said, "You sonsofbitches. This is your fault."

"Our fault?" Leroy said. "You was riding him."

"You goat-fucking sonofabitch, get me out of here."

Leroy's body sagged a little. "I knew that was gonna get around good. Ain't nobody keeps a secret. There was only that one time too, and them hunters had to come up on me."

They dug Torrence out from under the mule, and Frank went up the trail and got Old Dobbin and rode to the doctor. When Frank got back with the sawbones, Torrence was none the happier to see him. Leroy had gone off to the side to sit by himself, which to Frank meant the goat had come up again.

Old Man Torrence was mostly all right, but he blamed Frank and Leroy, especially Leroy, from then on. And he walked in a way that when he stepped with his right leg, it always looked as if he were about to bend over and tie his shoe. Even in later years, when Frank saw him, he went out of his way to avoid him, and Leroy dodged him like the smallpox, not wanting to hear reference to the goat.

But in that moment in time, the important thing to Frank was simply that he was still without a mule. And the race was coming closer.

That night, as Frank lay in his sagging bed, looking out from it at the angled wall of the room, listening to the crickets saw their fiddles outside and inside the house, he closed his eyes and remembered how Old Man Torrence's place had looked. He saw himself sitting with the pretty plump wife and the clean, polite kids. Then he saw himself with the wife inside that pretty house, on the bed, and he imagined that for a long time.

It was a pleasant thought, the wife and the bed, but even more pleasant was imagining Torrence's place as his. All that greenery and high-growing corn and blooming squash and thick pea and bean vines dripping with vegetables. The house and the barn and the pasture. And in his dream, the big mule, alive, not yet a confusion of bones and flesh and fur, the tail a broken flag.

He thought then of his mother, and the only way he could remember her was with her hair tied back and her face sweaty and both of her eyes blacked. That was how she had looked the last time he had seen her, right before she run off with a horse and some cornmeal and a butcher knife. He wondered where she was, and if she now lived in a place where the buildings were straight and the grass was green and the corn was tall.

After a while he got up and peed out the window, and smelled the aroma of other nights drifting up from the ground he had poisoned with his water, and thought: I am better than Papa. He just peed in the corner of the room and shit out the window, splattering it all down the side of the house. I don't do that. I pee out the window, but I don't shit, and I don't pee in the corner. That's a step up. I go outside for the messy business. And if I had a good house, I wouldn't do this. I'd use the slop jar. I'd go to the privy.

That didn't stop him from finishing his pee, thinking about what he would do or ought to do as far as his toilet habits went. Besides, peeing was the one thing he was really good at. He could piss like a horse and from a goodly distance. He had even won money on his ability. It was the one thing his father had been proud of. "My son, Frank. He can piss like a racehorse. Get it out, Frank. Show them."

And he would.

But, compared to what he wanted out of life, his ability to throw water from his johnson didn't seem all that wonderful right then.

Frank thought he ought to call a halt to his racing plans, but like so many of his ideas, he couldn't let it go. It blossomed inside of him until he was filled with it. Then he was obsessed with an even wilder plan. A story he had heard came back to him, and ran 'round inside his head like a greased pig.

He would find the White Mule and capture it and run it. It was a mule he could have for free, and it was known to be fast, if wild. And, of course, he would have to capture its companion, the Spotted Pig. Though, he figured, by now, the pig was no longer a pig, but a hog, and the mule would be three, maybe four years old.

If they really existed.

It was a story he had heard for the last three years or so, and it was told for the truth by them who told him, his Papa among them. But if drinking made him see weasels oozing out of the floorboards, it might have made Papa see white mules and spotted pigs on parade. But the story wasn't just Papa's story. He had heard it from others, and it went like this:

Once upon a time, there was this pretty white mule with pink eyes, and the mule was fine and strong and set to the plow early on, but he didn't take to it. Not at all. But the odder part of the story was that the mule took up with a farm pig, and they became friends. There was no explaining it. It happened now and then, a horse or mule adopting their own pet, and that was what had happened with the white mule and the spotted pig.

When Frank had asked his Papa, why would a mule take up with a pig, his father had said: "Ain't no explaining. Why the hell did I take up with your mother?"

Frank thought the question went the other way, but the tale fascinated him, and his papa was just drunk enough to be in a good mood. Another pint swallowed, he'd be kicking his ass or his mama's. But he pushed while he could, trying to get the goods on the tale, since outside of worrying about dying corn and sagging barns, there wasn't that much in life that thrilled him.

The story his papa told him was the farmer who owned the mule, and no one could ever put a name to who that farmer was, had supposedly found the mule wouldn't work if the pig wasn't around, leading him between the rows. The pig was in front, the mule plowed fine. The pig wasn't there, the mule wouldn't plow.

This caused the farmer to come up with an even better idea. What would the mule do if the pig was made to run? So the farmer got the mule all saddled, and had one of his boys put the pig out front of the mule and swat it with a knotted plow line, and away went the pig and away went the white mule. The pig pretty soon veered off, but the mule, once set to run, couldn't stop, and would race so fast that the only way it halted was when it was tuckered out. Then it would go back to the start, and look for its pig. Never failed.

One night the mule broke loose, kicked the pig's pen down, and he and the pig, like Jesse and Frank James, headed for the hills. Went into the East Texas greenery and wound in amongst the trees, and were lost to the farmer. Only to be seen after that in glimpses and in stories that might or might not be true. Stories about how they raided cornfields and ate the corn and how the mule kicked down pens and let hogs and goats and cattle go free.

The White Mule and the Spotted Pig. Out there. On the run. Doing whatever it was that white mules and spotted pigs did when they weren't raiding crops and freeing critters.

Frank thought on this for a long time, saddled up Dobbin and rode over to Leroy's place. When Frank arrived, Leroy was out in the yard on his back, unconscious, the seed salesman's hat spun off to the side, and was being moved around by a curious chicken. Finding Leroy like this didn't frighten Frank any. He often found Leroy that way, cold as a wedge from drink, or the missus having snuck up behind him with a stick of stove wood. They were rowdy, Leroy's bunch.

The missus came out on the porch and shook her fist at Frank, and not knowing anything else to do, he waved. She spat a stream of brown tobacco off the porch in his direction and went inside. A moment later one of the kids bellowed from being whapped, and there was a sound like someone slamming a big fish on flat ground. Then silence.

Frank bent down and shook Leroy awake. Leroy cursed, and Frank dragged him over to an overturned bucket and sat him up on it, asked him, "What happened?"

"Missus come up behind me. I've got so I don't watch my back enough."

"Why'd she do it?"

"Just her way. She has spells."

"You all right?"

"I got a headache."

Frank went straight to business. "I come to say maybe we ain't out of the mule business."

"What you mean?"

Frank told him about the mule and the pig, about his idea.

"Oh, yeah. Mule and pig are real. I've seen 'em once myself. Out hunting. I looked up, and there they were at the end of a trail, just watching. I was so startled, I just stood there looking at them."

"What did they do?"

"Well, Frank, they ran off. What do you think? But it was kind of funny. They didn't get in no hurry, just turned and went around the trail, showing me their ass, the pig's tail curled up and a little swishy, and the mule swatting his like at flies. They just went around that curve in the trail, behind some oaks and blackberry vines, and they was gone. I tracked them a bit, but they got down in a stream and walked it. I could find their tracks in the stream with my hands, but pretty soon the whole stream was brown with mud, and they come out of it somewhere I didn't find, and they was gone like a swamp fog come noon."

"Was the mule really white?"

"Dirty a bit, but white. Even from where I was standing, just bits of light coming in through the trees, I could see he had pink eyes. Story is, that's why he don't like to come out in day much, likes to stay in the trees, and do his crop raiding at night. Say the sun hurts his skin."

"That could be a drawback."

"You act like you got him in a pen somewhere."

"I'd like to see if I could get hold of him. Story is, he can run, and he needs the pig to do it."

"That's the story. But stories ain't always true. I even heard stories about how the pig rides the mule, and that the mule is stump broke, and the pig climbs up on a stump and diddles the mule in the ass. I've heard all manner of tale, and ain't maybe none of it got so much as a nut of truth in it. Still, it's one of them ideas that kind of appeals to me. Course, you know, we might catch that mule and he might not can run at all. Maybe all he can do is sneak around in the woods and eat corn crops."

"Well, it's all the idea I got," Frank said, and the thought of that worried Frank more than a little. He considered on his knack for clinging to bad notions like a rutting dog hanging on to a fella's leg. But, like the dog, he was determined to finish what he started.

"So what you're saying here," Leroy said, "is you want to capture the mule, and the pig, so the mule has got his helpmate. And you want to ride the mule in the race?"

"That's what I said."

Leroy paused for a moment, rubbed the knot on the back of his noggin. "I think we should get Nigger Joe to help us track him. We want him, that's the way we do it. Nigger Joe catches him, and we'll break him, and you can ride him."

Nigger Joe was part Indian and part Irish and part Negro. His skin was somewhere between brown and red and he had a red cast to his kinky hair and strawberry freckles and bright green eyes. But the black blood named him, and he himself went by the name Nigger Joe.

He was supposed to be able to track a bird across the sky, a fart across the yard. He had two women that lived with him and he called them his wives. One of them was a Negro, and the other one was part Negro and Cherokee. He called the black one Sweetie, the red and black one Pie.

When Frank and Leroy rode up double on Dobbin, and stopped in Nigger Joe's yard, a rooster was fucking one of the hens. It was a quick matter, and a moment later the rooster was strutting across the yard like he was ten foot tall and bullet proof.

They got off Dobbin, and no sooner had they hit the ground, than Nigger Joe was beside them, tall and broad shouldered with his freckled face.

"Damn, man," Frank said, "where did you come from?"

Nigger Joe pointed in an easterly direction.

"Shit," Leroy said, "coming up on a man like that could make him bust a heart."

"Want something?" Nigger Joe asked.

"Yeah," Leroy said. "We want you to help track the White Mule and the Spotted Pig, 'cause Frank here, he's going to race him."

"Pig or mule?" Nigger Joe asked.

"The mule," Leroy said. "He's gonna ride the mule."

"Eat the pig?"

"Well," Leroy said, continuing his role as spokesman, "not right away. But there could come a point."

"He eats the pig, I get half of pig," Nigger Joe said.

"If he eats it, yeah," Leroy said. "Shit, he eats the mule, he'll give you half of that."

"My women like mule meat," Nigger Joe said. "I've eat it, but it don't agree with me. Horse is better," and to strengthen his statement, he gave Dobbin a look over.

"We was thinking," Leroy said, "we could hire you to find the mule and the pig, capture them with us."

"What was you thinking of giving me, besides half the critters if you eat them?"

"How about ten dollars?"

"How about twelve?"

"Eleven."

"Eleven-fifty."

Leroy looked at Frank. Frank sighed and nodded, stuck out his hand. Nigger Joe shook it, then shook Leroy's hand.

Nigger Joe said, "Now, mule runs like the rock, that ain't my fault. I get the eleven-fifty anyway."

Frank nodded.

"Okay, tomorrow morning," Nigger Joe said, "just before light, we'll go look for him real serious and then some."

"Thing does come to me," Frank said, "is haven't other folks tried to get hold of this mule and pig before? Why are you so confident?"

Nigger Joe nodded. "They weren't Nigger Joe."

"You could have tracked them before on your own," Frank said. "Why now?"

Nigger Joe looked at Frank. "Eleven-fifty."

In the pre-dawn light, down in the swamp, the fog moved through the trees like someone slow-pulling strands of cotton from cotton bolls. It wound its way amongst the limbs that were low down, along the ground. There were wisps of it on the water, right near the bank, and as Frank and Leroy and Nigger Joe stood there, they saw what looked like dozens of sticks rise up in the swamp water and move along briskly.

Nigger Jim said, "Cottonmouth snakes. They going with they heads up, looking for anything foolish enough to get out there. You swimming out there now, pretty quick you be bit good and plenty and swole up like old tick. Only you burst all over and spill green poison, and die. Seen it happen."

"Ain't planning on swimming," Frank said.

"Watch your feet," Nigger Joe said. "Them snakes is thick this year. Them cottons and them copperheads. Cottons, they always mad."

"We've seen snakes," Leroy said.

"I know it," Nigger Joe said, "but where we go, they are more than a few, that's what I'm trying to tell you. Back there where mule and pig hides, it's thick in snakes and blackberry vines. And the trees thick like the wool on a sheep. It a goat or a sheep you fucked?"

"For Christ sakes," Leroy said. "You heard that too?"

"Wives talk about it when they see you yesterday. There the man who fuck a sheep, or a goat, or some such. Say you ain't a man can get pussy."

"Oh, hell," Leroy said.

"So, tell me some," Nigger Joe said. "Which was it, now?"

"Goat," Leroy said.

"That is big nasty," Nigger Joe said, and started walking, leading them along a narrow trail by the water. Frank watched the cottonmouth snakes swim on ahead, their evil heads sticking up like some sort of water-devil erections.

The day grew hot and the trees held the hot and made it hotter and made it hard to breathe, like sucking down wool and chunks of flannel. Frank and Leroy sweated their clothes through and their hair turned to wet strings. Nigger Joe, though sweaty, appeared as fresh as a virgin in spring.

"Where you get your hat?" Nigger Joe asked Leroy suddenly, when they stopped for a swig from canteens.

"Seed salesman. My wife knocked him out and I kept the hat."

"Huh, no shit?" Nigger Joe took off his big old hat and waved around. "Bible salesman. He told me I was gonna go to hell, so I beat him up, kept his hat. I shit in his Bible case."

"Wow, that's mean," Frank said.

"Him telling me I'm going to hell, that make me real mad. I tell you that to tell you not to forget my eleven-fifty. I'm big on payment."

"You can count on us if we win," Frank said.

"No. You owe me eleven-fifty win or lose." Nigger Joe said, putting his hat back carefully on his head, looking at the two smaller men like a man about to pick a hen for neck wringing and Sunday dinner.

"Sure," Frank said. "Eleven-fifty, win or lose. Eleven-fifty when we get the pig and the mule."

"Now that's the deal as I see it," Nigger Joe said. "I tell women it's eight dollars, that way I make some whisky money. Nigger Joe didn't get up yesterday. No, he didn't. And when he gets up, he got Bible salesman's hat on."

They waded through the swamp and through the woods for some time, and just before dark, Nigger Joe picked up on the mule's unshod tracks. He bent down and looked at them. He said, "We catch him, he's gonna need trimming and shoes. Not enough rock to wear them down. Soft sand and swamp. And here's the pig's tracks. Hell, he's big. Tracks say, three hundred pounds. Maybe more."

"That's no pig," Leroy said. "That's a full-blown hog."

"Damn," Frank said. "They're real."

"But can he race?" Leroy said. "And will the pig cooperate?"

They followed the tracks until it turned dark. They threw up a camp, made a fire, and made it big so the smoke was strong, as the mosquitoes were everywhere and hungry and the smoke kept them off a little. They sat there in the night before the fire, the smoke making them cough, watching it churn up above them, through the trees. And up there, as if resting on a limb, was a piece of the moon.

They built the fire up big one last time, turned into their covers, and tried to sleep. Finally, they did, but before morning, Frank awoke, his bladder full, his mind as sharp as if he had slept well. He got up and stoked up the fire, and walked out a few paces in the dark and let it fly. When he looked up to button his pants, he saw through the trees, across a stretch of swamp water, something moving.

He looked carefully, because whatever it was had stopped. He stood very still for a long time, and finally what he had seen moved again. He thought at first it was a deer, but no. There was enough light from the early rising sun knifing through the trees that he could now see clearly what it was.

The White Mule. It stood between two large trees, just looking at him, its head held high, its tall ears alert. The mule was big. Fifteen hands high, like Robert E. Lee, and it was big-chested, and its legs were long. Something moved beside it.

The Spotted Pig. It was big and ugly, with one ear turned up and one ear turned down. It grunted once, and the mule snorted, but neither moved.

Frank wasn't sure what to do. He couldn't go tearing across the stretch of swamp after them, since he didn't know how deep it was, and what might be waiting for him. Gators, snakes and sinkholes. And by the time he woke up the others, the mule and hog would be gone. He just stood there instead, staring at them. This went on for a long time, and finally the hog turned and started moving away, behind some thicket. The mule tossed its head, turned and followed.

My God, thought Frank. The mule is beautiful. And the hog, he's a pistol. He could tell that from the way it had grunted at him. He had some strange feelings inside of him that he couldn't explain. Some sensation of having had a moment that was greater than any moment he had had before.

He thought it strange these thoughts came to him, but he knew it was the sight of the mule and the hog that had stirred them. As he walked back to the fire and lay down on his blankets, he tried to figure the reason behind that, and only came up with a headache and more mosquito bites.

He closed his eyes and slept a little while longer, thinking of the mule and the hog, and the way they were free and beautiful. And then he thought of the race, and all of that went away, and when he awoke, it was to the toe of Nigger Joe's boot in his ribs.

"Time to do it," Nigger Joe said.

Frank sat up. "I saw them."

"What?" Leroy said, stirring out of his blankets.

Frank told them what he had seen, and how there was nothing he could do then. Told them all this, but didn't tell them how the mule and the hog had made him feel.

"Shit," Leroy said. "You should have woke us."

Nigger Joe shook his head. "No matter. We see over there where they stood. See what tracks they leave us. Then we do the sneak on them."

They worked their way to the other side of the swamp, swatting mosquitoes and killing a cottonmouth in the process, and when they got to where the mule and the hog stood, they found tracks and mule droppings.

"You not full of shit, like Nigger Joe thinking," Nigger Joe said. "You really see them."

"Yep," Frank said.

Nigger Joe bent down and rubbed some of the mule shit between his fingers, and smelled it. "Not more than a couple hours old."

"Should have got us up," Leroy said.

"Easier to track in the day," Nigger Joe said. "They got their place they stay. They got some hideout."

The mosquitoes were not so bad now, and finally they came to some clear areas, marshy, but clear, and they lost the tracks there, but Nigger Joe said, "The two of them, they probably cross here. It's a good spot. Pick their tracks up in the trees over there, on the soft ground."

When they crossed the marshy stretch, they came to a batch of willows and looked around there. Nigger Joe was the one who found their tracks.

"Here they go," he said. "Here they go."

They traveled through woods and more swamp, and from time to time they lost the tracks, but Nigger Joe always found them. Sometimes Frank couldn't even see what Nigger Joe saw. But Nigger Joe saw something, because he kept looking at the ground, stopping to stretch out on the earth, his face close to it. Sometimes he would pinch the earth between finger and thumb, rub it about. Frank wasn't sure why he did that, and he didn't ask. Like Leroy, he just followed.

Mid-day, they came to a place that amazed Frank. Out there in the middle of what should have been swamp, there was a great clear area, at least a hundred acres. They found it when they came out of a stretch of shady oaks. The air was sweeter there, in the trees, and the shadows were cooling, and at the far edge was a drop of about fifty feet. Down below was the great and natural pasture. A fire, brought on by heat or lightning, might have cleared the place at some point in time. It had grown back without trees, just tall green grass amongst a few rotting, ant-infested stumps. It was surrounded by the oaks, high up on their side, and low down on the other. The oaks on the far side stretched out and blended with sweet gums and black jack and hickory and bursts of pines. From their vantage point they could see all of this, and see the cool shadow on the other side amongst the trees.

A hawk sailed over it all, and Frank saw there was a snake in its beak. Something stirred again inside of Frank, and he was sure it wasn't his last meal. "You're part Indian," Frank said to Nigger Joe. "That hawk and that snake, does it mean something?"

"Means that snake is gonna get et," Nigger Joe said. "Damn trees. Don't you know that make a lot of good hard lumber. Go quiet. Look there."

Coming out of the trees into the great pasture was the mule and the hog. The hog led the way, and the mule followed close behind. They came out into the sunlight, and pretty soon the hog began to root and the mule began to graze.

"Got their own paradise," Frank said.

"We'll fix that," Leroy said.

They waited there, sitting amongst the oaks, watching, and late in the day the hog and the mule wandered off into the trees across the way.

"Ain't we gonna do something besides watch?" Leroy said.

"They leave, tomorrow they come back," Nigger Joe said. "Got their spot. Be back tomorrow. We'll be ready for them."

———

Just before dark they came down from their place on a little trail and crossed the pasture and walked over to where the mule and the hog had come out of the trees. Nigger Joe looked around for some time, said, "Got a path. Worked it out. Always the same. Same spot. Come through here, out into the pasture. What we do is we get up in a tree. Or I get in tree with my rope, and I rope the mule and tie him off and let him wear himself down."

"He could kill himself, thrashing," Frank said.

"Could kill myself, him thrashing. I think it best tie him to a tree, folks."

Frank translated Nigger Joe's strange way of talking in his head, said, "He dies, you don't get the eleven-fifty."

"Not how I understand it," Nigger Joe said.

"That's how it is," Frank said, feeling as if he might be asking for a knife in his belly, his guts spilled. Out here, no one would ever know. Nigger Joe might think he could do that, kill Leroy too, take their money. Course, they didn't have any money. Not here. There was fifteen dollars buried in a jar out back of the house, eleven-fifty of which would go to Nigger Joe, if he didn't kill them.

Nigger Joe studied Frank for a long moment. Frank shifted from one foot to the other, trying not to do it, but unable to stop. "Okay," Nigger Joe said. "That will work up good enough."

"What about Mr. Porky?" Leroy asked.

"That gonna be you two's job. I rope damn mule, and you two, you gonna rope damn pig. First, we got to smell like dirt."

"What?" Frank said.

Nigger Joe rubbed himself down with dark soil. He had Frank and Leroy rub themselves down with it. Leroy hated it and complained, but Frank found the earth smelled like incoming rain, and he thought it pleasant. It felt good on his skin, and he had a sudden strange thought, that when he died, he would become one and the same as the earth, and he wondered how many dead animals, maybe people, made up the dirt he had rubbed onto himself. He felt odd thinking that way. He felt odd thinking in any way.

They slept for a while, then Nigger Joe kicked him and Leroy awake. It was still dark when they rolled dirty out of their bedclothes.

"Couldn't we have waited on the dirt?" Leroy said, climbing out of his blankets. "It's all in my bedroll."

"Need time for dirt to like you good, so you smell like it," Nigger Joe said. "We put some more on now, rub in the hair good, then get ready."

"It's still dark," Frank said. "They gonna come in the dark? How you know when they're gonna come?"

"They come. But we gotta be ready. They have a good night in farmer's cornfields, they might come real soon, full bellies. Way ground reads, they come here to stand and to wallow. Hog wallows all time, way ground looks. And they shit all over. This their spot. They don't get corn and peas and such, they'll be back here. Water not far from spot, and they got good grass. Under the trees, hog has some acorns. Hogs like acorns. Wife, Sweetie, makes sometimes coffee from acorns."

"How about I make some regular coffee, made from coffee?" Leroy said.

"Nope. We don't want a smoke smell. Don't want our smell. Need to piss or shit, don't let free here. Go across pasture there. Far side. Dump over there. Piss over there. Use the heel of your shoe to cover it all. Give it lots of dirt."

"Walk all the way across?" Leroy said.

"Want hog and mule," Nigger Joe said. "Walk all the way across. Now, eat some jerky, do your shit over on other side. Put more dirt on. And wait."

The sun rose up and it got hot, and the dirt on their skins itched, or at least Frank itched, and he could tell Leroy itched, but Nigger Joe, he didn't seem to. Sat silent. And when the early morning was eaten up by the heat, Nigger Joe showed them places to be, and Nigger Joe, with his lasso, climbed up into an oak and sat on a fat limb, his feet stretched along it, his back against the trunk, the rope in his lap.

The place for Frank and Leroy to be was terrible. The dirt they smeared on themselves came from long scoops they made. Then they lay down in the scoops with their ropes, and Nigger Joe, before he climbed the tree, tossed leaves and sticks and dirt and bits of mule and hog shit over them. The way they lay, Frank and Leroy were twenty feet apart, on either side of what Nigger Joe said was a trail the hog and mule traveled. It wasn't much of a trail. A bit of ruffled oak leaves, some wallows the hog had made.

The day crawled forward and so did the worms. They were all around Frank, and it was all he could do not to jump up screaming. It wasn't that he was afraid of them. He had put many of them on hooks for fishing. But to just lay there and have them squirm against your arm, your neck. And there was something that bit. Something in the hog shit was Frank's thought.

Frank heard a sound. A different sound. Being close to the ground it seemed to move the earth. It was the slow careful plodding of the mule's hooves, and another sound. The hog, maybe.

They listened and waited and the sounds came closer, and then

Frank, lying there, trying not to tremble with anticipation, heard a whizzing sound. The rope. And then there was a bray, and a scuffle sound.

Frank lifted his head slightly.

Not ten feet from him was the great white mule, the rope around its neck, the length of it stretching up into the tree. Frank could see Nigger Joe. He had wrapped the rope around the limb and was holding on to it, tugging, waiting for the mule to wear itself out.

The hog was bounding about near the mule, as if it might jump up and grab the rope and chew it in two. It actually went up on its hind legs once.

Frank knew it was time. He burst out of his hiding place, and Leroy came out of his. The hog went straight for Leroy. Frank darted in front of the leaping mule and threw his rope and caught the hog around the neck. It turned instantly and went for him.

Leroy dove and grabbed the hog's hind leg. The hog kicked him in the face, but Leroy hung on. The hog dragged Leroy across the ground, going for Frank, and as his rope become more slack, Frank darted for a tree.

By the time Frank arrived at the tree trunk, Leroy had managed to put his rope around the hog's hind leg, and now Frank and Leroy had the hog in a kind of tug-of-war.

"Don't hurt him now some," Nigger Joe yelled from the tree. "Got to keep him up for it. He's the mule leader. Makes him run."

"What the hell did he say?" Frank said.

"Don't hurt the goddamn pig," Leroy said.

"Ha," Frank said, tying off his end of the rope to a tree trunk. Leroy stretched his end, giving the hog a little slack, and tied off to another tree. Nearby the mule leaped and kicked.

Leroy made a move to try and grab the rope on the mule up short, but the mule whipped as if on a Yankee dollar, and kicked Leroy smooth in the chest, launching him over the hog and into the brush. The hog would have had him then, but the rope around its neck and back leg held it just short of Leroy, but close enough a string of hog spittle and snot was flung across Leroy's face.

"Goddamn," Leroy said, as he inched farther away from the hog.

For a long while, they watched the mule kick and buck and snort and snap its large teeth.

It was near nightfall when the mule, exhausted, settled down on its front knees first, then rolled over on its side. The hog scooted across the dirt and came to rest near the great mule, its snout resting on the mule's flank.

"I'll be damned," Leroy said. "The hog's girlie or something."

It took three days to get back, because the mule wasn't cooperating, and the hog was no pushover either. They had to tie logs on either side of the hog, so that he had to drag them. It wore the hog down, but it wore the men down too, because the logs would tangle in vines and roughs, and constantly had to be removed. The mule was hobbled loosely, so that it could walk, but couldn't bolt. The mule was led by Nigger Joe, and fastened around the mule's waist was a rope with two rope lines leading off to the rear. They were in turn fastened to a heavy log that kept the mule from bolting forward to have a taste of Nigger Joe, and to keep him, like the hog, worn down.

At night they left the logs on the critters, and built make-do corrals of vines and limbs and bits of leather straps.

By the time they were out of the woods and the swamp, the mule and the hog were covered in dirt and mud and such. The animals heaved as they walked, and Frank feared they might keel over and die.

They made it though, and they took the mule up to Nigger Joe's. He had a corral there. It wasn't much, but it was solid and it held the mule in. The hog they put in a small pen. There was hardly room for the hog to turn around. Now that the hog was well placed, Frank stood by the pen and studied the animal. It looked at him with a feral eye. This wasn't a hog who had been slopped and watered. This was an animal who early on had escaped into the wild, as a pig, and had made his way to adulthood. His spotted hide was covered in scars, and though he had a coating of fat on him, his body was long and muscular, and when the hog flexed its shoulders to startle a fly, those muscles rolled beneath its skin like snakes beneath a tight-stretched blanket.

The mule, after the first day, began to perk up. But he didn't do much. Stood around mostly, and when they walked away for a distance, it began to trot the corral, stopping often to look out at the hog pen, at his friend. The mule made a sound, and the hog made a sound back.

"Damn, if I don't think they're talking to one another," Leroy said.

"Oh yeah. You can bet. They do that all right," Nigger Joe said.

The race was coming closer, and within the week, Leroy and Nigger Joe had the mule's hooves trimmed, but no shoes. Decided he didn't need them, as the ground was soft this time of year. They got him saddled. Leroy got bucked off and kicked and bitten once, a big plug was out of his right elbow.

"Mean one," Nigger Joe said. "Real bastard, this mule. Strong. He got the time, he eat Leroy."

"Do you think he can run?" Frank asked.

"Time to see soon," Nigger Joe said.

That night, when the saddling and bucking was done, the mule began to wear down, let Nigger Joe stay on his back. As a reward, Nigger Joe fed the mule well, but with only a little water. He fed the hog some pulled-up weeds, a bit of corn, watered him.

"Want mule strong, but hog weak," Nigger Joe said. "Don't want hog strong enough to go digging out of pen that's for some sure."

Frank listened to this, wondering where Nigger Joe had learned his American.

Nigger Joe went in for the night, his two wives calling him to supper. Leroy walked home. Frank saddled up Dobbin, but before he left, he led the horse out to the corral and stared at the mule. There in the starlight, the beams settled around the mule's head, and made it very white. The mud was gone now and the mule had been groomed, cleaned of briars and burrs from the woods, and the beast looked magnificent. Once Frank had seen a book. It was the only book he had ever seen other than the Bible, which his mother owned. But he had seen this one in the window of the General Store downtown. He hadn't opened the book, just looked at it through the window. There on the cover was a white horse with wings on its back. Well, the mule didn't look like a horse, and it didn't have wings on its back, but it certainly had the bearing of the beast on the book's cover. Like maybe it was from somewhere else other than here; like the sky had ripped open and the mule had ridden into this world through the tear.

Frank led Dobbin over to the hog pen. There was nothing beautiful about the spotted hog. It stared up at him, and the starlight filled its eyes and made them sharp and bright as shrapnel.

As Frank was riding away, he heard the mule make a sound, then the hog. They did it more than once, and were still doing it when he rode out of earshot.

It took some doing, and it took some time, and Frank, though he did little but watch, felt as if he were going to work every day. It was a new feeling for him. His old man often made him work, but as he grew older he had quit, just like his father. The fields rarely got attention, and being drunk became more important than hoeing corn and digging taters. But here he was not only showing up early, but staying all day, handing harness and such to Nigger Joe and Leroy, bringing out feed and pouring water.

In time Nigger Joe was able to saddle up the mule with no more than a snort from the beast, and he could ride about the pen without the mule turning to try and bite him or buck him. He even stopped kicking at Nigger Joe and Leroy, who he hated, when they first entered the pen.

The hog watched all of this through the slats of his pen, his beady eyes slanting tight, his battle-torn ears flicking at flies, his curly tail curled even tighter. Frank wondered what the hog was thinking. He was certain, whatever it was, was not good.

Soon enough, Nigger Joe had Frank enter the pen, climb up in the saddle. Sensing a new rider, the mule threw him. But the second time he was on board, the mule trotted him around the corral, running lightly with that kind of rolling-barrel run mules have.

"He's about ready for a run, he is," Nigger Joe said.

Frank led the mule out of the pen and out to the road, Leroy following. Nigger Joe led Dobbin. "See he'll run that way. Not so fast at first," Nigger Joe said. "Me and this almost dead horse, we follow and find you, you ain't neck broke in some ditch somewheres."

Cautiously, Frank climbed on the white mule's back. He took a deep breath, then, settling himself in the saddle, he gave the mule a kick.

The mule didn't move.

He kicked again.

The mule trotted down the road about twenty feet, then turned, dipped its head into the grass that grew alongside the red clay road, and took a mouthful.

Frank kicked at the mule some more, but the mule wasn't having any. He did move, but just a bit. A few feet down the road, then across the road and into the grass, amongst the trees, biting leaves off of them with a sharp snap of his head, a smack of his teeth.

Nigger Joe trotted up on Dobbin.

"You ain't going so fast."

"Way I see it too," Frank said. "He ain't worth a shit."

"We not bring the hog in on some business yet."

"How's that gonna work? I mean, how's he gonna stay around and not run off?"

"Maybe hog run off in goddamn woods and not see again, how it may work. But, nothing else, hitch mule to plow or sell. You done paid me eleven-fifty."

"Your job isn't done," Frank said.

"You say, and may be right, but we got the one card, the hog, you see. He don't deal out with an ace, we got to call him a joker, and call us assholes, and the mule, we got to make what we can. We have to, shoot and eat the hog. Best, keep him up a few more days, put some corn in him, make him better than what he is. Fatter. The mule, I told you ideas. Hell, eat mule too if nothing other works out."

They let the hog out of the pen.

Or rather, Leroy did. Just picked up the gate, and out came the hog. The hog didn't bolt. It bounded over to the mule, on which Frank was mounted. The mule dipped its head, touched noses with the hog.

"I'll be damned," Frank said, thinking he had never had a friend like that. Leroy was as close as it got, and he had to watch Leroy. He'd cheat you. And if you had a goat, he might fuck it. Leroy was no real friend. Frank felt lonesome.

Nigger Joe took the bridle on the mule away from Frank, and led them out to the road. The hog trotted beside the mule.

"Now, story is, hog likes to run," Nigger Joe said. "And when he run, mule follows. And then hog, he falls off, not keeping up, and mule, he got the arrow-sight then, run like someone put turpentine on his nut sack. Or that the story as I hear it. You?"

"Pretty close," Frank said.

Frank took the reins back, and the hog stood beside the mule. Nothing happened.

"Gonna say go, is what I'm to do here now. And when I say, you kick mule real goddamn hard. Me, I'm gonna stick boot in hog's big ass. Hear me now, Frank?"

"I do."

"Signal will be me shouting when kick the hog's ass, okay?"

"Okay."

"Ready some."

"Ready."

Nigger Joe yelled, "Git, hog," and kicked the hog in the ass with all his might. The hog did a kind of hop, and bolted. A hog can move quick for its size for a short distance, haul some serious freight, and the old spotted hog, he was really fast, hauling the whole freight line. Frank expected the hog to dart into the woods, and be long gone. But it didn't. The hog bounded down the road running for all it was worth, and before Frank could put his heels to the mule, the mule leaped. That was the only way to describe it. The mule did not seem cocked to fire, but suddenly it was a white bullet, lunging forward so fast Frank nearly flew out of the saddle. But he clung, and the mule ran, and the hog ran, and after a bit, the mule ducked its head and the hog began to fade. But the mule was no longer following the hog. Not even close. It snorted, and its nose appeared to get long and the ears laid back flat. The mule jetted by the fat porker and stretched its legs wider, and Frank could feel the wind whipping cool on his face. The body of the mule rolled like a barrel, but man, my God, thought Frank, this sonofabitch can run.

There was one problem. Frank couldn't turn him. When he felt the mule had gone far enough, it just kept running, and no amount of tugging led to response. That booger was gone. Frank just leaned forward over the mule's neck, hung on, and let him run.

Eventually the mule quit, just stopped, dipped its head to the ground, then looked left and right. Trying to find the hog, Frank figured. It was like the mule had gone into a kind of spell, and now he was out of it and wanted his friend.

He could turn the mule then. He trotted it back down the road, not trying to get it to run anymore, just letting it trot, and when it came upon Nigger Joe and Leroy, standing in the road, the hog came out of the woods and moseyed up beside the mule.

As Nigger Joe reached up and took the mule's reins, he said, "See that there. Hog and him are buddies. He stays around. He don't want to run off. Wants to be with mule. Hog a goddamn fool. Could be long gone, out in the woods. Find some other wild hog and fuck it. Eat acorns. Die of old age. Now he gonna get et sometime."

"Dumb shit hog," Leroy said.

The mule tugged at the reins, dipped its head. The hog and the mule's noses came together. The mule snorted. The hog made a kind of squealing sound.

They trained for several days the same way. The hog would start, and then the mule would run. Fast. They put the mule up at night in the corral, hobbled, and the hog, they didn't have to pen him anymore. He stayed with the mule by choice.

One day, after practice, Frank said, "He seems pretty fast."

"Never have seen so fast," Nigger Joe said. "He's moving way good."

"Do you think he can win?" Leroy said.

"He can win, they let us bring hog in. No hog. Not much on the run. Got to have hog. But there's one mule give him trouble. Dynamite. He runs fast too. Might can run faster."

"You think?"

"Could be. I hear he can go lickity split. Tomorrow, we find out, hey?"

The world was made of men and mules and dogs and one hog. There were women too, most of them with parasols. Some sitting in the rows of chairs at the starting line, their legs tucked together primly, their dresses pulled down tight to the ankles. The air smelled of early summer morning and hot mule shit and sweat and perfume, cigar smoke, beer and farts. Down from it all, in tents, were other women who smelled different and wore less clothes. The women with parasols would not catch their eye, but some of the men would, many when their wives or girls were not looking.

Frank was not interested. He couldn't think of anything but the race. Leroy was with him, and of course, Nigger Joe. They brought the mule in, Nigger Joe leading him. Frank on Old Dobbin, Leroy riding double. And the hog, loose, on its own, strutting as if he were the one throwing the whole damn shindig.

The mules at the gathering were not getting along. There were bites and snorts and kicks. The mules could kick backwards, and they could kick out sideways like cattle. You had to watch them.

White Mule was surprisingly docile. It was as if his balls had been clipped. He walked with his head down, the pig trotting beside him.

As they neared the forming line of mules, Frank looked at them. Most were smaller than the white mule, but there was one that was bigger, jet black, and had a roaming eye, as if he might be searching for victims. He had a big hard-on and it was throbbing in the sunlight like a fat cottonmouth.

"That mule there, big-dicked one," Nigger Joe said, pausing. "He the kind get a hard-on he gonna race or fight, maybe quicker than the fuck, you see. He's the one to watch. Anything that like the running or fighting better than pussy, him, you got to keep the eye on."

"That's Dynamite," Leroy said. "Got all kinds of mule muscle, that's for sure."

White Mule saw Dynamite, lifted his head high and threw back his ears and snorted.

"Oh, yeah," said Leroy. "There's some shit between them already."

"Somebody gonna outrun somebody or fuck other in ass, that's what I tell you for sure. Maybe they fight some too. Whole big blanket of business here."

White Mule wanted to trot, and Nigger Joe had to run a little to keep up with him. They went right through a clutch of mules about to be lined up, and moved quickly so that White Mule was standing beside Dynamite. The two mules looked at one another and snorted. In that moment, the owner of Dynamite slipped blinders on Dynamite's head, tossing off the old bridle to a partner.

The spotted hog slid in between the feet of his mule, stood with his head poking out beneath his buddy's legs, looking up with his ugly face, flaring his nostrils, narrowing his cave-dark eyes.

Dynamite's owner was Levi Crone, one big gent in a dirty white shirt with the sleeves ripped out. He had a big red face and big fat muscles and a belly like a big iron wash pot. He wore a hat you could have bathed in. He was as tall as Nigger Joe, six foot two or more. Hands like hams, feet like boats. He looked at the White Mule, said, "That ain't the story mule, is it?"

"One and the same," Frank said, as if he had raised the white mule from a colt.

"I heard someone had him. That he had been caught. Catch and train him?"

"Me and my partners."

"You mean Leroy and the nigger?"

"Yeah."

"That the hog in the stories, too, I guess?"

"Yep," Frank said.

"What's he for? A stepstool?"

"He runs with the mule. For a ways."

"That ain't allowed."

"Where say can't do it, huh?" Nigger Joe asked.

Crone thought. "Nowhere, but it stands to reason."

"What about rule can't run with the dick hard?" Nigger Joe said, pointing at Dynamite's member.

"Ain't no rule like that," Crone said. "Mule can't help that."

"Ain't no rule about goddamn hog none either," Nigger Joe said.

"It don't matter," Crone said. "You got this mule from hell, given to you by the goddamn red-assed devil his ownself, and you got the pork chop there too from the same place, it ain't gonna matter. Dynamite here, he's gonna outrun him. Gets finished, he'll fuck your mule in the ass and shit a turd on him."

"Care to make a bet on the side some?" Nigger Joe said.

"Sure," Crone said. "I'll bet you all till my money runs out. That ain't good enough, I'll arm wrestle you or body wrestle you or see which of us can shoot jack-off the farthest. You name it, speckled nigger."

Nigger Joe studied Crone as if he might be thinking about where to make all the prime cuts, but he finally just grinned, got out ten of the eleven-fifty he had been paid. "There mine. You got some holders?"

"Ten dollars. I got sight of it, and I got your word, which better be good," Crone said.

"Where's your money?" Leroy said.

Crone pulled out a wad from his front pocket, presented it with open palm as if he might be giving a teacher an apple. He looked at Leroy, said, "You gonna trade a goat? I hear you like goats."

"Okay," Leroy said. "Okay. I fucked a goddamn goat. What of it?"

Crone laughed at him. He shook the money at Nigger Joe. "Good enough?"

"Okay," Nigger Joe said.

"Here's three dollars," Frank said, dug in his pocket, held it so Crone could see.

Crone nodded.

Frank slipped the money back in his pocket.

"Well," Leroy said. "I ain't got shit, so I just throw out my best wishes."

"You boys could bet the mule," Crone said.

"That could be an idea," Leroy said.

"No," Frank said. "We won't do that."

"Ain't we partners?" Leroy said, taking off his seed salesman's hat.

"We got a deal," Frank said, "but I'm the one paid Nigger Joe for catching and training. So, I decide. And that's about as partner as we get."

Leroy shrugged, put the seed salesman's hat back on.

The mules lined up and it was difficult to make them stay the line. Dynamite, still toting serious business on the undercarriage, lined up by White Mule, stood at least a shoulder above him. Both wore blinders now, but they turned their heads and looked at one another. Dynamite snapped at the white mule and missed. White Mule snapped back at Dynamite's nose, grazing him. He threw a little kick sideways that made Dynamite shuffle to his right.

There was yelling from the judges, threats of disqualification, though no one expected that. The crowd had already figured this race out. White Mule, the forest legend, and Dynamite, of the swinging big dick, they were the two to watch.

Leroy and Nigger Joe had pulled the hog back with a rope, but now they brought him out and let him stand in front of his mule. They had to talk to the judges on the matter, explain. There wasn't any rule for or against it. One judge said he didn't like the idea. One said the hog would get trampled to death anyway. Another said, shit, why not. Final decision, they let the hog stay in the race.

So the mules and the hog and the riders lined up, the hog just slightly to the side of the white mule. The hog looked over its shoulder at Nigger Joe standing behind him. By now the hog knew what was coming. A swift kick in the ass.

Frank climbed up on the white mule, and a little guy with a face like a timber axe climbed up on Crone's mule, Dynamite.

Out front of the line was a little bald man in a loose shirt and suspenders holding up his high-water pants, showing his scuffed and broken-laced boots. He had a pistol in his hand. He has a voice loud as Nester on the Greek line.

"Now, we got us a mule race today, ladies and gentlemen. And there will be no cheatin', or there will be disqualification, and a butt-beating you can count on to be remembered by everyone, 'specially the cheater. What I want now, line of mules and riders, is a clean race. This here path is wide enough for all twenty of you, and you can't fan too much to the right or left, as we got folks all along the run watching. You got to keep up pretty tight. Now, there might be some biting and kicking, and that's to be expected. From the mules. You riders got to be civil. Or mostly. A little out of line is all right, but no knives or guns or such. Everyone understand and ain't got no questions, let up a shout."

A shout came from the line. The mules stirred, stepped back, stepped forward.

"Anybody don't understand what I just said? Anyone not speak Texan or 'Merican here that's gonna race?"

No response.

"All right, then. Watch women and children, and try not to run over the men or the whores neither. I'm gonna step over there to the side, and I'm gonna raise this pistol, and when you hear the shot, there you go. May the best mule and the best rider win. Oh, yeah. We got a hog in the race too. He ain't supposed to stay long. Just kind of lead. No problems with that from anybody, is there?"

There were no complaints.

"All right, then."

The judge stepped briskly to the side of the road and raised his old worn .36 Navy at the sky and got an important look on his face. Nigger Joe removed the rope from the pig's neck and found a solid position between mules and behind the hog. He cocked his foot back.

The judge fired his pistol. Nigger Joe kicked the hog in the ass. The mule line charged forward.

The hog, running for all it was worth, surged forward as well, taking the lead even. White Mule and Dynamite ran dead even. The mules ran so hard a cloud of dust was thrown up. The mules and the men and the hog were swallowed by it. Frank, seeing nothing but dust, coughed and cursed and lay tight against the white mule's neck, and squinted his eyes. He feared, without the white mule being able to see the hog, he might bolt. Maybe run into another mule, throw him into a stampede, get him stomped flat. But as they ran the cloud moved behind them, and when Frank came coughing out of the cloud, he was amazed to see the hog was well out in front, running as if he could go like that all the way to Mexico.

To his right, Frank saw Dynamite and his little axe-faced rider. The rider looked at him and smiled with gritty teeth. "You gonna get run into a hole, shit breath."

"Shitass," Frank said. It was the best he could come up with, but he threw it out with meaning.

Dynamite was leading the pack now, leaving the white mule and the others behind, throwing dust in their faces. White Mule saw Dynamite start to straighten out in front of him, and he moved left, nearly knocking against a mule on that side. Frank figured it was so he could see the hog. The hog was moving his spotted ass on down the line.

"Git him, White Mule," Frank said, and leaned close to the mule's left ear, rubbed the side of the mule's neck, then rested his head close on his mane. The white mule focused on the hog and started hauling some ass. He went lower and his strides got longer and the barrel back and belly rolled. When Frank looked up, the hog was bolting left, across the path of a dozen mules, just making it off the trail before taking a tumble under hooves. He fell, rolled over and over in the grass.

Frank thought: Shit, White Mule, he's gonna bolt, gonna go after the hog. But, nope, he was true to the trail, and closing on Dynamite. The spell was on. And now the other mules were moving up too, taking a whipping, getting their sides slapped hard enough Frank could hear it, thinking it sounded like Papa's belt on his back.

"Come on, White Mule. You don't need no hittin', don't need no hard heels. You got to outrun that hard dick for your own sake."

It was as if White Mule understood him. White Mule dropped lower and his strides got longer yet. Frank clung for all he was worth, fearing the saddle might twist and lose him.

But no, Leroy, for all his goat-fucking and seed salesman's hat stealing, could fasten harness better than anyone that walked.

The trail became shady as they moved into a line of oaks on either side of the road. For a long moment the shadows were so thick they ran in near darkness. Then there were patches of lights through the leaves and the dust was lying closer to the ground and the road was sun-baked and harder and showing clay the color of a poison-ivy rash. Scattered here and there along the road were viewers. A few in chairs. Most standing.

Frank ventured a look over his shoulder. The other mules and riders were way back, and some of them were already starting to falter. He noticed a couple of the mules were riderless, and one had broken rank with its rider and was off trail, cutting across the grass, heading toward the creek that twisted down amongst a line of willow trees.

As White Mule closed on Dynamite, the mule took a snapping bite at Dynamite's tail, jerking its head back with teeth full of tail hair.

Dynamite tried to turn and look, but his rider pulled his head back into line. White Mule lunged forward, going even lower than before. Lower than Frank had ever seen him go. Lower than he thought he could go. Now White Mule was pulling up on Dynamite's left. Dynamite's rider jerked Dynamite back into the path in front of White Mule. Frank wheeled his mount to the right side of Dynamite. In mid-run, Dynamite wheeled and kicked, hit White Mule in the side hard enough there was an explosion of breath that made Frank think his mule would go down.

Dynamite pulled ahead.

White Mule was not so low now. He was even staggering a little as he ran.

"Easy, boy," Frank said. "You can do it. You're the best goddamn mule ever ran a road."

White Mule began to run evenly again, or as even as a mule can run. He began to stretch out again, going low. Frank was surprised to see they were closing on Dynamite.

Frank looked back.

No one was in sight. Just a few twists of dust, a ripple of heat waves. It was White Mule and Dynamite, all the way.

As Frank and White Mule passed Dynamite, Frank noted Dynamite didn't run with a hard-on anymore. Dynamite's rider let the mule turn its head and snap at White Mule. Frank, without really thinking about it, slipped his foot from the saddle and kicked the mule in the jaw.

"Hey," yelled Dynamite's rider. "Stop that."

"Hey, shitass," Frank said. "You better watch that limb."

Dynamite and his rider had let White Mule push them to the right side of the road, near the trees, and a low-hanging hickory limb was right in line with them. The rider ducked it by a half inch, losing only his cap.

Shouldn't have told him, thought Frank. What he was hoping was to say something smart just as the limb caught the bastard. That would have made it choice, seeing the little axe-faced shit take it in the teeth. But he had outsmarted his ownself.

"Fuck," Frank said.

Now they were thundering around a bend, and there were lots of people there, along both sides. There had been a spot of people here and there, along the way, but now they were everywhere.

Must be getting to the end of it, thought Frank.

Dynamite had lost a step for a moment, allowing White Mule to move ahead, but now he was closing again. Frank looked up. He could see that a long red ribbon was stretched across in front of them. It was almost the end.

Dynamite lit a fuse.

He came up hard and on the left, and began to pass. The axe-faced rider slapped out with the long bridle and caught Frank across the face.

"You goddamn turd," Frank said, and slashed out with his own bridle, missing by six inches. Dynamite and Axe-Face pulled ahead.

Frank turned his attention back to the finish line. Thought: this is it. White Mule was any lower to the ground he'd have a belly full of gravel, stretched out any farther, he'd come apart. He's gonna be second. And no prize.

"You done what you could," Frank said, putting his mouth close to the bobbing head of the mule, rubbing the side of his neck with the tips of his fingers.

White Mule brought out the reinforcements. He was low and he was stretched, but now his legs were moving even faster, and for a long, strange moment, Frank thought the mule had sprung wings, like that horse he had seen on the front of the book so long ago. There didn't feel like there was any ground beneath them.

Frank couldn't believe it. Dynamite was falling behind, snorting and blowing, his body lathering up as if he were soaped.

White Mule leaped through the red ribbon a full three lengths ahead to win.

Frank let White Mule run past the watchers, on until he slowed and began to trot, and then walk. He let the mule go on like that for some time, then he gently pulled the reins and got out of the saddle. He walked the mule a while. Then he stopped and unbuttoned the belly band. He slid the saddle into the dirt. He pulled the bridle off of the mule's head.

The mule turned and looked at him.

"You done your part," Frank said, and swung the bridle gently against the mule's ass. "Go on."

White Mule sort of skipped forward and began running down the road, then turned into the trees. And was gone.

Frank walked all the way back to the beginning of the race, the viewers amazed he was without his mule.

But he was still the winner.

"You let him go?" Leroy said. "After all we went through, you let him go?"

"Yep," Frank said.

Nigger Joe shook his head. "Could have run him again. Plowed him. Ate him."

Frank took his prize money from the judges and side bet from Crone, paid Leroy his money, watched Nigger Joe follow Crone away from the race's starting line, on out to Crone's horse and wagon. Dynamite, his head down, was being led to the wagon by Axe-Face.

Frank knew what was coming. Nigger Joe had not been paid, and on top of that, he was ill tempered. As Frank watched, Nigger Joe hit Crone and knocked him flat. No one did anything.

Black man or not, you didn't mess with Nigger Joe.

Nigger Joe took his money from Crone's wallet, punched the axe-faced rider in the nose for the hell of it, and walked back in their direction.

Frank didn't wait. He went over to where the hog lay on the grass. His front and back legs had been tied and a kid about thirteen was poking him with a stick. Frank slapped the kid in the back of the head, knocking his hat off. The kid bolted like a deer.

Frank got Dobbin and called Nigger Joe over. "Help me."

Nigger Joe and Frank loaded the hog across the back of Dobbin as if he were a sack of potatoes. Heavy as the porker was, it was accomplished with some difficulty, the hog's head hanging down on one side, his feet on the other. The hog seemed defeated. He hardly even squirmed.

"Misses that mule," Nigger Joe said.

"You and me got our business done, Joe?" Frank asked.

Nigger Joe nodded.

Frank took Dobbin's reins and started leading him away.

"Wait," Leroy said.

Frank turned on him. "No. I'm through with you. You and me. We're quits."

"What?" Leroy said.

Frank pulled at the reins and kept walking. He glanced back once to see Leroy standing where they had last spoke, standing in the road looking at him, wearing the seed salesman's hat.

Frank put the hog in the old hog pen at his place and fed him good. Then he ate and poured out all the liquor he had, and waited until dark. When it came he sat on a large rock out back of the house. The wind carried the urine smell of all those out-the-window pees to his nostrils. He kept his place.

The moon was near full that night and it had risen high above the world and its light was bright and silver. Even the old ugly place looked good under that light.

Frank sat there for a long time, finally dozed. He was awakened by the sound of wood cracking. He snapped his head up and looked out at the hog pen. The mule was there. He was kicking at the slats of the pen, trying to free his friend.

Frank got up and walked out there. The mule saw him, ran back a few paces, stared at him.

"Knew you'd show," Frank said. "Just wanted to see you one more time. Today, buddy, you had wings."

The mule turned its head and snorted.

Frank lifted the gate to the pen and the hog ran out. The hog stopped beside the mule and they both looked at Frank.

"It's all right," Frank said. "I ain't gonna try and stop you."

The mule dipped its nose to the hog's snout and they pressed them together. Frank smiled. The mule and the hog wheeled suddenly, as if by agreed signal, and raced toward the rickety rail fence near the hill.

The mule, with one beautiful leap, jumped the fence, seemed pinned in the air for a long time, held there by the rays of the moon. The way the rays fell, for a strange short instant, it seemed as if he were sprouting gossamer wings.

The hog wiggled under the bottom rail and the two of them ran across the pasture, between the trees and out of sight. Frank didn't have to go look to know that the mule had jumped the other side of the fence as well, that the hog had worked his way under. And that they were gone.

When the sun came up and Frank was sure there was no wind, he put a match to a broom's straw and used it to start the house afire, then the barn and the rotten outbuildings. He kicked the slats on the hog pen until one side of it fell down.

He went out to where Dobbin was tied to a tree, saddled and ready to go. He mounted him and turned his head toward the rail fence and the hill. He looked at it for a long time. He gave a gentle nudge to Dobbin with his heels and started out of there, on down toward the road and town.